CHAOS

IN

I0668462

THE

BLINK

OF

AN

EYE

PART EIGHT:
THREE RESURRECTIONS

AWARD-WINNING
END TIMES SERIES BY
PATRICK HIGGINS

CHAOS IN THE BLINK OF AN EYE:
PART EIGHT – THREE RESURRECTIONS
COPYRIGHT © 2023 PATRICK HIGGINS

Library of Congress
Cataloging in Publication Data
Paperback ISBN: 978-0-9992355-9-1

Published by
www.ForHisGloryProductionCompany.com

Manufactured in the United States of America.
TO ORDER PATRICK HIGGINS' BOOKS IN PAPERBACK FORMAT
(AND SOON IN HARD COPY) AT DEEP DISCOUNT PRICES:

www.patrickhigginsbooks.com

All books purchased on the site will be personally signed by the author and dedicated to the readers. They make the perfect gifts for holidays, birthdays, anniversaries, Mother's Day, Father's Day, and on and on.

Order signed copies now for family members, friends and loved ones.

Prologue...

Then war broke out in heaven. Michael and his angels fought against the dragon, and the dragon and his angels fought back. But he was not strong enough, and they lost their place in heaven.

The great dragon was hurled down—that ancient serpent called the devil, or Satan, who leads the whole world astray. He was hurled to the earth, and his angels with him.

Then I heard a loud voice in heaven say: "Now have come the salvation and the power and the kingdom of our God, and the authority of his Messiah. For the accuser of our brothers and sisters, who accuses them before our God day and night, has been hurled down.

They triumphed over him by the blood of the Lamb and by the word of their testimony; they did not love their lives so much as to shrink from death.

Therefore rejoice, you heavens and you who dwell in them! But woe to the earth and the sea, because the devil has gone down to you! He is filled with fury, because he knows that his time is short" (Revelation 12:7-12).

Main Characters:

<u>Brian Mulrooney</u> – late 30s –Mulrooney was at Michigan Stadium with his childhood friend, Justin Schroeder, to watch the Ohio State-Michigan football game, when Schroeder suddenly disappeared along with thousands of others.

<u>Tamika Moseley</u> – 30 – Head nurse at safe house number one, who lost her two sons, Jamal and Dante, and mother, Ruth Ferguson, on the day of the Rapture.

<u>Charles Calloway</u> – mid 40's – Calloway was inside Tamika Moseley's cab when his colleague, Richard Figueroa, suddenly vanished while sitting in the back seat next to him. It didn't take long for Calloway to piece things together and realize it was the Rapture of the Church, and that he had been left behind.

<u>Clayton Holmes and Travis Hartings</u> – Co-founders the *End Times Salvation Movement*.

<u>Tom Dunleavey</u> – 65 – Former Catholic priest who tried consoling Brian Mulrooney the day after the disappearances. After both men had similar dreams for three straight nights, it ultimately led to Tom's leaving the Catholic church.

<u>Dick and Sarah Mulrooney</u> – Married for more than 30 years, the solid relationship they always had was showing small cracks in the dam, after their son Brian converted to Christianity and distanced himself from the Catholic church.

<u>Doctor Lee Kim</u> – Lead IT man for the website www.LASRglobal.org, and all other *End Times Salvation Movement* IT operations.

<u>Jacquelyn Swindell Mulrooney</u> – early 30s – Lost her husband at Michigan Stadium when he was killed by an object that fell from the sky, after a plane collided with a Goodyear blimp hovering above the stadium. Swindell also lost the child in her womb at that time.

<u>Jefferson Danforth</u> – 60 - Former President of the United States of America. His first wife, Melissa, was killed on board Air Force One when it was blown out of the sky. Jefferson later remarried his former White House chef, Amy Wong. Both are living in hiding at safe house number one in Chadds Ford, Pennsylvania.

<u>Salvador Romanero</u> – 33 – As the world mourned the loss of more than a billion people—either by death or disappearance—Satan raised up the young lawyer from Spain as his main agent in human form. No one knew it yet, but the young phenom was about to take the world completely by storm and become the unchallenged leader of the world...

<u>Doctor Meera Singh</u> – early 50s – *ETSM* Doctor at safe house number one, in Chadds Ford, Pennsylvania.

<u>Joaquim Guzman</u> – 16 – Married to Leticia, who was the first -to give birth at safe house number one, when she was only 12. Joaquim accepted the child as his own when he married Leticia. His parents were taken in the Rapture while working at the Kennett Square farm before it was turned into a safe house.

<u>Julio and Marta Gonzalez</u> – Julio (34) and Marta (32) were the parents of Leticia Guzman. Julio had owned a successful construction business in Providence, Rhode Island, before relocating to safe house number one with his family. He was one of two construction foremen on site.

<u>Tony Pearsall</u> – (39) – Construction worker from Nevada. He was one of the first to be invited to safe house number one and as a construction foreman.

<u>Hana Patel</u> – Late 20s – The first woman to give birth, post Rapture. Her husband Yogesh died after humiliating Salvador Romanero in a jam-packed arena in Dubai, with the whole world watching. He was later killed in the Philippines for his faith. Hana recently came to faith in Christ and is living in hiding with her daughter Cristiana.

<u>Yasamin Dabiri</u> – Late 20s – When the parents of the fourth child to be born, post Rapture, were killed for not naming their son, "Salvador", Yasamin was ultimately granted full custody of the boy.

<u>Benjamin Shapiro</u> – (68) – Benjamin was Salvador Romanero's personal physician, before his spiritual conversion.

1

THE FOLLOWING DAY

SALVADOR ROMANERO STOOD BEFORE the podium to address the many jubilant citizens filling the streets of Jerusalem, for the second straight day. The glow on his face that had resurfaced 24 short hours ago, leading up to the slaying of God's Two Witnesses, was still there, but his eyes were noticeably a few shades darker.

Now 33, his countenance very much resembled the way he looked when he first came to power, as the unchallenged leader of Planet Earth, three and a half years ago. The reason for this was threefold: the Two slain men lying in the street behind him, the supernatural power he felt flowing through every pore of his body—after seemingly a very long absence— and the secret mission that was skillfully being carried out with great success, that only his top people knew about.

The supernatural power pumping through him was the very same power that had caused him to predict that no rain would fall during the global vigil, following the disappearances three and a half years ago, which earned him the title of *Miracle Maker*.

It had also allowed him to boldly declare that children would populate the planet again, plus predict the two rounds of earthquakes that Salvador had "proclaimed" to have sent to Planet Earth—one targeted, the other global, sparing only the nation of Israel.

Most importantly, it had allowed him to finally kill his Two archenemies, forever silencing them. But whenever this supernatural power wasn't flowing through him, his predictions were nowhere near spot on, his failed declaration that rain would fall on Israel on his self-proclaimed holiday, being the most recent among them.

But when it was flowing through him, like now, Romanero felt invincible, especially after the powerful jolt that shook his body the instant the Two Witnesses were assassinated. It nearly knocked him off his feet. It overwhelmed him. He knew it would take time to adjust to it.

The cameraman zoomed in on Salvador the Great—a title he had once again earned in the minds and hearts of most of his followers. But he made sure that the slain bodies behind him remained in view for all to see.

"Wow! What a wonderful twenty-four hours we've had!" Romanero craned his head back to glance at the two lifeless bodies behind him, then gazed into the camera again gleefully, dreamily. "Just knowing those Two have been forever silenced should fill us all with hope for a better tomorrow. What a glorious sight indeed!"

He paused a moment to let his words slither into the minds of his many renewed supporters. "Doesn't everything feel different now? More hopeful? More euphoric? It warms me deeply inside seeing so much gift exchanging going on, after what took place here twenty-four hours ago. This is but a sign of what will soon become the reality for us all!"

Romanero grew even more determined. "We must mark this momentous occasion by building upon this new foundation of sorts, until it leads all of you who are still with me to the utopia of our dreams. Yes, it's time to get back to the important business at hand.

"In the spirit of celebration, as we resume our aggressive pursuit of detaining dissident Christ followers, another one of my greatest tasks will be to stabilize the global economy in the soonest possible time.

"There can be no denying that these past few months have been difficult for all of us. There isn't a person on the planet who hasn't been negatively impacted by this direct global assault on us, at the hands of the God *those* Two worship, worshiped rather…

"I don't think we need further convincing that their God is a vengeful and a hateful One!" Romanero snapped. "Now that we know for certain that the mental illness their millions of still-alive followers all suffer from is irreversible, I must reiterate the sooner they have been ridded from the world, *our world*," he shouted, motioning to everyone with his hands, "the sooner we will achieve our global objective!

"One thing I plan on doing is to offer a financial opportunity to help all compliant citizens get back on their feet as quickly as possible. Even as I speak, the final bugs are being worked out on a new, advanced facial-recognition app. While this technology is nothing new, similar technologies have been widely available for law enforcement agencies for many decades, it has never been so advanced, nor has it ever been made available to common citizens before.

"In case you are wondering, it's the very same technology that's being used in the surveillance cameras and scanners that are being used to police the planet. But whereas so many of them must be replaced after each new global tragedy, you'll soon have that same functionality at your fingertips.

"In essence, instead of waiting for dissidents to pass by our stationary surveillance cameras, you will soon have the opportunity to bring the cameras directly to them, plus be paid for your efforts! This app will also include an advanced facial Age Progression Shot, to project how the subject might look ten years from now, twenty years, or even how they might look with plastic surgery or any other facial makeovers."

Little did his followers know this technology would soon be utterly useless—none of them would survive the next three and a half years.

Romanero paused again to let his words sink in, then went on, "The goal, of course, will be to round up all rebel dissidents still living in hiding as quickly as possible, and bringing them *all* to justice. Simply put, they are an irredeemable bunch! We have countless millions of case studies at our disposal to back this claim, making this an opportunity worthy of your time and effort. And it's so simple, anyone can do it!

"So, here's the deal, once the facial-recognition app has been downloaded onto your smartphones, if you see anyone acting or behaving suspiciously in any way, simply take their picture then check it against the global app on your mobile devices.

"Even those who have welts or abrasions on their bodies which, as we all know, was the direct result of the five months of torture that was cruelly sent to our planet by the God those Two served," he said, with a sarcastic nod of the head, "cannot be trusted at this time. Some of them have since become Christians, if you can believe that."

Romanero and the Pope both knew that most humans on the planet were facing the bleakest of financial circumstances. With greed being greed, they would scan everyone with whom they came in contact, hoping they would ultimately be confirmed as enemies of the planet, so they could collect their reward money.

In short, they would end up policing one another, thus bringing the Antichrist and the False Prophet of the Bible one step closer to achieving their objective, which was nothing short of global domination. Vastly decreasing the human population was a vital part of making it happen.

Romanero continued, "Once an image has been uploaded onto the global database, the process itself shouldn't take more than a few seconds. If it comes back as a match, meaning that individual has been positively identified as an enemy of the planet, you will be instructed to contact authorities immediately.

"Once that individual has been detained, you will receive a one-thousand-dollar reward for your effort. It's that simple. This will continue for every dissident you help us capture.

"So, let's say, for example, that you stumble upon a group of dissidents out in public, or better yet, they lead you to their enemy camps, at a thousand dollars per person, the amount added to your global account at that time could be quite substantial, once their identifications have been verified and they have been placed in our custody.

"Some of you may be thinking, when compared to the five-thousand-dollar allowance that was added to your global monetary cards, upon activation, that a thousand dollars might seem small. But whereas the five-thousand-dollar allowance was a one-time disbursement, there will be no limit as to how much you can earn with this opportunity.

"Now, if the individuals in question put up a struggle in any way, before law enforcement arrives to apprehend them, you have my full blessing to subdue them at all costs. Even if it means killing the subjects, you will still collect your reward once a positive ID has been confirmed."

Romanero paused again, to let his diabolical comment resonate in their minds. "In the final analysis, whether law enforcement ends up silencing them, or you do it yourself matters not. All that matters is detaining them in the soonest possible time, as it will merely be a means to an end. Subsequently, if the search comes back as 'unverified', that person must still be detained until a positive match can be made.

"If the subjects in question are ultimately cleared, they will be deemed worthy and will be let go. But if that individual eventually becomes a heretic at any point in the future, the person responsible for their detainment at that time will be awarded the thousand-dollar payment. But for being the one to start the process, you will receive a five-hundred-dollar bonus in your global account, post haste.

"Now for the best part. In the five months in which our planet was under attack, by the God those Two served," Romanero said, pointing back at the Two corpses that he himself had ordered shot dead in the streets of Jerusalem a day ago, "aside from restoring Wi-Fi globally, the rest of that time was spent putting the final touches on the new cashless system I've been promising the past three years."

Romanero glanced over at the Pope who nodded his utmost approval. Since this was also his brainchild, he seemed almost giddy, as he approached the lectern, wearing his traditional priestly garments.

"Greetings global citizens!" he shouted above the enthusiastic crowd. "It thrills me to no end to announce that we are just a week away from implementing the mark globally! Finally, we are about to become one body of citizens in every sense of the word!

"And it all begins with the mark that will be unveiled one week from today! What an exhilarating time this is for all of us! Now, I know many of you have lost your global monetary cards in the past catastrophes that struck our planet, and you haven't been able to replace them yet.

"I'm also mindful that this has caused many of you to suffer. Let me assure you all that once you receive the new mark, either on your right hand or your forehead, that you will never have this problem again. Your body will be the only identification and verification you will ever need!

"By proudly displaying this mark on your bodies, not only will it prove your loyalty to the new global economy, government, and religion, but it will also allow you to buy, sell, trade, pay rent, seek legal advice, visit your doctors, and so on. Imagine going shopping or eating at a restaurant and leaving your handbags and wallets at home!"

The Pontiff couldn't ignore the glowing expressions he saw on the faces of everyone standing before him. "Impressive, I know. And since we already have control of your assets, everything will be transferred over for you, making this transition infinitely more seamless than it was last time, when you had to forfeit everything to local officials in your communities, before receiving your monetary cards.

"With that truth settled in your minds, let me reiterate to all who receive the mark 'willingly'", the Pope said, using his fingers in quotation marks, "that you will be deemed our true followers, and your loyalty to the new global economy, government and religion will never again come into question.

"Consequently, anyone wishing to participate in helping us locate Christian dissidents must first receive the mark. The instant you receive it, you can download the facial recognition app onto your smartphones and begin at once helping us locate them. With hundreds of millions of them still breathing air on the planet, this trillion-dollar opportunity will be ongoing until the last heretic has been identified and forever silenced.

"You can use these funds to help jump start the global economy, by fixing up your homes and businesses, purchasing new vehicles, and on and on, making this the perfect and final global reset for all compliant citizens. I get excited just thinking about how many new jobs this opportunity will create!

"Now, in no way will your participation serve to cancel the rations or any other assistance you've already been receiving. Those benefits will remain in place for all who receive the mark, until the planet has once again been declared financially stable.

"So, consider it your civic duty to help the cause, only in this case you will be paid for your efforts. Once everything has been transferred over to your new global accounts, the monetary cards you now have in your possession will be deactivated."

The False Prophet of the Bible glanced out at the crowd somberly. "On the other hand, those who do not receive the mark will not be able to buy, sell, trade, or receive paychecks from your employers. Instead, you will be placed on the 'Enemy of the Planet' list! So, if you're still on the fence, the time to climb down and get on board, so to speak, is now!

"I will return to Jerusalem a week from now to unveil the mark, dedicate the newly restored Temple, and present the New World Book of Life that will be based on the glorious future that all who follow Salvador Romanero can look forward to. Copies will be made available to you all. Until then, enjoy the ongoing celebration and may you all be blessed in Salvador's name..."

At that, the Pope backed away from the lectern, but he remained standing alongside the Antichrist of the Bible.

Romanero gripped the lectern and became more serious, stoic even. "You have all heard me end my past speeches with the words, 'May all of you who are still with me be blessed in my name.' Well, it's time to see who really is with me and who isn't. The sad truth is that not all heretics on the planet are Christ followers."

He paused to let his words resonate with his listeners. "It's no secret that there are many false converts living among us, who are presently in possession of the global monetary cards, who aren't Christian dissidents, but in no way are they my true followers, including some I had elevated to such lofty heights, if you can believe that..."

Salvador glanced out at the massive crowd before him, and saw the shocked expressions on so many faces, all wondering to whom he was referring. "The only way to eradicate this most grievous betrayal, and know for sure who is truly with me, will be by implementing the mark.

"This will be the final proof of your allegiance to the new global economy, government, and religion that will soon be in place. Naturally, everyone within my administration will be the first ones to receive it, followed by government officials, law enforcement, prison workers, military members, and all others working essential jobs.

11

"The children will be the last ones to receive the mark. Not only are they too young to buy, sell, or trade, I want them to receive it willingly just like the rest of you. I want true followers," the *Miracle Maker* declared, "not robots!"

The proud, arrogant expression on Romanero's face crumbled when, suddenly, a deep, soul-penetrating voice shook the atmosphere above him. "Fear God and give him glory, because the hour of his judgment has come," Yahweh's minister declared. "Worship him who made the heavens, the earth, the sea and the springs of water."

Everyone in Israel heard it loud and clear, as it boomed high above them. They glanced skyward, their eyes bulging, bodies quaking, before quickly ducking in fear.

After many breathless gasps, a hushed silence fell over the crowd...

2

SALVADOR ROMANERO AND THE Pope were clearly flustered by what had just happened in the sky above them. The glow on their faces was greatly dimmed, their eyes became another shade darker, and their change of posture was quite evident to all onlookers.

The Pope, who was approaching 70, looked as if he was stuck in the hunched over position for the longest time, before he finally found the necessary strength to steady himself, by latching on to Romanero's left shoulder, as his frail body shook uncontrollably.

Romanero took a few deep breaths, then gripped the lectern as tightly as he could, to keep his hands from also quaking, not to mention the rest of his body. "Well, that was interesting," he said, his voice quaking. "As much as I would love to remain in Israel for the seven days of celebration I have declared, to mark this momentous occasion," he lied, "I must return to New Babylon. We haven't a moment to waste!"

Salvador glanced back at the Two dead bodies behind him, hoping to redirect everyone's focus back to why they were all there in the first place—to celebrate their deaths—before his line of vision once again swung back and forth at the large crowd before him.

He cleared his throat, then ended with, "Now that those Two have been forever silenced, the celebration goes on. Even though we may not be here with you in person," he said, referring to himself and the Pope, "please don't let our absence dissuade any of you from enjoying the remaining six days of celebration to the fullest.

"You can rest assured knowing I'll be with you all in spirit. So let not your hearts be troubled. Help is on the way for all who are *truly* with me. May you all be blessed in my name."

It was evident to everyone that his words lacked confidence. No one had to ask why. All they had to do was look up.

Before Salvador left the podium, he was peppered with questions from the press. Since this was the first time in a very long time that reporters could question their leader, there would be no holding back.

One jubilant reporter asked him, "Your Eminence, what about the one hundred and forty four thousand Jewish men out there still slandering your holy name? When will they be silenced too?"

13

It was a valid question. Since they had faithfully backed the Two Witnesses all this time, now that God's Two mouthpieces were gone, many wondered what would become of them?

Romanero flinched, hoping no one had noticed it. "One step at a time," he said flatly, to the man from Dubai, with a forced smile on his face. "For now, we celebrate!"

Another jubilant reporter from Europe then asked him, "Were you stung by the locusts, your Eminence?"

The disheveled expression on the woman's face clearly indicated that she was still traumatized by what had happened to her, during those five terrifying months of unceasing torment she had suffered.

She was stung numerous times and still had the welt marks on her neck and body to prove it. For the most part, the physical pain was gone, but she still met with her psychiatrist twice a week to help get her past the emotional trauma.

Salvador shot a quick glance at his personal doctor, Benjamin Shapiro, before his eyes resettled on the female journalist in the crowd. "No, they didn't have any power over me," he lied again, still trying to brush off what had just happened. "But as an added precaution, I decided to conduct all global business underground, until they were gone. They were just too hideous to look at."

The female reporter flashed an endearing smile at him, relieved to hear the wonderful news. It reinstated her faith that he really was special, and was still worthy of following, despite the constant chaos in the world under his leadership.

Everything quickly changed when she glanced over at Salvador's private doctor and saw him shaking his head in disbelief.

The uneasy exchange between them prompted a follow-up question from her. "Forgive me, your Eminence, but since you just said the locusts were too hideous to look at, can you explain to us why they all bore a strong resemblance to your likeness?"

Seriously? Romanero gazed out at the woman incredulously, then grunted under his breath. "No comment…"

Another eager journalist from China, still trying to come to grips with the terrifying encounter, asked, "Can you tell us what just happened in the skies above, your Eminence?"

When Salvador remained silent, the next question came from a Jewish reporter stationed in Jerusalem. "Now that those Two are finally dead, when will it rain again in Israel? You know how desperately we need it!"

Romanero held out his hands. "No further questions."

The two world leaders were quickly surrounded by their entourages and escorted to a waiting chopper that would take them to Ben Gurion Airport, where a newly-constructed jumbo jet—that made *Air Force One* look like a child's toy—was waiting to take them back to New Babylon.

Before boarding the chopper, the *Miracle Maker* ordered the four journalists to be added to his "Kill List", for embarrassing him the way they had.

Although they all appeared to be on his side, and the questions had been innocently asked, purely out of concern for his and their overall safety, they would never leave Jerusalem alive...

Two of them would leave behind young children and live in partners.

FOR THE FIRST TIME since coming to power, one of Romanero's speeches was interrupted by what was classified by his top military minds, as an unidentified flying object.

Oddly enough, it looked nothing like the flying saucers that were shown in countless Sci-Fi flicks, since the dawn of television.

If anything, this flying drone, or whatever it was, was shaped more like an angelic being of sorts than a spaceship.

Had it come from another planet, or from another galaxy? Or was it something more sinister and nefarious than that?

Perhaps it was technologically generated by some of Romanero's dissenters, to trick his many supporters, hoping to pull them away from him. Perhaps they had found a way to stream the booming Voice through Blu-Tooth technology, which was hooked up to thousands of speakers, cell towers and alarm sirens.

No one knew for sure. Whether it was globally generated or other worldly, it was considered an immediate threat to humanity. This threat was infinitely stealthier than the sneak attack upon Israel three and a half years ago, which had postponed the peace treaty signing between Romanero and the nation of Israel, for three days.

But at least back then, they had a few minutes' notice, unlike now.

And there was no sonic boom or deafening sound this time, like when the meteor entered the earth's orbit a few months ago, causing global mayhem, shattering eardrums, and causing instant deafness to tens of thousands of human beings and animals.

Nor were there strong winds or extreme heat radiating from it, like the massive-sized ball of fire the meteor had generated, that incinerated plants and crops even hundreds of miles away.

No eardrums were pierced this time. Strangely enough, even those who were born deaf, who hadn't yet been eliminated by Romanero's forces for being subhuman, heard and understood the Voice with perfect clarity, as well as those whose eardrums were blown out by the recent meteor strike.

The Most High also granted all other special needs individuals, to include those with mental illness, the ability to comprehend the Message, so there wasn't a single soul on the planet who couldn't hear the Divine proclamation being made in the skies above.

For many, it would lead to their salvation...

With so many people living underground, and with some still residing in the most remote places—with no mobile devices, internet access, or electricity—whereas the voices of the 144,000 couldn't reach them, the voice of God's angelic messenger easily penetrated the deepest depths of the earth.

In short, there wasn't a place on the planet where the angel's voice couldn't be heard. Now that it had started its global mission, to preach the Gospel of Jesus Christ to a lost and sinful world, as a final act of Yahweh's mercy and grace, everyone would hear it with perfect clarity, so if they rejected the Message, they would be without excuse...

THE CHOPPER TOUCHED DOWN at Ben Gurion Airport. Just before his plane left Israel, for the short 805-kilometer flight to Salvador Romanero International Airport, in New Babylon, Romanero glared at one of his top military advisors on board the plane.

He pointed skyward. "Take care of that!"

"Yes, your Excellency," the highly decorated veteran said sheepishly, fully convinced that the God of Israel had sent the Voice, to proclaim the very Message that Romanero himself had outlawed.

How could he think otherwise, since peculiar scenes like this had become the norm in the Holy Land—all at the hands of Israel's God— ever since the *Miracle Maker* came to power?

"Immediately!" Salvador barked again. While Romanero was fully mindful of Who had sent it, what he didn't know at present was that the angelic messenger who had just begun boldly proclaiming the Message to the entire world, wouldn't be leaving his aerial pulpit anytime soon...

"Right away, your Excellency..." The man swallowed hard, then started making phone calls, silently wondering if he could successfully carry out his commander's order...*Could anyone?*

He feared the answer was no.

The instant Romanero's plane was cleared from Israeli airspace, the command was given to fire at will. Hundreds of surface-to-air-missiles were launched at the UFO, at Mach speed, hoping to destroy it.

Not a single missile struck the target. Each one passed through harmlessly, like airplanes breezing through clouds—only infinitely faster—before ultimately detonating far away from the mark.

Had Romanero's top military advisors only had direct access to the Word of God, they would have known that what they had just encountered was the first of three flying angels sent by Yahweh, to declare the Gospel to every person on Planet Earth, plus pronounce judgment on all who would reject the message.

They also would have known that what had made its presence possible in the first place, was that the heavenlies had finally been cleared of all demonic adversaries, when Revelation 12:9 was fulfilled after Yahweh's Two faithful Witnesses were slain: "The great dragon was hurled down—that ancient serpent called the devil, or Satan, who leads the whole world astray. He was hurled to the earth, and his angels with him."

Before that prophecy came to pass, Satan still had access to Heaven. While it was true that the dragon and his angels were cast out of Heaven at the time of their original rebellion, a state of war had always existed in the heavenlies since the devil's fall.

What started this end times intensification was when the raptured Saints passed through the realm of the Prince of the power of the air, three and a half years ago, when Christ came back for His Church.

Satan and his demons fought hard against Michael and his angels, trying to take back every last soul. But because of Christ's finished work on the cross, followed by His resurrection three days later, they weren't strong enough to succeed in their diabolical endeavor.

This warfare intensified significantly when the Most High destroyed Romanero's prisons during the global quake, essentially removing His tortured saints from the planet. Once again, Satan couldn't claim a single soul under the altar that had been ransomed by Christ Jesus.

Like all other redeemed souls throughout the ages, who were covered by the Blood of Jesus, the devil had no power over them! His constant accusations against the believers were always unsuccessful.

But now that Revelation 12:7-9 had come to pass, the end result was that the devil and his fallen angels had lost their place in heaven.

Another thing Romanero's top military advisors would have known had they only had access to the Bible, was that when Satan was cast down to the earth, with one-third of his devilish angels, the dragon entered Salvador Romanero and the Pope, significantly increasing both men's knowledge, and darkening their eyes, evilly displaying their diabolical souls to their scores of followers.

But by having zero access to the Word of God, all they could do at this juncture was speculate…

3

BUT NOT EVERYONE WAS buying what Romanero was offering. These still-on-the-fence supporters, as the *Miracle Maker* himself had dubbed them, weren't nearly as forgiving as the rest of his followers.

Many had lost everything under the man's leadership—some lost millions and even billions of dollars. What he was offering them was a measly drop in the bucket, an insult, really, when compared to the small fortunes that were lost on his watch. It would take a whole lot more than a thousand dollars per dissident to make them whole again.

And that was only one of the things bothering this growing group of global individuals. Even after being quarantined during a global pandemic, society eventually got back to the business of living.

But having endured catastrophe after catastrophe, in the three and a half years in which Romanero had ruled the planet, there was nothing to get back to now, including their livelihoods.

To make matters worse, most global citizens had long since developed cabin fever. Now trapped indoors and even underground for so long, teenagers, especially, could almost feel the walls closing in on them.

Prior to the dawn of the internet, most children and teenagers never wanted to be indoors. When their parents called them home, they usually bickered and moaned.

That all changed when they suddenly had access to the whole world with the touch of a button. Many of the things they had become addicted to over the years stemmed from having constant access to these things on their mobile devices.

They never had to venture outside to satisfy their lusts and addictions, like so many had to do before the internet ensnared the entire planet. All they had to do was turn on their phones from the comfort and privacy of their own homes, to instantly feed their online addictions, whether it be pornography, gambling, video games, and on and on.

On top of that, they got to create their own selfish little worlds online, by presenting themselves the way they wanted to be seen by others, instead of how they truly were. And they had total control over those they could invite into their virtual orbits, shutting out all others, making smartphones the most self-centered invention of all time.

With Satan at the helm, the internet had done a wonderful job of making the proud look even prouder.

Suddenly forced to accept the realization of just how hollow and insignificant their online personas really were, they wanted to put down their phones and go outside again. It was a true miracle that they were suddenly willing to power down their phones and venture outdoors, but their parents still felt it was too risky to agree to their desperate wishes.

Some parents wanted to take their children to the local parks and other recreational places, just to get out of the house for a while, but the thought of venturing outside caused their bodies to tremble in fear.

Even if they wanted to go outdoors, so many community playgrounds were severely damaged or destroyed, including the thousands that were constructed during the great rebuilding period that Romanero had promised his millions of followers around the globe.

Even in areas where local parks and playgrounds were still intact, parents of these toddlers feared leaving the house. Aside from the imminent danger they faced, the air their little ones would breathe could very well be toxic to their still-developing lungs.

And there weren't any shopping malls or toy stores to take their kids to for a change of pace, and for a much-needed mental break. The many malls and shops that had reopened, with great fanfare, after children started populating the planet again, were once again closed.

Would they ever reopen?

Despite Romanero's new round of promises that this new financial opportunity would jumpstart the economy, and create many new jobs planetwide, the jury was still out on whether it would happen...

And now that Hollywood was no longer—what the global quake didn't destroy, the meteor strike and tsunami took care of—the movie and entertainment industry had gone from crippled to totally paralyzed.

With the East Coast of America and the Mid-West being the only semi-inhabitable areas of land still left in the United States of America— much of the West Coast, Alaska and Hawaii had been completely wiped out—Hollywood executives who survived the mayhem were adamant that they would relocate to Atlanta, Georgia, to renovate the world-class studios that were already there, to honor their fallen colleagues.

While they kept brazenly promising to produce movies again, aside from the many "propaganda" documentaries that were made prior to the last rounds of global judgment, all projecting a bright and prosperous future for Salvador Romanero's loyal followers, the motion picture industry was otherwise forced into a complete standstill.

There were no movie theaters to go to, as a possible distraction from the chaos constantly pressing in all around them. Even if the handful of theaters that hadn't been destroyed could afford to reopen, the vast majority in the world would never be able to afford to pay the grossly inflated prices they would have to charge, just to break even.

Vacant for many months now, they looked eerily spooky to all passersby. On top of all that, there weren't any new TV shows, sitcoms, or movies being produced that could be streamed online.

Even if there were, how could their fictional stories possibly compete with what had become of the real world?

There were only so many reruns, including sporting matches, that one could watch before they lost their luster. How could society move forward when all they could watch were reruns? Reruns were a lot like leftover food. They were always good to have so long as there was something new and fresh to look forward to at some point in time.

For the limited few who still had the financial means to attend theme parks, sporting events, and other recreational events, there was no place for them to go to help break the monotony of life. Numerous television commercials had dominated the airwaves before the global quake, promising that theme parks would reopen, yet it still hadn't happened.

There hadn't been any progress made with professional sporting events either. Even though Salvador the Great kept promising they would resume someday, it still hadn't happened.

Spectators were desperate to attend these events, but there weren't any to attend, dashing their hopes yet again.

Even many of the world-class athletes who were once paid big bucks to play in these events, and were worshiped by millions of adoring fans, were thrust down off their high horses in shame and squalor.

21

With a sinking feeling that professional sports might never be played again, many of them fell into severe depression. Much like their fans, they kept chomping at the bit for their careers to resume, so they could once again use the God-given talents they had received at birth, instead of having them waste away.

But after waiting three and a half years for play to finally resume, many of them silently feared their careers were over for good.

How could they think otherwise, with calamity after calamity constantly rocking the planet on which they were treated as kings and queens, prior to the disappearances? It seemed that for every positive step they took forward under Romanero's leadership, they were ultimately thrust back a thousand steps, a thousand miles felt more like it.

To make matters worse, the fortunes they had amassed before the disappearances had dwindled down to nothing, including the countless millions they had subsequently invested into various stock markets and real estate ventures.

When they transferred their resources onto the global monetary cards, a little more than a year ago, like most other citizens on the planet, there wasn't much to transfer over. They were now destitute, and desperate to create new streams of income, without success.

Blessed in Romanero's name? What a joke! Even their podcast audiences had dwindled down to nothing. No one seemed to care about their personal problems. The millions who had practically worshipped them had more than enough to deal with in their own personal lives, than to remain emotionally invested in the lives of their former heroes.

Suddenly insignificant, many had already thrown in the towel and had stopped their daily exercise routines. Many had let themselves go and were grossly out of shape. They resembled those who had retired from their professions long ago. Others had lost so much weight that they looked like mere shells of their former selves…

What guarantees did they or anyone else have that this next reset would serve to turn things around, and finally allow them to reopen their doors? There were none!

Which would explain why many of his loyal followers were cautiously optimistic at best, regarding the celebration taking place in

Jerusalem, not to mention the many new promises being spewed out of Romanero's mouth, like poisonous venom from a snake.

They applauded how he had finally silenced his Two adversaries, by having them murdered in the streets, but after so many gargantuan setbacks with Salvador the Great at the helm of the ship, they would reserve praise or judgment on every new promise he would make to them, from this point forward. How could they not?

This increasingly growing group of individuals, including many Jews, were starting to pay closer attention to what the 144,000 kept preaching. As of yet, much like the Two Witnesses that Romanero had silenced the other day, nothing they ever said could ever be disproved.

Which could only mean they were preaching the Truth.

Unlike Salvador Romanero...

Tragically, for some who had lost everything, by ignoring the message that God's 144,000 sealed servants kept preaching, it would lead them to suicide.

SALVADOR ROMANERO WAS QUITE mindful of what these individuals were saying about him. He would let them vent their emotions, knowing it all came down to receiving the mark. Then he would know beyond certainty who his true followers were.

4

BUT IN A WORLD where most citizens were starving to death or dying from the constant plagues and pestilence bombarding the planet, with no jobs to go to, they applauded the *Miracle Maker* for the very timely opportunity he had just offered them.

Countless multitudes had been out of work since the disappearances. Those who were able to keep their jobs were suddenly unemployed, when their places of business were destroyed in the global quake.

Many companies that were fortunate enough to survive those two phenomena, were later destroyed by the meteor strike and the ensuing tsunami which had ravaged much of the world.

Businesses that had miraculously remained open despite it all, had to close their doors during the five-month demonic locust attack. Their employees were too frightened to come to work!

The end result of all of this was that most citizens on the planet were bordering on financial destitution.

With most household cupboards on the planet now threadbare, celebrating the murders of the Two troublemakers meant eating an extra Ramen soup. But at least they finally had a reason to rejoice again. It was as if a huge yoke had just been lifted off their shoulders.

They exchanged gifts with one another, many by way of bartering, or by signing promissory notes which would be made whole once they started earning income from this much-needed opportunity.

Despite that their collective nerves were rattled yet again, after witnessing something eerily strange transpiring in the heavens above, having already bartered everything that was worth something, they were becoming more desperate as the days passed.

Suddenly, an extra thousand dollars in their pockets, per capture, sounded like all the money in the world to them. They were grateful to the *Miracle Maker* and the Pope for the opportunity, and couldn't wait for next week to come, so they could go in search of Christian dissidents.

Without this opportunity, survival would be impossible!

Even those who once earned that much money in a day, or even in an hour or minute—including presidents and CEOs of some of these now bankrupt companies—would embrace this opportunity until things got better, and they could once again live their lives with gusto.

They would pour all their energy into finding and detaining Christians living in hiding, the instant the mark became available to them.

Even many of the world-renowned celebrities, and global leaders, that Romanero had invited to the Holy Land, to witness the slaying of the Two enemies of the planet, said in interviews that they were eager to join in the hunt for dissident Christ followers.

They promised to donate whatever they might earn to the charities of their choice.

In that light, Romanero was spot on. This really was the perfect reset. His speech had served to assuage the grief that most felt, after just losing everything again. Thanks to him, instead of sitting home and feeling sorry for themselves, this would be an easy way to get out and earn the income that was desperately needed.

And since the food and medicine rations they were already receiving wouldn't be forfeited by participating, even detaining one Christian per month would give them a little breathing room, and allow them to fix the many things that needed fixing, just as the Pope had declared.

Now, instead of watching Christian dissidents being slaughtered on the more than 10,000 livestream cameras, at Romanero's thousands of death camps—literally around the clock—to help pass the time until things eventually got better, they would soon be paid to help the cause.

Suddenly, these individuals were willing to overcome their fear of going outdoors and join the millions of others who would soon scour the country looking for Christian dissidents, upon receiving the mark and downloading the facial app technology on their smartphones.

With millions of little ones already walking, they could kill two birds with one stone—take their kids outside for some not-so-fresh air and earn a little extra income in the process.

In the end, it was all about the money. They were eager to begin…

MEGAN MCCALLISTER'S EYES FLASHED upon hearing this most wonderful news from Salvador Romanero. "Now we can stop worrying about trying to raise more money to find Brian," she said, squeezing

25

Rachel Stein's left hand, "and actually get paid for turning him in to the authorities…"

Rachel glanced over at her wife of just a few short, turbulent months, and nodded at her hopefully, even if skeptically. She was living proof that even new mothers were bordering on financial disaster!

With the inflation rate soaring to new unsustainable levels after each new catastrophe, the vouchers they received every month only brought them so far. There was always too much month at the end of the vouchers.

On top of all that, they both had been stung several times each during the five months in which the planet was under attack, by those vile monstrous locusts.

Rachel was the first to be stung. She became so furious with Megan that she took out her frustration on her. "Why does everything keep happening to me?!" she had screamed, crying hysterically. "Why can't it happen to you instead?"

Megan knew it was Rachel's way of reminding her that the only income she had generated since relocating to Pennsylvania, was the $5K disbursement she had received after transferring what little she had onto the global monetary card.

Other than that, she hadn't contributed anything else financially. *Hopefully this will do the trick*! she thought, inching closer to her wife.

In fairness to Megan, who was equally depressed herself, she was doing a wonderful job trying to help Rachel overcome her manic depression. She did all the cooking, cleaning, and most of the laundry, plus watched the baby whenever Rachel needed rest.

But what stung Rachel nearly as much as the locust stings was, having been assured on numerous occasions by the *Miracle Maker* himself, that new mothers would be well taken care of, she had faithfully followed all the rules.

That was the reason she decided to get pregnant in the first place. As a full-fledged feminist, she had no plans of ever getting married, let alone let some man impregnate her. But when women were urged to help repopulate the planet, she felt it was her global duty to do her part.

It took a while to adjust to this new mindset of sorts, but after feeling the baby kicking inside her womb for the very first time, the joy of motherhood took full control of her emotions, especially since she was treated like royalty everywhere she went, from the doctor's office to the supermarket, and everyplace in between. This made her feel even more honored to help the cause. She thanked her lucky stars every day.

Those days were long gone, along with the dreamy expression that was plastered on her face leading up to the birth of her son, Zachary. Rachel no longer felt special on any level.

In short, the woman who once brimmed so confidently with high hopes for a bright future, leading up to the birth of her son, was nowhere to be found. All these things combined was what had pushed Stein into her ongoing postpartum depression. Nothing could snap her out of it.

Even her dream of returning to her home state of Michigan and moving into the house that the *Miracle Maker* had promised her, after the six-month quarantine that all new mothers were subjected to had passed, now seemed a longshot at best.

The locust invasion, followed by the fallout created by the meteor strike, kept her stranded in Pennsylvania against her will, imprisoned inside her own apartment.

On top of that, they were out of money again. The combined $10K one-time disbursement they had received didn't last long. The original plan was that half of it would be put aside for when they returned to Michigan.

After purchasing a used 4-wheeler to better navigate the roads, and stocking the shelves with whatever essentials they could purchase at the market, or online, they ended up spending the rest of the money on making repairs to the apartment.

They didn't have much choice in the matter. With so much faulty wiring all throughout the complex, from the global quake, many of the outlets still weren't working properly, if at all. And while the owners were ultimately responsible for maintaining the condos, they managed to escape financial responsibility by filing for bankruptcy.

In the end, after being assured that they would never be asked to leave, they ended up spending $4K trying to make the apartment safer for Zach.

When the locusts flooded the area, some of the money was foolishly spent sealing more cracks in the walls. This did nothing to prevent them from gaining inside access and attacking the two women. Both had been stung a half dozen times each, even when they were sleeping!

But Zach wasn't stung once. Even after being assured that the locusts were gone for good, Rachel was still too traumatized by the horrific encounter to step foot outside the apartment, let alone attempt traveling back to her home state of Michigan with Megan, as wife and wife.

27

When Dick Mulrooney left them high and dry, without giving them the $500 he had promised, it started a dreadful spiral downward for the couple that hadn't stopped since.

After trying to cheer Rachel up for many months, thanks to their hero, hopefully this opportunity would finally help them get their lives back on track. "Think about it, honey, we know Brian, Jacquelyn and Brian's mother are living together. If Brian's father joined them, that could mean four thousand dollars in our pockets," Megan said, greed dripping from her words. "And if Charles Calloway and Tamika Moseley are also there, it could be potentially more than that!"

Rachel nodded with relief, just hearing the newfound confidence behind her wife's assuring words.

Still hopeful for a bright and prosperous future together, all they needed was to find a way to survive until the new utopia that Salvador the Great kept promising was finally realized. Perhaps this was it!

First their loving savior had silenced the two whackos in Jerusalem. Now he was offering them this wonderful opportunity one day later.

Yes, things were finally looking up for them. Finding Christian dissidents was the best news the couple had heard in a very long time, especially since it could potentially mean thousands of dollars in their account very soon, beginning with the arrest of Brian Mulrooney and his cohorts.

After all, Brian was the reason they were in Pennsylvania to begin with. Could this be it? After racking her brain senseless trying to find a way to carry her weight, financially speaking, Megan had a very good feeling inside. She smiled at the possibilities.

MANY ROMANERO SUPPORTERS ACROSS the planet started feeling hopeful again. Little did they know that two days from now their faith in him, as their messiah, would be shaken to the core yet again…

5

CLAYTON HOLMES AND TRAVIS Hartings wasted no time sending out an audio message to all *End Times Salvation Movement* members, who were still able to receive them.

Holmes began, "Well, here we are at the beginning of the midway point of the Tribulation period. With the mind-numbing judgments we've already endured, it's difficult imagining things getting any worse, but we all know they will. We ain't seen nothing yet!

"Man, oh man! Did you see the look on Romanero's face when the angel appeared high above him, boldly declaring Revelation fourteen, seven? As all of you already know, this is the first one. Two more angels are still to come. What a powerful reminder to us all that God is still in control. Imagine the shock on Antichrist's face two days from now, when the Two Witnesses are resurrected from the dead!

First, to see them breathing fire out of their mouths, knowing they'll be raised to life. Now to see and hear God's angelic messenger proclaiming the Gospel of Jesus Christ, for all to hear, I can't tell you how comforted I am by this. Seeing these powerful prophecies coming to pass before my very eyes, I can't help but feel like a first-generation Christian!

"The whole world is seeing Revelation fourteen, verse seven, coming to pass before their very eyes, even if they don't know the Source behind it. Even more exciting to me is knowing he is also fulfilling verse six, which declares, 'Then I saw another angel flying in midair, and he had the eternal gospel to proclaim to those who live on the earth—to every nation, tribe, language and people.'

"Talk about Matthew twenty-four, fourteen being fulfilled! To refresh your memories, Christ said in His sermon on the Mount, 'And this gospel of the kingdom will be preached in the whole world as a testimony to all nations, and then the end will come.'

"What better way to make sure everyone on the face of the earth hears it, than to set an angel in midheaven flying back and forth, day after day, proclaiming the eternal gospel of the kingdom! I get excited just thinking about how many new converts will come as a result!

"Long before the Rapture, many Christian pastors taught their flocks that this prophecy from our Lord was close to being fulfilled. The fact that we're still waiting for it to happen should indicate to us all that they were nowhere near as close as they had once imagined. Bottom line: we will be the generation to witness Christ's prophecy coming to pass.

"Beloved, if we think Romanero and the Pope, whom you must know will start playing a vastly larger role, were out to get us before Satan entered them, we ain't seen nothing yet! The fact that they just gave Planet Earth's most heinous evildoers the permission to do what they did best—commit violent crimes—only now they'll be paid to kill humans at will, you know, *us*, should tell us all we need to know!

"They already hate us! Imagine how motivated they'll be now that the Antichrist and False Prophet of the Bible have just put bounties on our heads? Another reason He wants Christians gone so badly, is so he can focus his attention on killing the Jews next."

No one could see the anguished expression on Clayton's face, but the desperation in his voice gave each listener the impression that their side was losing the battle, not winning it.

Their tried-and-true leader sounded exhausted, defeated. No one had to ask why. With the screws being tightened on their organization a little more each day, he no doubt felt the weight of it all squarely on his shoulders. Then again, every *ETSM* resident felt it.

With communications often stymied, and since Clayton and Travis had long since resorted to doing audio messages only, the vast majority of their residents hadn't seen their faces in quite some time.

With the ongoing rationing of food, and the daily stress, Clayton had shed more than 40 percent of his body weight off his 6'5" body, since the Rapture. His skin was sagging in some areas, namely in the stomach region. He almost looked unrecognizable! But all *ETSM* residents were thinner now.

"Not that any of you need to be reminded, but with the mark of the beast now imminent, once it has been willfully received by someone, they can hear the Gospel being preached a million times, but they won't be able to respond to it in a soul-saving way. This mark represents a finality of sorts, in that all who take it will be eternally doomed."

Holmes shook his head sadly. "For now, God's salvation window is still open for lost souls to get saved, but by just a sliver. As we all know, once they receive it on their arms or on their foreheads, there can be no turning back for them.

"Instead of still referring to them as the 'unconverted', we can know for sure at that time that they are our eternal enemies. Not that any of us will be out in public, but if any of you are displaced once the mark is available, you can know for sure those eternal enemies of God will surely be out capturing our images on their phones, so they can get paid for their efforts."

Holmes ended by warning, "Not to further frighten any of you, we're already reeling from the last rounds of judgments to strike the planet. Powerful as the last quake was, I feel the need to remind all of you who survive that long that God's final earthquake will cause every mountain to not only be shaken but be completely leveled.

"Listen to what the prophet Isaiah recorded in chapter twenty-four, verses nineteen and twenty, in the Book bearing his name. He frighteningly declared, 'The earth is shaken violently. The earth reels to and fro like a drunkard.' This coincides perfectly with Revelation sixteen, eighteen: 'There was a great earthquake, such as there had not been since man came to be upon the earth.'

"To give you all an added perspective, the earthquake that struck Japan in twenty eleven was so violent that some scientists claimed it shook the earth ten inches off its axis. If true, I can only wonder how far the earth was moved with the global quake we recently had. Three feet? Ten? However far, even it won't compare to what's still to come, not to mention God's many other judgments."

Holmes paused, then added, "As all of you know, there can be no praying away what is still-to-come. It is written and, therefore, it must come to pass. All we can do is prepare for it to the best of our ability.

"Only God knows who among us will still be alive when Christ returns. All I can say for sure is, as the world keeps spiraling into endless chaos, the Word of God hasn't changed one jot or tittle.

"So let me comfort you all with this powerful scripture from Second Corinthians four, 'We are hard pressed on every side, but not crushed; perplexed, but not in despair; persecuted, but not abandoned; struck down, but not destroyed. Therefore we do not lose heart. Though outwardly we are wasting away, yet inwardly we are being renewed day by day. For our light and momentary troubles are achieving for us an eternal glory that far outweighs them all. So we fix our eyes not on what is seen, but on what is unseen, since what is seen is temporary, but what is unseen is eternal.'

"Man, that's good! Let us cling tightly to this glorious promise from God to His children! I love you all so much and consider it the honor of a lifetime to be part of this amazing organization of believers! For how much longer, only God knows! But until that day comes, keep fighting the good fight. Pray for us as we pray for you. God is with us. May His grace, peace and protection be multiplied to you all. Here's Travis…"

"Greetings beloved!" Hartings began, "Given the dire circumstances we face each day, aside from welcoming all who are being sent to our properties from the one hundred and forty four thousand, using our printing presses to publish the Gospel message into many languages—which are being distributed by God's sealed servants in booklet form—caring for and protecting our precious children to the best of our abilities, and praying and fasting, from an organizational standpoint, there isn't much else we can do at this stage, except hunker down and keep growing in the scriptures, as we prepare for the worst.

"At any rate, thanks to God's divine provision, we were able to replenish much of what was lost in the global quake, during the five months in which God sent the locusts to torment all who weren't saved!

"Even amid the constant chaos, Genesis eight, twenty-two, which, to remind you declares, 'As long as the earth endures, seedtime and harvest, cold and heat, summer and winter, day and night will never cease,' is as true today as when it was written thousands of years ago, after the flood in the days of Noah.

"How awesome is our God for blessing us with a bountiful harvest! Even though we may never have the opportunity to grow crops outdoors again, we must praise our King for this very timely blessing!

"Now that we're in the final stages of being hunkered down for good, the one item that was overlooked at the outset was the need for replacement glass windows. Shortly before cash became illegal, and the unconverted world started using the global monetary card, we purchased five glass-making factories in Virginia, Texas, Montana, Oregon, and in California, so we could make glass windows ourselves. The two on the West Coast were subsequently destroyed in the tsunami.

"Believe me when I say, I'm no expert on the subject, but what I've recently learned is that glass is made from liquid sand, mixed with various chemicals. Once the sand's subjected to seventeen-hundred-degree temperatures, it turns into liquid. As the cooling process begins, the sand never returns to its grainy, gritty form, it remains a liquid.

"The glass we've been producing is tempered, much like bullet proof glass, to hopefully protect some of us from God's remaining judgments. It very much resembles the way it was made hundreds of years ago; in that

32

it will not be completely transparent. Nor would it ever pass governmental regulatory tests, but that's not the goal.

"We're also using this tempered glass to replace the many fish tanks that were lost in the global quake, and mason jars for storing food. Hopefully, they will fare better in the coming judgments…

"With that in mind, if anyone staying at your safe houses has experience in the glass-making field, or if they're willing to help us bring more truckloads of sand to our three remaining warehouses, have them contact me immediately. Naturally, safe houses that are presently being fortified with these items are those housing our precious children.

"For those of you who will not benefit from the glass windows we're making, I'll be posting a glass making tutorial video later in the day, which will show you a step-by-step process on how to do it on your own. But you'll have to obtain the sand for yourselves. But if there's one thing that we still have plenty of in this world, it's sand.

"As you might imagine, we'll need all the help we can get before the mark and subsequent facial recognition app become widely available. At that time, who knows if we'll be able to do it.

"That's all I have to say for now. Now that we've reached this point, we should expect things to happen in rapid succession, even more quickly than the first three and a half years, if you can believe that. But as all of you know, every day we wake up, we're one day closer to being with Jesus, where we'll never have to live in fear again.

"But until that day comes, we must always be mindful of just how dangerous it is living on a planet being ruled by an evil so dark that, save for those who lived in the days of Noah, before the flood, and perhaps those who were in Sodom and Gomorrah when God destroyed those two wicked cities, no other generation has encountered anything close to what we are dealing with, on a daily basis.

"As always, Clayton and I pray for you each day, always thanking God, the Father of our Lord Jesus Christ for each of you..."

At that, the message ended. Little did the two *ETSM* leaders know that every word they had just spoken was recorded by the enemy…

6

BRIAN AND JACQUELYN MULROONEY listened to Clayton Holmes' and Travis Hartings' dire message up in their bedroom. Both were seized with fear. They summoned everyone to the safe house number one sanctuary, then played it through the Bluetooth speakers so everyone could hear it for themselves.

The instant Travis finished speaking, Tamika Moseley became so frightened that she blurted out her husband, Isaac, "I don't want to spend another night alone."

Everyone sitting near the couple heard her loud and clear.

It had only been three weeks since Isaac became a resident at safe house number one, but the twenty-one nights he had slept in the shoddily reconstructed men's dormitory, felt more like two years to him.

It was the worst kind of torture to read the Bible with his wife each night, only to leave her at the main house and go back to the men's dormitory, especially with so much uncertainty in the air.

It was like sweet music to Isaac's ears. He shifted his weight in his pew in the third row. "Are you sure you're ready?"

Tamika glanced at him with a certain determination in her demeanor that demanded his full attention. Though she had initially willed herself to wait a full month before sharing the same bed with Isaac, Clayton and Travis had just changed everything. "Yes, but under one condition."

Isaac raised an eyebrow, then rubbed his chin very slowly with two fingers. His beard was slowly growing back. He wished his two front teeth he lost while trying to escape the angry group of Muslims that were camped outside his apartment building waiting to kill him, would grow back as well. He now spoke with a lisp at times. "And that is…"

"Before we share the same bed again, I'd like to renew our vows, so we can rededicate ourselves to each other…"

Isaac's face lit up. "When?"

Tamika let her eyes wander throughout the sanctuary. Everyone who could hear her listened with great interest. "Today, if possible…"

A grin crossed Isaac's face. "What can I say? You just made my day!"

Tamika glanced up at Tom Dunleavey in a front row pew. "Brother Tom, would you mind marrying us again?"

Tom craned his neck back at them. "It would be my pleasure! Since we're already in the sanctuary, why not do it before dinner is served in the cafeteria? I believe we're having salmon and vegetables tonight. We can celebrate your rededication there."

Tamika glanced at Isaac, who nodded excitedly, then flashed Tom a grateful smile. "Sounds perfect!"

Sarah Mulrooney interrupted, "Would it be okay if we joined you?" Dick shot a confused look at his wife. She reached for his hand. "Even though we've been sharing the same bed the past three weeks, now that we're true Christians, I feel it's the right thing to do."

Tom said, "Sure, so long as Isaac and Tamika don't have a problem with it."

The Moseleys nodded at each other. "We'd love that!"

"Let us begin then," said Tom, joyously, "without further delay!"

After the two casually dressed couples exchanged their renewal vows, Tom announced, "It is with great pleasure that I introduce our newest newlyweds, part two, Isaac and Tamika Moseley, and Dick and Sarah Mulrooney! Gentlemen, you may now kiss the brides!" He winced jokingly, then corrected himself. "Your brides, I mean!"

Everyone laughed then started clapping.

The former Catholic priest glanced around the sanctuary and couldn't overlook the new level of concern he saw on so many faces. He felt certain that since Romanero had just placed bounties on their heads, *ETSM* weddings would surely be on the rise, and he would be officiating plenty more of them in the coming days.

Like with all other marriages performed at safe house number one, none of them would ever be registered in the state of Pennsylvania.

Everyone made their way to the cafeteria for supper. Much like in the sanctuary, there was no reserved or preferential seating in the cafeteria. It was first come first serve. This was even true for Jefferson Danforth, which was perfectly fine with him.

The first time the front row was offered to him in the sanctuary, he waved it off declaring that he and Amy were merely servants, nothing more. He even asked them not to call him, "Sir," and even cooked meals for his co-residents in Christ every other day, as Amy worked in one of the seven daycare centers scattered about the property.

After the newlyweds were served their meals, Tom blessed the food, then everyone else got in line for their dinners.

Tamika put a forkful of salmon in her mouth and took her time chewing on it, before swallowing. Since they had salmon three times a week, delicious as it was, she said to Isaac, "I'd gladly trade it for a Reuben sandwich at Mitzi's deli!"

Brian heard the exchange and interjected, "Yeah, and after that, some fresh-brewed coffee and cheesecake!"

Tamika frowned. "I miss Craig."

"Me too. Just wish he would have…" Brian was unable to finish the sentence. He lowered his head, not wanting to think about what had become of his former childhood friend, eternally speaking.

Charles sensed what Brian was thinking and steered the conversation back on track. "What I wouldn't do for a few slices of New York City pizza right now!"

Mary Johnson interjected, "No, wait! How about a juicy cheeseburger deluxe at Five Napkin Burger!"

"Yummy!" said Sarah in reply. "Even just going to a local diner for a bite to eat sounds wonderful! I sure miss those days…"

Mary sighed. "I really miss going window shopping after my shift at the Waldorf. Manhattan had some of the best displays in the world. The money I used to spend at those places in my mind!"

"Glad those days are over!" said Donald, causing many to laugh.

Joaquim and Leticia Guzman were seated across from the Johnsons. Leticia asked Mary, "Does this remind you of our wedding night?"

Mary replied, "I was just saying that to Donald!" What had initially started with the Johnsons exchanging vows two Christmas Eves ago, had quickly turned into three weddings, when Joaquim and Leticia asked if they could also be married, followed by Deacon Stone and Miss Evelyn.

Leticia frowned. "I sure miss Deacon Stone and Miss Evelyn. They were a lovely couple…"

Donald saw Charles drop his head sadly. He was with them when they perished in the global quake. "Least we know they're in a better place."

Calloway glanced up at Donald and uttered a soft, sad, "Amen…"

Joaquim sat next to his wife, holding their son Julio Jr. on his lap. "Brother Tom's sense of humor sure surfaces at weddings. Normally he's more reserved, dry even."

Donald nodded in agreement. "Yeah, we still have the *Johnson and Johnson* baby oil he gave us as a wedding gift, which Tamika had to deliver to us, after Tom suffered a massive heart attack…"

Joaquim said, "I remember it well. What an intense night that was!"

Donald took a large gulp of water. "I'll say! I'm surprised there weren't more heart attacks after that surprise visit..."

Joaquim rubbed his entire face vigorously, using both hands. "I still remember how frightened I was when you, me, Brian, and Tony Pearsall raced out back with night vision binoculars, looking for the intruders only to see hundreds of people coming straight toward us!"

Mary sighed. "Certainly wasn't the ideal way to start a wedding."

Joaquim looked down at his plate. "Truthfully, I wouldn't have changed a thing. By far, it was my best day living here."

"Mine too," said Leticia. "I can still see the lit Christmas trees in the sanctuary, and wreaths hung on all the walls..."

Joaquim sniffed air in through his nose. "Wish I could still smell the deep-fried turkeys we had that night!"

Donald said, "Man! What I wouldn't do for some turkey, mashed potatoes, and all the fixins now!"

Mary added, "Yeah, and snow!"

Donald thought about what Joaquim had said and conceded to him. "I would have to agree with you. It was my best day here too..."

Leticia sighed. "Seems like so long ago..."

Dr. Meera Singh listened and cracked a smile. If there was one thing she was encouraged by, it was that her diabetes patients were all experiencing lower A1C readings, which she attributed to the smaller, healthier portions of food being consumed at safe house number one.

On top of that, the enormous amounts of junk food that most of them had consumed in the past were no longer part of their daily diets. Many of them no longer needed insulin or any other of the medications they always relied upon. Glucose levels had dropped significantly at all safe houses.

Then again, given the circumstances, even if their vitals and blood tests declared them healthier, the compounding stress they felt for always expecting the worst, didn't make them look or feel any healthier.

Julio Gonzales sat next to his wife, Marta, bouncing his daughter, Ruth, on his lap. He glanced over at the newlyweds and yelled, "Speech!"

"Yeah, speech!" Donald Johnson echoed.

Usually, this was where the best man gave his speech. But since there weren't any best men, Dick and Isaac stared at each other, both hesitant to be the first to speak.

Finally, Isaac cleared his throat and sat up a little straighter. "When we was married the first time, I took Tamika to Atlantic City, on a three day honeymoon. I confess the only thing on my mind on the two-hour bus ride was getting her alone in that hotel room!"

The way he said it so comically, so emphatically, caused more desperately needed laughter to reverberate all throughout the cafeteria.

Even Jefferson and Amy Danforth burst out in laughter.

Tamika elbowed her husband in the gut, and Isaac grew serious. "But that was then. I know our time together will be short but let me just say now that my promise to love and honor you so long as we both shall live, is one hundred percent true this time."

Isaac lowered his head and looked down at his worn-out shoes, which no groom would ever think to wear before the Rapture. "Unlike eight years ago when I violated my oath by converting to Islam, and leaving you all alone with two kids to raise, my goal this time will be to leave the consummating *Round Two* decision up to you," he said, once again lisping all consonants, "My goal from this day forward will be to do my very best to make you feel loved and protected in my arms each night. That will be just as good to me as making love."

Tears trickled down Tamika's cheeks knowing he was being truthful this time.

Everyone in attendance was deeply touched by Isaac's heartfelt declaration to his wife.

Dick gulped hard, realizing it was his turn to say something. *How can I possibly top that?* He cleared his throat and gazed deeply into Sarah's eyes. "Much like Isaac, I'm grateful for this second chance with you, my dear. Who would've thought it possible a few short months ago? On many levels, even among the craziness, the last three weeks we spent together were three of the best weeks of my life."

Dick glanced over at Isaac. "After everything you and I have been through these past few months, it only figures that we've rededicated our marriages together. You've become a true friend and a brother to me."

Isaac pressed his lips together and didn't bother wiping the tears from his eyes. "Right back at you. God has answered our prayers!"

Dick grinned at him without showing his teeth. "Yes, He has!"

Brian lowered his head and started weeping, still amazed that God had answered all their prayers in this regard. It was a true miracle!

Dick kissed his wife on the lips, then continued, "At any rate, I never thought I'd see the day when God would use the religion that had torn us apart, to ultimately bring us back together again."

"I can relate!" said Isaac. "Only in my case, I was the one who left Tamika in the name of religion. But when I think about how God used a former Muslim to travel to New York, to die for me, hoping that I would get saved as a result, it still blows my mind! Wow! Just wow!"

Dick let his eyes wander about the cafeteria. "I would also like to take this time to apologize to those of you who were at my son's wedding in Michigan. I made a complete fool of myself that day. The anger I harbored toward you all back then was intense.

"I never thought the day would come when we would end up being friends, let alone living together on the same property. I'm sure some of you are thinking the same thing. Isn't God good?"

"So good!" Lila Choharjo shouted.

Dick nodded at his son, then confessed to Sarah, "But my biggest regret since the whole world changed, was my foul behavior on the day I tore the Bible you were reading to shreds, in front of Chelsea."

Sarah's lips quivered at the mention of their late daughter's name. She wiped tears from her eyes with the sleeve of the sweater she was wearing.

Dick confessed, "Turns out you weren't the only one keeping a secret back then. As you were reading the Bible without me knowing it, I started having dreams about Renate, after Romanero and the Pope urged young girls and women of all ages to get pregnant and do their part to repopulate the planet."

"Oh?" Sarah was shocked to hear this. Her nose crinkled. "What kind of dreams were you having?"

"That Renate gave birth to a son." Dick glanced over at Brian. "You were the father, but you weren't part of the picture. The best part about it was that Renate promised to let me raise my grandson as a Catholic."

Dick snickered and shook his head sadly. "Prior to the Rapture, I never would have entertained such a notion. I would have woken from that dream calling it a nightmare. But when the two of you left the Church, it suddenly sounded promising to me, sort of like a replacement legacy of sorts. I was convinced it would happen at some point."

Dick lowered his head. "Then Renate took her life and that dream ended, which only added to the anger I felt toward you for leaving the church. Now I'm convinced my dream was purely Satanic."

He glanced back at Sarah. "I already told you when I came to Pennsylvania searching for you, I stayed with Renate and Rachel..."

Sarah nodded at him, fully mindful that all eyes were on them.

39

"Turns out Renate told Megan about the dream. She reminded me of it one night after a full day of searching for you. She begged me to impregnate her. She even dangled the proverbial legacy carrot before my eyes, saying instead of being a grandfather, I could be a father again."

Sarah flinched in her chair hearing this, then braced herself. "And?" Her voice cracked.

Dick leaned back and fiddled his thumbs a moment before saying, "Megan kept trying to convince me that getting her pregnant would be the perfect revenge on Brian, for everything he did to destroy our families. At that time, I was in total agreement with her, at least the part about Brian destroying our families, that is…"

Brian wasn't the least bit surprised to hear this.

Dick went on, "But mostly, I think she was jealous because Rachel was just weeks away from giving birth, and she wanted to get pregnant herself. She said she was dead broke, and getting pregnant was her only hope of survival."

Sarah looked a little uncomfortable having this conversation with her husband, with so many others listening. "So, what happened next?"

"Nothing happened. When she tried seducing me, I told her I would think about it, just to get her to stop begging me. I woke early the next morning and left the apartment, knowing I'd never return."

Dick looked down at his half-eaten dinner plate. "I'm sure they're still mad at me for not giving them the money I promised. There's no doubt in my mind they won't hesitate to turn us in for the bounty Romanero's offering, if they ever discover this location."

Sarah asked, "Do you think they know you're here?"

Dick took a deep breath and exhaled. "Can't say for sure. But if they do find out, it will motivate them even more…"

Silence filled the cafeteria, as everyone took a moment to process what they had just heard. For Brian, seeing his parents being so transparent with each other was further proof that both had been changed by the power of the Holy Spirit.

Finally, Tamika said glumly, "Since we're all baring our souls, I won't deny the thorn in my side is the guilt I still feel over Amos' death. How could I not when he went to New York just for me?"

Isaac squeezed Tamika's left hand with his right hand, then sighed.

Meera interjected, "It's not your fault. Neither of you. Amos went to New York willingly. Besides, do either of you think he would want to come back to this place?"

Isaac and Tamika both nodded no.

"Frankly, I'm jealous I'm not where he is now. His days of living in fear are over. As much as I miss Amos, imagine how awesome it will be when we're all reunited on the other side, living in perfect peace and safety, in the protection of our loving Savior!

"One thing I know for certain, when that time comes, if either of you try apologizing to him, I can already envision him waving it off, especially since God used his death to rescue you and Dick."

A smile curled onto the *ETSM* doctor's lips. "Imagine the eternal treasures he stored up for laying down his life for two brothers, especially since you both got saved as a result? In that light, it was God's will that it happened, just as Amos kept persisting, and not your fault. You must believe this!"

Tamika lowered her head and started sniffling. She opened her mouth to speak but no words came out.

Marta Gonzalez said, "I'll never forget Amos' first visit here on our daughter's wedding night. I never saw someone eat so much snow in all my life!"

Her comment caused more laughter to fill the cafeteria.

Lila Choharjo giggled. "He sure knew how to keep things lively."

Since it was a special occasion, to close out the wedding celebration, Marta Gonzalez made sure to bake enough peach and apple pies for everyone to have a slice.

After that, everyone not working the late shift or standing guard went back to their residences…

7

ISAAC SCOOPED TAMIKA UP in his arms and carried her all the way to the main house. She still walked with a limp from when the cafeteria wall came crumbling down on top of her during the global quake, but that's not why he did it. He wanted to be romantic.

Isaac was still blown away by what had been discussed at supper. Given the present climate, being surrounded by enemies at every turn, it was the best gift either couple could have received from their dinner guests. There was this redeeming quality about being so transparent with one another. Neither had ever felt such raw closeness before.

One thing was certain: the topics that were broached this night, were never discussed at any wedding they had ever attended before the Rapture, unless it came in the form of gossip.

Back then, not only were they too busy doing a million different things to spend much quality time with friends and loved ones, but they were too prideful and too ashamed to even consider being so open and honest with each other, especially with so many others listening.

Some would have preferred numbing themselves with booze or drugs over being transparent in front of others, especially with friends and family members. It was a freeing sensation to be sure.

The Moseleys joined the Danforths, the four Mulrooneys, Charles Calloway, Tom Dunleavey, Meera Singh, and Lila Choharjo in the living room for another group chat, before calling it a night.

Much like the cafeteria conversation earlier, it was lively and engaging, as Brian and Jacquelyn brought the newer residents up to speed on how they discovered the property, three and a half years ago.

The Danforths had already heard much of it before, but they still listened with great interest, as the Mulrooneys retold some of the remarkable history that had been shared at this place, both good and bad.

Dick and Isaac had already heard much of it from their wives, but every time the story was retold, new elements were always added.

There was a pause in the conversation, until Isaac turned to face Jefferson Danforth. "I guess it's my turn to bare my soul," he said. "Truth be told, honored as I am to have you attend our wedding, I was never fond of your politics. I certainly didn't vote for you."

"Gee, thanks, Isaac," Danforth said jokingly, causing some to laugh.

Isaac scratched his nose. "I still remember seeing you on TV in Brussels, when you urged all Americans to celebrate Thanksgiving. You even promised us everything would eventually be okay." He shook his head, without trying to look disrespectful, then admitted, "I said to myself that day, 'What a joke!'"

Jefferson held out his hands. "I was trying to resuscitate a distraught nation. Truth be told, I was even more terrified by what had unfolded in Belgium than with the disappearances, which we now know was the Rapture of Christ's Church. Turns out, every bad thought I had about Salvador Romanero back then was spot on."

"I always thought he was evil myself," Isaac replied, still trying to wrap his mind around the fact that he was speaking to a former American President. He was grateful for the non-scripted insight. "Then again, most Muslims did!"

Danforth shook his head in disgust. "Did you ever think the day would come where someone's life would be worth merely a thousand dollars?"

Charles Calloway opined, "With all due respect, if they ever discover you're still alive, I'm sure the bounty on your head would be substantially higher than that, perhaps in the millions..."

Amy Danforth shivered at the thought, and leaned into her husband as far as she could go.

Jefferson knew his comment had terrified her. He slightly pivoted, "Speaking of elections, at least I can say I was never voted out of office."

Isaac thought about it then asked, "Wouldn't that mean your two now-dead predecessors never had the constitutional authority to be sworn in as President in the first place?"

Jefferson stared at the wall opposite him, as if reliving some past memory in midair. "Not much any of us can do about it now..."

Amy Danforth took a sip of water. "Who would want that job now anyway? I would never want to be First Lady of this country now..."

Jefferson grinned at his wife. "Technically, my dear, since I'm still alive, you *are* the rightful First Lady of the United States, even if no one knows it but us," he said, arcing his hand, meaning everyone listening.

Isaac's tone became softer, and more endearing. "I know there will never be another American election, but if there was, and you ran for office, I'd vote for you in a heartbeat..."

"You and me both," said Tamika. "How could we not after the many awesome things you did for this organization?"

Isaac added, "Plus you attended our wedding!"

Jefferson was choked up. "Truth be told, there's no other place I'd rather be than here with all of you."

Amy nodded agreement. "I couldn't wait to leave the last safe house! We were always stuck underground, and there were only a handful of us staying there. I feel so much more connected here and blessed to care for so many children."

Dick took a small sip of water. It was time to ask the question that had tortured him more than any other, since he arrived three weeks ago. It could wait no longer. "Since we're being so open and honest with each other, my question is about Chelsea." He grimaced. "Is she really in hell now?"

The warm, fuzzy feeling that had filled the room was gone.

Sarah braced herself, as a prolonged silence filled the living room.

For someone who never felt comfortable confessing her sins to Catholic priests, as evidenced by the fact that she went to confession one time for every ten times Dick went there, Sarah felt perfectly safe pouring out her heart and soul in front of her brothers and sisters in Christ, including the former President of the United States of America.

And she looked extremely comfortable doing it. There was only one question she dreaded being asked, and Dick had just asked it.

Brian and Sarah lowered their heads sadly. It was impossible to reconcile that the three of them were saved, yet the youngest family member was now suffering in torment.

Dick understood the suicide part, and the serious consequences that followed such a decision. But until his recent conversion, he still believed in a place called purgatory. He kept hoping and praying that his daughter was there, as part of her penance, however long it would take, before she could finally be admitted into Heaven.

Now that he no longer believed in such a place, the silence still hanging thick in the air confirmed to him that the answer was yes.

Finally, Sarah gasped, then sighed deeply through her nose. "It's my fault. Chelsea inherited it from me."

Tom asked, "Why do you say that?"

Sarah looked up at the ceiling. "Do you know how many times I gazed in the bathroom mirror contemplating that very same thing, wondering if I would still be alive in the next few minutes? But in the end, what always stopped me was that I couldn't do it to my family."

Brian shot an uncomfortable glance at his father, silently thankful that the question wasn't asked in the cafeteria. Had this topic come up prior to the Rapture, they both would have been baffled by it.

Sarah added, "Even after I was saved, I asked God on several occasions to take me out of this world, especially after leaving my husband only to discover that my own daughter had taken her life. I'm sure many of you saw the gut-wrenching video she made."

Silence filled the room until Tamika broke it. "I think we can all relate to that, Sarah, I was there many times myself! We've all dealt with similar situations. All we can do is be there for each other, and comfort one another through these terrifying times, until we finally see our blessed Savior face to face."

Sarah wiped tears from her eyes. "But why did my daughter take her life? Now that I know the eternal consequences, it doesn't seem fair. It still haunts me to this day."

Dick sighed. "I admit I don't know how to act in this regard. I want to be mad at God for taking Chelsea from us. Is that a sin?"

Sarah shrugged her shoulders, not knowing whether it was or not. "Do you know how many times I've had similar thoughts?"

Tom interjected, "Not to come across as insensitive to either of you, but God didn't take Chelsea away. It was a decision she made on her own. I assure you both that the Most High would never condone suicide."

He grimaced. "I can't tell you how many young Catholic girls I had counselled before the Rapture, who may not have been suicidal, but after getting pregnant before marriage, tried blaming God through their rivers of tears, for letting it happen to them.

"Even the young men responsible for getting them pregnant tried blaming God for what they had done of their own free will. While I never went along with them in this regard, so many others had…"

Tom shook his head sadly. "Looking back, I now see just how messed up the Church was, mostly because of the low view so many had toward God. So much so that it was suddenly okay to blame Him for the sins we committed in life."

He sighed. "To answer your question, Dick, about whether it's a sin to blame God for our sins and actions in life? I would have to say yes."

Tom's reply brought a lump to Dick's throat.

Sarah flinched at first, then it was as if a huge weight had been lifted off her chest. "You're right, Tom! How can any of us blame God for our sinful actions? Even though Chelsea practically blamed me and Brian in her goodbye video, it was her decision to take her life, not ours…

"I won't deny my decision to leave Chelsea may have planted the suicide seed in her head. But brother Tom just helped me realize that on those handful of days when I was consumed with suicidal thoughts myself, had I actually gone through with it, it would have been my decision and therefore my fault, not God's or anyone else's."

The room grew silent again. Sarah eyeballed Dick with an expression on her face that begged for understanding. "Can you forgive me for the psychological damage I caused you, for leaving you high and dry with only goodbye letters to read? Even though I felt I had to leave you for spiritual purposes, I could have used a different approach."

Dick buried his face in his hands and had a good cry for his daughter he knew he would never see again. The pain was unbearable.

Sarah wiped a stray tear from her left eye and rubbed her husband's back. "The one thing I kept thinking about during those times was something Brian told me before I left New York to come here."

Dick swallowed back confusion. "And that is?"

Sarah glanced around the room. It was evident that everyone wanted to hear what would come out of her mouth next. "He said he would rather be in Heaven with Jesus than with Chelsea in hell. He also included you at the time."

Dick winced, clearly taken aback by what Sarah had just said. He wasn't the only one. It sounded a bit harsh, insensitive even.

Sarah patted his hand, knowing what he was thinking. "When I first heard those words come out of his mouth, it jolted me too. I had great difficulty wrapping my mind around it. But once I finally understood what he meant, while it didn't take the pain or guilt away, it forced me to refocus on how blessed I was to be one of God's children.

"The last thing he wanted was for you or me to die in our sins like Chelsea. After I got saved, that became my constant prayer for you."

As if on cue, Baby Sarah broke the moment when she started crying. She was hungry and wanted to be fed. Jacquelyn dried her eyes with a tissue, then excused herself to go upstairs to feed her daughter.

Isaac got up off the couch. "Goodnight y'all." He carried Tamika up to their bedroom, careful not to trip on a crack in the stairway that still hadn't been fixed since the global quake.

When they reached the top step, he gently placed her feet on the carpeted floor.

46

Tamika kissed him on the lips. "Welcome to your new bedroom. It used to be nice before the quake. Four of us slept here in bunk beds. We lost two sisters that night."

Isaac let his eyes drink in the room. He saw the plywood covering the part of the floor that gave way during the global quake, and mentally noted not to step on it. "Sorry for your loss."

Tamika sighed. "Least they're in a better place. Now it's just you, me, Cocoa, and Rev, short for 'Revelation'".

Tamika found the feline roaming the grounds after the global quake. Since he didn't have a name tag on, she renamed him. She felt bad for Rev's former owners, she really did, but there wasn't a chance she could go looking for them to return their pet cat back to them, especially since he was Cocoa's new playmate.

Isaac glanced up at the ceiling. The newly constructed roof consisted of uneven beams of wood that came from one of the fallen trees, and sheet metal, plywood and broken bricks that were plucked out of the small mountains of debris that had piled up across the property.

In no way was it a professional job, but Isaac didn't need to ask why. It was all about survival now, not comfort.

Tamika followed her husband's eyes upward. "Only reason the roof doesn't leak is that it hasn't rained since the global quake. And with so little insulation, the room's always drafty. But it's so much better since we received the shipment of new windows.

"I'm just grateful to have a bedroom to sleep in again. After the quake, I slept on the living room floor with Lila, and a handful of others, until the roof was fixed a few weeks later, sort of fixed, anyway."

Isaac placed his right arm around his wife. "Believe me, this is so much better than when I stayed at Dick's house back in New York. And it sure beats sleeping in a walk-in refrigerator any day!"

Tamika glanced at her husband incredulously, then sat on the lower bunk bed. "What?! I knew you slept at the restaurant, but a walk-in refrigerator?"

"Oh, I didn't tell you about that?" Isaac explained, "When my former Muslim brothers wanted me dead, I was so frightened that I left my apartment in the middle of the night, without a penny to my name. The only place I could think to go was the restaurant where I worked."

Tamika was perplexed. "But why the refrigerator?"

"If you saw how bad the restaurant was after the quake, you would have done the same thing. I kept fearing that if the building shifted again, even slightly, what was left of the roof would've come crashing down on me. I figured the refrigerator was the safest place for me.

"I set up a cot I found in the storage closet, then jimmied a few small branches in the door hinge, so the freezer door wouldn't suddenly close and trap me inside. I slept there for more than three weeks! Compared to that place, this is like the Taj Mahal…"

Tamika grinned at Isaac. "Well then, glad you like it, honey."

Isaac kissed his wife hard on the lips. "All that matters is that we're back together again."

His comment earned him a smile, and another long kiss on the lips.

After being separated for more than five years, they both seemed a little nervous now that they were about to spend their first night together, as husband and wife, part two.

Tamika changed into pajamas, then snuggled as close to her husband as she possibly could, grateful for this second chance that God was giving them.

Isaac held his wife, vowing to her over and over that he would never leave her again.

Tamika smiled in the darkness. It felt good to hear those comforting words coming from him, especially since she believed him this time, unlike in the past when she only believed he was being truthful half the time, if that!

True to his word, the thought of consummating their renewal vows never once crossed Isaac's mind. He would give Tamika as much time as she would need before taking the next step. It would happen when she was ready, and only then!

Little did the couple know as they drifted off to sleep in each other's arms, that their days of having a private bedroom at safe house number one were numbered…

8

NEW BABYLON

SALVADOR ROMANERO'S PERSONAL DOCTOR kept tossing and turning on his bed in his palatial bedroom, his mind too crammed with thoughts to possibly sleep.

When Benjamin Shapiro first heard the booming Voice flying high above the many gatherers, making his dire proclamation during Romanero's global address in Jerusalem, about "fearing God and giving him glory, because the hour of his judgment has come," at first, he foolishly thought it was a warning to all dissidents living in hiding, that they had better fall in line or face the *Miracle Maker's* fierce judgment.

Shapiro even nodded optimistically at the booming Voice above. Talk about perfect timing—just as his boss was addressing the world!

How could he have thought otherwise, after everything that had transpired over the past 24 hours leading up to the invasion of sorts in the atmosphere above?

Like everyone else on Romanero's staff, he was on top of the world. The highlight for Benjamin was when his boss challenged Israel's God in his speech leading up to their executions, either to prove or disprove His omniscience, by sparing His Two Witnesses before they were killed.

Along with everyone else on the planet, he watched and waited with bated breath, to see which side was speaking the truth and which side wasn't.

When Israel's God let His Two servants die, it bolstered Shapiro's confidence in the *Miracle Maker* all the more.

With those two finally out of the way, he felt very strongly that the final hurdle had just been overcome, and they could at last proceed full steam ahead with the new utopia his boss was building, in which Benjamin was fully committed to help bring into existence.

That is, until he saw Salvador shrinking in horror upon hearing the Voice, and everything came crashing down on top of him.

Benjamin became so terrified by his fearful reaction that he had been unable to come to grips with it ever since. It only lasted a second or two, but it was undeniable. It was like a gut punch to him. The Pope had a similar reaction. But he wasn't Benjamin's savior. Only Salvador was!

49

He couldn't wait to leave Jerusalem and get back to New Babylon, so he could think straight again. Only it never happened.

That was only one of many things Dr. Shapiro wrestled with this night. Equally disturbing was the bold-faced lie his savior had told at the end of his speech, about not being stung by those hideous creatures, in the five months in which they had terrified the entire planet.

Just like the rest of his followers, Romanero was also stung by them, six times, in fact, before he finally retreated underground with Jurgen Staat, Li Ping, and a handful of others.

Nothing could kill them! They tried everything—exterminators, various poisons, tasers, even fly swatters—but nothing worked! And since they never stopped flying, they couldn't be stomped on. The only time they stopped flitting this way and that, was when they were stinging their subjects.

If Salvador Romanero truly was godlike, as he constantly proclaimed himself to be, why would he deceive anyone by saying he wasn't stung by them? His multitudes of followers had all been stung themselves—multiple times in fact—and would surely sympathize with him.

So why hide it from them? What benefit would that serve? For the life in him, Benjamin Shapiro still couldn't understand why his boss and sole patient had done it.

And why did the flying angel, or whatever it was, suddenly appear when Romanero was addressing the world from Jerusalem, just after he boldly declared that his mark would soon be available?

Once again, Benjamin didn't have a logical answer to his question.

Whatever the reason, he just wanted to sleep so he could forget all about it, but those questions kept running through his mind like slow poisonous drips.

When he was finally able to drift off to sleep, he was rocked by a dream which had nothing to do with the torturous thoughts that had ensnared him ever since the plane left Jerusalem earlier in the day.

Nor did it have anything to do with the soul-shredding cataclysmic events constantly besieging the planet, all on Romanero's watch. This was something Shapiro couldn't deny, not even to himself.

In his dream, Benjamin saw himself sitting alone on a wooden bench at a recreation park, situated a quarter mile away from his home in Bucks County, Pennsylvania.

Before the disappearances, he would often go there for quiet time, after a long day at the office, until his life was drastically changed for what he thought was the better.

Even though he hadn't been back home for more than two years, it wasn't uncommon to have such dreams about his homeland.

But what made this dream so bizarre was that suddenly, out of nowhere, someone whom he hadn't seen or heard from in many years appeared, seemingly out of nowhere, and sat next to him on the bench.

It was his nephew, Jakob.

Without any kind of formal greeting and without making eye contact, the young man looked straight ahead with no emotion whatsoever on his face. "You're living a lie, Uncle," he said somberly, morbidly.

Benjamin saw himself stiffen on the bench, shaking his head incredulously. As the personal physician to the most powerful man on the planet, a man who was drastically improving life for all his followers—at least that was the hope—how could his nephew say such a blasphemous thing?

He twisted his head one way, then the other. "I'm living a lie?!"

Jakob nodded. "Yes."

Benjamin shook his head sarcastically. "Okay, humor me, which lie are you referring to, Jakob?"

"Because of your constant denial of Yahweh God, everything in your life is a lie! If you don't reverse course, and trust in Yeshua for the salvation of your soul, it will lead you straight into eternal destruction."

Benjamin snorted in astonishment. "Ha! Are you referring to the God the Two dead bodies in the street in Jerusalem once worshiped?"

"I am…" came the reply, matter-of-factly.

Benjamin became puffed up with pride and decided to protest more. "Who are you to say this to me, nephew? Do you know I have direct access to the man who considers all who worship their God his archenemies?"

"I do…" came the reply again, in a voice that was unafraid.

Benjamin glared at him then pressed on, "So, you're also aware that telling me this could bring a world of trouble down on you, if it ever gets back to my boss?"

Finally, Jakob made eye contact with him. Just when Benjamin thought things couldn't get any stranger, he declared to his uncle, in a voice that was full of conviction, "I am one of the hundred and forty four thousand sealed servants of the Most High God! Antichrist has no power over me."

Antichrist?! Dr. Shapiro's eyes widened on the park bench, shocked by what had just come out of his nephew's mouth. Try as he might, he couldn't speak.

Silence hung thick in the air, forcing Benjamin back inside his head. In what could be considered as the irony of all ironies, not only did Jakob proclaim to be one of the 144,000 young Jewish males publicly speaking eternal judgment over his boss; he brushed off his threat about bringing a world of trouble down on him, like it had never been made.

I'm living a lie?! "Okay, Jakob, let's say for argument's sake that you are one of them," Benjamin asked arrogantly, not wanting to believe it. When Jakob didn't answer, he glanced over at him, but his nephew was no longer there. He was gone. Poof!

Dr. Shapiro clutched at his chest gasping for air, as a spine-tingling fear shot through him that no medication could remedy.

He looked down at his feet. His mind raced back to how baffled everyone on Salvador Romanero's surveillance team were, after the 144,000 troublemakers were transported to various locations around the world, after sitting under the tutelage of the Two global enemies at the Wailing Wall, in Jerusalem.

Using high-tech surveillance, all 144,000 young males were positively identified upon arriving at their new global locations. Only no one knew what mode of transportation they took to get there, except that it wasn't on boats, trains, or airplanes!

Whatever they used to get to those places, it quickly became apparent to those monitoring them that they weren't looking to hide anywhere.

If anything, they wanted to be seen and heard, as they defiantly preached their outlawed messages of hate and division.

Even more mind-boggling was the instant they stopped preaching, it's like they became ghostlike, much like his nephew had just done. *Is Jakob really one of them? If so, is my boss really powerless from silencing them, like Jakob had said?*

That was the question that finally rustled Dr. Shapiro from his sleep. He gulped hard, daring not to venture a guess, even if he didn't like what his gut kept telling him.

What gnawed on him the most and offended him ever so deeply about the dream, was that he had always considered himself to be a man of integrity, whose life was governed by the truth. His honesty was such that he couldn't help but loathe liars and fake people. *I'm living a lie?!*

Benjamin Shapiro wasn't perfect by any stretch of the imagination. Nor did he proclaim to be. As a lifelong atheist, he was proud of the hedonistic lifestyle he chose to live and felt no need to apologize for it. Since he only had one life to live, he was fully determined to do the things that pleased him the most, without ever questioning them.

When Salvador Romanero suddenly appeared on his radar screen, his way of thinking quickly changed pertaining to all things spiritual. Benjamin saw the young man not only as a man of truth, but as *the* Man of Truth, with a Capital *M* and *T*.

But if he really was the Man of Truth, why did he blatantly lie to everyone in his speech earlier, by saying he hadn't been stung by the locusts? It was a question to which Dr. Shapiro had no answer. Weren't truth and lies polar opposites?

As much as Benjamin wanted to share his spooky encounter with someone, who could he possibly turn to? Certainly not Salvador Romanero or anyone else from within his administration, including those he had grown the closest to over the past three years, Li Ping and Jurgen Staat among them!

He couldn't call his ex-wife. He hadn't heard from her in many years. When his divorce was final two decades ago, she took their three children to Arizona for a few years, before they ultimately resettled in Southern California. Surely, they knew about his lofty promotion by now, and about his spiritual conversion.

But as hardcore atheists themselves, perhaps his conversion had pushed them even farther away from him, if that was even possible!

Benjamin shook his head sadly, wondering if they were dead or alive? He blinked the thought away and rubbed his throbbing forehead. Now wasn't the time to relive his past failures. His brain was already too crammed to allow any other debilitating thoughts to enter inside.

The only other person he could think of telling was his brother Seth, who happened to be Jakob's father, and Benjamin's only brother.

Whereas Seth had ultimately caved into their father's constant urges to become a religious leader, thus keeping the lineage in check which began with their grandfather, Ehud, Benjamin never felt led to follow them by becoming a rabbi himself.

He wanted to be a leader in life, to be sure, but certainly not in the field of religion! How could he, when he vociferously objected to everything in the Book from which his grandfather, father, and only brother had taught? Nothing had changed over the years.

Even at an early age, everyone in the family knew how badly Benjamin wanted to become a physician. He was grateful that his late mother had always urged him to follow his dream and lifelong obsession, which he did.

After graduating from the University of Pennsylvania medical school, summa cum laude, he was hired at Thomas Jefferson Hospital in Philadelphia, where he remained for more than 20 years, before starting his own private practice in the Philly suburbs. To say he was supremely confident in his abilities would be an understatement.

Without a doubt, Benjamin Shapiro's crowning achievement in life came when Salvador the Great chose him among thousands of other candidates, to be his personal physician. He considered it the blessing of a lifetime.

The fact that he had risen to such prominence by gaining direct access to the most powerful man on Earth, further confirmed to him that becoming a physician had been the right choice to make. He even had his own mansion in New Babylon, which further punctuated his success!

But the most stunning thing to happen was how he had gone from being an outspoken atheist all his life, to worshiping the young phenom as the one true god of the universe, in just a few short months.

The more the renowned physician heard the *Miracle Maker* speak, the more convinced he became that this man was someone worthy of dedicating the remainder of his life to, in the service of his choosing. He even called Salvador the Great his personal lord and savior.

When Seth first heard about Benjamin's spiritual conversion, he thought his brother had a mental breakdown, much like the many others who had been brainwashed by the young Spaniard.

"The only worship you're known for," the longtime rabbi had countered, "is self-worship!"

The two brothers were quite outspoken about their beliefs or lack thereof. It seemed every time they got together; arguments always ensued. But when Benjamin had decided to follow the young phenom from Spain, it led to the most heated arguments between them.

"So let me get this straight, Benjamin," Seth had fumed, "after a lifetime of rejecting Yahweh, not to mention your Jewish roots, you choose to follow that Gentile!" He had paused before adding, "He is no god, I assure you!" At that, Seth hung up on his brother.

It was the last time they had spoken to one another. Both were prideful, stubborn men who would rather ignore one another, instead of being the one to take the first step to improve what had always been a rocky relationship between them.

Benjamin turned off the night lamp on the glass table next to his massive bed, hoping to sleep again, already knowing it would be impossible. *I'm living a lie?*

9

THE FOLLOWING DAY

AFTER A FITFUL NIGHT OF tossing and turning, Benjamin Shapiro sat up in bed and scratched his throbbing head, still confused by the unsettling dream he had a few short hours ago.

He went to the master bathroom to shower. When he was finished, he stared at his tired image in the mirror.

He had a large nose, long sideburns, and a long thin face. He wore bifocal glasses which did nothing to hide his bushy eyebrows. Without having his toupee on, he looked much older than 68.

But beyond those familiar facial features, he couldn't ignore the confusion splashed all over his pale face.

Benjamin checked his watch for the time: 5:18 a.m. It was early but he knew Seth would be awake. As much as he dreaded the thought of calling his brother, he didn't know who else to turn to.

With that mental justification, Benjamin showered then plucked his cell phone from his gold silk robe and tapped the call button. As it rang, he already dreaded the outcome. *What will he think when I tell him I had a dream about his son, who proclaims to be one of the 144,000 evildoers in the world preaching outlawed messages?*

On the sixth ring, Seth finally answered. Benjamin didn't have to ask why it took him so long. Seeing his brother's name appear on his mobile phone, he was no doubt trying to talk himself out of answering it.

After exchanging brief emotionless pleasantries, Seth asked his brother, "To what do I owe this honor?" *Dishonor*, he thought, keeping it to himself.

Benjamin exhaled loudly into the receiver. "It's about Jakob…"

Seth became tense. "What about my son?"

"I had a dream about him last night…"

Seth flinched, then braced himself. "And?"

"This might sound strange to you, but he told me he was one of the hundred and forty four thousand young Jewish males constantly speaking unforgivable blasphemies against Salvador Romanero. Is it true?"

Seth gasped at his brother's question but remained silent, knowing it couldn't remain a family secret forever. But in this case, he was ever mindful of the ramifications this discovery could ultimately present, now that his brother knew.

Seth had already disowned his son, but he didn't want to see Jakob go to prison before ultimately being beheaded, for his sinful actions.

Benjamin pressed on, "Well?"

Finally, Seth confessed, "When Jakob started sitting under the tutelage of those Two," he scoffed bluntly, in a forced Middle Eastern accent, which sounded funny coming from a native New Yorker, "I refused to speak to him. On several occasions, I tried bringing him back to his senses, but the boy wouldn't budge an inch."

Seth shook his head sadly, embarrassingly. "How mortifying that my own flesh and blood has become a mouthpiece for Yeshua," he shouted into the receiver—his face red with fury. "Thanks to those Two, nothing will change his mind!"

So, it's true! Benjamin thought to himself. "At least they're dead now, right? Now we can all move on!"

Seth shook his fists skyward. "I can't tell you how many arguments I've had with those Two over the past three and a half years! Even in death the hatred I feel toward them, for falsely indoctrinating my son, incenses me to no end! So many Jews are being brainwashed because of their teachings!"

Hmm, thought Benjamin, carefully affixing his hairpiece with the help of the mirror again, as if someone might actually mistake it for real hair. For all his riches, the one thing he never upgraded was the toupee.

Whereas Seth looked like a rabbi in every sense of the meaning, with his balding head and long gray beard, Benjamin was clean shaven with a ridiculously looking blonde toupee on his head, which, in and of itself, was rather odd, since he was never a blonde to begin with.

When he was a younger man, the hair on his head was dark brown. The reason Benjamin wore the toupee was that he wanted it to make him look 20 years younger, which it didn't. It was no secret that he had a very high opinion of himself. Clearly, vanity was one of his weaknesses.

He said, "It seems people of all nations and tongues are listening to them very carefully and believing in their God. Many who used to be on our side have since gone into hiding after listening to their preaching. I believe it's easily into the tens of millions, perhaps even higher than that, including many Jews."

The longtime rabbi wiped a tear from his eye. "They took my son from me," he bemoaned, through soft sniffling. "So far as I'm concerned Jakob's dead to me, just like the Two he chose to listen to over my sound teachings. May Yahweh have mercy on his soul and bring him back to the Truth!"

He sounds just like my boss! Benjamin snorted into the phone. "Are you saying you don't forgive Jakob?"

Seth knew his brother was prodding him on, like he had often done during their debates. "Forgive him! Ha!" he scoffed. "How can I forgive my son, when he tossed away so many years of theological education, after just a few short months under their dangerously bizarre tutelage? Now he openly proclaims *Yeshua* to be Israel's Messiah? YESHUA! That Man is anathema to us Jews!"

Seth's palms became sweaty as more anger rose to the surface. He took a few deep breaths to calm himself down, then chewed on his lower lip to keep himself from exploding again. "No one was more joyous than me when *your* boss silenced those Two men for good! If there's one thing I have in common with Salvador Romanero, it's our shared hatred of them! But that's the only good thing I'll say about him!"

"Actually, I'm also grateful to your boss for ridding Israel of the fanatical Muslims that had occupied our land, until the Dome of the Rock was destroyed. I can honestly say this is the first time since I relocated my family here that we've experienced near perfect peace in our streets. The constant tension we all felt on a daily basis vanished the day the Muslims vanished.

"Romanero deserves all the credit for that. But I'll never credit him for sparing Israel from the global quake. It was Yahweh who spared us. Just like *Yeshua* isn't the Savior we've all been waiting for, neither is your boss!" Seth's voice dripped with contempt. "He's a skillful politician, I'll give him that, but how can he be Israel's Messiah when he isn't even a Jew?!"

Usually, this would be when Benjamin would scold his brother for speaking such atrocities about his sole patient. But he didn't, mostly because he wasn't so sure what to think anymore. How could he possibly think straight after what had transpired over the past 24 hours?

Never in a million years would Benjamin have ever predicted that someone from his own bloodline and genealogy would end up being one of those evildoers. In his highly revered position, he knew exposing this truth to his boss would mean death to his nephew.

Then again, according to Jakob, not so.

When Seth relocated his family from New York City to Israel a few years before the disappearances, Jakob was only five years old. After just one day of taking in the sights in Jerusalem and seeing so much Jewish history materializing before his very eyes, it was then that the youngster felt that he belonged to a chosen people.

He was so impacted that day that he doubled down on his commitment to want to follow in his father's, grandfathers, and great grandfather's footsteps, by becoming a rabbi himself.

Most who knew Jakob considered him a boring introvert who never touched alcohol, never dated women, never uttered profanities, or did the many things that most considered to be normal human behavior. If ever there was a goodie two shoes, it was Jakob.

Benjamin often joked with his nephew in the past saying, "How could people like you die when you never even lived?"

In the decade or so that Jakob had studied the Torah, mostly under his father's strict tutelage, he was shy, timid, and humble.

Everything about his demeanor changed after just a few short weeks of listening to those Two Witnesses at the Western Wall. He certainly wasn't argumentative like this before his spiritual conversion.

What made it even worse was that the voice Jakob had found was being used to promote a false Savior and blaspheme his boss.

But Seth also hated Romanero, which was why the two had never met for lunch or dinner, on the many occasions when his brother was in Jerusalem with the *Miracle Maker*. Benjamin had no intention of meeting Seth when he returned to the Holy Land, a week from now.

When Israel was the only country to be spared from the global quake two years ago, Seth rejoiced along with everyone else, even if he didn't know who deserved the credit at that time, Romanero or Yahweh…

The confusion he temporarily felt was removed when Salvador the not so Great promised that rain would fall on Israel, on his new birthday.

When it never came, the anger Seth felt toward the so-called *Miracle Maker* intensified. "What man changes his own date of birth?" he often asked himself. "Only criminals did!" he kept concluding.

Benjamin asked, "What are your thoughts on the loud Voice filling the atmosphere making its dire proclamations? Seems nothing can silence it or make it go away." *Or no one*, he thought, with an uneasy flinch, *apparently, including my boss!*

"For now, I have no comment on it," Seth said flatly, clinically. The longtime rabbi was well versed in the Torah, but since he had never read the New Testament—he forbade anyone from reading it, including his long-lost son—he was just as clueless as the next unconverted person, about what was happening in the skies above.

The call ended and nothing had changed between them. A chasm still existed between them that both brothers doubted would ever be crossed.

Benjamin was presently unmindful that he would soon be forced to choose between his only brother or his nephew Jakob...

WHEN DR. SHAPIRO ARRIVED at his office in New Babylon, everyone knew he wasn't himself. Then again, ever since Romanero had announced in his speech that not all dissidents were Christians, and not everyone was with him, to even include some he had offered such lofty positions, the paranoia level had mushroomed among everyone within his inner circle.

All were fully mindful of what disloyalty to their boss meant. Yet, whenever someone inquired, even though Benjamin was coming apart at the seams, he waved them off, justifying his disposition by a sleepless night.

While it was true that he hadn't slept much, what had put the dour expression on his face more than that was his nephew invading his dreamworld, all the while proclaiming to be one of the 144,000 young Jewish males out disgracing their boss, not to mention that he was still grappling with the bold-faced lie Romanero had told the reporter.

How could anyone rest comfortably under such conditions?

LATER THAT EVENING, BENJAMIN woke up in a cold sweat, after being rocked by yet another dream, in which he saw himself on the same park bench situated a short walk from his house in the States.

Once again, Jakob appeared out of nowhere...

Much to his dismay, this dream was even more bizarre than the first one had been. *Not dead? What in the world?*

Benjamin scratched his head in confusion. What had spawned Jakob's inconceivable comment was when he challenged his nephew with this question, "If you are one of God's sealed servants, as you proclaim, how can you possibly justify your position, when your Two spiritual mentors were forever silenced? Don't you serve the very same God as they?"

"They still serve Yahweh God, Uncle..." said Jakob in reply, evenly.

Benjamin blinked hard a few times, thinking he was hearing things. "How can that be, Jakob, they're dead?"

Jakob looked deep into his uncle's troubled eyes. "Not for long, Uncle."

The expression on Benjamin's face went from confusion to full-blown anger. He shook his head incredulously. *If you say so...* "Believe me, Jakob, they're dead! I'm a doctor! I should know!"

Jakob gazed even more deeply into his uncle's eyes, as if searching them. For the first time ever, there was a hint of confusion there. "The only reason Antichrist was able to accomplish what many had died trying to do, was that Yahweh temporarily withdrew His supernatural protection from His Two Witnesses. Soon, very soon, you will see them come back to life, Uncle."

"Come on, Jakob, use your sense," Benjamin had countered, sarcastically. "You're more intelligent than that!"

Instead of being offended, Jakob's face lit up. "Again, I say, soon you will see it for yourself. The whole world will, in fact, before the next sunset. And there will be nothing Satan or Antichrist can do to stop it."

"Okay, I'll play along," Benjamin said, mockingly, "but what if you're wrong?"

"If I'm wrong, Uncle," Jakob said sincerely, "it would mean Yahweh's Word was wrong. I assure you that's not the case!" He paused for a moment, then warned his uncle again, "You're working for the devil himself. Flee from Antichrist while you can. Receive Yeshua as Lord and Messiah. Only then will you truly be free..."

Benjamin scoffed at his nephew's remark. "Free? Ha! Need I remind you, Nephew, that all who trust in that mythical Figure are either dead, in prison, or fearing for their lives in hiding! Further, all things Jesus have been scrubbed from the face of the Earth, and all who still choose to follow Him are nowhere near anything close to being free!"

When Jakob didn't reply, Benjamin added, "I confess that Romanero isn't perfect, but at least I can see him and hear his voice. He is my leader, my savior..." Unlike all past declarations Benjamin had made about the *Miracle Maker*, this one lacked conviction.

"I assure you, Uncle, his reign will soon be over, and he will be cast into hell with his leader, the devil, the Pope, and all the other devilish men and women who follow his lead." Jakob paused, then added, "Including you."

61

That was when Benjamin woke in a cold sweat. As frightened and desperate as he was to share this new nightmare with someone, there wasn't a chance he would call his brother Seth again.

But Benjamin Shapiro wasn't the only Jew on the planet being confronted by the 144,000 young males fearlessly preaching their outlawed messages planetwide.

Yahweh's sealed servants were meeting with family members and friends and sharing the true Gospel message with them.

Some, like Jakob, had only invaded the dreams of one individual.

Others were given multiple lives to invade and confront.

Aside from performing their daily preaching duties, Yahweh was using His sealed servants to gather His Remnant, by using Isaiah 53, as the main bridge connecting the Old Testament to the New—by offering undeniable proof that it all pointed to one Person, one Messiah, Yahweh's Son, Yeshua HaMashiach.

They also quoted Revelation chapters 7 and 14, to confirm to those of Yahweh's choosing that they were indeed part of the 144,000 that were prophesied about 2,000 years ago, in the Book they were forbidden from reading.

Prior to being visited by them, recipients of these deeply confusing dreams, which ultimately led to meetings, never bothered listening to the vitriolic hate speech that constantly spewed out of the mouths of Yahweh's sealed servants.

They were listening very carefully now...

10

THREE AND A HALF DAYS AFTER THE TWO WITNESSES WERE KILLED

"'NOW WHEN THEY HAVE finished their testimony," the 144,000 declared in unison, globally, "the beast that comes up from the Abyss will attack them, and overpower and kill them. Their bodies will lie in the public square of the great city—which is figuratively called Sodom and Egypt—where also their Lord was crucified.

"For three and a half days some from every people, tribe, language and nation will gaze on their bodies and refuse them burial. The inhabitants of the earth will gloat over them and will celebrate by sending each other gifts, because these two prophets had tormented those who live on the earth.'"

Someone shouted at one of God's sealed servants who was preaching near the Wailing Wall, "Your side already lost! Why don't you find something better to do with your life, something more productive?!"

Another heckler then yelled to another one of the 144,000 troublemakers, "Hopefully, Salvador the Great will silence all of you next!"

If they were fearful for their lives, they didn't show it. Instead of fleeing their agitators and going into hiding, they kept preaching boldly and fearlessly, just like their brothers were doing planetwide. But instead of stopping at Revelation, chapter 11, verse 10, like they had done the past three days, they included verses 11 through 13 this time.

"'But after the three and a half days the breath of life from God entered them," they declared, "and they stood on their feet, and terror struck those who saw them. Then they heard a loud voice from heaven saying to them, 'Come up here.' And they went up to heaven in a cloud, while their enemies looked on.

"'At that very hour there was a severe earthquake and a tenth of the city collapsed. Seven thousand people were killed in the earthquake, and the survivors were terrified and gave glory to the God of heaven.'"

"Shut up!" many shouted angrily at them. Some even spit on them.

Most people had already tuned them out.

Many of the Jewish leaders and rabbis who were among the large gathering celebrating at the Western Wall, were quite mindful that the Old

Testament expressly forbade the practice of refusing proper burial to anyone. It was considered both a curse on the corpses and a sign of blatant disrespect.

As far as these rabbis were concerned, even though their bodies were starting to decay, they had profaned and tormented too many good people, to deserve a proper burial.

They applauded the young Gentile from Spain for putting their bodies on display like this, thus dishonoring his Two enemies, and holding them in the highest contempt for the whole world to see.

One rabbi shouted above the crowd, "Yeah, yeah, yeah, blah, blah, blah!" at the young man, before directing his attention back to the Two slain men. "What was that? Oh, wait, you didn't say anything, you're dead!" he scoffed, mocking the dead bodies.

Laughter roared throughout the Western Wall area.

The sealed servant replied by quoting Matthew 23:37, "Jerusalem, Jerusalem, you who kill the prophets and stone those sent to you, how often I have longed to gather your children together, as a hen gathers her chicks under her wings, and you were not willing.'"

"Prophets?" the same rabbi scoffed, "Who, them? Ha!"

More laughter erupted throughout the Western Wall area.

"The only Prophets you love are dead ones, because Prophets never come to bring good news, only judgment," Yahweh's sealed servant replied, with emphasis.

In the height of arrogance, Romanero allowed it all to be broadcast on international television. He didn't know it yet, but by ignoring the devil yet again, it would come to his dismay, as the mass jubilance in the streets of Jerusalem was about to come to an abrupt end…

It started with a slight flinching of the leg of one of the Two slain Witnesses. No one noticed it at first, not even the large group of celebrants circling the corpses. They were too high or inebriated to notice. Many of them had barely slept the past three and a half days.

After enduring so many months of pain and constant hardships, it felt good to celebrate something again. And this was truly an event worth celebrating! They sang songs that were written about the *Miracle Maker*, and danced, and spewed unintelligible blasphemies at the Two dead bodies which were cordoned off with rope.

Some of them even flicked alcoholic beverages at them!

When it happened again, one woman in her early 20s, who was as close as she could get to the two dead bodies, stopped dead in her tracks. She lowered the facemask she had on. The last thing she wanted was to smell their rotting, decaying corpses. "Did you see that?"

"See what?" her boyfriend replied, hiccupping.

She folded her arms over her chest, wondering if her sleep-deprived mind might be playing tricks on her. "I think one of them just moved..."

He pointed down at the two corpses. "Who, them?" he snickered through his facemask. "Ha! Now I know you're drunk, sweetheart!"

Suddenly, out of the corner of her eye, there was more movement, only from the other one this time. "It happened again!" she shouted; her voice full of fear.

Her boyfriend lowered his facemask and took a long swig from his half-empty whiskey bottle. "Yep, you're drunk alright!" He leaned in to kiss her.

She swatted away his advances, then became frighteningly still. "I'm telling you! I saw them both move!"

"Hello," he said sarcastically, "they've been dead for three days!"

This prompted a facemask wearing guard to glance down at the corpses. After being hailed as heroes the past three days, and celebrated all throughout the Holy Land, this was the first time the twelve guards who were responsible for killing the Two Witnesses, were back on duty.

They were positioned behind the corpses, so they wouldn't obstruct anyone's view. After a few seconds had passed, he snorted frustration at the imbecile who had said it.

Just as he was lifting his eyes to resume scanning the area, it happened again. His eyes widened; fear gripped his entire body.

"Whoa!" he shouted. His hands trembled so fiercely that he dropped his automatic weapon to the ground, alerting his eleven comrades in arms that something wasn't right. They quickly aimed their guns at the crowd waving them back and forth, ready to fire if need be.

Suddenly, there was movement in the rest of their extremities. Their stiff limbs became limber, as the Two rocked their bodies one way then the next, causing a prolonged hush to fill the streets of Jerusalem.

The whole world watched in horror as the Two slain men came back to life before their very eyes!

What in the world? became the petrifying thought of most, now stunned into utter silence. *Could it be?*

"See, told ya!" the inebriated woman said again to her boyfriend, scratching her head, as the rest of her body was chilled to the core.

The 25-year-old man wiped his eyes with filthy hands. Realizing his eyes weren't playing tricks on him, he became so terrified that his heart gave out on him. He fell dead to the ground a few feet away from the Two slain Witnesses.

His girlfriend dropped to her knees and started pounding on his chest, hoping to revive him, but to no avail. She moved her long black hair away from her face to give him CPR followed by more chest compressions, when suddenly, her eyes were forced skyward, when a loud voice shouted from Heaven saying, "Come up here!" just as the 144,000 had warned, causing her own heart to give out next.

This voice was even louder than the unidentified flying object, or voice, or whatever, still spewing constant blasphemies in the sky above, its message identical to what the 144,000 kept preaching.

Everyone heard it loud and clear, and trembled in fear, causing numerous heart attacks to occur on every continent.

Without uttering a word—their earthly ministry was completed when the Antichrist temporarily silenced them—the Two men stood to their feet and lifted their arms skyward toward Heaven. Their countenances were changed, and their faces beamed like the sun for all to see, as they started levitating skyward, without a single gunshot wound or dried blood on their bodies, or without a single trace of decomposition.

An eerie hush fell across the city, as everyone waited to see what would happen next. Even if they could talk, what could they possibly say?

This led to even more heart attacks, not only in the Holy City, but planetwide.

Once they were taken up to Heaven, a massive earthquake rocked Jerusalem, sending even more soul-stopping shockwaves reverberating all throughout the planet, quickly reaching all seven continents.

Many watched, as a crater-sized hole appeared in the ground where the Two were resurrected, swallowing everyone within close proximity whole, including the twelve guards who were responsible for killing Yahweh's Two Witnesses three and a half days ago.

Each shot fired that day, by the six men-six women crew, had successfully hit their targets, riddling their bodies with many bullets.

Now that their lives had just been ended, the twelve guards were painfully mindful that the Two they had assassinated really were God's

Two Witnesses. They also knew they would have to give an account for their grievous vile acts before a just and holy God.

In short, all twelve had eternal blood on their hands...

When buildings started crumbling all throughout Israel, from the 9.0 quake that shook their tiny country to the core, many became so terrified that they gave glory to the God of Heaven.

Yet, much like Pharaoh had done on several occasions, when Yahweh used Moses to send more plagues, instead of repenting of their wretched ways, and trusting in Yeshua as Messiah, their hearts remained dead set against Him, with "dead" being the operative. From a spiritual standpoint, they weren't converted, only frightened for their lives.

Providentially, as some blasphemed the God who did this to them, many Jews fell on their knees in repentance, crying out to Yahweh, begging for His forgiveness.

To witness the Two Men who were clearly dead, the past three and a half days, suddenly rise to their feet before being taken skyward, there could be no denying now that they belonged to the God of Israel...

It was a remarkable scene and an amazing revelation seeing these newly converted souls who had supported Salvador Romanero all this time, now transferring their loyalty and allegiance to Yahweh God.

They praised the Most High and gave Him all the glory right there in the streets of Jerusalem...

11

NEW BABYLON

SALVADOR ROMANERO WAS IN his personal quarters when it happened. The rage and humiliation he felt watching his Two enemies being resurrected from the dead on his large TV screen, with the whole world watching, was incalculable.

When Satan was recently cast out of Heaven, and forever banished from the Throne of God, it was then that the devil entered Romanero and the Pope. He filled his agents in human form with godlike powers and increased their knowledge to levels that had never been attained by mere humans before.

Until just recently, Salvador had always prayed that the supernatural power he felt before the Two Witnesses were killed, would never leave him. Now that he felt the Master Deceiver's power full throttle, it was so intense he wished he could control it or occasionally tone it down, but he couldn't. It left him feeling jittery most of the time. And the constant body twitches made it impossible for him to rest at night.

But the worst part about having this dark supernatural power flowing throughout his entire being, without dilution, was that he was suddenly aware of certain things he wished he didn't know. He was starting to sense just how dark this power really was!

Romanero always knew the possibility existed that he might be on the losing end of the battle, but the fact that his side outnumbered the enemy by at least ten to one, always made him feel optimistic that they would be victorious in the end.

He was starting to sense for the first time that the war between his master and the Most High God of Israel, might not end well for his side.

This, in turn, made him feel less secure about the new utopia he kept promising for all his followers up to this point…

Had he only read and understood the Book he had outlawed a year and a half ago, at his master's behest, he would have known all about his grim outcome. But as a lover of the darkness, even from childhood, just one glance at the Christian Bible would twist his stomach in knots.

Romanero was mindful that it foretold about these days. He knew bits and pieces of what it said. But once he rose to power and prominence, and suddenly had direct access to the Master Deceiver, he never felt the urge to read it for himself.

Up until now, he always had complete trust that the devil would enlighten him at every turn. He no longer felt that way. How could he after this major breach of trust? His rage took on a whole new meaning.

Romanero screamed at Satan at the top of his lungs, "Why didn't you tell me this would happen?! You assured me that I would have the power to kill them! I even challenged the God they served, daring Him to rescue them both from imminent death!

"Why do you let me feel omnipotent at times, by allowing me to perform mighty miracles, even shaking the kingdoms of the Earth, only to humiliate me again with the whole world watching? Three days ago, I felt invincible! Now I feel like a fool again!"

Romanero's body twitched violently as he paced the massive room, trying to piece it all together. The many great boasts he had uttered just before the Two were slain, now felt like acid being poured on his tongue. Even worse, he allowed it all to be aired on live television!

Salvador screamed at Satan again, "You keep promising that we will exalt our throne above the stars of God, yet I can't even neutralize the God of Israel's sealed servants!"

He became so enraged by this realization that he ransacked his own palace. He smashed dishes, glassware, and even priceless artifacts that were given to him as gifts from global leaders, all the while wondering how he could possibly overcome this major setback.

It wasn't until many hours later when Romanero had finally calmed down, that the Master Deceiver reasoned with his chief agent in human form. He explained what had happened was necessary to prepare him for even greater things. This was the final sifting and separation period.

Satan then reminded his underling that once someone took the mark, it would be impossible for them to defect to the other side. Therefore, he should place all his focus on achieving that objective.

But after suffering his most humiliating setback thus far, the *Miracle Maker* needed to do something huge, to reestablish his role once again as leader of the world.

Romanero went live from his palace in New Babylon, using the new global push alert system that allowed his voice to override everything his followers were doing on their smartphones, and on all other mobile devices, leaving them no choice but to listen.

What he liked most about this new feature was that he could reach his global audience in real time—either with audio or also with video—without being peppered with questions from reporters afterward.

Whenever Salvador or the Pope would address the world from New Babylon, from this point forward, it would be done using this format.

Using only the audio feature this time, Romanero came straight to the point, "Due to the unfortunate circumstances in Jerusalem, the Temple dedication will be delayed for two weeks. Some of the areas surrounding the Temple were badly damaged in the quake and will need to be repaired before we can gather there again.

"The Temple itself wasn't damaged. Under no circumstances would I have allowed that to happen. But just to be safe we will delay it for a while, so the scores of spectators who will surely gather for the Temple dedication, and for the unveiling of the mark will feel protected.

"Make no mistake, the God of Israel is responsible for sending the quake, which led to the massive loss of life of so many in Jerusalem," he said, without mentioning the resurrections. "But just know that when the final count is in, they will discover that a tenth of Jerusalem was leveled, and exactly seven thousand people were killed as a result.

"I regret to inform that many of my top advisors who proudly served you were among the seven thousand to perish in the quake, at the hands of Israel's God. Among them were Li Ping, Jurgen Staat, Israel's Prime Minister, and many of my key Jewish supporters. They were gathered at a private location three kilometers away from the Temple, when the quake ended their lives.

"Many who follow the God of Israel proclaim that He is a jealous God. They are absolutely right! He is a jealous God, and a small thinking God, whose religion is available to only one race of people. And with his many laws and restrictions, it's no wonder that most Jews chose not to follow Him throughout the ages!

"The new global religion that the Pope himself will head up will be open to everyone, not just the few. Unlike Israel's God, we will make the world a better place for all global citizens. In that light, if I were *Him*, I would be jealous too!

"Despite this minor setback, we must keep our eyes on the prize, which is the new reset once the mark is administered. This technology is already in place and is in the final stages of being streamlined globally.

"Once it has been set up in your area, if you do not have access to transportation, or if the roads are still too badly damaged, or if you're suffering from health issues, simply make an appointment and someone will come directly to your home.

"Finally, for those of you who wanted to be among the first to receive the mark, let not your hearts be troubled. Just as the Pope has promised, everyone who shows up for the Temple dedication will still be the first ones to receive it. What a glorious day that will be! Until then, may you all be blessed in my name..."

At that, the microphone was turned off. Now sensing that his time as leader of the world might be extremely short, the Antichrist of the Bible was even more determined to bring as many souls down to the pit with him as he could. *If I'm going down, I'm not going down alone!*

AS SHOCKWAVE AFTER SHOCKWAVE reverberated all across the planet, God's 144,000 sealed servants weren't the only ones to know in advance about what had transpired in Jerusalem the past three days.

They also knew 7,000 would perish in the quake. Romanero's so-called prediction wasn't rocket science. It was written...

Even though they couldn't share it with anyone other than themselves, every Christ follower on the planet—whether living in hiding or in prison—fully expected it to come to pass, exactly how it was written by the Disciple John, on the Island of Patmos, 2,000 years ago.

They rejoiced and praised God with all their hearts and souls, for performing this mighty resurrection miracle.

Whereas Antichrist's followers were left reeling yet again, the millions of Christians suffering in Romanero's new death camps, were further strengthened seeing how God's timetable was right on schedule.

It gave them the added strength to press on toward the goal, which was an eternity with their King, the Lord Jesus Christ. *Hallelujah!*

FOR SALVADOR ROMANERO'S STILL-on-the-fence supporters, every minute they had to wait before finally hearing from their leader felt like an hour. And this was his way of comforting them?

It didn't go unnoticed by anyone that he never explained how or why his Two enemies came back to life, or Who was responsible for performing this undeniable miracle, with the whole world watching.

He never even mentioned it, in fact!

And where was the sympathy for the many on his staff who'd perished in the quake? If anything, Romanero sounded like a TV anchorman reading a script, without a hint of emotion behind his words. It was almost as if he had already discarded them.

After feeling so exuberant the past three days, their nerves were on edge once again. Even his promise of a seven-day celebration was cut in half, leaving them feeling hopeless yet again, deceived really.

Partly because of this, his address fell mostly on deaf ears…

12

THE NEXT DAY

DR. BENJAMIN SHAPIRO LISTENED to his boss give his lackluster address to the masses, on his mobile phone. It offered him little hope that his boss really was in control of things like he always proclaimed to be.

Like so many of his followers, it left him scratching his head in confusion, with more questions swimming through his mind than answers. What angered him the most about the speech was when Romanero called what happened in Jerusalem a minor setback.

Dr. Shapiro was at home when the Two were seemingly resurrected from the dead. He watched it all unfolding on his massive TV screen in his exercise room. He was on the treadmill when the Two came back to life. Without finishing the full hour that he had programmed into the treadmill, he shut it down, and started gasping for air in horror, and clutching at his heart, hoping it wouldn't give out on him.

His first thought was, how could Jakob have possibly known they would be resurrected precisely how he had said they would, with the whole world watching? That had to count for something, right? And how did he know that 7,000 would perish as a result?

Even though his boss had since confirmed it to everyone, since Jakob had already told him, it was received by Benjamin as second-hand news.

He blinked that thought away and rubbed his throbbing forehead, as another dreadful thought invaded his mind. *Had I not left Jerusalem the other day, would I be dead too?*

Benjamin was saddened to discover that the vast majority of Romanero's staff had perished in the Jerusalem quake, including some he had felt a special closeness to. Just like that, they were gone. Even before his boss confirmed it in his address, seeing so many destroyed buildings on his TV screen, he already felt it deep in his bones.

Benjamin wondered why this, too, had happened on Romanero's watch? Equally disturbing was that his boss had signed a seven-year peace treaty with Israel, then solidified his commitment to them by sparing them during the global quake. So why would he allow an earthquake to rock their tiny country now? What sense did that make?

It was almost as if the God of Israel was mocking the *Miracle Maker*.

73

Shapiro couldn't help but wonder what other lies his boss had told since he started working for him? But it wasn't only Romanero's lies that that had him shaking his head in confusion. It was also his inability to answer the many questions that were asked of him in Jerusalem, four days ago.

Why couldn't he silence the Voice from above? And why couldn't he definitively answer the reporter's question about the 144,000 being silenced? Why couldn't he answer the question about when it would finally rain again in Jerusalem, after his bold promise that it would rain on his new birthday had never materialized?

On top of that, why couldn't he explain to the other reporter what had happened in the skies above—and was still happening—despite that Romanero's forces tried shooting it out of the sky, without success?

These questions had consumed Benjamin ever since he left the Holy Land, with Romanero and the Pope. But now they gnawed on him like a hungry dog chewing on a bone.

But what bothered him the most was the baldfaced lie his boss had told after being asked if he had been stung by the locusts. Having personally treated his sting marks and abrasions—not to mention his own—all he could do was lower his head in shame. And why did those demonic locusts all bear a strong resemblance to his own likeness?

When Benjamin heard him justifying the deaths of so many who worked for him, by placing all blame at the feet of Israel's God in his address, it rubbed him the wrong way. At least initially it did.

Then it dawned on him. If so, wouldn't that prove that Yahweh was more powerful than Romanero? Clearly, He had vindicated His Two faithful Witnesses, by resurrecting them with the whole world watching.

Then to send the devastating quake, which had caused so many of Romanero's true followers to perish, there could be no doubt in his mind that Israel's God was mocking his boss.

For the first time since becoming Salvador Romanero's private doctor, Benjamin silently questioned his patient's so-called supernatural powers. Everything that once felt holy and pure to him now felt anything but those things. Now convinced that his boss was both a liar and a fake, this thought crushed him in the deepest chambers of his spirit.

On top of everything else, for the first time in his adult life, Dr. Shapiro felt like a failure. Having climbed the highest ladder that anyone in his position could climb, and finally seeing it for what it was—sheer emptiness—he suddenly felt trapped in an endless web of evil and deceit.

Benjamin sensed deep in his spirit again that he had to escape out from underneath the man's evil clutches before it was too late…

What came as no surprise was when he was finally able to drift off to sleep at 3 a.m., he was once again visited by his nephew on the same park bench on which they had met in the first two dreams.

Benjamin had fully expected to see him again and hear the, "I told you so" speech. But it never happened. Instead, Jakob had insisted that it was time for them to meet in person.

When Benjamin offered to meet him in Jerusalem, Jakob had replied, "You won't find me there, Uncle. We can meet right here on this park bench."

Benjamin's eyes bulged. "In Pennsylvania?"

Jakob nodded. "It's where Yahweh sent me to do His business."

Benjamin asked, "What day will we meet? And what time?"

Jakob answered, "Once you are there, Uncle, I'll find you."

The way he had said it with such assurance was what had woken Benjamin from the dream. *So that's why I kept seeing him there?*

On the one hand, he couldn't overlook the fact that these conversations all took place in dreamland, which happened to be the one dimension of his life over which he had no control. On the other hand, everything that Jakob had told him would happen in the real world, had come to pass precisely as he had said it would in his dream world.

With his mind made up to travel to America, Benjamin wondered if his nephew would be there to meet him on the park bench when he arrived? He wasn't sure. Then again, he was suddenly unsure of so many things, with his boss topping the list.

The first thing he did when he arrived at his office was to request a lunch audience with Salvador, which was granted.

In the five hours he waited to meet him, he couldn't concentrate on anything else. It was eerily strange how few people were also in the building with him. So many of them had perished in the Jerusalem quake.

As the noon hour approached, Benjamin took a seat at Romanero's table. Just as they were about to eat, suddenly, the Voice rocked the atmosphere above New Babylon, "Yahweh is my rock and my salvation; he is my fortress, I will not be shaken. My salvation and my honor depend on Yahweh; he is my mighty rock, my refuge.

"Trust in him at all times, you people; pour out your hearts to him, for Yahweh is our refuge. For the Lord takes pleasure in His people; He will beautify the humble with salvation. The fool says in his heart, 'There is no God.'"

Both men remained fearfully silent as Yahweh's angelic messenger's deep, booming voice caused even the table they were seated at to shake.

Shapiro's eyes were fixated on his boss the entire time, as he trembled in fear again at the sound of the Voice.

Salvador saw his doctor staring at him with what could best be described as a look of disappointment chiseled onto his face. "What's wrong Benjamin? You don't look well."

Dr. Shapiro looked up at the ceiling and swallowed hard. His boss looked different to him now, more inwardly conflicted, more human. "I can't stop thinking about what happened in Jerusalem…"

"Which part?" This was asked matter-of-factly.

Benjamin cleared his throat. Once again, his question had struck him the wrong way. "Where do I begin? The resurrections? The ensuing quake? The deaths of so many of my good friends? Don't you find it a little strange that the location at which the five thousand VIPs were gathered, was nowhere near the Wailing Wall?"

Benjamin paused, then added, "It's not like they were collateral damage like the many celebrating at the Wall before the quake. That part's easy to understand, but not the rest. And why was Israel's Prime Minister killed, after you signed a seven-year peace treaty with the man? He would be the last person I would ever think would perish at the halfway point of the agreement. Do you find it as bizarre as I do?"

Salvador took a moment to consider what his doctor had said. "Good thing we left when we did!" This was said without the slightest sense of empathy.

Benjamin had just stuffed a wheat cracker loaded with hummus in his mouth and nearly spit it on the table, clearly taken aback by his insensitive answer. It was a cruel and heartless thing to say.

He took a moment to collect his thoughts. "Forgive me for saying this, your Excellency, but it almost seems as if…"

Romanero leaned up on his chair and squared his shoulders. "Yes?"

Benjamin sighed deeply. "Well, it seems targeted, your Excellency."

Romanero leveled his eyes on his personal physician, ever so suspiciously. "What are you getting it Benjamin?"

Dr. Shapiro frowned. "I'm just trying to wrap my mind around it all. I'm having difficulty accepting that many of my friends and colleagues were killed, when they were there to celebrate the deaths of the Two

Witnesses. Now they're dead too! How should I act when this marvelous city you have built for us, is suddenly less populated by thousands of your top minds and other staff members..."

Romanero was already in a foul mood, from once again being forced into damage control. This wasn't helping. "I understand your feelings. It's been a difficult twenty-four hours for all of us."

Benjamin took a few deep, exasperated breaths and exhaled. "I think I need a break so I can properly mourn the loss of my friends and colleagues. I haven't had a vacation since I became your personal physician. I feel burnt out.

"Grateful as I am to serve you in this capacity, your Excellency, I feel if I don't take a little time to recharge my batteries and properly grieve now, it will have a drastic effect on my health later, not to mention my dedicated service to you."

Romanero took a sip of guava juice. "What about your speech about the cancer-fighting microchip?"

"Truth be told, I haven't even started writing it. How can I when it's been a whirlwind of late? I need to be still a while so I can concentrate."

Romanero couldn't argue his point.

Benjamin wasn't sure what his boss was thinking. He went on, "Now that you've moved the date back two weeks, I think this would be a good time for me to go someplace quiet, so I can rest my mind and body and concentrate on writing the speech."

Salvador nodded that he understood. Still mindful of the awkward exchange the two of them shared when he lied to the press, even though he knew he could trust no one until after the mark was administered, his request sounded logical enough. "Where will you go?"

"I'm thinking back to the States. This way, I can rest at home a few days then work on my speech in peace and quiet, without any distractions. That's precisely what I need right now, your Eminence, a little peace and quiet. I miss taking daily walks to the local park. I used to do a whole lot of thinking on those walks. I feel certain that's what I need right now to recharge my mind, body and spirit."

Benjamin knew he would be GPS monitored, so it was best to be up front with his boss, so when they tracked him to the park, it wouldn't cause red flags to go up.

Romanero threw up his hands and leaned back on his chair. "You're a doctor, you should know, right?"

Benjamin nodded gratefully. "Thank you for understanding, your Eminence."

Romanero asked, "When would you like to leave?"

"Today, if possible. I don't feel up to performing my duties. Unless, of course, you need me for something."

Salvador took a moment to mull it over in his mind, then said, "Permission granted. You can take one of the planes. I'll arrange transportation for you once you arrive in the States."

Dr. Shapiro grinned just enough for his boss to see it. "Thank you, your Eminence. That's very generous of you."

"Just make sure you're back a few days before the Mark is administered. As my personal physician, I'll want you standing by my side in front of the newly constructed Temple, in Jerusalem, so you can give your speech after the Pope gives his."

"Yes, your Excellency…"

Romanero flashed his legendary smile, which no longer appealed to Benjamin, especially with his eyes projecting increasing darkness. "How exciting that you will also be among the first to receive the mark?"

Benjamin hesitated and looked down at his feet. The anger he saw in his eyes, which he could only assume was from the Voice they both heard to start the meeting, made it impossible to hold the man's gaze. It frightened him. Finally, he tipped his eyes up at his boss. "Yes, of course. Now, if you'll excuse me, I need to pack my things."

"As you wish. I just hope when you return from your vacation to the States, you'll be well rested and ready to resume your duties here."

"That makes two of us, your Eminence…" Shapiro said, thankful that his boss couldn't monitor his dreams. *Or could he?*

Benjamin left Romanero's palace silently wondering if he would be added to his "Kill List", for questioning his boss the way he had, and for his uncertainty which he knew Salvador no doubt sensed?

But that wasn't the case. What Salvador was thinking instead was that he needed the very same thing his physician needed now, peace and quiet.

But ever since Satan had entered him, those two things kept eluding him a little more with each passing day...

13

THE NEXT EVENING

"THANK YOU, LORD!" DONALD Johnson shouted, upon reading the message on his SAT phone.

After sending numerous emails and text messages, and even resorting to stalking her on social media, using a fictitious name, Analyn Tibayan had finally replied to one of his messages.

Her reply was short and to the point: *Who is this?*

Donald literally wept tears of joy. Her timing had been perfect, which meant it had truly come from God. He typed, *This is your Ninong, Donald.*

After a few more exchanges, it led to the VPN video chat between them. Per Dr. Lee Kim's strict instructions, this was the only mode of communication *ETSM* residents were allowed to use, when contacting unsaved friends and family members. Not only did they have a 100 percent success rate, by having video calls, both sides could know for sure they were chatting with the real person.

After exchanging pleasantries, Donald asked, "Why did you avoid me last time I was there? And why haven't you replied to any of my messages since?"

Analyn grimaced. "The reason I avoided you," she said, her voice deflated, "was that I met a man online from Australia..."

"Before the disappearances?"

Analyn nodded her head in shame. "When Romanero opened all borders for anyone wishing to relocate to other countries, we finally got to meet in person. Long story short, I got pregnant..."

Analyn gasped, then lowered her head in shame. "The only reason I had sex with him was that I was convinced he truly loved me. But in the end, it was nothing more than a well-crafted lie on his part."

Donald asked, "How do you know he was lying?"

Analyn took a deep breath. "I received a message one day on one of my social media accounts from another Filipino woman, demanding that I stop contacting her husband. I was so heartbroken that I wanted to kill myself, especially when I discovered I was pregnant..."

Analyn paused, expecting her ninong to lash out at her, but he didn't. If anything, the compassion she saw on his face comforted her immensely.

She lowered her head again. "Now you know why I avoided you all this time."

Donald pressed his lips together. "You even blocked me. You left me no choice but to message you anonymously."

"Sorry. I was so ashamed of myself and knew you would be disappointed in me for acting so foolishly." Eyes pleading for mercy, she asked, "Can you forgive me, Ninong?"

"Of course, I forgive you!" Johnson knew whatever had put that somber expression on her face, it went far beyond asking for his forgiveness.

Mary heard the commotion in the small cottage living room and got out of bed, careful not to wake Luke, who was purring away like a small kitten in the crib next to the bed.

She found her husband engaged in a deep conversation on his SAT phone. "Who are you talking to, honey?" she asked.

Donald turned the phone so his wife could see the young woman on his screen. "I finally got ahold of someone in the Philippines. This is Analyn Tibayan. She was one of my former students."

Before Mary could reply, Analyn asked, "Who's that, Ninong?"

"My wife, Mary."

"Wow, congratulations!" Analyn wanted to look joyous, but she was too beaten down to resemble anything close to that positive emotion.

"Thanks, Analyn. We got married a little more than two years ago."

Mary sat next to her husband and listened. The sadness she saw on the young woman's face was about to be taken to a whole new level.

Donald said, "I'm so relieved you survived the recent catastrophes. I can only imagine how bad it was in your country. Every time a new tragedy strikes the planet, I think of the Philippines."

Analyn slumped her shoulders. "You wouldn't recognize it if you were here, Ninong. So much of my country was destroyed. Even the Mall of Asia that you used to take me to for ice cream, is no longer there."

Mary asked, "How old is your child? Did you have a son or daughter?"

Analyn looked away as tears flooded her eyes. She lowered her head and started softly sniffling.

Donald and Mary looked at each other shaking their heads, both sensing the worst.

With the saddest expression on her face, she bemoaned, "My daughter was swept away in the flood waters from the tidal waves. She was ripped right out of my arms. My parents too. We fled to higher ground, but it wasn't high enough. They're gone. Everything is gone. All is lost…"

Analyn lost control of her emotions and wept bitterly for the thousandth time since it happened.

Donald's face crumpled in anguish. He thought back to the unbridled joy he felt after converting her to Mormonism, when she was still a teenager, a year and a half before the Rapture took place. That was when her parents, whom he had also converted, asked him to be her ninong, which, essentially, was like being a godfather to their daughter.

Mary's heart burned within her. "So sorry to hear that. What was your daughter's name?"

Analyn looked down at her lap. Her lips quivered. "Juliana."

Mary's shoulders slumped this time. "Are you okay?"

Analyn couldn't hold Mary's stare and looked down at her lap. "No, I'm not. On top of everything else, I just found out my boyfriend's been cheating on me with another man. I feel so worthless. I'm tired of this life. I just want to die."

The way she said it pierced the Johnsons deep down in their souls. The next words out of Analyn's mouth shook them both to the core of their being.

She wiped her moist eyes with a sleeve of her shirt, and very calmly said, "The only hope I have left is to receive the mark, so I can help Romanero find Christian dissidents. On the day he announced it, I was about to drink something poisonous. Salvador is my only hope…"

Donald shot a quick glance at Mary, then leaned up on his chair. He gazed into his phone screen. "Whatever you do, Analyn, do *not* take that mark!"

Analyn shook her head incredulously, unable to comprehend why her ninong had said that to her. "I have no food or money. My global monetary card was lost in the flood. I haven't been able to replace it yet. I've had a bad toothache for many weeks, but I can't go to the dentist. If I don't take the mark, how can I eat? I'm tired of looking in dumpsters for food to eat. The only way I see out of it is by taking the mark…"

Donald felt a sharp pain in his chest. "I know how you feel, Analyn. It's been a terrible time for all of us." He took a deep breath and exhaled. "What if I told you I'm one of the dissidents Romanero's looking for?"

Analyn's eyes widened. "He's killing Mormons too?"

"I'm no longer a Mormon…" Donald cleared his throat and sat up a little straighter. "Please hear me out. Everything I ever told you about Mormonism was a lie. I didn't know it at the time, but by helping spread that false religion, I was representing Satan's kingdom instead of God's."

Analyn blinked hard a few times. "How can you still believe in God with so much evil in the world? Now, on top of everything else, you tell me the religion I learned from you is a false one?"

Donald said, "You asked me earlier if I'll forgive you. Now I ask the same of you. Will you please forgive me, for misleading you spiritually."

When Analyn didn't reply, he tried reasoning with her, "After the disappearances, which I now know was the Rapture of Christ's Church, I read the Christian Bible from cover to cover, then repented of my sinful ways and trusted in Christ alone for my salvation."

Analyn stared skeptically into her phone. "I don't know, Ninong…"

Donald panicked. "Please listen to me, Analyn, if you think your situation is bad now, it's nothing compared to what awaits each doomed sinner on the other side, including everyone who takes the mark…"

Analyn sighed into the phone. "Doomed sinners?"

Donald shook his head. "That's the fate of all who die without Christ's forgiveness on this side of the grave. If you still profess faith in Mormonism, you'll never have God's eternal assurance."

Analyn brushed off a shiver. "If Mormonism is a cult like you say, and you were representing Satan, what is the fate of my daughter and parents?"

Donald winced at the question, and shot a desperate glance at his wife, as his mind raced back to when Brian told Jacquelyn shortly after the Rapture that her first husband, Tom Swindell, was in hell awaiting God's eternal judgment. Brian then told her that if she didn't repent of her sinful living and trust in Jesus for her salvation, she would follow him there someday. He now knew how his good friend felt that day.

Mary sensed what her husband was thinking, and rubbed his shoulders, then ran her fingers through his gray hair knowing how much he liked it. Even that couldn't erase the anguish on his face.

"Your daughter *is* with Jesus now."

Analyn braced herself. "And my parents?"

Donald gulped hard. "Well, if they perished believing what Mormonism teaches, because of people like me, I would have to say no. It isn't Christ centered. But only God knows their hearts."

Analyn's chest heaved up and down as she reached for her next breath. What little wind she still had left in her sails, had just been extinguished. "I can't deal with this now, Ninong. Ever since my boyfriend left me, I feel all alone with no one or nowhere to go. I'm constantly groped by men and women whenever I leave my sleeping quarters. I always fear being raped by someone. I've never been more frightened in all my life."

More pain stabbed at Donald's heart. "Can I pray for you?"

Analyn felt spiritually betrayed by him and started weeping again. "Perhaps another time. Sorry, but I have to go now." She ended the call.

Donald stared at the blank phone screen for a few moments, then buried his face in the palms of his hands and wept. The guilt he felt for misleading this young woman, and so many others, by having them join what he now knew beyond a certainty was a cult, was unbearable at times.

He dried his eyes with a renewed determination to do all he could to share the true Gospel message with her, and the many Filipinos he had converted to Mormonism in the 13 years he spent there.

His prayer starting today would be that his Maker would open this door for him…

14

THE JOHNSONS WOKE EARLY the next morning, and went to the cafeteria for breakfast, before Mary started her shift at one of the daycare centers that were spread about the property. Everyone could feel the tension between the married couple.

Tamika had just finished having breakfast with Isaac. The two were on their way to work. This would be the start of Isaac's fourth week standing guard at the front of the property. What she saw on Donald's and Mary's faces concerned her deeply. "Is everything okay, you two?"

Donald took a sip of water. "Something happened last night, and we would like your opinions on it…"

"On what?" asked Brian.

After everyone had gathered around, Donald and Mary shared their experience from the night before.

Isaac and Tamika remained behind in the cafeteria and listened, as the Johnsons explained what had transpired between themselves, and the young woman in the Philippines.

Once they were up to speed on the situation, Donald said, "I know this is no time for believers to venture outdoors, let alone travel halfway around the world, but I sense very strongly that I need to go to the Philippines as soon as possible. If only you could have seen Analyn last night, you would fully understand my dilemma."

Mary sighed deeply, then shivered at the notion of traveling all that way in this chaotic world. It was the last thing she wanted now. She glanced up at the ceiling and rested her index finger on her lip, to formulate wat she would say to the group.

Finally, she said, "If God's calling Donald to the Philippines, I'm not against it. I saw the young woman's face, and I agree that she desperately needs help. But as committed as I was to go with him before the last round of God's judgments struck the planet, the thought of leaving this place and traveling halfway around the world now frightens me to no end."

Mary set her jutting jaw in that certain way she was known for at moments like this. "Besides, I feel needed here, not only for Luke, but for all the other children. You all know about my past. Most of you do anyway. After being an orphan all my life, I finally found my true family here at safe house number one."

84

She paused, then added, "The last thing I want is to be stuck halfway around the world in a foreign country, when the seven bowl judgments start rocking the planet. With so many young children to care for, this is where I want to be, whether I live or die! Is it wrong to want my husband here with me and Luke when it happens?"

Donald was quite mindful that his wife still suffered from separation anxiety. "Of course, I want to be here with you, Mary, that goes without saying, but we can't leave Analyn there like that."

Mary threw her arms up in the air. "You heard what she said, Donald. The Philippines is no longer recognizable!" The tension on her face and in her voice was palpable. "You and I both know the next round of God's judgments will be even worse. I'm scared."

Donald couldn't argue with her logic. What person in their right mind would want to travel halfway around the world at this point in history? "I don't know what to expect over there. But Analyn's all alone living in a dilapidated boarding house with no water or electricity, always fearing someone will rape her or worse."

Mary frowned. "Yes, but you will be risking your life, and this family, for someone who isn't even saved, and may never get saved…" Her voice trailed off.

Donald got up off the bench and paced the floor. He said to Tamika, "When you called Amos' death a thorn in your side the other day, the instant you said it, the many folks I've misled in the Philippines flooded my mind. Now suddenly, after all this time, one of them replies to one of my messages. How could God's hand not be in it?"

Donald placed his hands on his wife's shoulders, and gently massaged them. "They are the thorns in my side, Mary. I'll admit it's a big risk, but I have to at least try to rescue as many of them as I can. The longer I wait, the better organized the enemy will be."

Mary placed her hands on the table, then steepled her fingers. "Why can't we ask an ETSM member over there to share the Gospel with her?"

Donald became incredulous. "Who, Mary? We haven't heard from anyone over there in many months. We don't know who's still alive or dead. Analyn needs help now. I'm not thrilled about traveling all the way to the Philippines as a Christ follower. I have the same reservations you have. But I can't just sit back and do nothing."

Donald sighed deeply. "I know God has forgiven me for preaching a false gospel to them, but I can almost feel their blood on my hands. That said, I feel it's my duty to make every attempt to share the Gospel with whoever I may see when I'm there. If any of them truly converts to Christianity, I'll do my best to bring them back here to the States."

Mary's lips started quivering. "What if you get caught?"

Donald kissed her stress-induced wrinkled forehead. "That's where prayer comes in, honey."

After listening to them very carefully, Brian asked Mary, "Not to overstep my bounds, but does your situation remind you of anything?"

Mary shot Brian a confused look. "Not off the top of my head. What do you mean?"

"Think about it, had Charles and I not gone to New York to rescue Tamika, way back when, there's no telling where she might be now, or if she would even be alive." Brian glanced at a teary-eyed Tamika, before his eyes volleyed back to Mary. "If you recall, that was when Charles met you at the Waldorf-Astoria, before Braxton brought you here with my mother, which ultimately led to your getting married to Donald. Can you deny it was all part of God's plan?"

Mary lowered her head in defeat.

Brian looked at Tamika again. "I'll never forget how frightened you were back then. I heard it in your voice on the phone. There was a time when I thought you might suffer a nervous breakdown, especially when you saw your image on the TV in her hotel room."

Tamika lowered her head, and silently thanked God again for her two dear brothers in Christ.

Isaac placed his right hand on his wife's shoulder. He knew most of the details about her daring escape from New York City, but Brian had just helped him put another piece of the puzzle in place.

Brian shifted his attention to Donald, to hopefully encourage him in his decision. If anyone needed support right now, it was him. "Imagine how fearful Analyn is after losing her daughter in the tsunami that ravaged her country. Imagine how petrified she must be. No doubt she'll remain that way until someone finally rescues her."

Johnson shook his head in agreement. He took it as further confirmation that it was what God was calling him to do.

Donald sat next to his wife and reached for her hand, then lowered his head. "Let us pray. Oh, great and wonderful Heavenly Father, Analyn desperately needs Your healing touch right now. You know how much she's suffering. Despite her broken heart and grim financial situation, calm her spirit as only You can.

"If it's Your will that I go to the Philippines, I know You will open a safe passageway for me, so I can win Analyn to You, and hopefully others. Until that day comes, if it comes, penetrate her weary heart, and break the constant hopelessness she feels inside, in Jesus' name I pray, Amen…"

"Amen!"

Mary lowered her head in defeat, knowing Brian was right. There was no point in arguing any further. "When will you leave?"

Donald kissed his wife on the cheeks again. "As soon as I can. Once the mark becomes available, it will be even more difficult for us to venture outdoors, let alone travel halfway around the world."

Manuel Jiminez approached them. "Perhaps this is my signal to try and make it back to Mexico, and join our brothers and sisters there…"

"That would be fine with me," said Donald in reply. "Let's send it up the chain of command and see what happens."

Before standing guard at the back of the property, Donald sent a secure text message to Analyn. *I'm working on coming to the Philippines for you, and hopefully some of the others as well. It will take a little time to put a solid plan in place, but once I have one, I'll let you know.*

Until then, whatever you do, please don't take the mark until after we meet. If you do, cruel as it sounds, we will be eternal enemies, and there will be nothing I can do to help you. Please, that's all I ask. I hope to see you soon. Until then, take care of yourself…and know that I'm always praying for you.

15

IT TOOK FIVE LONG, unsettling days before Donald Johnson and Manuel Jimenez finally left safe house number one, in Chadds Ford, Pennsylvania for the state of Florida, under the cover of darkness.

The reason for the lengthy delay—five days was like an eternity with the implementation of the mark of the beast looming—was that this would be a four-pronged attempt at relocating *ETSM* members.

Aside from sneaking Donald on board a cargo container ship for Singapore, and Manuel boarding a fishing vessel for Brownsville, Texas, they also secured passage for Hana and Cristiana Patel in India, and for Yasamin and Navid Dabiri, who had been living underground, in Dubai, waiting for the signal to be given to bring them to America.

If everything went according to plan, once it was confirmed that Donald was safely on board the ship, Hana would set sail to Singapore 35 days later, on a small fishing vessel from Chennai, India, as Yasamin and her son would sail to Singapore, from Dubai.

The plan was that all three would arrive in Southeast Asia on the same day. Donald would meet the two international fugitives who had already been added to Salvador Romanero's Top Ten Most Wanted list, for their ultimate betrayal and desertion, and all three would be taken to an *ETSM* safe house for a night or two, before the two women and their small children would be smuggled on board the same cargo ship that Johnson would take to Singapore.

Once they were safely on board the ship, Johnson would then board a 30-foot motorized sailboat that was owned by a fellow Christian from Russia. Sergei Ivanov had already agreed to take him to the Philippines, to hopefully rescue Analyn, and bring her back to the States.

It was a complex plan to be sure. What made it infinitely more complex was that since one-third of all ships and fishing vessels were destroyed in the past calamities, many of the Christian contacts they had made before the meteor strike and ensuing tsunami, had either lost their lives or their vessels as a result.

As many prayed and fasted, Dr. Lee Kim networked around the clock with fellow believers on both sides of the world. Through various secure channels, God finally led them to new believers in the faith, who were willing to attempt transporting fellow believers on their boats and ships, until the mark was administered in the coming days or weeks.

The fact that these brave selfless men were willing to risk their own lives, by smuggling the two female fugitives halfway around the world, was commendable to say the least.

Clearly, everyone involved was taking a massive risk by attempting such a monumental task. All things considered, the five days it took to set the plan in motion seemed rather miraculous.

They thanked God for His provision, and were comforted knowing that many believers would be praying for them around the clock.

Johnson and Jimenez were presently headed south on I-95, in South Carolina, 55 miles north of the Georgia border. They took turns driving, senses on full alert, constantly praying that they wouldn't be pulled over by law enforcement at some point along the way.

If they were stopped, the instant they were identified as dissidents, or even as unidentified subjects, guns would be drawn, and they would either be taken into custody or shot dead in their vehicle by the arresting officers.

Since Romanero had already given common citizens the authority to kill Christian dissidents who dared put up a struggle, the officers involved would never face stiff questioning from their superiors after the fact.

If anything, they would be congratulated for ridding the planet of two more heretics and would receive a thousand dollars each upon receiving Romanero's soul-damning mark, once it became mandatory.

If that happened, their rescue plan would be squashed before it ever got off the ground.

With most roads still under construction, and most convenience stores and service stations no longer in business, and with no way of paying at the pump, they brought two 36-gallon steel fuel tanks full of gasoline with them, so they wouldn't have to stop to refuel along the way.

Normally, one would be enough to get them there, but they brought two tanks, just in case. As an organization, their gasoline supplies had slowly dwindled to near nothing, but with their days out in public clearly numbered, what sense would it make trying to conserve it? The goal was to use as much of the fuel transporting *ETSM* members to their final locations as they possibly could, without getting caught.

At this point, there was no debate as to whether they should drive a gasoline powered or electric car. Even those who were staunch environmentalists before the Rapture dared not weigh in on the matter.

How could they when all they had to do was glance in any direction to see the global destruction at every turn? Being sympathetic toward the environment now was as fruitless as trying to construct a new home on a garbage dump! Even their electric cars would soon be worthless.

As was fully anticipated, they encountered several delays along the way. The worst one was at the halfway point in South Carolina, just north of Santee. Road construction signs were replaced with road closure signs. The lengthy bridge crossing Lake Marion was one of the numerous casualties caused by the global quake, two years ago.

Most locals believed the bridge would never be repaired and had long since resorted to traveling by boat from one side to the other.

Many ferryboat operators in the area had turned the glaring problem into a new business venture, by also transporting cargo and vehicles.

The biggest challenge they faced was that most locals were destitute and couldn't afford their services. But with multitudes soon to be out in full force, hunting for Christians, the hope for these boat owners was that they would then use their services, which in turn would positively affect their bottom lines.

"After all, this used to be the Bible Belt," they had reasoned, hoping to further convince one another that their plan would eventually succeed.

Johnson and Jimenez would have loved to take a boat across Lake Marion—it would have saved them at least three hours—but with cash outlawed, and since neither man possessed global monetary cards, they had no means to pay for the service. They couldn't even stop at a restaurant if they got hungry. They had to bring food with them.

Donald looked over at Manuel in the passenger seat. "All things considered, I would have rather left from a port in New York or northern New Jersey, rather than travel all this way to Florida!"

Manuel said, "Personally, I would have preferred driving to Brownsville or El Paso, Texas, and crossing the border under the cover of darkness, then have one of our residents drive me to the Guadalajara safe house. I'm not crazy about taking a boat to Mexico. But since we don't have any new contacts at those locations, what choice do I have?"

Donald checked all three mirrors. "It is what it is, right?"

Manuel nodded in agreement. "Right!"

If there was one cause for optimism, faint as it was, after hearing Romanero's comment about bringing the cameras to the dissidents, instead of waiting for them to pass by the numerous surveillance cameras and checkpoint cameras policing the planet, did that mean they were no longer functioning?

Johnson and Jimenez didn't know, but they would always remain vigilant, as if all cameras were still functioning, knowing it could be yet another trap the Antichrist of the Bible was setting for them.

It seemed whenever Manuel glanced over at Donald, his good friend was wiping more tears from his eyes, with an old rag he kept using as a handkerchief of sorts. He didn't have to ask why…

It had only been 16 hours, but Donald already missed his family. What made it even more excruciating for him was whenever the couple made eye contact over the past five days, Mary would start crying hysterically, and beg him not to leave her.

She kept saying she had a foreboding that once he left, they would never see each other again. There was a time or two when he nearly threw in the towel and agreed with his wife's desperate pleas.

With only so many more sleeps before either one of them were killed or until Christ returned, his daily prayer would be that he would get to hold his wife and son in his arms again.

Without a doubt, leaving them behind was the most excruciating decision he had ever made in life. Was it really goodbye?

Although Donald wished he was still in Pennsylvania, where his heart was, whenever he thought about Analyn, and her incredible situation, he regained his focus. She needed to be rescued!

It took 27 grueling and exhausting hours before Johnson and Jimenez finally arrived at the designated meeting location, just north of Jacksonville.

David Wilcox was there waiting for them. After quick introductions were made, Wilcox handed them both old camouflage-patterned baseball caps, then opened a vacant garage door that no one had used for decades. He motioned for Johnson to park his vehicle inside.

Once the two had climbed into the back of Wilcox' 4-wheeler, he turned the headlights on and sped off, taking mostly dirt roads which led them straight to the woods, and ultimately to the subterranean safe house at which the three would reside for the night, along with 30 of his fellow residents.

The next morning, after only getting five hours of sleep, the three men consumed two MRE breakfasts each, consisting of maple and brown sugar oatmeal, sausage with gravy biscuits, and trail mix packages with almonds, coconuts, dried bananas, and pineapple and papaya chunks, before David drove them back to their vehicle at 4 a.m.

Jiminez filled the fuel tank with gasoline, then the three men prayed for each other's protection before Manuel left for Tampa.

Donald hugged his good friend. This would be their first time being apart since both became residents at safe house number one, way back when. "Who would've thought we'd arrive in Chadds Ford on the same day, only to leave on the same day?"

"I know, right?" Manuel said, hoping they both would make it safely to their destinations.

What Donald saw in Manuel's eyes indicated that he wasn't so sure. "God be with you, brother. I'll be praying for you daily."

Manuel looked up and down the street to make sure no one was watching or listening to them. "Likewise, brother. If we don't see each other again on this side, I'll see you on the other side…"

Donald grinned at him. "You can count on it…"

Little did Manuel Jimenez know how prophetic Donald's words would turn out to be.

When he pulled away, Wilcox and Johnson hurried back into the garage and changed into the uniforms that were provided by Vishnu Uddin, a fellow believer from Bangladesh, and a seaman on the massive container ship on which he and Donald would both sail to Singapore.

When they arrived at the dock, Donald was mildly impressed that it was still functioning at near capacity.

Smuggling illegals from A to B on cargo container ships had been done for many decades, even long before the Rapture took place. But since the meteor strike and tsunami, it had increased exponentially.

Since Romanero had opened all borders a few years ago, there were no longer illegals being sought, only dissidents.

Before the meteor strike and subsequent tsunami, Christian dissidents wishing to relocate halfway around the world had to pay the ridiculous fee of $250K, per passenger. Had the *ETSM* not been blessed with new connections, none of this would have been possible.

Donald said to David, "Thanks for everything, brother. I hope to see you again when I return in a few months, hopefully not alone." With the mark of the beast a little more than a week away from being administered globally, his tone of voice lacked confidence.

Wilcox understood completely. "My pleasure, brother," he said sincerely. "I'll be praying for you every day."

Vishnu was nervous and signaled with his hands that they had to get a move on.

The two men hugged, then Wilcox drove off.

Uddin said to Donald, "Follow me. Keep your head down until we reach the stowaway compartment."

Donald swallowed hard, and followed the man to the massive container ship, stride for stride, praying for God's protection every step of the way...

16

WITH MANY OF THE crew still sleeping, Donald and Vishnu made it down to the stowaway compartment without incident.

Now that they were on board, the reality sunk in even more of what would become of Vishnu, if they ever got caught.

All it would take would be for one of his fellow crew members to spot them, and it would be all over before it even started.

No turning back now! Vishnu opened the steel door and hurried Donald inside, quickly closing the door behind him.

"Here it is," the seaman said, in his thick accent, "your new home for the next seven weeks or so. I know it's cold, but once the engines are on, it will get stuffy in here at times. If it does, turn on those fans," he said, pointing up to them, "to suck in more air and oxygen from the outside.

"If you need to air out the room, open those vents. The reason for the steel screens covering them is that we have a serious rodent infestation on the ship, especially down here on the bottom deck. It seems to have only worsened since the tsunami, I'm afraid. I'm a little surprised we didn't see a few rats already."

Donald chuckled sarcastically. "Thank God for that!"

Vishnu wanted to laugh at Donald's reply, but his pulse was racing too hard in his ears to chuckle. "Those buckets over there should be used as makeshift toilets, or if you feel nauseous or seasick. I'll collect the buckets from you as often as I can, plus bring fresh buckets of water for bathing and washing your clothes.

"But whatever you do, do not attempt to drink it. It will surely make you sick. Thankfully, you have plenty of bottled water to drink. In case you don't know, your leaders had the supplies delivered to David Wilcox, who passed them onto me to smuggle on to the ship. It wasn't easy, but I got it done, praise Jesus," he said softly.

Donald nodded that he already knew that.

Uddin went on, "Don't be alarmed if I'm unable to check on you for the remainder of the day. The first and last days are always the busiest for the crew. Whenever I can, I'll knock on the door three times, pause a moment, knock two more times, pause again then knock four more times. That's how you'll know it's me. Understood?"

Donald nodded that he did.

"If you're wondering why I chose that combination, it's for Romans three, verse twenty-four. But to best understand verse twenty-four, it must be combined with verse twenty-three. 'For all have sinned and fall short of the glory of God...'"

Donald finished it for him, "'...and all are justified freely by his grace through the redemption that came by Christ Jesus.'"

"Amen, brother!" said Vishnu, fist-bumping Donald. "The only time I'll padlock your door on the outside will be if I ever sense danger. Other than that, it will remain unlocked."

Donald asked, "Will I ever get to go top deck for fresh air?"

"I'll do my best to make it happen, but it'll have to be at night under the cover of darkness, when most of my crew mates are sleeping."

"I understand," came the reply. What else could he say?

Vishnu glanced at his smart watch. "I should go now. I'll check on you whenever I can, and bring whatever food and water I can manage to sneak away from the kitchen, starting tomorrow. But you have plenty of snacks and Ramen soups to hold you over for now. The microwave works quite well."

Donald said, "Thanks for everything you're doing for me. I know you're taking a huge risk."

"It's my honor, brother!" Uddin said, meaning it.

It was evident to Donald that it really was his honor. "Let me comfort you with these words, keep fighting the Good fight. Pray for me as I pray for you. God is with us!"

Even among the constant chaos, those words comforted Vishnu deep in his soul. He hugged his brother in Christ, then left, so he could take a three-hour nap and shower before roll call...

When Uddin closed the container door, Donald looked around the relatively small room. It had two steel-framed twin beds, a small table and two chairs, two battery-operated lamps, and the microwave. Nothing more.

Johnson grimaced, feeling like he had just been locked away in a prison cell, much like his countless brothers and sisters who were detained in Romanero's death camps, the world over.

Only they would never leave their cells. Then again, it's not like he would be gaining his freedom upon reaching Singapore. Far from it!

But unlike his brothers and sisters in prison, at least his room was fully stocked with enough food and other supplies to last the 13,000 mile or 11,869 nautical mile trip, with plenty to spare for the two women and their children on their voyage back to the States.

He just prayed he would be able to endure being confined in this relatively small space, for the next seven weeks.

With nothing else to do, Donald refocused on the complex plan. The only way he would consider this trip a success would be for four things to happen. 1) the small fishing vessel Manuel would board in Tampa would arrive safely in Brownsville, Texas, and he would be safely smuggled to the safe house in Guadalajara, Mexico, 2) Donald would arrive safely in Singapore and help smuggle Hana and Yasamin on board this container ship back to the States, 3) when he arrived in the Philippines, Analyn wouldn't have the mark of the beast on her right hand or forehead, and she would convert to Christianity, 4) everyone involved would ultimately end up where they were headed unimpeded.

If those four things happened, even if Analyn was the only one he got to win to Christ, he would rejoice, knowing he had left the 99 to rescue one lost sheep. *Thy will be done, Lord...*

AT 2:00 A.M., THE container ship was in the Caribbean Sea, headed south toward Panama. Vishnu knocked on Donald's compartment door. Without even opening it, Donald knew it was him by the 3-2-4 signal he gave. He opened the door to find his brother in Christ holding a propane lamp in his left hand.

Vishnu whispered, "Would you like to go top deck now?"

"I would love that!" It hadn't even been one day, and Donald already felt a little stir crazy. He still had his uniform on, so he was good to go.

"Once we get up there, don't look up. There are always two men standing guard at the highest point of the ship. They will surely see us. If they ask questions, I will handle it..."

"Got it."

When they were on the top deck, the look on the dark-skinned man's face told Donald he was deeply troubled. Vishnu came straight to the point. "Not surprisingly, I was informed during roll call earlier that the mark will be ready to be implemented by the time we arrive in Singapore."

Donald fully expected to hear him say this, but that didn't prevent a million thoughts and questions from filling his exhausted brain. Fear shot through him knowing that when they arrived at their destination, many would already be out scouring the country searching for them.

Uddin added, "About the only good thing is the crew won't have to receive it, until we arrive back in the States."

Donald stared out at the darkened expanse of the ocean. "Why's that?"

"So many docks and fishing piers were destroyed by the massive tsunami, all throughout Asia, including Singapore. Last time I was there, there wasn't even a port to pull into. It was completely obliterated. The entire country is in shambles. Much of what we're transporting on this cargo container are relief supplies for them..."

Vishnu sighed. "This gives us seven weeks to figure out how we're going to smuggle the two women on board on my return trip."

Donald suddenly felt even more trapped on this container ship and wondered for the hundredth time since leaving safe house number one, if he had made the right decision by attempting this bold venture. It made him long for his wife and son even more.

Vishnu looked out into the darkness. "If there's one good thing about the docks being obliterated, it's that loading and unloading cargo is so much more difficult for crew members assigned to those tasks. Instead of using the hydraulic container lifts at the docks, like we've always done, everything must be transferred to and from the ship anchored out at sea, by other sea vessels, before they can be hoisted onto the container ship hydraulically. This takes so much longer to load and unload than usual. It's back breaking work to say the least."

Donald tilted his head in the man's direction. He was clearly confused. "How is that a good thing?"

Vishnu explained, "It makes it a little easier to smuggle stowaways on board among all the commotion."

Donald was hoping for a more comforting answer, but it would do for now.

Uddin added, "If there's another benefit we have, it's global cooling."

Donald was confused again, and asked, "How is that a benefit?"

"Christians still in the workforce can wear long sleeve shirts, sweaters, and even jackets, in countries where we seldom needed them prior to the Rapture. This way, we can cover our bodies so no one will notice that we weren't stung by the locusts that were released from the bottomless pit a few months ago! If the temperatures were hot, we would certainly come under the suspicion of the enemy."

"Simply amazing!" Donald shook his head in all directions like a bobblehead doll, as he thought about what he had just heard. "God always provides a way for His children. He never ceases to amaze me!"

"Amen to that!" said Vishnu, in reply. "Even so, we must be very careful every step of the way. One false move by either of us could spell trouble. Naturally, we'll need to be twice as careful when Hana and Yasamin are in our care. The sooner we can get them out of Singapore, the better."

Donald breathed the salty sea air in through his nostrils. "Believe me, brother, that will be my daily prayer."

"Mine too…"

Donald placed his left hand on Vishnu's right shoulder. "Now that we know for sure the mark will be available when we arrive in Singapore, I plan on contacting my superiors, and asking them to let you stay at our safe house in Pennsylvania, once you return to the States."

The look on Vishnu's face conveyed to Donald that this was the best news he had been told in quite some time. "Thank you, Donald…"

"No, Vishnu, thank you! You're taking quite a risk for me."

Uddin spotted some of his crewmates scrambling about. "We need to get you back to your room before someone sees us!"

Donald nodded that he was ready, then followed Vishnu back down to the lowest part of the ship…

17

CHADDS FORD, PENNSYLVANIA

AT 6 A.M. SHARP, Joaquim Guzman and Lila Choharjo relieved Tony Pearsall and Joaquim's father-in-law, Julio Gonzalez, of their guard duty at safe house number one. Both men had been watching the front of the property since midnight and were starved for sleep.

Ever since Clayton's and Travis' grim reminder after Romanero's speech, that they would soon be hunted in masse, everyone at safe house number one was required to stand guard. Those who could, that is.

Soon after the change of guard took place, Joaquim and Lila spotted a man out in the distance headed straight toward them. Both were mindful of a similar instance that took place a while back, when Jakob suddenly materialized at safe house number one, startling Titus and his late friend, Remo, shortly before the global quake.

Different from that time was that whereas Jakob had seemingly appeared out of nowhere, rightly proclaiming to be one of Yahweh's chosen 144,000 sealed servants, this man—whoever he was—was crawling very slowly toward them, on his hands and knees, causing fear to pulsate through the two unarmed guards.

When the subject was less than 20 feet away, Guzman shouted, "Stop right there!"

The filthy-looking middle-aged Caucasian man raised his right hand in surrender. His knuckles were covered in blood. "I need water, please!"

"Who are you?" the 17-year-old demanded to know. Joaquim knew for certain that Jakob hadn't sent him there. If he had, the first words out of his mouth would have been their organization creed. But instead of reciting it, he asked for water. Whoever this man was, since he apparently hadn't been invited by God's sealed servant, there wasn't a chance they would let him onto the property until he recited it.

"Please, I need water!" he begged.

Lila shot a confused, fearful glance over at Joaquim. It was apparent to her that this man was suffering from massive dehydration, not to mention from severe exhaustion. "First tell us who you are!" she barked, trying to shield the compassion she felt for the man who appeared to be a breath away from total incapacitation.

"My name's Rick Krauss," he said, through heavy gasps. "I'm an ETSM member. Some of your residents know me, and can confirm this if they're still alive…"

Joaquim gulped hard; fear shot through him. "Yeah? Like who?"

"Brian and Jacquelyn…" he said, through more heavy gasps.

"Brian and Jacquelyn?"

"Mulrooney."

"How do you know them?" Joaquim barked.

Lila winced, not at all pleased with Joaquim's response. It implied to this stranger that they might actually know the Mulrooneys. She shook her head silently praying that this man wasn't the enemy.

"Please, I need water…" he begged again, rather hoarsely.

"First answer the question!" Joaquim barked, his eyes searching for marks or abrasions on the exposed parts of the man's body, which was mostly covered in dirt.

"Please," he pleaded again, his chest heaving up and down with each inhale and exhalation. "My throat's so sore and dry, I can hardly talk."

Joaquim persisted, "Tell us something that will prove you belong to us!"

Without hesitation, Rick very hoarsely said, "Keep fighting the Good fight…" He paused to take a deep breath. "Pray for me as I pray for you…" He took another deep breath. "God is with us."

Finally! Joaquim relaxed and handed the man a canteen full of water.

The two guards kept a steady eye on their subject, as he guzzled it out of the canteen as quickly as he could. It was the first clean water he had consumed in many days. Most of what he had drunk since his exodus from the state of Michigan came from creeks and rivers, which were full of ashy volcanic soot, which had caused him many bouts of diarrhea.

Krauss drained the canteen dry, then took a few more deep breaths, still amazed at how he had ever survived the long journey. He wanted to give up too many times to count. He sat on the ground to give his bloodied and bruised hands a break.

Joaquim asked him again, "How do you know Brian and Jacquelyn?"

"We went to church together in Michigan, before they moved to Pennsylvania to manage this safe house," Krauss said, in between more heavy breaths. "I even attended their wedding. Are they still alive?"

When neither guard answered, he added, "Tom Dunleavey also knows me. He used to stay with me when he was on the run from the Catholic Church. If they're here, they can confirm it for you."

Joaquim ignored his answer for the time being, believable as it sounded. He still couldn't be too careful. He pressed on. "How did you find this location?"

"I got your address from Pastor Jim Simonton, the man who married Brian and Jacquelyn. He gave it to me before he died."

"Died?"

Rick Krauss nodded sadly. "He was killed in the global quake…"

"Sorry to hear that," said Joaquim. Since both guards had met Pastor Jim Simonton, when he was at safe house number one for Joaquim's wedding two Christmases ago, it boosted the man's credibility a bit.

Even so, they could take no chances. Joaquim was ready to pounce on him if it ever came to that. Then again, in his condition, this man wouldn't stand a chance to defend himself even against an infant.

The former Hollywood actress grabbed her walkie-talkie. As much as Lila hated to wake Titus, this was an emergency.

"Yeah," he barked, wiping sleep from his eyes, waking his wife, Ingrid, in the process.

"Sorry to disturb you, Titus," she said quietly, not wanting to disclose another name of someone residing at safe house number one to this stranger, "but we have a visitor at the front gate, a man from Michigan, who claims to be an ETSM member. He said he knows Brian, Jacquelyn, and Tom Dunleavey. He even recited the organization creed."

Titus bolted up on his bed. His pulse raced in his ears. "Name?"

"Rick Krauss. Sound familiar?"

Titus stretched his arms above his head. "Doesn't ring a bell."

"Who is it, honey?" Ingrid asked her husband.

Titus held up his pointer finger at her, silently asking her to wait. They had just finished guard duty, and had just settled into bed, after clearing the dozen new converts that Jakob had sent their way at the rear of the property, under the cover of darkness.

The two became practically inseparable after Titus' good friend and counterpart, Remo, ended up being one of the many casualties at safe house number one, during the global quake. Ingrid later became Remo's replacement. The couple were married during the five-month period when the unconverted world fell under attack. Tom Dunleavey married them.

Titus and Ingrid listened intently, as the man kept pleading with Lila and Joaquim, "Tell him Charles Calloway and Tamika Moseley also know me."

101

Krauss didn't know if they were living there or not. The only ones he knew for sure were the Mulrooneys, Tom Dunleavey and some of his former parishioners at the Catholic church, in Ann Arbor.

Lila asked Titus, "What should we do with him?"

"Take him to the camouflage shed. I'll call Jacquelyn."

"I don't think he has the strength to make it that far."

Titus rubbed his throbbing head, mostly due to sleep deprivation. "Have Joaquim carry him there until I get back to you."

"Copy that," said Lila. "Oh, and Titus?"

"Yeah?"

"You may want to tell Jacquelyn to bring Brian or Tom with her."

"Why's that?"

"It may take a second set of eyes to identify him. You'll see when you get here."

"Roger that! I'll get back to you soon…"

"Please hurry, Titus."

Titus couldn't ignore the fear in Lila's voice. "Roger that…"

Jacquelyn was lying in bed next to Brian, when Titus' voice crackled through the walkie-talkie on the drawer next to the baby's crib, where baby Sarah lay sleeping. "Can anyone hear me?"

Jacquelyn jumped out of bed, and grabbed the walkie-talkie off the table, hoping his voice wouldn't wake her daughter, who had just dozed off after her morning feeding. "Yes, we hear you. Is everything okay?"

Titus came straight to the point. "Do you know anyone named Rick Krauss?"

Jacquelyn's eyes doubled in size. She couldn't believe what she was hearing. "Why do you ask, Titus?"

"Because there's a man at the front entryway who proclaims to know you and Brian, with that name. Said he knows Tom Dunleavey too."

Jacquelyn's heart rate accelerated. *Could it be?* "If it's the Rick Krauss I know, he was one of my brother Dennis' good friends in life, before the Rapture, and one of the most-dedicated prayer intercessors at the church Brian and I attended before we relocated here."

"Can you and Brian come to identify him?"

"Brian's not feeling well again…"

"Bring Tom then."

"Why should I bring Tom?"

"Lila said he looks unrecognizable. That's all I know for now…"

"Sure," Jacquelyn said, without further inquiring. "If Tom's still down in the living room, I'll ask him to join me."

"See you soon." Titus radioed Lila. "Be there shortly."

"Copy that," said Lila, without taking her eyes off her subject. Then to Joaquim, "They'll be here shortly."

Jacquelyn and Tom arrived at the front of the property a few minutes later, then walked the short distance to the camouflage shed.

Not surprisingly, Titus and Ingrid were already there. He also asked Shamus Harmon to join them, in case they needed added muscle.

Harmon was from Boston. His family of eight was reduced to five on the day of the Rapture, when he lost a son, two daughters, and four grandchildren. All had left the Catholic Church before the disappearances. After slowly piecing it together, Shamus realized what had happened, and repented of his sinful lifestyle.

Once his wife, two sons and daughter did the same, they left the Catholic church and eventually became residents in Chadds Ford.

The Harmons were only one of three "complete" families living at safe house number one. All were in the construction business.

When Jacquelyn and Tom first laid eyes on the subject, neither could identify him. He was ghastly thin; at least 50 pounds lighter than when they last saw him. His hair was long and matted, and he had a full beard, unlike before.

The confusion Lila saw on their faces caused even more panic to mushroom through her. It screamed, "Quickly before someone notices us!" She cleared her throat. "Well?" The fear in her voice was evident to everyone, including this stranger in their midst.

Tom squinted at him for a few seconds, then folded his arms across his chest. "I can't be sure if it's him or not, Lila..."

Rick looked up at Tom. The very sound of his voice brought tears to his eyes. They mixed in with the dirt that was caked on his face, creating a muddy stream riding down his cheeks, partly because he was dirty and partly as a camouflage of sorts.

"Brother Tom! Oh, thank God it's you!" Krauss declared, still unable to believe how he had survived the tumultuous 850-mile journey from the Upper Peninsula of Michigan to Southeastern Pennsylvania, in enemy territory, mostly on foot.

Tom bubbled over with joy. "It is you!" He pointed at Rick and said to Lila, "That man is one of the finest men I've ever known. He let me

103

stay at his house before I relocated here. We would pray and read the Bible together every night, before sleeping."

Rick wiped his face with a filthy sleeve. His lips were severely chapped from the cold temperatures. "I can't tell you how happy I am to see you again! Never thought I'd see the day. I pray for you every day."

Joaquim, Lila, and Titus all sighed relief, as Rick shifted his focus to Jacquelyn. "Nice to see you again. I've missed you! Where's Brian?"

Jacquelyn identified his voice, raspy as it was, and wept tears of joy. "He's with our daughter."

"Daughter? Congratulations," came the reply softly, evenly. Rick was too exhausted to exert the joyful energy he felt inside, brief as it was.

"Thank you," she said. Then, "How'd you find us, Rick?"

Rick ran his fingers through his filthy hair. His mouth was stretched in a yawn. "I'm too exhausted to explain it now. If you'll allow me to sleep and take a shower, I'll fill you in on everything…"

Jacquelyn nodded at him empathetically. "Yes, of course! If anyone needs rest, it's you…"

Tom asked, "I have just one more question for you, Rick. Where's Pastor Simonton?"

Rick glanced up at him solemnly, then paused to draw more air into his lungs. He was so tired and fatigued that he kept slurring his words. "He was killed in the global quake…"

Jacquelyn gasped. "That's what we always sensed…" Desperate as she was to hear every detail about Rick's harrowing encounter, now wasn't the time. He needed rest.

Titus said to Joaquim, "Let's bring him inside before someone spots us out here."

When it became apparent that this man couldn't stand on his own two feet, Joaquim hoisted him up on his right shoulder and carried him all the way to the main house at the rear of the property to where the Mulrooneys lived.

When they arrived there, he laid their new guest on the living room couch, ever so gently.

Within seconds, Rick was snoring away...

18

RICK KRAUSS WOKE FROM his deep slumber 14 hours later, to find Brian and Jacquelyn sitting on the loveseat opposite him. Brian had his daughter on his lap, grinning at his friend in amazement.

Rick sat up on the couch. "Hey Brian! Are you ever a sight for sore eyes! Wasn't sure I'd ever see you again."

"Likewise. Did you sleep well? It sure sounded like you did."

"Like a rock! Best sleep I've had in months. Is that your daughter?"

Brian beamed. "Meet baby Sarah."

"What a beautiful little girl! I can see both of you in her."

Brian kissed the back of his daughter's head. "Thank you. We feel so blessed to be her parents."

Jacquelyn said, "We're eager to hear all about your encounter. But first feel free to shower and eat something."

"That would be great," said Rick, with a long yawn. "Sorry for stinking up the house. I'm sure the odor is pulsating off me. The only time I was able to clean myself was in some of the creeks and rivers I encountered along the way, mostly at night, so no one would see me. Man was that water cold! And full of ashy soot!" he uttered, with no emotion.

Brian waved him off. "Think nothing of it, brother. Just glad you're here."

Jacquelyn said, "You can use our bathroom upstairs."

Rick asked Brian, "Do you have something I can wear? I never wanna put these clothes on again!" He pointed at his long, matted beard. "I'll need scissors and a razor for this. Never had a beard before."

The Mulrooneys chuckled at the way he said it. "I'm sure that can be arranged."

Jacquelyn said, "In the meantime, I'll go to the cafeteria and bring you some food."

"I really appreciate it," came the reply, somberly. Even though Rick had succeeded on his journey, he still displayed a defeated expression on his face. At any rate, with so much sleep under his belt, he was able to climb the stairs without needing assistance.

When he came back down 30 minutes later, he was both clean and clean shaven.

Brian joked, "Wow! It really is you, Rick!"

Krauss laughed. He wasn't surprised to see that the crowd size had expanded in his brief absence. But what did shock him was seeing Jefferson Danforth seated on the couch, holding hands with an Asian woman he could only presume was his wife.

Rick knew the former U.S. President was an *ETSM* member, but he didn't know where he was residing. "It's an honor meeting you, Sir."

"Likewise, Rick. This is my wife, Amy."

Rick nodded at her. "Nice meeting you, Ma'am…"

"Please call me, Amy."

When Rick saw Brian's father, his shock knew no bounds. His mind still vividly recalled how poorly he had acted at his son's wedding, and the many threats he had made before storming out of his church in Michigan. He was the last person he expected to see at this place!

Brian noticed his discomfort. "My father's saved now, praise God!"

Brian's comment earned him a smile, weary as it was. "Nice to see you again, Sarah. I never got the chance to meet you at the wedding."

Sarah snorted, "Sure was a crazy day…"

Rick nodded in agreement with her. The poor woman looked 10 years older now than she did back then.

Charles Calloway and Tamika Moseley were also there, along with someone Rick didn't know. "Hey, Tamika! Nice to see you again. We didn't get to say bye last time."

Tamika smiled wearily at him, knowing he was referring to when she was whisked away from the wedding, and taken to Tennessee with Charles and the late Braxton Rice, before ultimately being relocated to Pennsylvania. "You too, Rick. Meet my husband, Isaac."

Rick raised an eyebrow at her, then extended his hand towards Isaac. "Pleasure to meet you, Isaac."

"You, as well, Rick…" They shook hands.

After the introductions were made, Tamika said to Rick, "When we're finished here, I'd like to examine you and check your vitals."

"She's the head nurse here," said Isaac, ever so proudly.

"Wow, Tamika, you're so full of surprises!" Still mindful of the many lies that had been spread about her, he couldn't be happier for her, despite that she was a hunted woman for her faith in Jesus.

Rick filled his belly with more food than he had eaten in many weeks, and consumed two cups of black coffee, then signaled that he was ready to share his harrowing experience with everyone.

"Can you tell us what happened to Pastor Simonton now?"

Krauss shook his head sadly. "Like I told you and the others earlier, Tom, he was killed in the global quake. Only a handful of us survived. I was out patrolling the area when it happened. Had it not been for a tree that was uprooted, I would have been a goner too.

"I somehow managed to grab onto one of its branches as it fell to the ground. I clung to it for dear life, as it covered a huge crevice. I barely escaped. Brother Jim wasn't so fortunate. He was underground when it happened. When we finally dug him out of the rubble two days later, he had several broken ribs and a collapsed lung."

Krauss took a small gulp of water. "Jim knew he was dying. The last thing he told me, as I held his hand, was to search for this address on his encrypted SAT phone, so I could inform you all of what happened to our safe house." Rick stared at the wall opposite him. "I would have gone through protocol and emailed those at the top before attempting to come here uninvited, but we had no power.

"After spending a few weeks helping the other survivors fix what could be repaired on the property, I went in search of a Wi-Fi signal. Not even ten minutes after I left the safe house, I heard a faint noise in the sky. The closer it got, the louder it became."

Rick scratched his throbbing forehead. "When the bomb struck the safe house, I was thrown off my bike and nearly killed as a result."

Tamika swallowed back fear. "Bomb? What bomb? Could it have come from the meteor that broke apart at the last second?"

Rick shook his head. "It happened long before then. I was already in Western Pennsylvania by then. All I can say is it was massive. So much worse than even the global quake, if you can believe that. It did far more damage to the safe house. Perhaps it was intentional."

Rick paused to take another sip of coffee. His audience was held completely captive by his account. They were spellbound. "I don't know if anyone else survived other than myself. I seriously doubt it." Eyes pleading for understanding, he added, "I wanted to go back to check on them, but even being three miles away the damage was unspeakable. I wouldn't be surprised if the crater was a quarter mile in diameter."

Tom said, "We understand, brother..."

Rick nodded his thanks at him. "Since I didn't know where any of our other safe houses were located, I had no choice but to try finding you. It took roughly six months to get here. Just knowing I was within close

107

proximity to some of our other safe houses, yet not knowing where they were, was deflating at times!"

Tears filled Rick's eyes. "I can't tell you how many times I felt like giving up. Just glad now that I didn't…"

Brian was flabbergasted. "Where's your bike?"

Rick shook his head sadly, then shrugged his shoulder. "Halfway through Ohio, the tires became so threadbare that I was afraid to ride it. But with cash illegal, where could I go for a spare tire? I pushed that bicycle for three days before I finally ditched it."

More tears flooded Rick's eyes. "This will probably sound strange to you, but I felt like Tom Hanks in the movie, *Castaway*, when he lost his best friend and companion, Wilson, which happened to be a stupid volleyball. Mine was a bicycle. Even so, I cried for many hours on end."

Embarrassed expression on his face, especially with a former U.S. President listening, he added, "I can only imagine how idolatrous this probably sounds to you all, but that's how lonely I felt, and terribly afraid being in enemy territory! The sadness I felt was indescribable."

Krauss shook his head in bewilderment. "Funny the things that fill our minds at times. At any rate, I was fortunate to be picked up by a few kind strangers along the way. But with most roads still impassible, they were only able to drive me a few miles at a time…"

He paused, seeing the concern splashed on all their faces. "My body was covered in mud so no one would notice I didn't have sting marks."

"Good thinking," Brian remarked.

Rick nodded. "But I saw their sting marks, and knew I had to be extremely careful. Once they receive the mark of the beast, they will be doomed. I've prayed for each of them every day since, asking God to rescue them before it's too late."

Rick sighed, still dazed from the grueling trip. "Thankfully, they let me charge my phone in their cars. Since most roads were destroyed, I had to take many detours, which nearly doubled the distance. I can't tell you how many times the GPS on my phone had to recalculate. I finally ended up writing the directions on a piece of paper and stuffing it inside my coat pocket. I knew it was careless, but what other choice did I have?"

They nodded that they understood the risk he took.

"Believe me when I say, I was more nervous about the enemy finding that piece of paper than anything else. I was determined to protect this location at all costs and would have shredded it into many pieces if it ever came to that, or even eaten it."

Jefferson Danforth crossed one leg over the other and rested his hands on his lap. "That's quite an adventure you went on, Rick. I'm sure you're exhausted just sharing this with us..."

"I'll say! Just last night, I slept under a tree in a field less than a mile from here. Close as I was, I didn't have the strength to walk another step. I would have texted you, but the phone battery was dead." Rick sighed. "Just glad I made it here before the mark was administered..."

"Amen to that," Danforth said, with a nod of his head.

Rick shook his head wearily. "I still feel dizzy and emotionally drained from the long trip. And discombobulated."

Jacquelyn said, "Feel free to sleep again if you want. This is your home now. What's left of it, anyway..."

Rick grinned at Jacquelyn. "I think I may do that, Jacquelyn..."

Tamika asked, "Can I at least check your vitals first? If they're not too bad, you can hold off on a full examination until you're well rested."

Rick yawned into his fist. "By all means, nurse..."

As Tamika checked his vitals, everyone else got back to what they were doing, before Rick woke from his long slumber.

Little did they know, three days from now, the *ETSM* would receive confirmation about the safe house, at which Rick Krauss was a resident, had indeed been bombed by the enemy, just like he had proclaimed.

It would come from the unlikeliest of sources...

19

DR. BENJAMIN SHAPIRO LANDED at Philadelphia International Airport, at 9:55 a.m. He wasn't surprised to see a limousine waiting for him on the runway, along with a police escort.

As much as he wanted to send them away—his purpose for the trip was to be left alone—since Salvador Romanero had made all the necessary arrangements, it wouldn't look good if he did.

Before getting off the plane, Benjamin sent a quick text message to his boss, feigning his appreciation for thinking so highly of him.

The chauffeur, a man named Vito, was honored to be Benjamin Shapiro's driver. After introducing himself to the Miracle Maker's personal physician, and practically bowing down before him, the middle-aged man of Italian descent, loaded the man's belongings into the trunk, and left at once for his residence in Bucks County, accompanied by a police escort.

Vito tried engaging in conversation with his passenger about the mark that would soon be unveiled, but he seemed unwilling to discuss it with him. When they arrived at the house, four armed men were already standing outside the residence, guarding, and protecting it.

Vito opened the car door for his VIP passenger, then carried his belongings to the front door of his residence. "If you need to go anywhere, just text me. I'll take you anywhere you want to go, at any hour of the day."

"Thanks, Vito, but I have my own cars," Benjamin replied, oddly comforted to be hearing a Philly accent again. "Although it's been a while since I last drove them. They may need jump starts."

Vito often spoke using his hands. When he nodded at his VIP passenger, his hands moved up and down as if they were nodding too. "Like I said, if you need me at any time, don't hesitate to call me, Doctor…"

Benjamin opened the front door to his house. "I appreciate it, Vito." He closed the door thinking, *how would this man treat me if he knew the real reason I was here?*

At any rate, he was thankful that he had retained the maid service company before relocating to the Middle East. There wasn't a trace of a musty odor in the house from being unoccupied for so long.

He couldn't ignore the patched-up cracks in the walls in some places, from the global quake, which he fully expected to see, having frequently monitored his residence on his phone in New Babylon.

The roof also had to be replaced, and the swimming pool in the back yard needed a new coating of cement before it could be filled with water again. Other than that, aside from the foot-wide gaps in the grass, for the most part, his house had survived the brunt of it.

Benjamin took a short nap, to hopefully offset the jetlag he felt, then got dressed. He took his time affixing his toupee to his scalp, placed a few items in a plastic bag, then grabbed a can of chicken noodle soup from the cupboard that hadn't yet reached the expiration date.

His brain told him he was hungry, but he was too anxious to eat. His stomach was still doing backflips over his meeting with his nephew. He placed it on the counter for when he returned later.

Benjamin left the house and spent some time chatting with the four-armed guards. Two of them offered to accompany him on his walk, but he politely refused the offer, telling them he wanted to go alone.

He walked the quarter mile to the park he often frequented when he still had his practice, all the while wondering if Jakob would be there or not. Since everything leading up to this point took place in his dreamworld, not to mention that there was no set time or date, it wasn't an unrealistic thought.

Mindful of the potential danger a meeting like this could pose, he went inside what was left of the park restroom. Two of its walls were covered with blue tarpaulins, no doubt from the global quake.

Benjamin plucked a fake beard, dark sunglasses, and an old straw Amish hat out of the bag that he had purchased three decades ago on a daytrip he took to Lancaster County, with his ex-family, and put them on.

He looked at his poor reflection in the dim mirror on the wall. "Talk about sticking out like a sore thumb!" he scoffed to himself. *What Amish person wore a wig?* He removed the hat, practically tore off the toupee, placed it inside the bag, and put the straw hat back on.

Satisfied that he looked nothing like his normal self, Benjamin walked the short distance to the park bench and took a seat.

His eyes drank in the familiar scenery. It felt good to be back in the States, far away from the craziness going on in the Middle East.

After waiting a few agonizing minutes, he didn't know how to act in this situation, Jakob approached him without any sort of disguise on.

"Shalom, Uncle!" Jakob took a seat next to him. His first observation was that his uncle who had always brimmed with self-confidence, who always walked with determined strides, no longer appeared to be the ego-centric man everyone knew him to be.

If anything, he looked shaken to the core, and totally unsure of himself. Insecurity came off him like radiation.

"Hello Jakob," Benjamin said, trying to contain his astonishment. "Aren't you concerned about being recognized by anyone?"

This was the first time Jakob had ever seen his uncle Benjamin without his wig on. He was mildly surprised by it. "I already told you; Antichrist has no power over me or my sealed brothers. But if you really were safe in his care, why would you feel the need to wear a disguise?

"As one of the most important people on the planet, shouldn't you be free to go wherever you want without the fear of being spied on? Where's the trust?"

Benjamin flinched at his nephew's comment. His eyes darted nervously left to right, looking for someone who might possibly be spying on them. "Your father's not at all pleased with you…"

"Yes, I know. I never thought the day would come when I would be estranged from my own family, my father especially. He was always my hero. It all started when I began listening to Yahweh's Two Witnesses."

Jakob rested his hands on his lap. "I pray daily that Yahweh will open Papa's eyes to the true Gospel Message. Every time I tried sharing it with him, it only led to greater separation between us. The hatred he has toward me is stronger than anything I can ever remember."

"What if I told you your father's praying the same thing for you?"

"I'm sure he is, Uncle," Jakob said sadly.

Benjamin was flabbergasted. His arms dropped flatly at his side. "Never thought I'd see the day when my own brother would be at war with his son! He constantly bragged on you until he became convinced that you were brainwashed by the Two who were resurrected in front of the whole world, just like you had predicted..."

Was he brainwashed? Benjamin flinched at the thought and studied his nephew's face very carefully. Whereas his brother Seth was quite enraged when they discussed it on the phone, Jakob was calm and collected. "Can you further explain the mayhem that took place in Jerusalem last week?"

Jakob knew what his uncle was getting at. "The only reason Antichrist was able to temporarily overcome my Mentors at the Western Wall, was because Yahweh gave him the power to do it. Without Jehovah's express permission, it would have never happened."

Jakob eyeballed his uncle. "Everything that's happening in the world was prophesied more than two thousand years ago, in perfect detail, in the Book that Antichrist felt so compelled to outlaw. The reason he did it was that the Word of Yahweh clearly indicts him as being Satan's chief human agent, and the Most High's eternal enemy."

Jakob's face became even more aglow. "Even I was prophesied about in Yahweh's Word, as being one of His one hundred and forty four thousand sealed servants."

Benjamin winced upon hearing this, then quickly shrugged it off, having never read that Book anyway. He pointed skyward. "And that?"

Jakob nodded affirmatively. "Also foretold thousands of years ago in the Word of Yahweh. Now that Jehovah is once again dealing with His chosen people, He is once again using angelic messengers to share the Gospel of salvation to gather His Remnant, along with many others from every nation, tribe, people, and language."

Benjamin was confused and asked, "Remnant?"

Jakob nodded affirmatively. "His chosen Israelites." He paused, then quoted, Zechariah 13:8-9 to his uncle: "'It will come about in all the land,' declares the Lord, 'that two parts in it will be cut off and perish; but the third will be left in it. And I will bring the third part through the fire, refine them as silver is refined, and test them as gold is tested. They will call on My name, and I will answer them; I will say, 'They are My people,' and they will say, 'The Lord is my God.'"

Benjamin shifted uncomfortably on the park bench, then coughed into his fists several times. Each cough made his jowls flap a bit.

Jakob noticed his uncle's confusion. He backpedaled, "The messenger you keep hearing in the sky above, is the first of three angels."

"Three angels?"

Jakob nodded affirmatively again, then looked up. "He is the first of three. Yahweh has positioned his messenger in midheaven, where he will fly there continually in the sight of everybody."

Benjamin was still confused. "Midheaven?"

Jakob explained, "It's the highest point where the greatest visibility will occur across the face of the earth, for all to see. Back and forth he will fly in midheaven, as the earth rotates so the whole world can hear him preaching, when he reaches their locations.

"You saw with your own two eyes how powerless Antichrist's global militaries were at shooting him down. They will remain completely powerless from stopping what Yahweh has ordained."

Benjamin flinched at his nephew's words but kept listening.

Jakob went on, "Yahweh is using His messenger to call the world to salvation, through Yeshua HaMashiach. Once all three of them have been revealed, they will warn humanity day and night, before the seventh trumpet has been blown, thus signifying the seven bowl judgments."

Once again, Benjamin had no idea what his nephew was talking about. "Bowl judgments?"

Jakob nodded affirmatively. "If you think this planet has experienced its full dose of Yahweh's judgment, Uncle, think again. It will soon get even worse!"

"Okay, so when will the two other angels come?" Benjamin felt like Ebenezer Scrooge in *Dickens' A Christmas Carol.*

"Soon enough. In case you haven't noticed, the Gospel he proclaims is the same Gospel message we preach, Uncle."

Benjamin looked skyward. "What is this Good News you refer to?"

Jakob's face became aglow again. "It's the Good News that tells lost sinners how they can enter into the eternal kingdom of God, the kingdom that has been opened by Messiah. It's the only one that offers eternal life. Only those who repent of their sins and believe in Him can enter. Everyone else will be eternally doomed."

Benjamin flinched again. "That sounds a little cruel to me..."

Jakob thought to counter his uncle, by reminding him of just how vile and deceptive Antichrist was. Instead, he said, "Even after the many great evils that are being perpetrated against Yahweh, the door to the kingdom is still open. There's still time to repent and believe. Yahweh is so gracious, Uncle. To the very end He is calling people to salvation.

"Now that He is once again focused on His chosen people, He's using men and angels to spread His message. And that message is 'Turn from Antichrist to Yeshua.' Even though His Word was banned from the planet, everyone is hearing about the grace, forgiveness, and salvation He offers to all who believe and repent, so all who reject it will be without excuse."

Benjamin wanted to say something, but his mind was having great difficulty processing everything his nephew had just told him.

Jakob easily saw the deer in the headlights look on his uncle's face. It was time to stop for the day. He handed his uncle a booklet that had been printed on the *ETSM* printing press. "Take this home with you."

114

The Way? Benjamin read the bland looking cover and squirmed on the bench again. "What is it?"

"Read it. It will further explain the Gospel message to you. I would suggest you begin in Isaiah fifty-three, followed by the four Gospels in the New Testament. Let's meet here again the same time tomorrow so we can further discuss it."

Benjamin gulped hard, his eyes once again surveying the park, wondering if he should take it or not? Finally, he gripped the booklet with both hands and got up off the bench.

Jakob said, "Oh, and one more thing…"

"Yes, Jakob?"

"Leave the disguise at home tomorrow. Even if they are watching, Uncle, they can't see me. All they will see is you sitting on this park bench alone wearing a disguise. It makes you look suspicious."

Without uttering another word, Benjamin walked away scratching his head in amazement. Or was it befuddlement? Both sensations always felt similar to him. When he reached his residence, his first thought upon seeing the four guards was what Jakob had said about the lack of trust being extended to him. *Are they there to protect me, or to keep me in line?*

He stuffed his copy of *The Way* into his jacket, nodded at them and went inside. The four guards exchanged confused glances. When Dr. Shapiro left the house earlier, he was wearing a toupee. Now he wasn't.

But they never bothered asking for a reason, and Benjamin never offered an explanation. He had far more pressing things on his mind than to be concerned about his appearance.

After taking another nap, Benjamin had chicken noodle soup for dinner, then spent the rest of the evening reading the 120-page booklet his nephew gave him, until he eventually dozed off. What woke him in the middle of the night this time wasn't Jakob, but God's second angelic messenger that his nephew had told him would soon follow…

SALVADOR ROMANERO ALSO HEARD it loud and clear, when it was positioned over New Babylon. Only he was awakened by it this time. He jumped out of bed as quickly as someone might, after encountering a cockroach crawling up their leg.

This voice differed slightly from the first voice, yet it was equally soul piercing. It was already bad enough that Salvador heard the first angel making his Gospel proclamations every day, without fail.

115

Now that the second one had come in the middle of the night, would he be tortured daily by this one as well? He feared so...

Once again, the Most High God had granted the ability to those who were deaf, and all other special needs individuals—including those with mental illness—the same ability to hear and comprehend the Message, with perfect clarity, as God's angelic messenger made his Divine proclamations known in the skies above.

Romanero never bothered ordering his military to try striking it down this time, like he had done with the first unidentified flying object.

Bottom line: he didn't want to be humiliated again...

20

THE FOLLOWING MORNING

BENJAMIN SHAPIRO WALKED THE short distance to the park bench situated a quarter mile away from his house, looking even more ashen than he had the day before. When Jakob appeared, he lowered his head and confessed to his nephew, "I heard the second angel last night…"

Jakob quoted Revelation fourteen, verse eight to his uncle, 'Fallen, fallen is Babylon the great! She who has made all the nations drink of the wine of the passion of her immorality.'"

Benjamin grew fidgety on the bench. "What does it mean, Jakob?"

Jakob was mildly surprised that his uncle wasn't wearing his toupee again. It made his long gray sideburns look entirely out of place. Not counting his bushy gray eyebrows, it was the only hair left on his head or face. "Like I told you yesterday, Yahweh's first angelic messenger is offering people one final opportunity to respond to the Gospel Message. But since most continue to reject that Message, angel number two is now pronouncing judgment and damnation on all who follow Antichrist."

Benjamin asked, "What did he mean by, 'Fallen, fallen is Babylon the great?'"

"Babylon refers to the worldwide kingdom of Antichrist. The repetition of the word, 'Fallen, fallen' shows the intense nature of the judgment. Notice what else it says, 'This evil system has made all the nations drink of the wine of the passion of her immorality.'"

Benjamin clasped his hands together. "What does that mean?"

"Aside from the unspeakable immorality going on in the world, the real issue here is fornication on a spiritual level, which is unfaithfulness to God. And the whole world will drink the wine of the passion of this spiritual defection from the one true God."

Benjamin asked, "How can that be? I'll admit New Babylon was badly damaged in the global quake, but it has since been rebuilt. So how can this second angel make this claim?"

Without hesitation, Jakob answered, "Antichrist will surely achieve his goal of turning New Babylon into the political, economic, and religious world empire he so badly desires. And his image will be in Jerusalem. But it won't last."

Benjamin didn't need to inquire about this. He was fully mindful of the statue of Romanero's image, that the Pope had commissioned during the five months in which the world was under attack by the locusts, which would be placed inside the Temple in Jerusalem when it was dedicated. It would have the ability to speak and even reason, as if it were real.

But right now, he was too focused on what the second angelic messenger had said the night before, to give it much thought. He found himself shrinking on the park bench in horror.

Jakob fully expected this sort of reaction from him. He went on, "Next time Yahweh destroys it, it will be for good. The second angel is simply foretelling of its entire collapse, which will surely happen. Mark my words, this utopia Antichrist keeps promising to his true followers will never be realized. If you keep placing your trust in that man and his false system, you'll soon discover just how flawed and damning both are!"

Benjamin gulped hard, feeling like Ebenezer Scrooge again. Another shiver shot through him. "What about the third angel?"

"Angel number three will pronounce damnation, which will be the final warning which Yahweh will use to lead many to salvation."

"What final warning will he give, Jakob?"

From memory, Jakob recited, "'If anyone worships the beast and his image and receives a mark on his forehead or upon his hand, they, too, will drink the wine of God's fury, which has been poured full strength into the cup of his wrath. They will be tormented with burning sulfur in the presence of the holy angels and of the Lamb.

"'And the smoke of their torment will rise for ever and ever. There will be no rest day or night for those who worship the beast and its image, or for anyone who receives the mark of its name.'

"Yahweh's Word also tells us Antichrist will mark out his people on the forehead or on the hand with his number. And the whole world will worship the beast and the image that the false prophet sets up."

Benjamin's eyes bulged. "Really? It says that?"

Jakob nodded at his uncle. "In the book of Revelation, chapter thirteen, which is in the booklet I gave you yesterday."

Having already fingered his way through *The Way*, Benjamin remembered seeing it at the end. He countered, "Are you even aware of the groundbreaking technologies which are part of a chip that will be implanted, soon after the mark has been received? We believe it will ultimately cure cancer. I've been asked to give a speech explaining this new technology at the Temple dedication in Jerusalem."

The expression on Jakob's face indicated to Benjamin that he wasn't the least bit interested in hearing about it. His reply proved that much. "This microchip you speak of, Uncle, which you proclaim will ultimately cure cancer and perhaps lead to eternal life, is nothing more than spiritual deception at the highest levels."

Jakob noticed his uncle stiffen on the bench; his pride challenged. He went on, "While it may help fight cancer to some degree, it will ultimately lead to the destruction of each soul that takes it into their bodies. The instant someone receives the mark, followed by the chip, there can be no turning back for them. Be they men or angels, they will not be able to believe."

Jakob turned to face his uncle. It was time for the dagger. "What you must understand is that Antichrist will not remain in power too much longer. In just under three and a half years, the one you presently serve will be forever silenced…"

Benjamin winced at his nephew's words; his pulse quickened in his ears. "Three and a half years? What are you talking about, Jakob?"

"That's how much time Antichrist has left on this earth, before he falls under Yahweh's judgment. Anyone who takes the mark and subsequent chip you seem so excited about into their bodies shall likewise fall under Yahweh's judgment and will not survive the next three and a half years.

"This includes you, too, Uncle, if you don't change your allegiance from the beast to the Lamb. But if you still choose to worship Antichrist after hearing the Truth, you *will* drink of the wine of the wrath of God. Whoever drinks it will be tormented with fire and brimstone."

Jakob paused a moment, when his uncle started coughing after air got caught in his lungs. "Take a few deep breaths, Uncle…"

Benjamin took a few moments to compose himself before attempting to regain some ground in the debate, which had been one sided up to this point. "Why should I believe you, Jakob?"

"For all the reasons I just gave you, Uncle. And here's something else for you to consider, that I'm sure will also come as a shock to you."

Benjamin swallowed back another large gulp of fear. He couldn't deny that Jakob was supremely confident in his beliefs. "What is it?"

"Antichrist is coming for the Jews next. Make no mistake about it. He spent the first three and a half years of the Tribulation period protecting the Jews. But he will spend the next three and a half years trying to destroy them. The first half of the Tribulation has affected the entire world. The second half, also known as the Great Tribulation, will affect mostly Israel. The Jews are about to see this firsthand…"

Benjamin sat motionlessly on the bench. Had the earthquake not destroyed a tenth of the city of Jerusalem, killing even Israel's Prime Minister, he would have vehemently argued against this point.

The one thing he always appreciated about his boss was that he allowed the Jews to resume sacrificing to their God, after the Dome of the Rock was destroyed.

He might have challenged his nephew by saying, "I may not believe like you do, Nephew, but I'm still a Jew, and I appreciate Romanero's love for our kind," but something caused him to remain silent.

Jakob explained, "Before the disappearances, the three Abrahamic religions—Christianity, Judaism, and Islam—constantly fought over Jerusalem. All three kept claiming that tiny parcel of land as their own. It's the most contested piece of real estate on Earth.

"You already know what Antichrist did to the Muslims. Mark my words, once the Christians are gone, with exception to Yahweh's Remnant, the Jews will be the next to be wiped off the face of the Earth."

Benjamin asked, "Okay, let's say for argument's sake that you're right. Why, then, is he using a systematic approach?"

Jakob answered, "The only way Antichrist can be wholly worshiped in Jerusalem, as Israel's true king, will be for those three religions to be forever silenced. With one of the three already wiped out, and the second soon-to-be gone, his main focus will be on exterminating the Jews next."

Dr. Shapiro dry heaved; he felt sick to his stomach. As excited as he was about the unveiling of the mark, he was even more optimistic about the chip. It was so full of promise…*Should I even attempt to write a speech now?* He rubbed his face with both hands, even beneath his glasses, to release the pressure that had built up inside his head. "Is there anything else I should know?"

Jakob nodded. "Antichrist hates even his own followers, including the children he proclaims to love so much."

"That's difficult to believe, Jakob. He practically worships children, nearly as much as the world worships him! Everyone knows this…"

"It's all a lie, Uncle, a facade. Antichrist knows by now that he is on the losing side, and the end result for him will be eternal damnation. If he loves them so much, why would he willfully condemn their souls to eternal damnation as well? What kind of love is that? If he truly loved them, he would set them free."

Jakob watched his uncle shifting wildly on the bench again. He pressed on. "Let's consider everything that's happened under Antichrist's relatively short reign. In just three and a half years, nearly half the world population has been wiped out, a third of the seas and fresh water have been polluted, people keep dying from famines and plagues and earthquakes. Millions of believers have been murdered and beheaded.

"How much more devastation will you need to see, Uncle, before you turn away from Antichrist? How much more warning?"

Depression fell squarely on Benjamin's shoulders. It was all starting to come together for him. "How foolish I was to think that monster loved the children, let alone the Jewish people."

Another cold, sobering shiver shot through him. Benjamin surveyed the area again, then started trembling. The more he listened to his nephew speaking, the more foolish he felt for following that man, and filthy for living such a sinful lifestyle. "Your wisdom astounds me, Jakob. As much as I want to refute your words, I can't. Everything you tell me keeps happening." He gasped. "I can't say the same about Romanero…"

Jakob stared at his uncle compassionately. "I am only one of Yahweh's servants. But because I preach His word, everything I tell you will come to pass exactly how I say it will, for it is written."

When Benjamin finally found the strength to speak, he asked his nephew, "What will be required of me, Jakob?"

Jakob answered, "Worship the Creator, not the one He created. You fear Antichrist when you should be fearing Yahweh. Satan didn't create the universe. Yahweh did. He's the One you should worship, Uncle!

"The first angelic messenger you heard again last night, keeps warning you to turn from Antichrist and turn to Yahweh, because He is the One who made the heaven and the earth and the sea and the springs of waters, not Antichrist.

"This false savior you worship is merely Satan's agent in human form. Make no mistake, he is every bit as human as you and me! So why worship someone who was created in the image of the same living God I serve, only he doesn't belong to Yahweh. The god he bows down to is the devil himself!

"Antichrist likes taking credit for things for which he was not involved. But I assure you, Uncle, that the One who started it will end it. The One who created it is in charge of it. The One who brought it into existence is the One who will put it out of existence.

"He is the One to fear, not Antichrist or Satan. The price you will pay for worshiping that mere man will be an eternity in hell, forever separated from the One who created you."

"Yeshua Himself said, 'Do not fear those who destroy the body, but fear Him who is able to destroy both soul and body in hell.' Antichrist has already killed millions of bodies, but he hasn't killed a single soul.

"He doesn't have that power. But his soul will surely be damned for all eternity, along with everyone who follows him and submits to his authority."

Like layers being peeled off an onion, Benjamin could no longer control his emotions. He had been too blinded, too loyal to Salvador Romanero to see the man for who he really was, the great deceiver and the Antichrist of the Bible. *Three and a half years?*

Jakob saw the utter brokenness in his uncle's overall demeanor. He liked what he saw. "While it's true that Yahweh has been using dreams to gather His true believers, in no way do these dreams have anything to do with being saved. Only by receiving Yeshua as Lord and Messiah can you be saved from the everlasting lake of fire. It's important that you understand this, Uncle."

Benjamin gulped hard, then nodded that he understood. All he could think to say was, "Lord, have mercy on me, a sinner!"

It was then that the Most High Yahweh God changed his heart and opened his spiritual eyes and ears to the Gospel of Yeshua HaMashiach.

21

GATLINBURG, TENNESSEE

AS BENJAMIN SHAPIRO MADE his way to Gatlinburg, Clayton Holmes, Travis Hartings, and Dr. Lee Kim were summoned to the cabin in Oak Ridge, at 6 a.m., by Moishe, who was the first of the 144,000 sealed servants to appear on the *ETSM* radar screen.

The first time Clayton and Travis met the young Jewish preacher at the cabin, it took them two and a half hours to travel from Ellijay, Georgia to Oak Ridge. But it took a mind-bending three days to travel back to the tiny Georgia safe house, after the global quake shook the entire planet.

Even two years later, many of the roads were still in disrepair. They had to take many detours, but at least they didn't have to turn back at any point along the way, like they had to on several occasions last time.

This was Lee Kim's first ever meeting with Moishe. His last visit to Oak Ridge was when they had smuggled Jefferson Danforth there before the former U.S. President was whisked away to Coeur d'Alene, Idaho, before ultimately settling at safe house number one, in Chadds Ford, Pennsylvania, with his wife, Amy.

Turbulent as everything was back then, it couldn't compare to now. It was about to get even worse...

Moishe greeted them warmly, "Shalom!"

"Shalom, Moishe! So nice to see you again!" said Clayton. Whereas he and Travis looked so much older and thinner than the last time they were together, Moishe hadn't changed one bit.

Surely, the Lord was preserving him on all levels. Moishe hugged his three visitors, then invited them inside for breakfast.

Travis was surprised that the coffee he had brought to the cabin last time was still in the kitchen cabinet. Just seeing the container forced his mind back to the last time he tried brewing coffee at this place. What had caused him to realize that something was terribly wrong, had little to do with the kitchen faucet not working.

When he looked outside the kitchen window and saw the foothill mountains in the near distance practically split in half, and the massive fault-line crevices in the ground—which were still clearly visible—he became so frightened that he nearly fell to the kitchen floor.

While the shock he felt that morning had long since worn off, just seeing the widespread damage again made him marvel at how he and Clayton had survived the global quake, let alone slept through it all.

Hartings poured two cups of coffee for himself and Lee, then joined Clayton and Moishe, who weren't coffee drinkers, at the breakfast table. "It's well past the expiration date, but at least it's coffee."

Lee nodded his thanks to Travis.

Moishe came straight to the point. "The reason you're here is that you will be meeting with someone later today who recently converted to our faith. His name is Benjamin Shapiro."

The three *ETSM* leaders looked at each other and shrugged. The name didn't ring a bell with any of them.

Moishe removed all confusion for them. "He's Antichrist's personal physician. At least for the time being."

Travis was taking a sip of coffee and nearly spit it out of his mouth. "Salvador Romanero?"

"Yes. He is also the uncle of one of Yahweh's sealed servants presently residing at your safe house in Chadds Ford, Pennsylvania. I believe you all know Jakob."

The three men nodded that they did.

"Benjamin has been in Pennsylvania the past few days, meeting with Jakob, which ultimately led to his spiritual conversion, praise Yahweh!"

"Wow! That's terrific news! Does Romanero know?"

"Not yet." Moishe pushed his plate aside and folded his hands on the table. "There's no easy way to say it, brothers. Your organization is in imminent danger."

Clayton was clearly deflated hearing this. He leaned back and placed his hands behind his head, elbows out, shaking his head in fear.

Travis and Lee both felt their hearts pounding away in their chests.

Travis asked, "What kind of danger are we in, Moishe?"

"I'll let Doctor Shapiro tell you all about it."

Clayton gulped hard, then asked, "Will he come here to the cabin?"

Moishe shook his head. "You will meet him roughly an hour away from here, in Pigeon Forge."

Travis said, "I know where it is. Been there many times."

"Actually, you will meet him a few miles east of Gatlinburg, at a hiking trail. He will wear purple and green hiking gear. That's how you will know it's him. You will hand him a letter which will direct him to a hotel in Gatlinburg, where the four of you will meet."

Lee asked, "Why couldn't we have met him in Pennsylvania?"

Moishe took a small sip of tea, then looked at Lee over his teacup. "To keep up with appearances. The reason Benjamin left New Babylon in the first place was that he started having dreams about Jakob. It started on the night Yahweh's first angelic messenger interrupted Antichrist's speech in Jerusalem.

"When my Two Mentors were resurrected, just like Jakob had told him they would be, followed by the Jerusalem quake, Benjamin said he felt this great evil pressing in on him, suffocating his spirit.

"When he later discovered that many of his friends and colleagues had perished in the quake, he asked Antichrist for a leave of absence. He told him he wanted to go back to Pennsylvania, where he was born and raised, so he could clear his head and focus on a speech he was supposed to write, detailing the many benefits the chip will provide for all who receive it.

"But after spending three days with Jakob, that speech will never be written, not by Benjamin anyway. He's too busy reading the booklet your organization has printed."

Moishe paused upon seeing the elation on the faces of the three men. From an organizational standpoint, it felt good to finally have something to celebrate again.

Moishe went on, "At any rate, he told Antichrist he was having difficulty concentrating with so much attention being brandished upon him. He said he wanted to do some hiking in Tennessee to clear his mind. Antichrist offered to fly him here, but Benjamin told him that even with the ongoing road construction, a long drive, followed by a few days of hiking the trails would do him good.

"When Antichrist offered to send the security detail to Tennessee with him, Benjamin told him they were part of the reason he was having difficulty concentrating on his work, and their presence wouldn't be necessary.

"He agreed to Benjamin's wishes but warned him that he better be fully prepared to explain the many benefits the chip will offer to all who take it, when they meet in Jerusalem less than two weeks from now.

"In truth, Jakob sent him in our direction, so he could meet with the three of you. He left his house last night and drove all through the night. He should arrive at the meeting location the same time as you."

Clayton asked Moishe, "What does he know about us?"

Jakob explained, "He knows you represent a large Christian organization that he now wishes to be a part of, before he ultimately relocates to the Middle East to be with Yahweh's chosen people.

"Yahweh is really starting to move among His people. The Most High is using this time to gather the rest of His Remnant from the clutches of Antichrist. Even though His Word has been outlawed by the Son of Perdition, He's using His sealed servants and angels to share His salvation message to every nation, tribe, and tongue."

"Revelation seven, verses nine and ten?"

Jakob nodded at him. "Precisely. Yahweh has countless scores of angels at His full disposal, to do whatever He pleases, for it is written. Angels were involved in the giving of the law. They have been involved in the care of believers and in ministering to the saints."

Travis sipped his coffee. "In the New Testament, an angel visited Zacharias telling him that his wife would conceive a son whose name would be John."

Lee added, "Yeah, and not too long after that, an angel visited Mary to tell her she would give birth to the Savior of the world. Another angel later confirmed to Joseph that Mary was being truthful with him. Angels even announced the birth of Messiah, scores of them, in fact."

Clayton then added, "We see angels praising God all throughout the book of Revelation, fighting demons, enacting judgments, and bringing messages from God."

Moishe nodded at his three fellow believers. "Correct! Very recently, angels were involved with removing Satan from the heavenlies. And even at the time of God's final judgment, angels will be the reapers who will gather people at the end for judgment, as well as gathering the elect into the kingdom." He grinned at them. "So, why should we be surprised by what we see transpiring in the skies above?"

The three *ETSM* leaders paused to let the conversation sink in a little further. Finally, Lee asked, "What kind of danger are we in, Moishe?"

Moishe reiterated, "I'll let Dr. Shapiro tell you all about it. All I'll say for now is that Antichrist is working diligently behind the scenes to silence Christians, so he can focus on the Jews next."

All three men already knew that. They would just have to remain patient until they met with Benjamin.

Moishe took the final bite of his bread. The way he chewed on it, savoring each bite, before swallowing it, gave them the impression that he was eating manna from heaven. Perhaps he was…

With breakfast over, Moishe said, "As always, make sure Benjamin recites your organization creed before taking the next step with him. Jakob had him write it down before he left. We know Antichrist is monitoring his every move, so we must always be careful."

"Absolutely!" said Clayton, "that goes without saying…"

Moishe nodded at him. "When your meeting is finished, come back to the cabin. The three of you can share the basement for the night."

"Thanks, Moishe," Travis said, on behalf of the three of them. He still found it a little strange that they were being invited to spend the night at the cabin that was the very first purchase made by the *End Times Salvation Movement*.

When the three *ETSM* leaders drove off the property, the location that had always been so special to Travis, felt even more special now that one of Yahweh's sealed servants had taken full occupancy of it.

Had the days not been so full of chaos and uncertainty, it would have been impossible for him to wrap his mind around what was transpiring.

But now that he understood what was going on in the world, precisely as it had been recorded in the Bible, it made perfect sense to him…

22

MEANWHILE, DOCTOR SHAPIRO ARRIVED at the hiking trail location 10 miles east of Gatlinburg, Tennessee, without the use of a chauffeur this time, and parked his car at the agreed upon meeting location.

It was one of the few trails in the Great Smoky Mountains that was still accessible, which hadn't been demolished in the global quake.

Travis Hartings was already perched on a large rock a quarter mile up the trail, when Benjamin began his ascent. With the use of binoculars, he spotted him in the green and purple hiking gear that Moishe said he would be wearing. It made him stand out, but that was the point.

Not that it mattered much, only a handful of other folks were there. Hartings descended the small incline and headed straight toward the man. When he was five feet away from him, he said, "Howdy!"

That was the greeting Benjamin was told to expect. His eyes darted nervously from left to right. Seeing no one spying on him, he coughed into his right fist. "Keep fighting the Good fight. Pray for me as I pray for you. Yahweh is with us."

Benjamin felt slightly awkward reciting it, partly because he always thought he was fighting the good fight prior to his conversion, so his words lacked conviction. Even so, they came from the heart.

Upon hearing the creed, Travis handed him a folded-up piece of paper, then resumed walking down the small incline.

Benjamin shoved it in his coat pocket, then started his ascent up the mountain, searching for the best location to read it without having any of the still-functioning spy cams seeing him pulling it out of his pocket.

His instructions were clear: *After you finish hiking, check into the Great Smoky Mountain Lodge and Resort, in Pigeon Forge, and request the largest suite they have. Request two keys. Once you're checked into your room, go out to your car and place the spare key under the front driver's side tire. My associates and I will retrieve the key, then meet you in your room a few minutes later.*

Since the three *ETSM* leaders couldn't be seen in public, nor could they pay for a hotel suite in this cashless society, they found it morbidly amusing that Salvador Romanero's personal physician—at least for now—would be footing the bill, so to speak.

Doctor Shapiro, knowing he was being monitored by GPS, hiked the trails for three more hours, before leaving for Pigeon Forge.

When the hotel owners became aware of who had just entered their once-successful establishment, they couldn't believe their good fortune.

The elderly couple bubbled over with joy, even though they were bordering on financial destitution. The wife said, "My name is Charlotte. This is my husband, Jasper. We're honored to have you staying with us! Just wish we would have known in advance…"

Benjamin noticed the marks and abrasions covering their bodies, from the locust stings. "Truth be told, I don't want anyone knowing I'm here. I'll be conducting a classified meeting up in my suite, in an hour or so. The last thing I need would be for someone to alert the media. I trust you won't tell anyone about my arrival, including on social media."

Charlotte's face lit up. She hadn't felt this joyful in too long to remember. "We won't tell a soul! Cross our hearts!"

Benjamin nodded his thanks to her.

Jasper asked, "First time in Pigeon Forge?"

"It is…" said Benjamin, nonchalantly.

Jasper explained to his VIP guest, "In its heyday, it was quite the tourist attraction. Now it looks like a ghost town. Even the once world-class theme park, *Dollywood*, is in total disarray. Then again, most of our town is in disrepair.

"From a structural standpoint, our hotel was one of the few in Pigeon Forge to escape the mayhem. But with no guests filling our rooms, we're barely hanging on. Right now, we're at ten percent capacity. We were at eight percent last week."

Charlotte typed on the keyboard in front of her. "I've sealed off the entire top floor just for you, Doctor!"

"That's very generous of you," Shapiro said, half expecting it.

"It's our pleasure! We're huge Romanero supporters! We can't wait to receive the mark and download the app next week, so we can help with the cause. We believe many Christian dissidents are hiding in the vicinity. We plan on getting it on day one!"

Eyes begging for assistance, she handed him his room keys. "Please tell us once we receive the mark, everything will be okay soon after that, and we can hire more of our staff back. We can't go on much longer like this."

Not if you take the mark, he thought to himself somberly. As one who loathed liars, Benjamin wasn't about to lie to them now. He still felt bad for lying to his soon to be former boss when he was back in New Babylon, about agreeing to take the mark when his mind was already made-up that he wouldn't take it. Although it was a necessary lie, it was a lie, nonetheless. It didn't sit well with him.

Now convinced that Romanero was the Antichrist of the Bible, he cleared his throat and, without providing the hotel proprietors with even a hint of assurance that things would turn around for them once the mark was administered, he said, "Naturally, when my visitors arrive, we're not to be disturbed."

Charlotte shot a confused glance at her husband, not at all satisfied that he didn't offer them any assurance whatsoever. "Absolutely, sir!" she said, in her twangy voice, "If you need anything, anything at all, don't hesitate to let us know."

Shapiro nodded his appreciation at her and went up to his room without saying anything else.

After a quick shower, Benjamin went down to the parking lot, at precisely 11:30. He knew Romanero was tracking him with GPS, but his silent prayer was that his boss wasn't spying on him the same way he was with countless millions of Christians planetwide.

He dropped his second room key to the ground, trying to make it look like an accident. He slid it behind the front tire, then went back up to his room without even glancing over at the hotel proprietors.

Lee Kim collected the key, relayed the room number to his two brothers in Christ, and went inside. When he reached Dr. Shapiro's suite, he pushed the door security guard out, so Clayton and Travis wouldn't have to knock when they arrived.

Lee scanned the room with a handheld device, searching for cameras and listening devices, but found none.

When Clayton and Travis arrived, Lee turned the TV volume up as high as it could go, as Clayton and Travis dragged four dining room chairs into the massive-sized bathroom, then arranged them in a square.

Clayton turned the shower on and the exhaust fan, then motioned for everyone to proceed there. After brief introductions were made, Holmes asked them to join hands as he opened the meeting in prayer.

When he was finished, Benjamin placed his hands on his lap. "So, you're the organization behind the LastShotAtRedemption website?"

130

The way he said it was a bit unnerving. The fact that until just recently, this man was the personal physician to the Antichrist of the Bible compounded the uneasiness they felt.

The three *ETSM* leaders relaxed. Moishe had confirmed to them that this man was Jakob's uncle, and that he had been genuinely converted. That was good enough for them.

Travis folded his arms across his chest. "Did Romanero link us to the website?"

"Yes, he did, but that's not what prompted my question." Shapiro looked at Doctor Lee Kim. "When you introduced yourself, I recognized your name as being on Romanero's Kill List. You were added to it a few days after Yogesh Patel's plane was blown out of the sky, over Manila."

Even though Lee already knew that, now that Romanero's physician had just made it official, he gulped fearfully.

Shapiro pointed at Clayton and Travis. "The two of you are on it too. He wants all of you silenced as soon as possible!"

The two leaders glanced at each other. This wasn't earth-shattering news. Clayton asked, "We hear you've been having dreams…"

Shapiro nodded at Clayton, then adjusted his weight on the chair. "My nephew Jakob, whom I hadn't seen in many years, kept visiting me at a park in Pennsylvania that I hadn't been to in more than two years."

Travis asked, "What was the content of your dreams?"

Shapiro shook his head, as if still trying to piece it all together. "Long story short, Jakob told me I was living a lie. He then warned me that if I kept following Antichrist—he refused to call him anything but that—I would be eternally doomed.

"The next night he visited me again, saying the Two Witnesses would be resurrected the day before it happened. He also predicted the earthquake. When both happened exactly how he had foretold it, my first thought was, Romanero was never spot on like that."

The way the three men nodded at him, confirmed Shapiro's suspicion that they also knew it would happen. "It was then that I wanted to meet Jakob in person. I told him I would fly to Jerusalem, but he told me to go back to Pennsylvania, and we would meet on the same bench on which we had met in my dreams.

"My first impression upon seeing my nephew was, despite the somber expression on his face, he was aglow. It was as if his countenance had drastically changed since the last time that I saw him.

131

"It was there that Jakob gave me an in-depth explanation of the Voice that had disrupted Romanero's speech in Jerusalem. He also warned that two other angelic messengers were still to come.

"Strangely enough, the second one appeared that very night." Shapiro frowned. "I always thought I spoke the truth; I wholeheartedly believed in it. It pains me to admit I had no idea what 'real' truth was. I came to realize God's Truth was so alien to my nature."

Benjamin shook his head sadly. He felt like weeping. "Thanks to my nephew, I'm convinced Romanero really is the Antichrist of the Bible."

With his left hand, Shapiro rubbed his cheeks all the way down to his chin, then repeated the process three times, as if to release some of the pressure that had built up. "He's on to you, even more than you know."

Hartings said, "Moishe told us, only he didn't provide any details."

Shapiro leaned as far back on the chair as it could go without tumbling over. "Do you remember what Romanero said in his speech just before he ordered the slaying of the Two Witnesses?"

Holmes eyeballed the man who technically still was Antichrist's personal physician. "Which part? He said many things. Are you referring to the thousand-dollar bounty he's offering for turning in Christians?"

"I'm afraid that was only the tip of the iceberg," Shapiro said. "The facial recognition app he offered to his followers, as a means of earning income, was a mere pittance since he's already been using that technology to spy on dissident camps, but on an infinitely larger scale."

Hartings gulped hard. His eyes widened fearfully. "Dissident camps?"

Benjamin nodded yes. "Do you remember his remark about the strong measures that were being taken to speed up the process of locating defiant Christ followers, at the places at which they were hiding?"

The three men braced themselves, fully sensing they were about to discover what had put that glum look on his face…

Lee Kim squirmed on his chair. "What strong measures did he take, Doctor?"

Benjamin Shapiro crossed one leg over the other and shot the three *ETSM* leaders an agonizing look. "In the five months Romanero was forced underground, to avoid being stung any further by the…"

Clayton interrupted him, "He was stung too?"

Benjamin rolled up his shirt sleeves. "See these scars?"

This was the first time the three *ETSM* leaders had seen them up close and personal. Just one glance was all it took for them to silently praise God again, for sparing them from those hideous afflictions.

Dr. Shapiro rolled his sleeves back down. "I assure you those flying beings armed with determined minds or instincts or whatever they were that did this to me, did it to Romanero as well."

Holmes asked, "If he was a true miracle maker, why couldn't he heal himself?"

Benjamin's nostrils flared. "Exactly! This is something I've grappled with ever since he lied to that reporter in Jerusalem, about not being stung by them. I was with him when he was stung six times while inside his new palace, so I can say with conviction that his retreat underground wasn't voluntary, as he proclaimed in his speech. He was forced underground writhing in agony."

Shapiro shifted his weight on the chair again. "Was he ever glad when they were finally gone! All of us were! Nothing could kill those demonic beings! Even though Romanero's scars have since been surgically repaired, I assure you he was stung by them, many times in fact! The pain he suffered was excruciating!"

Benjamin shivered at the terrifying memory and stretched his arms above his head. "Another thing I couldn't understand until just recently was since those otherworldly beings all resembled my boss, wouldn't it have made more sense if they attacked his enemies instead of his own followers?" He gasped. "But they didn't..."

Travis raised an eyebrow. "Very good point you make..."

Benjamin shrugged his left shoulder. "At any rate, when Romanero became aware that those belonging to Jesus were immune to their stings, and Christians were free to go about their business and stock up on essentials and grow crops, as everyone else was forced indoors in agony, it incensed him to no end.

"So much so that aside from putting the finishing touches on the new Mark everyone must receive if they want to buy, sell, or trade, the rest of his time was spent with his team of scientists and engineers perfecting the ultra-miniaturized technologies he had access to, before plotting his next level of revenge on Christians..."

Lee Kim became even more fidgety, as his mind slowly started piecing things together. "What ultra-miniaturized technologies are you talking about, Doctor?"

Shapiro shook his head fearfully. "In a nutshell, miniature drones also known as microfliers."

Lee Kim gasped loudly, and it was as if the air had left the room...

133

23

TRAVIS HARTINGS SQUIRMED VIOLENTLY on his chair, and shot Dr. Shapiro a frightened, sideways look. "Microfliers?"

Lee Kim knew what they were and didn't need any further explanation. "I remember hearing about them long before the Rapture. If my memory serves, I believe the smallest ones were roughly the size of a grain of sand, and were originally intended for monitoring air pollution, airborne diseases, and environmental contamination."

Shapiro nodded at him. "I remember them well myself. They were guided by the wind, much like a maple tree's propellers spinning like helicopters harmlessly to the ground. They've come a long way since those days…"

Lee nodded at Dr. Shapiro. "I remember it was all the buzz when they became motorized. I knew back then that they would ultimately be used for surveillance purposes. Talk about the perfect spying tool!"

Shapiro took a large gulp from his water bottle, then cleared his throat. "Your senses were spot on, Lee. But I assure you the former models cannot come close to competing with what Romanero has access to. Not only are these newly advanced microfliers the smallest-ever human-made flying structures known to man, they're also GPS guided and have been mounted with pinhead-sized cameras and microphones, to record and even livestream as directed."

Seeing beads of sweat forming on Kim's forehead, Shapiro added, "They're also embedded with limitless memory for storing all data that is collected. All have been linked directly to the facial and voice recognition app that Romanero recently offered to his followers."

Lee clasped his hands together to keep them from shaking so much. *Moishe was right! We are in imminent danger!*

Benjamin went on, "Romanero took full advantage of your carelessness by spying on you with these motorized microfliers, with great efficiency I might add."

Kim's eyes widened fearfully. He didn't need Dr. Shapiro to expound on what he meant by "carelessness". While they were always careful when away from their safe houses, they had become too lax at home. In short, they had let their guard down, something the late Braxton Rice would have never allowed. "When did it begin?"

Shapiro rested his hands on his lap. "Roughly around the midway point of the five-month period. Truth be told, the way you took control of the room when you first arrived, turning the TV volume up full blast, dragging me into the bathroom, and turning the shower on, in the back of my mind I thought perhaps you already knew about the microfliers."

"Not at all," Lee Kim said emphatically, defeatedly.

Shapiro circled the top of his bald scalp with his right hand, as if trying to release the increased pressure build up. "Well then, your low-tech maneuvers make me harken back to simpler times, gentlemen, better times, before the whole world went crazy. In a way, it's comforting."

As the lead IT man, Dr. Kim wanted to be offended, but he wasn't. "We don't have much choice. We can't freely roam the planet setting up surveillance traps at will. Nor can we trust our technology."

"I understand, Lee." Shapiro grew serious again. "Romanero used that time to his benefit, by ordering more than a billion of them to be dispatched to the far corners of the Earth, searching for dissidents out growing crops, making deliveries, and so on and so forth. What made his timing so perfect was that the demonic locusts had no power over the microfliers. Nor did the colder temperatures affect them."

Travis looked up at the vaulted ceiling, his body trembled in fear, already sensing they hadn't heard the worst part yet.

Shapiro grimaced. "That's not all. Romanero's top scientists took it one step farther by modifying a batch of them and increasing their size to take the form of insects of all sizes—gnats, mosquitoes, bees, dragonflies, butterflies, even hummingbirds. They've already been tested on tens of thousands of Christians with great efficiency."

Clayton leaned up on his chair. "Tested? How?"

Shapiro easily saw the fear in his eyes, and confessed, with a frown, "Many of these insect drones were engineered to inject poisons into their targets, to incapacitate them before being apprehended by local authorities, only to wake up in one of Romanero's death camps, knowing their lives were about to come to a brutal end, by way of guillotine."

Shapiro sighed. "Millions of Christians met their demise that way. After a while, instead of incapacitating their targets, the microfliers were reprogrammed to spot welts or abrasions on their bodies. When none were found, those individuals were followed back to their hiding places.

"Once an enemy camp was spotted, the drones would remain stationary, hovering above recording everything within their scope, gathering as much intel as they could, hoping it would lead them to even more enemy camps. They obtained so much footage!"

Lee shook his head incredulously, knowing this day would come. "To the best of my knowledge, I don't believe any of our VPN calls were compromised in any way, all were secure…"

"You may be right," Shapiro replied somberly, "but since the air above many of your safe houses was saturated with scores of microfliers, they recorded everything that was being said and listened to."

Benjamin grimaced. "Didn't you find it a bit strange when Romanero admitted in his speech, that he felt he could no longer trust the scores of surveillance cameras and sensors that were mounted to all new construction, for the sole purpose of tracking humans? Why confess something like that to the enemy?"

Before anyone could answer, he added, "I'll tell you why. He was already using these microfliers to spy on tens of thousands of dissident camps long before he gave that speech. I assure you it had nothing to do with the frustration he felt for constantly having to replace the cameras and sensors after each new calamity rocked the planet."

Shapiro bit the lower right side of his lip. "Like I said, what he's offering his followers for finding Christian dissidents is peanuts, compared to what's already been uncovered behind the scenes."

The look on Clayton's face conveyed to everyone in the room that this was the worst possible news he had heard since the *End Times Salvation Movement* was formed. He asked, "And you can definitively confirm that our organization is under surveillance?"

Shapiro folded his arms across his chest. "I'm afraid so, Clayton. They even know about the three glass factories you purchased in Virginia, Texas, and Montana, not to mention the two that were destroyed on the West Coast." He paused and waited until he knew he had their full attention, to say, "They also know President Danforth is still alive and staying with you in Chadds Ford…"

Clayton said to Travis, "This is bad!" The fear in his voice was quite pronounced.

Shapiro shook his head in shame. "I confess that when I first got wind that some of these dissident camps had been discovered, even though I've always been a staunch defender of one's personal liberties, since you were the true enemies of the planet, I wanted you all gone just as much as everyone else did! If these microfliers could help speed up the process, I was all for it."

Benjamin rubbed his chin very slowly. "Then came the Voice from above followed by dreams about my nephew, and here I am…"

Hartings swallowed back a huge gulp of fear, as he thought back to the last audio message he and Clayton had sent out. His mouth became dry as cotton. His stomach started churning violently. He excused himself to get water for everyone in the living room area…

When Travis returned, Clayton asked, "How did they find us?"

Shapiro took a large guzzle of water and cleared his throat. "While it's certainly true that your website was what put your organization on the map, what started closing the net on you was when authorities recovered the cell phone of a real estate agent from Pennsylvania, who was killed in Wilmington, Delaware on the night of the Universal Children's Day explosions."

Holmes and Hartings shared more fearful glances. Both knew what the other was thinking: Rhonda Kimmel.

Shapiro noticed the uneasy exchange between them and deduced that they knew the realtor. He explained, "A file was later discovered on the woman's phone, ultimately linking five-hundred properties that were all listed for sale in the U.S. and Canada. All were occupied by Christians before the disappearances. It was originally called the 'Chadds Ford Mission', but later changed to the 'Montpelier Mission', after a thorough investigation was conducted on the woman's phone."

Travis glanced over at Clayton. The level of concern he saw in his partner's eyes was nearly enough to stop his heart from beating.

Even though the three *ETSM* leaders had eternal assurance and there was no need to fear being killed, now that they had been discovered by the Antichrist, they couldn't help but tremble in fear.

Now that Shapiro, too, was an enemy of the planet, what he saw on their faces frightened him to no end. He went on, "Apparently, she was part of a vast network of realtors trying to sell the locations. Even though she had only personally sold the property in Chadds Ford, after scouring through her text messages, she described her clients as being friendly but strangely different, even suggesting to her fellow realtors that they might be like the 'whackos' who occupied the properties before they were vaporized."

He paused, then added, "Her words, not mine. At any rate, that was when they realized they had a potential treasure trove in their hands. When Romanero was briefed on this, he sensed these properties were somehow

137

connected to your website and ordered the immediate dispatching of scores of microfliers to spy on each location."

The three *ETSM* leaders shared more frightened glances, before Travis thought, *I need to warn everyone! Brian Mulrooney and Charles Calloway need to know Romanero knows Danforth is living there!*

Lee Kim asked, "Are you absolutely sure about this?"

Shapiro sighed deeply and took another large gulp from his water bottle. "I'm afraid so. The conversation wasn't intended for my ears. I only heard bits and pieces of it, when I was treating Romanero's sting marks underground, and overheard him discussing some of the strike locations that would soon be carried out.

"The only reason it stood out in my mind in the first place, was that Montpelier reminded me of a place in Vermont where I used to take my family skiing every Christmas. It's a quaint little town situated roughly twenty miles south of Stowe. We used to drive there for lunch."

Holmes and Hartings were mindful of Montpelier and didn't need this geography lesson now. They were too shellshocked to think about skiing trips at this point in history.

Realizing he had gone off on a tangent, Benjamin refocused, "When it was confirmed that all five-hundred locations had new occupants living on them, Romanero ordered the drones to keep spying on them, hoping someone would ultimately be identified, either visually or vocally.

"It didn't take long before they got positive hits, when the facial recognition technology identified many of the new mothers in the global system. You know, the ones who forfeited the care he had been providing for them, choosing instead to go into hiding."

All three of them nodded fearfully that they understood.

Dr. Shapiro took another large gulp of water. "I don't have to tell you how enraged he was upon hearing this. It was then that all those locations were placed on the strike list.

"Initially, much like he used the insect drones to incapacitate tens of thousands of Christians before apprehending them, he likewise selected a few locations to be bombed, as target practice, but only those situated in remote locations which were believed to be without children.

"He figured no one would be able to connect the dots among the mass devastation rocking the planet, especially since those properties were out in the middle of nowhere. All were destroyed by two-thousand-pound bunker buster bombs."

Hartings looked down at his feet and sighed. "Rick Krauss…"

"Was thinking the same thing myself," Holmes replied, with a deep sigh of his own. "If anything, it further confirms what he said happened to his safe house, in the Upper Peninsula of Michigan."

Lee Kim asked, "Would you happen to know which locations were bombed?"

Shapiro shook his head. "All I know is after the first few targets were successfully obliterated, Romanero ordered a cease-bombing."

Dr. Kim scratched his chin. "Why's that?"

"He believes the one hundred and forty four thousand sealed servants are sending new converts to your places for cover, including many runaway children who have since left his protection.

"Since he hasn't been able to convert a single Christian in his prisons, he is fiercely determined that all kids being raised in dissident camps will worship him once they have been removed from those places. This is at the top of his list, the megalomaniac that he is."

Travis asked, "When will they come for our children?"

Shapiro shook his head in confusion. "Not sure, but we must assume it won't be long now. Once the children have been removed, the order will then be given to blow them all to smithereens, simultaneously..."

"Are we still being spied on?"

"If I heard Romanero correctly, I would have to say no. The purpose of spying is to not get caught. Why potentially harm the mission by having the enemy discover what you're doing? Knowing Romanero the way I do, I'm sure he wants you all to remain in the dark about it, leading straight up to the all-out blitzkrieg on all locations...

"However, I can say that the microfliers are always out searching for new enemy camps. Full disclosure, your organization isn't the only one being spied on. There are many others. He plans to wipe them all out on the same day. The man's insane!"

After a brief pause in the conversation, Dr. Shapiro said, "I do have some good news to share with you..."

Hartings smirked. "Oh yeah? What is it?"

"Before I left Pennsylvania for Tennessee, my nephew advised me that I should use my power to reallocate many of the things I had full access to, to help Yahweh's chosen children. It took a while, but I finally managed to send massive quantities of supplies and medicines that were being housed in one of his underground vaults, to various undisclosed locations, including here in the States.

"Once the order was carried out, I manipulated the computer to show that they were lost during the last rounds of God's judgment. Many of these life-sustaining essentials have been earmarked for your organization."

Shapiro took another chug of water. "I've also managed to redirect many of the military-strength insulated fallout shelter capsules Romanero's been shipping all over the planet for many of his key people, in preparation for the global blitzkrieg.

"Let's face it, there's never been a time in human history when hundreds of thousands of bombs were dropped on strike zones all at once." Benjamin paused, still blown away at the words that just came out of his mouth. "Since Salvador has successfully merged all militaries into one global one, he already has everything he needs to pull it off. They're just waiting for the order to be given...

"These capsules are insulated on the outside to withstand a twenty-kiloton nuclear blast. And they're large enough to house a dozen people, namely those who may be in poor health and won't have the strength to make it off the property. Needless to say, they must be dispatched before Romanero discovers what I did. I just need to know where to have them shipped."

Travis said to Clayton, "Looks like we just found our next President Danforth."

Clayton nodded at his partner, knowing exactly what he meant, they had found their next global supplier.

Shapiro looked at the massive mirror on the wall. It was completely steamed over from the warm water. He could no longer see his reflection. Even the face of his smart watch was steamed. "So, where do I go from here? Where will I stay?" The fear etched on his face and the panic in his voice was evident.

Clayton said, "That's already being arranged."

Benjamin's forehead furrowed. "Can I at least stay on one of your properties in Pennsylvania? Call me sentimental, but now that my days of living in the Middle East are over, I'd like to live out my remaining time, short as it may be, in the state of my birth."

Travis answered, "Sure, but you cannot step foot in any of our properties until after the GPS locator in your body has been removed. Once that happens, you can never communicate with Antichrist again, let alone go back to New Babylon, or even to your house in Pennsylvania."

"I already figured that much. Where will I reside in Pennsylvania?"

Clayton said, "At the Chadds Ford safe house."

Benjamin nearly choked on the saliva in his mouth. "The location on Romanero's strike list?"

The way he said it nearly caused Clayton to burst out in laughter. But clearly this wasn't the time for laughing and joking. "Yes. Just until we can sort through it all and take it before the Lord. Besides, that's where your nephew resides."

Shapiro raised an eyebrow, comforted by this admission. "Am I to just drive there?"

"Of course, not! By the time you return to Pennsylvania, you'll have your instructions. But do not change your plans here in Tennessee. Since Romanero expects you to go hiking for a few days, to clear your head, give the man what he expects."

With the meeting adjourned, the three *ETSM* leaders were happy for this inside glimpse into the inner workings of Antichrist, as told to them by his soon-to-be former doctor. It was like gaining a 3-D perspective.

Clearly, with exception to the Word of God itself, this was the best intel they had ever obtained on the enemy since becoming a Christian organization...

141

OAK RIDGE, TENNESSEE

THE RIDE BACK TO Oak Ridge was spent mostly in silence, as the three *ETSM* leaders tried piecing everything together in their minds which, thanks to Benjamin Shapiro, were completely blown.

All three were thinking of the best approach when sharing the terrifying news with everyone else in the organization, without causing unbridled panic to set in, already knowing it would be an impossible endeavor. One thing was certain: everything was about to change.

When they arrived back at the cabin, they took turns briefing Moishe on everything that had been discussed with Dr. Shapiro in Pigeon Forge.

Moishe was already mindful of what they had been told and could tell they were still trying to process everything. It was a lot to take in all at once.

Travis looked deeply troubled. "May I ask?"

Moishe nodded at Hartings to proceed.

"The one thing I can't understand is when we first met you here, you assured us that all places housing children would be safe. We've been sending children to those places ever since. What should we do now?"

Moishe very calmly said, "All children will be safe, dear brothers, only some of your locations will change. Much like Yahweh's chosen people will soon be forced to flee from Jerusalem, many Gentile believers living in hiding will have to do the same.

"This will be the final shift. All children residing in Chadds Ford, for example, must be relocated to Kennett Square soon! That location will become the new safe house for children living in that area."

Clayton said, "We were foolish to let our guards down by thinking our safe houses would be safe during the five-month period the enemy was hunkered down indoors."

Lee Kim and Travis Hartings exchanged defeated glances. Both were amazed that despite their most extensive planning at the outset, only a few of their carefully laid plans had been realized.

They weren't surprised that the LSAR website had been taken offline. They had no control over that decision. But so many other things also hadn't worked out the way they had hoped. This was especially true with the thousands of drones they had acquired.

Now that they were being spied on by microfliers, Dr. Kim feared the copious amounts of time, effort, and money that he and his staff of scientists and mathematicians had invested into programming their drones was about to be flushed down the drain.

They had fully anticipated using them during the Great Tribulation, to deliver intel from one *ETSM* location to another, plus drop their Gospel booklets over the largest population areas.

All were programmed to self-destruct if they ever crashed to the ground, or if they were intercepted by the enemy.

Lee gasped. "Forget about using our drones now! The only other option will be for couriers to hand deliver messages from one location to the next, you know, Paul Revere style…"

Travis sighed. "Yeah, like Rick Krauss. Only he didn't have a horse to ride on."

Clayton nodded agreement but remained silent as he tried mentally calculating their next move. It was late and everyone was exhausted.

Before calling it a night, Clayton recorded a message for everyone. When he was finished, Travis began the tedious task of alerting all leaders at their properties about this most dreadful discovery.

BRIAN MULROONEY WAS ASLEEP in bed, recovering from yet another cold, when he received an encrypted one-word text message from Travis Hartings: *URGENT!*

It was just after 10:30 p.m. Brian shot up on the bed and gulped hard. His eyes widened with fear, and his heart pounded through his chest.

He replied on his SAT phone: *What's wrong, Travis?* He thought to wake Jacquelyn, as he awaited Hartings' reply, but she was exhausted from taking care of Sarah. Their daughter had another tooth coming in, which had made her cranky most of the day.

Now that they both were sleeping, he didn't want to wake them.

Finally, after waiting nearly three minutes, Travis replied: *Go to the basement of your house. Bring Charles with you. Let me know when you're there. Bring earbuds with you. Whatever you do, don't call me or Clayton!*

Brian glanced rather oddly at his phone screen for a second or two, wondering what had caused his leader to sound so panic-stricken. With his health slowly but steadily declining, part of him didn't want to know.

143

He very quietly got out of bed, grabbed his asthma inhaler and earbuds off the bureau, and tiptoed downstairs, to find his father engaged in deep conversation with Charles Calloway and Tom Dunleavey. This was something they did each night. The living room had quickly become their favorite meeting place.

Brian put his right pointer finger up to his mouth. "Shh…"

Dick flinched, then asked his son, "What's wrong?"

Brian pointed at his SAT phone and shrugged nervously. He motioned for Charles to follow him, using the same finger.

Calloway got up off the chair and followed Brian down to the basement.

Tom and Dick remained seated on the couch that had one of its legs broken off during the global quake. Julio Gonzalez Sr. had since nailed the leg that had snapped off back to its frame, but the phone books that were used to keep the couch propped up before the leg was repaired, remained there for added support.

They were curious as ever to know what was going on, hoping they would know soon enough. Whatever it was, it wasn't good...

Once Brian and Charles were down in the basement, Mulrooney sent a text message to Travis: *We're here now*...

Travis replied. *I just sent you another recorded message from Clayton. After you and Charles listen to it, WITH EARBUDS ON, you'll know what to do. I'll contact you again when the time is right. For now, stay safe and SMART!*

Brian swallowed hard again, then let Charles read Travis' three messages, before giving his big brother and spiritual mentor one bud for his ear, so they could both hear it at the same time.

Mulrooney touched the play button with his right pointer finger. "Greetings beloved! I wish I had good news to deliver to you all, but I'm afraid that's not the case. It couldn't be worse, in fact. As much as Romanero has prevailed upon Christians all this time, we ain't seen nothing yet! Our organization is in deep trouble.

"Getting to the point, Travis, Lee, and I were just informed by someone with direct knowledge of the situation, that many of our properties have been spied on the past few months with miniature drones, which are better known to the scientific world as microfliers.

"I'll spare you the details for now, except to say that some of these microfliers are the size of tiny pinheads, while others resemble flies, mosquitoes, and various other insects. It pains me to inform you that many of our locations are on Romanero's radar screen, including yours."

Even though Brian and Charles knew something like this would happen at some point, they nevertheless shared looks of total disbelief.

"From what we were told, this spying campaign has been ongoing since the five-month plague, so chances are good that whatever has been discussed at your location since that time has already been recorded.

"According to Lee, it's unlikely that they've breached our system and gained access to our encrypted SAT phone activity. But what can be confirmed is that many of our conversations have been recorded by these microfliers, as they hovered above many of our properties spying on us.

"Chances are good that some of the miniature drones have entered inside some of your cottages, armed with audio and video capabilities. We must also assume that our on-property walkie-talkie communique were captured and recorded."

Clayton gasped loudly. "From what we were told, before he destroys all safe houses that have been positively identified, Romanero wants to take our children from us. As of yet, we don't know when it will happen, only that it will surely happen at some point."

Brian's eyes widened fearfully; he started hyperventilating and took a puff from his asthma inhaler.

"About the only thing the enemy doesn't know is that we know they're spying on us. While it doesn't give us a huge advantage, it gives us a little time to prepare. Our source doesn't believe the locations that have already been identified are still being spied on, because they don't want us to catch on to what they're doing.

"Only God knows how many microfliers might be hovering above all our other locations, even as I speak. That said, chances are good they have obtained so much information on our organization.

"I know this comes as a frightening revelation, but it's better to know we're being spied on than to become sitting ducks when it ultimately happens. I know it's not much to cling to, but at least it's something.

"Quoting Revelation thirteen, ten, 'If anyone is to go into captivity, into captivity they will go. If anyone is to be killed with the sword, with the sword they will be killed.' Only in our case, the sword will be guillotines or bombs being dropped on our safe houses.

"That's all I have to say for now. Make sure to let all the adults at your location listen to this message. Do not, I repeat, do not let anyone listen to

145

it without earbuds on, and do not contact any other safe houses under any circumstances. We'll take care of that.

"For now, do your best to carry on as if you didn't know you were being spied on. And avoid all communication with us until we know what steps to take next. I love you all."

Brian rubbed his suddenly throbbing forehead. He took a few deep, exasperated breaths. "Why don't you bring Tom and my father down here, so they can listen to it first, as I wake Jacquelyn, my mother, Isaac and Tamika…"

Charles nodded at Brian, and followed him back upstairs…

25

ISAAC AND TAMIKA MOSELEY were still awake in bed enjoying each other's company, after finally consummating the marriage.

Tamika rolled over and stared at Isaac, silently wishing they could remain together until Jesus came back for them. As appealing as that sounded, both were committed to approaching every new sunrise as a sign that they still had work to do in the Lord's service.

Now that they were both tried and true Christ followers, Tamika felt even more married now than she did last time. She immediately took to the new and improved, saved version of her husband.

Isaac leaned over and kissed her hard on the lips a few times. "I can't wait till we see the boys again, and they see that we reconciled."

"Momma too!" Tamika smiled at him in the dimly lit bedroom. With his two front teeth missing, it made him look a little older, but Tamika didn't mind. His overall features meant nothing to her now. It all came down to what was on the inside. "What a glorious day that will be!"

She got up out of bed and opened the window to let in some air. She was thankful that Joaquim Guzman and Tony Pearsall had made three trips to the glass factory in Virginia, which allowed them to replace most of the windows on the property that had become casualties of the global quake, including the ones in her bedroom.

Since it was tempered glass, it wasn't nearly as clear as the former windows, but it was so much better than having the window frames covered with plastic. They also replaced every fish tank that was lost in the quake, and fully restocked them with tilapia and catfish.

Tamika was oddly surprised at this late hour to hear a bird chirping gleefully on a tree branch, a few feet from the second-floor bedroom window. Then again, at this point in history on this insane planet being ruled by insane leaders, it only figured.

She didn't know this wasn't as uncommon as it seemed. Even before the Rapture, it happened on occasion. Sometimes when birds were confused, or when male birds were looking to mate or protect their territories, they were known to chirp or sing at night.

Whatever the reason, it was enough to rouse Revelation from his sleep, as Cocoa purred away, not wishing to be bothered.

Tamika scooped her adopted pet feline up in her arms, and stroked his fur. Eyes searching for the culprit outside making all that noise, his ears were perked up at full attention.

Tamika said to the bird, "If you knew what this planet was still in for, you wouldn't be chirping right now, you'd wish you were dead!"

She then directed her attention to Rev. "Be careful, Rev, as much as you'd like to eat that bird, we may have to eat you someday. You, too Cocoa," she added, seeing her cuddled in the corner of the room. "Just kidding, my loves, I won't let anyone eat either of you!"

Tamika gently placed the cat back on the carpet and stretched her arms above her head, not knowing how true her words about wishing to be dead would be this day, for many *ETSM* residents.

There was a knock on the doorframe leading to their bedroom.

"Who is it?" Isaac asked.

When the person who kept persistently knocking didn't answer, Isaac got out of bed and stuck his head out of the curtain, to find Brian standing there with a fear in his eyes that was alarming.

He put his right pointer finger to his mouth. "Shh…" Using the same finger, he motioned for the married couple to follow him.

"Give us a minute to get dressed," said Isaac, his voice shaky.

Brian left them and knocked on the doorframe leading to his parents' room.

"Yes?"

When Brian didn't reply, Sarah pulled back the curtain to see her son holding his right pointer finger to his mouth. "Shh…"

"Are we in danger?"

Brian whispered, "Yes, we are. I need you to get dressed and go downstairs. I'll join you after I wake Jacquelyn."

Sarah shot her son a confused sideways look. This exchange between them reminded her of the night Brian persistently knocked on her door—when there still was a door to knock on—on the night America fell under attack. He ordered her down to the basement where she was made to put on a hazmat suit of all things.

Sarah put on her robe, then followed Isaac and Tamika downstairs. Brian and Jacquelyn joined them a few seconds later.

When they reached the basement and listened to the message for themselves, all were filled with unbridled fear.

After hearing the terrifying message for themselves, Titus scanned the sanctuary for listening devices, as Shamus Harmon, Julio Gonzalez Sr., and Tony Pearsall rushed off to scan the rest of the 27-acre property, including the air above, and finding none.

It was then that Chadds Ford residents were awakened by someone knocking on their cottage doors, their pointer fingers to their mouths, directing them to the church sanctuary.

Upon arriving at the sanctuary and listening to Clayton's terrifying message, with earbuds pushed deep in their ears, many became short of breath; their hearts pounded inside their chests like beating drums.

This was the worst possible news! The urgency factor had just been increased by a sum that couldn't be fully factored in human terms.

Brian and Charles were seated on chairs on the stage in the sanctuary, and easily saw the fear in everyone's eyes. Even the former President of the United States looked terrified, Amy Danforth too.

"What will we do now, Brian?" Leticia Guzman asked in a soft panic, in case they were still listening. "How can we stay here if we're being spied on?"

Brian took a puff from his inhaler. "Where else can we go? It's not like we have other options. We're a hunted people."

Marta Gonzalez was sitting next to her daughter. "Clayton said in his message that it's better to know than to become sitting ducks. That's precisely how I feel now, like a sitting duck!"

Brian nodded at her empathetically, trying to appear calm when he was just as panicked himself. "I understand how you feel, Marta, but Clayton also said he seriously doubts we're still being spied on."

"But that could always change," Marta said, her voice quaking, as she clung to her daughter, Ruth, on her lap. "I thought our children would be safe here, Brian?"

Mary Johnson's face quaked in anguish. "Jakob assured us this place would be protected. That was the main reason Donald and I conceived in the first place…"

Brian twisted his lips one way then the other. "I'm sure Jakob will tell us what to do and where to go, when the time is right…"

Lila Choharjo asked, "Was the Kennett Square safe house spied on?"

Charles answered the question for Brian, "We all heard what Clayton said about not contacting anyone for now. All I can say is it wasn't part of the five hundred properties that were purchased at the outset. "But since numerous food deliveries have been made to our safe house, the past three years, from Kennett Square, it's highly possible. In time, we'll know...

"For now, we need to pray for God's protection, as we all absorb and process this latest blow, and watch everything we say and do, as if the microfliers were still hovering above the property, even if they aren't."

A tear escaped Mary's right eye. As the days passed, it was more difficult to keep her emotions in check. Ever since Donald left them, Luke became even more clingy and started crying more frequently, and for longer periods of time. *Now that we've been spotted, will they take Luke from me next, leaving me all alone again, before they behead me?*

Sarah Mulrooney was sitting next to Mary and saw her hands and knees trembling. She grabbed Luke from her arms and put him on her lap, giving her friend time to compose herself. It was as if the two women had switched personalities. When they first arrived at safe house number one, way back when, Sarah looked and very much felt like Mary did now.

Jacquelyn asked her husband, "How can we ever rest comfortably again knowing that insect drones can hover above us at any time spying on everything we do?"

"Try not to think about it now," Brian said softly, more tension building on his face just thinking about his wife's growing concerns.

Jacquelyn let out a loud gasp that everyone in the sanctuary heard. The more Brian kept telling her not to think about it, the more her mind kept reliving every last detail! How could she not think about it when she felt like she was living in a glass house, with her enemies staring at her licking their chops lying in wait for the right time to strike.

She couldn't remember a time when she felt more vulnerable than she did right now. She felt certain that she wasn't alone in her thinking.

Jacquelyn just hoped that when the enemy invaded, and bombs started falling on safe house number one, that the end would come quickly for them all. It suddenly sounded like a good way to go.

As much as she loved this place, it was time to start mentally and emotionally disconnecting from safe house number one. She knew it was a selfish thought, but her wish all this time about wanting to survive until Jesus returned, so she and Brian could raise baby Sarah, seemed less appealing to her now.

Silence fell upon the dimly lit sanctuary, as everyone shared looks of fear and disbelief. They were slightly comforted when Jakob entered the sanctuary and walked up to the stage.

Said he, "I know this comes as frightening news to you all, but the children will remain safe. Nothing has changed in this regard, only the location has, which will be in Kennett Square. It's being supernaturally protected by Yahweh and will not be impacted by Antichrist's bombing campaign.

"Much like Yahweh's chosen people will soon be forced to flee from Jerusalem, many Gentile believers living in hiding will have to do the same. This will represent the final shift.

"For now, like Charles said, you should resume your lives like you did before you heard the news. We do not want to give the enemy a foothold, by letting them think we're on to them.

"One more thing, tomorrow we will welcome a new resident. This man is a recent convert, who just happens to be the one who informed us about what Antichrist has been doing to us behind the scenes."

"Who is it?" asked Jefferson Danforth.

"You will see tomorrow. Until then, I encourage you all to keep resting in Yahweh's eternal promise, that He is sovereign, and in complete control of the situation."

At that, Jakob left them...

It was late and everyone was tired, but no one wanted to leave, not until they prayed together as a group, and processed everything they had just been told.

After spending a full hour together in prayer, the crowd started thinning out, little by little. Some would remain in the sanctuary all night praying to God and seeking His guidance in this all-important matter...

But whether they remained in the sanctuary or went back to their cottages, having already endured so much tragedy and despair, they were more subdued than anything else, like battle-hardened veterans fighting on the front lines in enemy territory.

Only now, their location had been positively identified by the enemy of their souls. It was yet another grim reminder that, with each passing day, the end was drawing closer and closer for all Christ followers...

26

BENJAMIN SHAPIRO OPENED THE front door and saw a young woman standing outside holding a delivery bag, looking increasingly nervous.

He looked both ways and nodded at the four armed guards that it was okay. He took the bag from her and sniffed in the aroma. "I hope it tastes as good as it smells."

"Me too, sir..." came the reply.

"Wait! Let me give you a tip for your prompt service. Would you like to come inside? It's cold out there."

"Thank you, sir," came the reply gratefully, nervously, hoping she wouldn't blow it. Dressed in plain clothes, she was really an *ETSM* nurse who had been staying at a safe house in the Adirondack Mountains, in upstate New York, caring for more than 200 toddlers.

The property was near Lake Placid and was one of the 500 locations that was discovered on Rhonda Kimmel's cell phone. It, too, was targeted to be destroyed along with safe house number one, and many others.

Her instructions had been vague. All she knew was that her purpose for being at Dr. Shapiro's home in Pennsylvania was to remove the GPS locator from his body, then proceed to the Kennett Square location, where she and the children were all being reassigned.

She was briefed in advance that Dr. Shapiro was Salvador Romanero's physician, and once the locator was removed from his body, his boss would be instantly notified, even at 3 a.m., the present time in New Babylon. Soon everyone would know...

Once Benjamin removed his long sleeve shirt, it only took her a few seconds to locate the GPS locator inside his body. She numbed the area on his right arm, but with four armed guards standing outside the house, she wasn't sure if she could wait around until it finally kicked in.

Dr. Shapiro sensed what she was thinking and nodded at her to proceed. As she began the tedious process of carving it out, he put a pencil in his mouth and chomped on it as hard as he could. Even that didn't help ease the pain. But it had to be done.

After successfully removing the locator from his right arm, mindful that it was both motion and heat sensitive, she put it in a plastic baggie, then placed it in a bowl of hot water to hopefully maintain his body temperature, until after he escaped.

It was reminiscent of what Dr. Jameel Khan had done, when he removed the GPS locators from Hana and Cristiana Patel's bodies, after Hana had made her online declaration for Christ, roughly two months ago. The *ETSM* nurse cleaned and bandaged Shapiro's arm, then hurried to the front door, before the guards became suspicious.

Benjamin put his shirt back on and followed behind her. "Thanks for the prompt delivery," he said, loud enough for the guards to hear him.

A warm smile formed on her face. "You're welcome, sir. And thanks for the generous tip! I really appreciate it!"

"Stay safe out there." Benjamin went back inside and stared outside his living room window and watched her drive down the block. Once she was out of sight, he rushed outside again. "Which way did she go?"

One of the guards answered, "That way, sir. Is everything okay?"

Benjamin sighed. "Can you believe she left her phone here?" His voice indicated that he wasn't pleased by the woman's carelessness.

Another guard asked, "Why don't you call the restaurant or delivery service company?"

Because there isn't a restaurant or delivery service company to call, he thought, before saying, "I'd like to save her a trip if possible…"

"Would you like me to try catching her, so your food doesn't get cold?" asked Jack Nelson, the guard in charge.

"Nice of you to offer, but it shouldn't take long," he said in reply, opening the garage door.

Benjamin climbed inside his Mercedes SUV, which was already packed with the things he would need, mostly clothing, and pulled away, knowing he would never step foot inside that house again.

He met the woman two blocks away from his house and gave her phone back. "Thanks again, for removing the GPS locator from my body. God be with you, my sister…"

"God be with you too," she said, nervously looking in the rearview mirror. At that, they parted ways, knowing time was of the essence.

Benjamin Shapiro arrived in Chadds Ford an hour later. By then the four guards had already been alerted. But even before Nelson received a text message from his supervisor, he knew something wasn't right. Thirty minutes had already passed, and Dr. Shapiro still hadn't returned.

One of the guards jokingly asked, "Where did the good doctor finally catch up with the delivery driver, in Center City, Philadelphia?"

The guard standing beside him burst out in laughter. "Maybe he's on his way to Atlantic City!"

Their smiles faded when Nelson received another message from his supervisor. It caused fear to swim through them all. It said: *According to his GPS locator, he never left the house. The reason I contacted you in the first place was that his body temperature keeps dropping to dangerous levels. Are you sure he isn't in the house?*

Jack replied: *Positive. He left a half hour ago.*

Hmm, something isn't right... came the next reply.

Nelson gulped hard at his supervisor's morbid reply, then went into panic mode. He alerted his three colleagues to surround the house, as he entered inside already knowing he wouldn't find Benjamin there.

But what he found was the man's GPS locator in a plastic baggie, floating in a bowl of lukewarm water on the kitchen table.

Nelson also checked the delivery bag. To his astonishment, there was no food inside. But what he did find inside was a copy of *The Way*. Dr. Shapiro even dedicated it to him: *The only secure future you can ever have can be found in the pages of this Book! I hope you'll read it, Jack!*

Nelson informed his supervisor of these odd discoveries, omitting the "book dedication" part, and silently wondered if he and his three colleagues would still have their jobs, once Romanero became aware of what had just happened on their watch...

Meanwhile, when Dr. Shapiro pulled his vehicle to a stop, on U.S. 202, Shamus Harmon and Tony Pearsall were already there waiting for him. Shamus pointed Benjamin in the direction of a small open field, where a 4-wheeler being operated by Joaquim Guzman was waiting to take him to his new residence, temporary as it would be.

"What about my things?" asked Benjamin.

"Don't worry," Harmon said, not knowing he was speaking to Salvador Romanero's now former doctor, "we won't forget them."

Benjamin nodded his thanks to the man, and rushed off toward the 4-wheeler, as Harmon got behind the wheel of their new resident's car, and drove it to a location where it would soon be burnt to a crisp.

Tony Pearsall followed him there, then helped him remove the man's belongings from the Mercedes SUV, before setting the vehicle ablaze, and heading back to safe house number one, hopefully without incident.

"Hold on tight!" shouted Joaquim.

Without asking any questions, Dr. Shapiro jumped on the back of the 4-wheeler. He held onto the young man as tightly as he could, as Joaquim skillfully navigated the 4-wheeler through the hilly terrain of the darkened woods, leading to the back entrance of safe house number one where new members were smuggled in at night.

When they reached the river, which was nearly bone dry, the young man slowed the vehicle and gently guided it across to the other side.

A few minutes later, they reached the back entryway to the safe house. Titus and Isaac were already there waiting for them. The iron gate was already open so they wouldn't have to stop.

Once they were on the property, Joaquim took his time guiding the 4-wheeler over the wooden planks covering the large craters that were created by the global quake, as they proceeded to the sanctuary.

Benjamin sighed relief seeing his nephew waiting outside for him. "Shalom, Uncle! Welcome home, for the next few weeks, anyway."

They embraced. "Thank you, Jakob…"

Jakob was impressed that his uncle wasn't wearing his toupee. Even his sideburns were gone. After being regenerated by the power of the Holy Spirit, he decided to never wear it again—it reminded him too much of his former self. "Let's go inside so I can introduce you to everyone…"

Titus finished sweeping the sanctuary for listening devices and gave Jakob the green light to proceed. "Shalom everyone! This is the man I told you about yesterday. Meet Doctor Benjamin Shapiro. Not only is he my uncle on my father's side, until a few days ago, he was Antichrist's personal physician."

Many loud gasps filled the completely full sanctuary.

Tamika's eyes widened. Her shock knew no bounds. She wasn't the only one. Everyone had astonished looks on their faces.

In a way, because this man had recently been in the inner circle of the Antichrist of the Bible, most residents were more enthralled meeting Dr. Shapiro than when they met Jefferson Danforth for the first time.

Benjamin cleared his throat. "It's a pleasure being here with you all. Thanks for offering me a place to stay, even if only temporarily. And to think it all started with dreams about my nephew. Actually, since it started in Jerusalem, I'll begin there…"

Everyone remained on the edge of their seats from start to finish, as Dr. Shapiro took his time bringing everyone up to speed on how he was able to leave Romanero in New Babylon, to the three days he spent with Jakob in Pennsylvania, followed by the three days he spent in Tennessee with Clayton Holmes, Travis Hartings, and Lee Kim.

Benjamin saw a young woman in the front row holding a baby on one leg, and a copy of *The Way* on the other leg. It was Leticia Guzman.

He pointed at it. "I can't fully express to you all just how impacted I was reading that booklet! By the time I arrived in Tennessee, I was already a believer. But in the three days I spent hiking the trails, I made sure to take it with me. I did some of my best reading and meditating during those times. I know your organization is responsible for printing it."

Brian said, "But we have you to thank for the large paper shipment."

"All glory to Yahweh!"

Several Amens filled the sanctuary.

Benjamin smiled. "When Jakob gave it to me, he challenged me to read Isaiah fifty-three, then compare it to the four Gospels. By doing so, I saw a clear connection between the suffering Servant described in Isaiah fifty-three, and the life of Yeshua, as recorded in the four Gospels."

Benjamin shook his head in amazement, as tears flooded his eyes. Before his conversion, he seldom showed emotion. Everything was different now. "Every molecule in my body was filled with a sensation I had never experienced before. I knew it was God's love smothering me. For the first time ever, I felt free. My soul was so alive."

Everyone in this sanctuary had also experienced that amazing sensation themselves. They shared in their new resident's joy.

Benjamin's eyes narrowed after recognizing Jefferson Danforth seated at the midway point of the sanctuary. "The reason I'm not shocked seeing you here is that Romanero knows you're still alive. He also knows you're living at this location…"

Jefferson wasn't entirely surprised to hear this. It was just a matter of time. Amy, on the other hand, became terrified.

Jefferson scratched his chin. "I met the man three times. Once in Brussels, once at the U.N., and once at the White House. I never felt comfortable being in his presence."

Shapiro grimaced. "You're not the only one! Everyone in his inner circle fears him. At least they did, until most of them were killed in the Jerusalem quake. I presume you knew Jurgen Staat and Li Ping…"

Jefferson nodded that he did. "We used to be quite cordial until Romanero came on to the world scene. Once that happened, everything changed for the worse, including our companionship."

Shapiro said, "The joy they felt at the outset for being in his inner circle was replaced with constant dread. It got to where they hated being in his presence. He was always so unpleasant to be around.

"Publicly, they praised Romanero, but in private they feared him. It had gotten to where the former U.N. Secretaries-General no longer felt their opinions mattered to him.

"What Romanero says in public and how he acts in private are two very different things. In private, he's always angry and agitated."

Danforth said, "That's how I always perceived him…"

"I was with him during the global quake when much of the new utopian city he was in the process of completing was leveled, including his palace. Was he enraged! Now that I'm saved, I couldn't imagine Jesus throwing a temper tantrum like I saw that day."

Shapiro shook his head, still feeling foolish for following that man, and for thinking he was a savior of all things. "I'm sure you can still recall how he told everyone that he allowed it to happen, so everyone could rebuild together. Nothing could be further from the truth.

"Even though he took credit for sparing Israel, I assure you he wasn't happy about it. But from a political standpoint he used the global quake to his advantage so beautifully.

"Ever since Satan entered the man, he has become increasingly paranoid. He trusts no one. Mostly due to this, he wants all dissident camps destroyed in the soonest possible time, before word leaks out about his plan. If for only that reason, I believe he was relieved that so many of his staff perished in the Jerusalem quake.

"But I would have to say the one thing that gnaws away on him more than anything else is knowing that while he has the power to kill scores of Christians, he doesn't have the power to break the loyalty to the One we serve. I think that's why he was so incensed to discover that while everyone else on the planet was constantly subjected to the venomous stings of those demonic creatures, himself included, Christ followers weren't tormented by them!

"I didn't see him on the day the Two Witnesses were resurrected, but I was told that he went berserk." He sighed. "How foolish I was to think that monster loved the Jewish people. Or children for that matter. The man's diabolical!"

Everyone in the sanctuary felt privileged to hear this man provide this valuable insight into the workings of Salvador Romanero.

They welcomed their new brother in Christ warmly and praised God for rescuing him from the Antichrist of the Bible.

157

27

AFTER TWO LONG, TERRIFYING, uncertain months in hiding, at the subterranean safe house situated just outside Tirupati Andhra Pradesh, India, 83 miles northwest of Chennai, the signal was finally given for Hana and Cristiana Patel to make their daring escape to America.

With local and global authorities once again in full pursuit of her, Hana now knew how her late husband had felt before his tragic death, when he had held that undesirable, spine-tingling title as the most wanted person on the planet. She was presently unaware that a man named Benjamin Shapiro had recently usurped that title from her.

There wasn't a day that had passed when Hana didn't suffer sustained anxiety attacks. Had she been able to go outside for a few minutes each day, it surely would have helped assuage the physical and mental anguish she battled most days. But by having one of the most recognizable faces on the planet, she didn't have that option.

The only ones who ever left the safe house since they relocated there just before the meteor strike, were the handful of young men who went out to scout the surrounding area, wearing disguises, to make sure they weren't in harm's way, even though everyone still alive on the planet was in harm's way, every second of every day.

The only good thing was that the flood waters from the tsunami, caused by the meteor strike, never reached as far as their new subterranean safe house, like they feared might happen at the outset. Had that happened, their hideout would have been turned into a watery grave.

Adding to the overall stress Hana felt was that her daughter didn't like being trapped underground any more than she did. Of the 1,500 square-foot of sectioned-off subterranean space they had access to, Hana and Cristiana shared their small section of space with three other mothers and their children—one boy and two girls.

The youngsters made the best of it, but there was only so much space, which they used to play with their toys, color, and play hide and seek, as if it was their own personal playground.

Cristiana, soon to turn three, was starting to talk in short sentences. Whenever she grew tired of subterranean life, or bored with her playmates, she would whine to her mother saying, "I wanna go home, Mama," meaning to the house in which she had happily lived, before they were forced underground.

Clearly, Cristiana preferred that sprawling residence over this dreadful place. What child wouldn't? What grownup wouldn't?

"I know, sweetie, but we're going to a much better place," Hana would always reply, not sure whether she believed it, or if they would even make it to America.

Hana couldn't believe how quickly her daughter had grown. She sighed. It had been two years since her husband was killed by the same man from whom she was presently living in fear. But she took solace knowing that they would see each other again.

Hana didn't know much about the escape plan to America. All she knew was that she and her daughter would be dropped at the fishing pier in Chennai, where Yogesh had worked all his life, before she won the contest, which had drastically changed their once simple lives.

From there, they would sail to Singapore on a moderately-sized fishing boat that was owned by a fellow brother in the faith, and longtime friend of Dr. Jameel Khan—the doctor who had removed the GPS trackers from Hana's and Cristiana's bodies, just before they went into hiding.

Upon arriving in Singapore, they would meet with Yasamin and her son, and Donald Johnson, before sailing to America.

If everything went according to plan, the stowaway compartment that Donald Johnson was presently occupying, on his long voyage from the U.S. to Singapore, would be the very same space that Hana, Yasamin, and their two children would share on the way to America.

Thanks to their American brothers and sisters in Christ, once they boarded the container ship for the States, they would find it stocked with all the essentials they would need during their extensive time at sea.

Other than that, Hana didn't know much else. except that if they arrived safely in Singapore, they would stay at an *ETSM* safe house, until the next step could be taken to smuggle them to the States.

But if Donald Johnson ended up being detained by one of the crewmen on board the cargo ship he was presently sailing on, chances were good that Hana and Cristiana would be stranded in Singapore until they were ultimately caught, killed, or until Christ came back for them…

Clearly, she was taking a massive leap of faith for even attempting this daring escape with her daughter.

With the plan set in place, they celebrated Cristiana's third birthday a month and a half early. It was a simple celebration to say the least. One of the women had made a rice and coconut milk cake for her. Cristiana was also given two lollipops.

Hana let her daughter enjoy one of them earlier, but would hold on to the second one for when they arrived at the pier.

At 1 a.m., Ahmed informed Hana that it was time to go. She changed into baggy blue jeans, an oversize sweater, and old sneakers.

One of the new mothers staying at the subterranean hiding place cut her long black hair earlier in the day, spiked it, and dyed the tips blonde, to disguise her as a punk-rock teenage boy.

Before climbing up out of the hole, everyone formed a circle around Hana and Cristiana and laid hands on them, as Ahmed prayed for their safe passage.

Mindful of the huge risk Hana was taking, they easily saw the fear in her big black eyes, and once again silently questioned why she was so adamant on traveling halfway around the world in the first place.

They knew she had to leave India, but why couldn't they remain in Singapore once they made it there, or hide out in a neighboring country like Pakistan or Nepal, or even Bangladesh?

Most thought Hana was being foolish for attempting to sail all the way to America with her young daughter, as the most wanted fugitive on the planet. They knew how badly she wanted to meet Brad and Joan Henriksen, but would it be worth the massive risk she would be taking for herself and her daughter, just to make it happen? They feared not.

After sharing a lengthy, tearful embrace, Ahmed and Dr. Khan led them out of the safe house.

Many wiped tears from their eyes, knowing this would be the last time they would ever see each other until they were all reunited with Jesus someday. Cristiana was like a daughter to them. She would be sorely missed. The saddest goodbyes were when Cristiana hugged her playmates for the last time. There wasn't a dry eye among them…

Hana carried her daughter to the van and quickly climbed into the middle row of seats. The back row was covered in whatever they would take on the boat with them, baby toys to help occupy the time, and other essentials she would need for her daughter, while en route to Singapore.

Ahmed and Jameel both wore long pants and long sleeve shirts, so no one would see that they had no welt marks on their bodies. They also wore baseball caps.

But if they were pulled over by the police, none of that would matter. They would be detained until a proper identification could be made. Upon discovering that the young teenage boy in the back wasn't a punk rocker, but was Hana Patel in disguise, it would be all over for them!

Ahmed was mindful that citizens were urged to contact authorities immediately, if they spotted vehicles with tinted windows that were covered in any way to prevent detection of the passengers inside them.

The car windows weren't tinted, but since there hadn't been any rain, the entire vehicle was covered in filthy ash and dirt. But since most other vehicles on the road were just as filthy, they weren't overly concerned about arousing suspicion because of the unclean vehicle they were riding in. That was the only thing they weren't worried about.

Senses on full alert, the safe house spiritual leader was noticeably nervous as he navigated the van on the damaged roadways, in silence, constantly checking his mirrors to make sure no one was following them.

Hana and Dr. Khan also felt increasingly anxious. But not Cristiana. Having been holed up underground for so long, the most-famous child on the planet stared out the window, drinking in whatever sights she could see in the darkness, curious as ever, as they made their way to Chennai.

She was totally unaware of their dire predicament or of her own notoriety, for that matter.

The three grownups, on the other hand, were grateful for the darkness outside. Not only for protection purposes, but also because they didn't want to see how their city had been reduced to a pile of rubble.

What took a little more than two hours to travel from Chennai to the underground safe house in Tirupati Andhra Pradesh last time, took five hours this time. The closer they got to their hometown city, the more widespread the devastation became.

With more streetlights working, just one glance was all it took for the three adults in the car to be convinced that had they not escaped mere moments before the meteor strike, they surely would have perished.

Hana knew to expect the once-sprawling cosmopolitan city to be severely damaged from the meteor strike and subsequent tsunami wave, but seeing it with her own two eyes, she couldn't control her emotions.

Tears fell from her eyes one after the next.

When they passed the now world-famous hospital at which Hana had given birth to her precious daughter, she wasn't the slightest bit surprised to see that it had been completely destroyed.

And while she couldn't see the house she had received as a gift after giving birth to Cristiana, the entire area had been leveled. Even had it still been standing, there was no way she would point it out to her daughter.

Hana thought to herself, *Surely, we would have died...*

From there, it took another hour before they finally made it to the fishing docks. Seeing the many boats and ships of all shapes and sizes strewn on the shoreline, it provided them with a stark visual reminder that one-third of all ships had been destroyed from the massive tsunami, precisely as it was written in the Bible.

The larger container ships that had washed up on shore easily destroyed everything in their pathway, including the old shack the Patels had lived in before winning the contest. It was where Cristiana was conceived before the so-called *Miracle Maker* announced the contest.

Seeing this forced even more tears from Hana's eyes. The only neighborhood she had ever truly known was totally unrecognizable, gone!

A few moments later, Ahmed spotted the captain and two crew members of the boat the two Patels would take to Singapore.

He motioned with his right hand for Hana to lie down on the bench seat with her daughter, then nodded at the three men but kept going.

Eyes darting left and right, he drove southbound then made the first right turn he could, then headed west away from the Bay of Bengal.

He drove a half kilometer before making another right and heading north, then drove another half kilometer and headed east toward the fishing pier again, essentially driving in a square.

When he turned right to head south again, he pulled the van to the side of the road, then motioned to Hana that it was time for her to make her move. "God be with you, my sister," Ahmed said, in a soft whisper. "We will be praying daily for your safe arrival."

With exception to Cristiana, these were the first words anyone had uttered since leaving the safe house.

Hana looked completely terrified. "Thank you. I'll be praying for you as well. All of you. I will miss you all."

Eyes drinking in his surroundings, Ahmed was clearly on edge. "Regardless of what may happen in the coming days, I take comfort knowing we will see each other again."

Hana uttered a soft, "Amen," blinked tears from her eyes, then kissed her daughter on the forehead. *Now for the hard part!* She pointed in the direction of the fishing vessel. "See that boat over there, sweetheart?"

Cristiana squinted in that direction, then nodded.

"That's the boat we will sail on. Ahmed and Doctor Khan will take you there now. I'll join you shortly, okay?"

Cristiana's lips started quivering. Tears flooded her eyes. "I wanna go with you, Mama..."

Hana shot a desperate glance at Ahmed, before her eyes settled back onto her daughter. "I know, sweetheart, but I need you to be brave now. Can you do that for Mama?"

Cristiana nodded again, but ever so sadly.

Hana pointed at a large plastic bin in the back seat. "I need you to be a good girl and climb inside that bin for me." She braced herself.

Cristiana frowned. "I don't want to, Mama."

Hana took a deep breath to prevent from bursting out in tears. "I know, sweetie, but it has to be this way for now. Once you're inside the bin, Ahmed and Dr. Khan will carry you to the boat."

Cristiana became emphatic. "No, Mama, I don't want to..."

Hana twisted her lips on the right side of her mouth. "You won't be in there long, I promise! As soon as we're on the boat you can come out, okay? Take your teddy bear with you so you're not alone."

Hana removed the lollipop from her pocket and gave it to her daughter to suck on. She had planned on giving it to her once the boat left the dock but, clearly, it was needed now. "This is for being a good girl."

Cristiana put the lollipop in her mouth, without ever taking her eyes off her mother.

Hana took a deep breath. "I'll join you shortly." Seeing more tears filling her daughter's eyes, she added, "I promise, sweetheart, okay?"

Cristiana nodded sadly again.

"That's my baby girl..." Hana kissed her daughter on the cheek, wiped more tears from her eyes, then got out of the car. Head down, she walked briskly, her heart pounding in her chest every step of the way, praying no one would recognize her.

She prayed her daughter wouldn't become so fearful that she would start screaming hysterically at the top of her lungs, and try kicking the lid off the container. If she did that, it wouldn't end well for any of them.

"Protect us, Lord, as only You can," Hana uttered under her breath, feeling even more vulnerable by not having the security team she had hired when she thought she was something special. When she had them on staff, she never needed them! Now that she needed them, they weren't there to protect her! *Surely, even they hate me now!*

Hana blinked that dreadful thought away, swallowed hard, then picked up the pace a bit, fear and adrenaline pumping through her frail and weakened body every step of the way.

The instant Ahmed pulled the van over, two men approached him, then quickly unloaded Hana's belongings from the back of the passenger van. Dr. Khan pointed to the bin that Cristiana was in, so they would be extra careful handling it.

Once everything was removed from the vehicle, Ahmed and Jameel waited until Hana and Cristiana were safely on board the fishing vessel, before beginning the tedious task of driving back to the safe house in Tirupati Andhra Pradesh...

28

MEANWHILE, DESPITE BATTLING ROUGH seas much of the way, the container ship on which Yasamin and Navid Dabiri had been sailing—from Dubai to Singapore—the past three days, was scheduled to arrive in Southeast Asia twelve days from now, hopefully on the same day the others arrived.

That day couldn't come 8fast enough for the 29-year-old woman, who achieved international acclaim after gaining custody of her son, when his biological parents were killed for not naming the newborn, Salvador, not even as a middle name.

Yasamin felt certain that Donald Johnson was experiencing the very same unpleasant conditions. Only he boarded his ship five and a half weeks before they boarded theirs. Just thinking about it exhausted her.

Her constant prayer was that she and Navid would have the stamina to endure the next grueling leg of the trip.

It had only been three days, but the task of keeping her son entertained, while being confined to this tiny metal compartment, was already taking a toll on her.

Yasamin took a swig from her water bottle and thought back to her daring escape from her high-rise condominium in the heart of Dubai.

Like everything else in her life of late, it proved no easy task. Once the GPS trackers were successfully removed from their bodies, with the use of a scalpel, Yasamin and Navid were smuggled to an *ETSM* safe house situated just outside the city, where they waited underground for 38 days, until Donald Johnson was well on his way, and the signal was finally given to take them to the cargo ship under the cover of darkness.

The disguise Yasamin wore during her escape from her condo was as a dark-skinned, obese, elderly woman, so her skin tone was more comparable to her son Navid's.

When the toddler first saw his mother wearing it, she looked so different to him that he became frightened, until Yasamin sang his favorite song to calm him down. With so much heat on her, everyone involved in her escape knew that even with a disguise on, it would be impossible to attempt something of this magnitude, once the sun was up.

Frightened as she was being whisked from the safe house in Dubai to the container ship, it didn't compare to the nerve-shredding experience of leaving her condominium for the last time. Even with the disguise on, her body trembled like never before, her greatest fear being Navid.

Thankfully, he fell asleep in her arms, as she carried him down to the getaway car. It was as if God had sealed his mouth shut.

At least I don't have to wear my grandmother disguise down here, Yasamin thought, with a prolonged sigh.

Now fully convinced that Salvador Romanero wasn't a savior, but the devil in disguise, Yasamin could no longer call her son by his name. After her spiritual conversion, which was solidified when she watched Hana Patel's online declaration, she changed his name from Salvador to Navid, to honor her late husband, who was lost in the Rapture.

She was powerless from changing the name on his birth certificate, but now that she knew beyond certainty that their citizenship was in Heaven, she couldn't care less about a stupid earthly birth certificate!

When compared to the bright future they both had to look forward to, it meant nothing!

But for now, life remained one constant struggle for the young mother and her son. Like a tidal wave, they came one after the next. The past three days at sea were especially difficult for her. Despite battling constant seasickness, due to the abnormally choppy seas, to make matters worse, she and Navid both had fevers—headache, diarrhea, and nausea.

Plus, she was having her monthly menstruation, which compounded the dread she felt even more. Yet, with toddlers being toddlers, instead of resting more, like she had hoped he would, Navid was always energetic, despite being sick.

Yasamin marveled at how children usually only complained at the worst times, when they weren't feeling well. Other than that, they weren't pretentious. Nor did they seek the sympathy of others. All they wanted to do was play. Drained of all energy, this didn't bode well for her. As her son always wanted to play, all she wanted to do was sleep.

The room had a twin bed inside, two battery-operated lamps, a small table and two chairs, enough food and water to last the entire trip, a few toys, and children's books to read to her son, and her Bible, which was disguised as a World Atlas book, just in case.

It wasn't easy being an international fugitive stowaway on a large container ship, with a young boy who didn't understand what was happening, or why they had been confined to this tiny stowaway compartment, especially now that he was walking.

Being forced to live in this limited space had resulted in a few temper tantrums the past few days.

Even though Yasamin was assured that the room was virtually soundproof, whenever Navid would cough, cry, or scream when he didn't get what he wanted, fear would always mushroom through her.

She prayed each time that no one on board the ship would hear him.

Thankfully no one had thus far…

Even so, whenever Navid became unruly, Yasamin would read him a story. Even before Romanero banned all things "Jesus", much like American books, Middle Eastern kids' story books she read never mentioned the Savior of the world.

Yasamin made sure to constantly tell her son about Jesus, and the Kingdom they would soon inherit by being God's children. She explained it so simply that he easily understood it.

The greatest disadvantage she faced by having never given birth, was that she was unable to produce milk in her breasts for Navid, for when he was tired and cranky or wasn't feeling well. She had plenty of water and powdered milk to give to her son. Even so, not being able to produce it on her own was something she greatly regretted.

While Yasamin certainly wasn't looking forward to the excruciating 50-day voyage to the States, at least she wouldn't be alone for that part of the journey. Hana would be with her.

Even better, Navid would have a new playmate, Lord willing, and the two women would be there to help each other, when they felt they were at their breaking points.

More than anything, Yasamin looked forward to communicating freely with Hana, instead of exchanging generalities online, like they had both done since meeting in the Middle East, before the two decided to escape the clutches of the man both had worshiped until recently.

Whenever Navid was sleeping, Yasamin kept her face buried in the Word of God. With two battery-operated lamps dimly illuminating the pages, she started in Genesis on the first day of their pilgrimage, and was already halfway through the Old Testament.

167

It was difficult concentrating at times, with a head cold and fever, but all things considered; it was a good accomplishment…

But whenever she took a break from reading, loneliness would always set in. Now that life had come to a near screeching halt on this massive ship, she had plenty of time to think, really think.

The one face that flooded her mind the most was her late husband. Now convinced that she would see Navid again, she longed for that day to come. She missed him to the point of aching for him.

Yasamin stared at the wall opposite her. It still blew her mind that she didn't do more research after he vanished into thin air on that terrifying day. Even more mind numbing was how she didn't make it her life mission to find out where her husband ended up going.

When it was announced that what had happened was Christian in nature, even that wasn't enough to pique her curiosity enough to explore the possibilities for herself.

In her defense, she was in mourning for the longest time. And part of her lack of interest stemmed from the fact that they both came from Muslim upbringings. When news got out that it was a "Christian" thing, it added to the angst both families felt when Navid vanished into thin air.

But the biggest reason she didn't further investigate what had become of her husband back then was, aside from her spiritual blindness, she was equally blinded by the extravagantly lavish lifestyle she had been handed, from Salvador Romanero, before her mind could fully catch up to what was really going on.

Yasamin sighed. In the end, she was too greedy to care. She blinked that morbid thought away and thought about the man she was convinced Yahweh had used to wake her up spiritually, Aarush.

It all began with dreams about him. Aarush, which means, 'Bright', worshiped with her husband underground, just outside of Teheran, before the Rapture. Yasamin shook her head in amazement.

She went from being convinced she was communicating with a madman, even if only in her dreams, to following in his footsteps and becoming a Christ follower herself. Whereas he was ultimately killed for his faith in Christ, here she was traveling on a ship to America with her son, for having the very same faith that had cost Aarush his life.

Navid and Aarush would be proud of me…

29

BRUSSELS, BELGIUM - 3 DAYS BEFORE THE MARK

HANS GREINHOLD LAY IN bed, his mind racing and his soul stirring like never before. It was three nights before he was scheduled to return to his supervisory position, at one of Salvador Romanero's newly constructed prisons, after being away from the job for nearly two years.

The last day that Greinhold had worked was on the day before the global quake. As much as he hated being away from the action for even one day, he was totally sleep deprived and needed 24 hours to recharge his batteries. Strangely enough, it had been his first day off in more than three months. Had he been on duty that day, he surely would have perished along with everyone else.

But Hans didn't walk away from the global quake unscathed. He was eating dinner with his family, when the floor started trembling beneath him. He was badly injured when a China cabinet that had been leaning up against a dining room wall came crashing down on top of him.

He suffered a severe head injury which kept him in a coma for nearly a year. His doctors and nurses weren't optimistic that their patient would ever recover. When Hans finally came to, they rejoiced on his behalf.

Prison guards were being treated nearly to the level of respect and importance as law enforcement officials and even new and expectant mothers. In the eyes of many, by killing Christian dissidents, they were heroes on the front line who needed to be celebrated.

When one of them was injured, they received the very best of care...

Greinhold discovered upon regaining consciousness that he had a new prosthetic leg up to the knee, to replace his left leg, which was severed off when a jagged piece of glass from the fallen cabinet fell on him. Had first responders not gotten to him in time, he surely would have bled out.

He was also informed at that time that his live-in girlfriend and their three teenage children were all killed in the quake. He mourned bitterly over them, and even attended grief counseling sessions online, as he recovered from his many injuries.

Upon being informed that every single detention center on the planet housing Christians had been utterly destroyed, and that his fellow colleagues had also perished, Hans ultimately concluded that they were front line soldiers who were all killed in the line of duty for their country. Since they served the entire planet, all were remembered as global heroes.

But instead of seeing it as a judgement on what they were doing to Christ followers, the quake served to further justify Greinhold's position all the more. He wasn't the least bit remorseful that not a single prisoner had survived. He was in total agreement with everyone else that they must have been even more vile than Hans had first thought, for the universe to cast every single one of them out of existence like that.

The global quake merely helped speed up the process...

When Christians were first being detained, and word got out that Romanero had given prison guards the permission to do whatever they wanted to those sub-humans before they were eliminated from society, Greinhold filled out an application that very same day.

It only took one interview for his soon-to-be supervisors to conclude that the man seated before them was a true sadist. The more they explained the mind-bending level of torture he would be required to inflict on his captives, if he ever got promoted to the next level, the more diabolically darker his eyes became.

Whereas so many of his co-workers couldn't stomach what took place in the bowels of the prison, most were contented to remain at Level A, which would allow them to rough up their detainees, rape them, extinguish lit cigarettes on their bodies, and things like that, as part of the interrogation process. That was more than good enough for them.

But not Hans Greinhold. The thought of removing his detainees' limbs and various other body parts made him feel drunk with power.

It became evident to his interviewers that he wasn't interested in being a Level One torturer, which was a position that no longer existed in Romanero's newly constructed death camps.

More than anything, Hans wanted to become a supervisor someday, so he, too, could join in the fun by electrocuting his prisoners and removing their limbs without a hint of mercy, or without the fear of retribution. What more could an unemployed ex con ask for?

When he ultimately reached that prized position, there was nothing he enjoyed more than watching his detainees squirming on steel chairs, completely terrified of what would soon become of them.

Hans thirsted for it and felt honored to be on Romanero's frontline in his death camps. There was no one more wretched than he was.

Yet, for all the pleasure he had derived from it, the part he could never figure out was how those Christians could remain loyal to their God, despite the unrelenting pain and anguish they were constantly subjected to under his swift command. How could it be?

There wasn't a night that passed that Greinhold didn't have terrifying dreams about it. It got to where he feared going to sleep at night. So much so that he often tried staying awake until sunrise.

He succeeded on occasion, but the body could only refuse sleep for so long, before it shut down and he eventually dozed off, only to reenter his own torture chamber of sorts inside his head.

Those terrifying dreams always started with visions of Ajit Laghari, and the pained anguish he saw on the Christian martyr's face, knowing what would soon become of him. From there, his mind would drift toward the thousands of Christ followers that he himself had personally tortured and violated mercilessly, until they were ultimately put to death.

Their images haunted his mind, one after the next, torturing him with the same level of heart-stopping fear that he himself had put into each of their hearts. As much as he tried looking away from them in nightmare land, it was as if his head was stuck in a vise, and he couldn't move it in any direction.

Hans was convinced beyond a shadow of a doubt that after having strong electrical currents ripping through their bodies, even the most hardened of gangsters and criminals would have confessed to anything—even false charges being brought against them—just to stop the torture.

But not these Christians. Though many of them had appeared to be timid in nature, even after being constantly tortured—even having their tongues cut out—they remained firm in the faith, unwilling to renounce their Lord and Savior.

Until fairly recently, Greinhold never understood that part...

Hans was still recovering from his injuries when he first heard one of the 144,000 Jewish preachers outside the hospital, spewing his outlawed gibberish. Everyone knew how much he hated those men.

But in his bedridden condition, where could he go to escape the sound of his voice, when it easily penetrated the walls, filling his room, rendering him restless? He tried covering his ears with his pillow on several occasions, but it never worked. He had no choice but to listen...

Strangely enough, as the days passed, the more he listened to the young Jewish male, the more he felt this hungering inside to want to know more about the One he called his Messiah, whom Greinhold knew was the ultimate enemy of the planet, the Lord Jesus Christ.

In time, he came to realize how His true followers had all found the necessary strength to overcome any situation, even unto death. It was more of a resignation, like they would soon be going to the very Place that all had confessed would be their eternal destination during the interrogation process. In short, it had nothing to do with this wickedly evil world, and everything to do with the world to come.

After being subjected to the young Jewish man's preaching for more than a month, Hans started feeling sinful, filthily sinful deep down in the soul. Suddenly, the life he had been living, that had always felt right to him, now seemed vile, unredeemable.

Yet, among all the frightening things the young man had preached about, he also spoke of a peace that surpassed all understanding for all who belonged to the God he served, through Yeshua HaMaschiach.

Hans listened very carefully and with great interest to those parts of his sermons. When he came to understand how God had the power not only to forgive his lifetime of murderous debauchery, but that He was willing to save someone as depraved as him, despite it all, the question he kept asking himself was, *who would want to save someone as despicable as me?*

After feeling totally condemned in his trespasses, the Holy Spirit intervened and Hans was finally brought to his knees in worship and sincere repentance.

It took him nearly a half hour to lower his body out of his hospital bed, every second a stark reminder of just how badly damaged his body was, but he nevertheless felt this strong conviction to get down on his knees and beg God for his forgiveness, through Christ Jesus

Hans was in his mid-forties. He had brown shoulder length hair, and a beard and mustache that was always neatly groomed, partly to cover a scar on his left cheek that had resulted from a fistfight during an ice hockey game. He punched his opponent so hard that he fell backwards onto the ice, but not before the man's left skate ripped into his left cheek on the way down. It took many stitches to sew his flesh back together.

Hans believed long before his spiritual conversion that the Two Witnesses and the 144,000 were special men, and the God they served was so powerful that not even Salvador Romanero could control or silence them. The proof of this was that the Two Ancients in Jerusalem whom Romanero had temporarily silenced, ultimately came back to life, and ascended into Heaven with the whole world watching, just like the young man outside the hospital kept saying they would.

Clearly, no one was as powerful as their God—not even Salvador Romanero! Even though the *Miracle Maker* had declared in his post-resurrection speech that their ascension skyward was nothing more than smoke and mirrors, Hans was now convinced the only ones using smoke and mirrors to deceive the masses were Romanero and the Pope.

When Hans truly repented of his countless wretched sins, he felt changed. He even quit smoking pot, cigarettes and drinking alcohol on that day. Even so, he couldn't overcome the guilt he felt from having killed so many Christians. He wanted to believe he was truly saved, but Satan kept messing with his mind, by making him think he was beyond God's redemption.

Greinhold was still in the hospital learning how to walk again, when the demonic locusts were released from the bottomless pit. They easily breached what little security barriers most hospitals on the planet tried to set in place, to hopefully prevent them from getting inside and attacking everyone. They had failed miserably.

Hans watched in horror as every doctor, nurse and patient in the hospital started writhing in pain, with pus-filled welts and abrasions covering parts of their bodies. Nothing could kill those demonic beings!

When Hans wasn't stung by them, not even once, that was when he was finally convinced that he was saved for real. This conviction was further galvanized when he started receiving text messages from his fellow prison guards, complaining that they were all being stung on the job, but their captives weren't being stung.

Greinhold rejoiced and praised the Most High God under his breath, then voluntarily checked himself out of the hospital the following day, saying he wanted to continue the tedious rehabilitation process at home.

Had he not done so, those who were caring for him would eventually discover the reason he was welt and abrasion free was because he was a Christian dissident and, therefore, an enemy of the planet.

The end result was that he would end up in one of Romanero's death camps, not to resume guard duty, but as one of its prisoners.

Shortly before the meteor strike, as he was still recovering at what was left of his home, he watched Hana Patel's soul-stirring testimony online, even though he never followed her on social media.

This was partly due to the hatred he had harbored toward her husband, for what he did to Salvador Romanero, with the whole world watching.

Hans wanted Yogesh to be tortured in his prison, much like his spiritual mentor, Ajit Laghari, had been, before ultimately meeting his demise. But before that could happen, the private plane on which Patel was traveling was blown out of the sky just over the Philippines.

Although Romanero had ordered it shot down, Greinhold thought the man got off far too easily that day. He no longer thought that way.

He was also convinced that it was God's will that he watched Hana's silent "cue card" proclamation, before it was taken offline.

The fact that she was nearly 20 years younger than he was, yet she was willing to sacrifice her own life, if it meant leading others to Christ Jesus, was commendable.

Since his spiritual eyes and ears were already open at that time, her powerful witness for Jesus didn't serve to save his soul from utter destruction. But what it did was give him a spiritual backbone, instead of merely acting like a Christian jellyfish.

Up until then, as Hans kept milking the rehabilitation process for as long as he could, he wrestled with whether he should go into hiding with the rest of the Christians, upon being released from the hospital, or follow through with what he kept seeing in his dreams the past three nights.

Now on the eve of returning to work, after such a long absence, Greinhold trembled at the thought of following through with his plan.

But with the mark just days away from becoming mandatory for all prison guards, he couldn't put it off any longer.

Hans was told that if he didn't feel up to going back to work, someone would come to his house, as a courtesy, to administer the mark from the confines of his home. But if that happened, no one would ever know about it. If, on the other hand, he had the guts to follow through with his plan, chances were good that many would hear what he had to say…

In the end, with the countless heinous acts he had committed upon God's true children constantly stabbing at his newly saved soul, he chose to be obedient to the dream.

Greinhold sighed, then uttered to himself, "Lead the way, Lord…"

30

JERUSALEM, ISRAEL

DESPITE THE MANY SCAFFOLDS and large construction equipment that was scattered across the Holy Land, throngs of people enthusiastically lined the streets for the Temple Dedication.

They were also there to receive the long-awaited mark. They all felt honored to be the first ones on the planet to officially receive it.

Many of the areas that were too badly damaged by the Jerusalem quake, were cordoned off to the public. But aside from those unavoidable eyesores, all grim reminders that they were living in an extremely chaotic world, it was indeed a glorious day in the Holy Land.

Whereas the last Temple took nearly 50 years to construct, this one was finished in just three and a half years. Every last detail was carried out to perfection, as it had been recorded in Ezekiel, chapter 40.

No expense was spared in constructing the palatial grounds. Not even King Solomon's temple compared to it, nor did the magnificent construction of the Egypt of old. It was a remarkable achievement, human ingenuity at its finest, in fact.

Among the festive crowd was a small group of Jews who lived in the Holy Land. Fed up with Salvador Romanero, and his empty promises, they were there for an entirely different reason.

The quake that rocked the Holy Land gave them all the proof they needed that he wasn't protecting their tiny country. On top of that, he never paid homage to their Prime Minister who had perished in the quake.

When Romanero was forced to reschedule the Temple dedication, it was then that they started hatching plans to assassinate him on his next visit to their country. They knew they had no chance of taking him out when he landed at Ben Gurion airport early this morning.

They also knew that with security being so airtight, they wouldn't be able to use drones or any other type of technology to accomplish their mission, regardless of where the attempt was made to finally put that man out of his existence.

175

In the end, with a full month to think things through and hatch a plan, it was decided that their best shot at killing Romanero would be when the Pope dedicated the Temple.

It would be similar to the way Romanero ordered the assassinations of the Two Witnesses a little more than a month ago. Only there would be no pomp and circumstance this time.

Another thing they knew was that they weren't the only ones hoping to assassinate him. Countless others from all over the world also wanted the man dead. But these six men wanted to be the ones to do it on their own home turf, as the saying went.

Like soldiers at war, if they lost their lives defending their homeland, like the six gunmen fully anticipated happening, so be it.

Enough was enough! It was time for Romanero to go.

As the Pope was still greeting new friends and dignitaries, the order was given to proceed. Many in the crowd started shouting obscenities at the Pontiff, as six highly skilled gunmen produced guns from under their shirts, and aimed them, not at the Pope, but at Salvador Romanero.

One armed guard, seeing six red dots trained on Romanero's face, fearfully alerted his colleagues on the ground protecting the two world leaders. They quickly sprang into action, skillfully taking out the gunmen one by one.

Just before the sixth gunman was killed, the fatal shot was fired, hitting Romanero just above his left temple. He fell hard to the ground; his blood and miniature bone fragments were splattered everywhere.

Loud screams ensued, as panicked people ran off in all directions. Those who didn't flee the area, stared at the Pope to see if he, too, had been shot. Seeing that he hadn't been, they waited to see what would happen next.

With the whole world watching, online and TV, the Pontiff promptly walked over to where Salvador Romanero lay slain and knelt beside him.

Even before Satan recently entered him, the Pope was mindful of what was happening. He knew that in order for Salvador Romanero to qualify as humanity's savior, he would have to be resurrected from the dead just like Christ was.

Now that Satan was controlling his body more than he was, the Pope knew he would have the power to heal him. He laid his hands on Salvador's head wound, then whispered in his ear, "Now they will truly worship you!"

Suddenly, with the whole world watching, there was slight movement. Was their leader still alive? They knew it wasn't rigor mortis. That wouldn't occur for at least two hours after death.

After witnessing the fatal shot with their own two eyes, they couldn't imagine their leader surviving it. Then again, since two other resurrections had already taken place from this same location, would this be the third one? They hoped it would...

To their great joy and relief, Romanero's body moved again. A few moments later, he slowly sat up, as the Pope covered his bloodied head with a towel.

Thunderous shouts of joy, relief, and adoration floated skyward, for the Pope, for healing their beloved leader, who had suffered a fatal gunshot wound to the head, as they all witnessed it happen.

After a while, Romanero stood to his feet, removed the towel from his head, and stretched out his arms like Christ did on the cross, after being seemingly resurrected from the dead.

Many who had fled the area after the gunshots were fired, heard the loud cheering, and came back to see what was going on. They made it back just in time to see Romanero back on his feet. Many became so emotional that they fell to the ground in worship of him.

Defiant expression on his face, Romanero declared to the Jews gathered at the Temple, "Where is Yeshua now? Where are the Two who recently ascended to be with their so-called Savior?

"If they truly cared for their followers, why aren't they here with you now? Unlike them, I'm here to stay. I will never leave you or forsake you. All who come to me will never hunger or thirst. I am the way to eternal life."

Romanero's words shocked each listener, and mesmerized his many followers, further confirming to them that he really was Heaven sent.

As the six slain gunmen were removed from the crowd, before the Temple could even be dedicated, Romanero entered inside and exalted himself as god, thus restoring the faith his many followers had placed in him. This was yet another proof that their spiritual blindness regarding the ways of God, was off the charts.

The Pope declared to the crowd that had very quickly reassembled, "I hereby dedicate this remarkable Temple to our blessed savior, Salvador Romanero! Now that he has become the final sacrifice, I also hereby declare that there will be no animal sacrifices at this place.

177

"Hasn't Israel's God already killed enough of our precious pets and animals, by demanding that millions of them be sacrificed to Him over the centuries, for His warped pleasure? Hasn't He killed more than enough animals with the plagues and judgments He has sent to our planet?"

The Pope paused for effect, then added, "Therefore, I can no longer, in good conscience, allow the slaughtering of innocent animals to take place from this altar, or from any other location for that matter. Not only is it cruel and unreasonable, but I find it quite inhumane!

"With that in mind, whatever animals were brought here to be sacrificed to the God of Israel, please take them home with you when you leave, for they will not be sacrificed at this place. Now that Salvador has been resurrected from the dead, no other sacrifices are required to atone for mankind. He is the final sacrifice!"

Many rabbis and other religious Jews in the crowd tore at their clothes shouting, "Blasphemy!" to high heaven.

When Romanero had enthusiastically allowed them to resume animal sacrifices to their God, after the Dome of the rock was destroyed, he had garnered the full support of Jews everywhere.

They had greatly anticipated sacrificing to Yahweh and dedicating the New Temple to Him. Now this slap in the face from his right-hand man?

Not only had he just put an end to something that had already been promised to them, now he was demanding that they worship Salvador as God! They felt betrayed by these two men at the very highest level.

It was painfully evident to them that their intention wasn't to dedicate the Temple; but to desecrate it!

SCATTERED AMONG THE CROWD were four of Yahweh's 144,000 sealed servants. One of them shouted 2 Thessalonians 3-4 for all to hear, "'Don't let anyone deceive you in any way, for that day will not come until the rebellion occurs and the man of lawlessness is revealed, the man doomed to destruction. He will oppose and will exalt himself over everything that is called God or worshiped, so that he sets himself up in God's temple, proclaiming himself to be God.'"

Then another one of them declared Revelation 13:16-17 aloud, "He causes all, both small and great, rich and poor, free and slave, to receive a mark on their right hand or on their foreheads, and that no one may buy or sell except one who has the mark or the name of the Beast, or the number of his name."

178

Then another one of them declared Daniel 9:27 aloud, "He will confirm a covenant with many for one 'seven.' In the middle of the 'seven' he will put an end to sacrifice and offering. And at the temple he will set up an abomination that causes desolation, until the end that is decreed is poured out on him.'"

Finally, the fourth young man declared Daniel 11:31 aloud, "His armed forces will rise up to desecrate the temple fortress and will abolish the daily sacrifice. Then they will set up the abomination that causes desolation.'"

Everyone in attendance heard them with perfect clarity. It caused a prolonged hush to fall upon Jerusalem...

179

31

THE POPE TOOK A few moments to compose himself, after hearing the young Jewish males making their bold statements against him.

Their voices stabbed at his blackened soul. But knowing he didn't have the power to silence them, he had no choice but to remain patient until they were finished.

It took a while, but he was finally able to find his voice to address the stunned crowd again. Said he, "Okay, let's get back on schedule. Starting next week, the mark will be available planetwide, beginning with all essential workers! But even if you aren't employed at those places, don't let that stop you from receiving it as quickly as possible.

"The instant you receive it, your global passport will be activated. You will no longer need to carry outdated passports or driver's licenses. Everything you will ever need will already be on your bodies. Even more amazing is that you will never again have to worry about checking exchange rates. Now that we are truly one global body, no longer will we have foreign or third-world countries! Yes, indeed, the future is bright!"

The Pope smiled glowingly for all to see. "Naturally, those receiving the mark today must freely acknowledge that you are hereby pledging your full allegiance to the new world religion, government, and economy. From this day forward, these new global entities will be the only ones that will be recognized anywhere on the planet.

"Further, only those receiving the mark will have continued access to the free global internet that everyone on the planet has enjoyed up until now, including the many dissidents living in hiding.

"The reason Salvador had extended this courtesy to them in the first place, was so they would see the kindness in the heart of the very one they keep vilifying. Those days are over. They are about to be cut off. Upon receiving the mark, you will be given an access code which will allow you free and constant access.

"But the greatest benefit other than the mark itself, is that those who receive it will be eligible to receive the microchip injection that has been widely talked about the past few months," the Pope declared, as the whole world watched and listened.

"Doctor Benjamin Shapiro, who all of you know was Salvador Romanero's personal physician until just recently, was supposed to give a speech detailing the countless benefits the microchip will offer to all who take it into their bodies.

"Unfortunately, he recently developed that same mental illness that so many dissidents on the planet have contracted. This was confirmed to us when he sent a scathing e-mail to everyone on Romanero's staff the other day, urging them not to take the mark.

"Why would anyone of sound mind urge others against taking it, when only those who receive it can buy, sell, or trade?" the Pope asked the humungous crowd before him. He scoffed. "Does he want everyone to starve to death?"

The Pope shook his head in confusion. "While I didn't write a speech detailing the many benefits of the chip, since that man is considered an international fugitive, and no longer part of this administration, I will provide you all with a brief explanation on it. A more detailed explanation will be provided, once it becomes available to the masses.

"For now, let me just say that once the microchip has been injected into the body, it will begin an immediate search and destroy mission, rooting out and destroying all illnesses and cancer cells, eliminating them one by one, restoring all bad cells thus bringing perfect health, which will naturally lead to much longer life and life more abundantly. It will also serve as a backup GPS locater.

"As the microchip aggressively restores your bodies from within, our global military will keep working day and night eliminating all external cancers, until we finally become a vibrant body of citizens the likes the world has never known." He wanted to add that by the time the microchip became available, most dissident camps would be completely wiped out, but since it was a secret mission, he wouldn't expound on it at this time.

"In fact, I'll go so far to say that, with exception to those who might tragically be killed by external sources in the future, this microchip will bring immortality to all who receive it. So let us all give pause to the very notion of perfect health for all of eternity..."

The Pope paused and glanced out at everyone. What he saw on most faces staring back at him strengthened him considerably. Finally, he said, "I hereby declare that anyone refusing the mark will be unable to buy or sell anything! Nor will they be able to receive medical treatment from doctors, dentists, nor will they be able to seek the counsel of lawyers. Like I stated on my last visit here, there will be no exceptions to this decree!

"For all you counterfeiters out there, make no mistake in no way will you be able to duplicate the mark by trying to put inauthentic tattoos on your bodies just so you can go outdoors. The penalty for anyone foolish enough to try it will be death. No exceptions!"

The Pope let his eyes wander the crowd again. His excitement knew no bounds. "At this time, I would like to unveil this magnificent statue of our savior which will be placed inside the Temple. This statue looks like Salvador, talks like Salvador, thinks like Salvador, and reasons like Salvador. It will have the ability to talk, answer questions, and reason with all who worship it, as if bowing down to the savior himself.

"When his parents named him at birth, they were unaware that they were being directed by a higher power to call him Salvador, which means, 'savior." That's how he should be addressed from this point forward.

"Finally, I am most pleased to announce that the new Bible has been finished. I feel so blessed to have the very first copy! Everyone who receives the mark today will receive a copy to take home with you."

The Pope declared ever so joyously, "Now that our fearless leader has been brought back from the dead, which all of you got to see for yourselves, you will also discover upon reading it, that it was prophesied in this new global gospel I hold in my hands. How amazing is that!

"Once I return to New Babylon, one of my daily rituals will be to read it to you all, little by little, from start to finish, throughout the entire year. It will become required reading from this point forward."

The Pope declared to the stunned crowd gathered before him, "If you have ever wondered why the date for Resurrection Sunday had always fluctuated on the calendar in the past, it's because the world has been waiting all this time for the one true savior to walk among us.

"Today, you got to see with your own two eyes that, by his death and resurrection from the dead, Salvador Romanero is that savior! Let this day mark our new Resurrection Sunday. I hereby decree this to be a permanent day of celebration of Salvador's resurrection!

"So, as I close, my hope is that you will enjoy the remainder of this new Resurrection Sunday! You may now line up to receive the mark and collect your bibles. May we all be blessed in the holy name of our savior and messiah, Salvador Romanero."

Just then, the voice of Yahweh's third angelic messenger boomed in the atmosphere above, "If anyone worships the beast and his image and receives a mark on his forehead or upon his hand, they, too, will drink the wine of God's fury, which has been poured full strength into the cup of his wrath. They will be tormented with burning sulfur in the presence of the holy angels and of the Lamb.

"'And the smoke of their torment will rise for ever and ever. There will be no rest day or night for those who worship the beast and its image, or for anyone who receives the mark of its name.'"

The Pope was nearly thrown to the ground. He became so terrified by the sound of the Voice that all he could do was tremble in fear.

For many Catholics, just seeing their leader cowering like this, it was the last straw for them.

Many of them were tempted to leave the Church three years ago, when the Pope stood side by side with Salvador Romanero on Christmas Eve, and brazenly declared to the large gathering in Vatican Square, that December 25th would no longer be recognized as the observation of Christ's birth, but as Salvador Romanero's new birthday.

Fully mindful of the severe persecution all Church dissenters were suffering, they sheepishly backed down. But no longer.

But it wasn't just Catholics who were fed up with Romanero and the Pope. Many rabbis who had fully supported the two world leaders and had constantly vilified the flying angels and the 144,000, were listening very carefully now, as they kept shouting Yahweh's message of salvation, without interrupting! Their hearts were being stirred like never before...

183

32

THE SANCTUARY AT ETSM safe house number one, in Chadds Ford, Pennsylvania was full of residents. They were gathered to watch what had happened in Jerusalem on the projection screen behind the stage.

Newsflashes were still posted on the screen: THIRD RESURRECTION TAKES PLACE IN JERUSALEM IN LESS THAN A MONTH!

"Ha!" scoffed Charles Calloway, at the newsflash, "Two and a half resurrections is more like it! And even that's giving Satan too much credit!"

Calloway was seated up on the stage with Tom Dunleavey, as the two men tried explaining what just happened in Jerusalem, to all newcomers to safe house number one, who were still infants in the faith.

Charles began, "Don't believe for a second that God was fooled by any of this! What happened in Jerusalem only happened because Yahweh granted limited power to the Pope to deceive the masses. In other words, what happened today happened because God allowed it to happen, plain and simple! Like Jakob told us last month from this very sanctuary, only Yahweh can create life and bring dead people back to life."

He added, "What you must understand is that everything Jesus did in the thirty-three years he walked the planet, Antichrist always tries imitating. Now that Romanero is the same age that Yeshua was when He was crucified, it's no coincidence that he was assassinated and resurrected at the very same age, as we all watched.

"The False Prophet received credit for healing his headwound and bringing Antichrist back to life. Now he will be worshiped by the masses too. In reality, all we saw was a strong illusion. But it was strong enough that multitudes believe they had witnessed a true miracle, like we did for real, when God resurrected His Two Witnesses.

"Many who were on the fence about receiving the deceptive mark, will surely take it now. But just like one third of the angels were swept out of heaven by Lucifer's tail, one third of the resurrections we witnessed this month were deceptively fake."

Benjamin Shapiro was seated in the front row. He shook his head incredulously. "Jakob told me this would happen. He also said the Jews were about to see firsthand, that the first three and a half years that

Romanero spent protecting them, would now be followed by three and a half years of him trying to destroy them."

Calloway sighed. "Sadly, he is correct…"

Tom Dunleavey then said, "In no way did Satan, the Antichrist or the Pope usurp God or outdo Him. Whatever power was given to the Pope to heal Romanero, if indeed he was dead at all, didn't surprise the God we serve. While it surely was satanically induced, like Charles said, it only happened because the Most High God allowed it to happen."

Dick Mulrooney was also seated on a front row pew. He asked, "Are you suggesting it was a sleight of hand trick?"

Tom replied, "I don't know, Dick. All I know is that our God is sovereign. And this means nothing ever escapes His attention. Nor does anything happen apart from His complete knowledge and understanding."

Many in the sanctuary shouted, "Amen!"

Dick shook his head sadly. "I don't need any convincing that this Pope is evil, it isn't a hard stretch. But it's still difficult for me to accept that none of them were ordained by God."

Tom folded his hands on his lap. "I know how you feel. In all my years as a Catholic priest, no one defended the Papacy any more vehemently than me.

He grimaced. "But if the lineage of the Papacy truly was predicated on being the Vicars of Christ, there would have never been a bad Pope. With so much evil having been perpetrated by so many of them, how could they even broach the possibility of being infallible, when they were just as human as we are. And just as flawed.

"After I finally got saved for real, I wrestled with that very same question. It was difficult for me to accept that the man the Catholic church had elevated to a deity level was entirely manmade, and not some representation of the Disciple Peter, for whom Christ said upon that rock He would build His church.

"In no way was Christ foretelling about the Catholic church, like many of us were taught to believe. He was referring to Peter's faith in Him, not any Pope succeeding the Disciple. Did you notice Jesus didn't say He would build Peter's church? He said He would build *His* church!

"I assure you, Dick, that no Pope ever carried out their missions like the Disciple Peter, the Apostle Paul, and all others who represented Christ during the early Church years had done. We only have to look on the outside to see just how different their worlds were.

185

"Whereas every Pope got to live in worldly opulence, the Apostle Paul, and all others who followed Christ, forsook the world to advance the Kingdom of God. They denied 'self' and carried their crosses daily.

"They were humble servants who didn't seek the things of this world. They knew friendship with the world was enmity with God." Tom sighed. "Can we say that about any Pope? The answer is no. Most had become so full of themselves that they left no room for Christ.

"In that light, while none of us are the slightest bit surprised that this Pope is the head of the false, new world religion, what I've recently come to realize is that every Pope before him all had their unregenerate fingerprints all over the Papacy.

"Much like the generational curses we read about in the Bible, when it comes to the lineage of the Papacy, the curse that began with the very first Pope had carried on through every Pontiff since, before finally reaching its culmination with this Pope."

Tom paused, then asked, "How could we think otherwise when the very last Pope that the Catholic Church will ever know, has just resurrected the Antichrist of the Bible?"

Rick Krauss shouted from the third row, "Wow! That's deep, brother Tom."

Tom nodded his appreciation at him, still amazed that Rick had survived the grueling trip to Pennsylvania in the first place.

Benjamin Shapiro sighed, as he massaged his kneecaps with his two hands. "I've always had a bad feeling about the Pope. Something about him just never felt right to me."

Tom replied, "And for good reason, Benjamin. The Pope is never once mentioned scripture, not in a good way, anyway. In Revelation four, the four living creatures never stop saying, 'Holy, holy, holy is the Lord God Almighty, who was, and is, and is to come.

"We never hear four holies being proclaimed, only three. If the Pope truly was the vicar of Christ, as the entire lineage of popes have openly proclaimed throughout the centuries, wouldn't there have been a fourth 'holy' designated just for them?"

Dick scratched his scalp. "Hmm, very interesting point you make."

Tom took a small sip of water from his bottle. "Again, if all the Popes who have ever lived, were the combined 'vicars of Christ' why wasn't it recorded in the Bible, not even once?

"As we'll soon get to live with our Redeemer, for all eternity, the one thing we'll *never* hear being uttered by anyone, will be a fourth holy.

Therefore, only God the Father, Christ the Lord, and the Holy Spirit, should ever be worshiped and prayed to. No one else…"

Isaac said, "That's good stuff, brother Tom."

Tom grinned at Isaac and went on, "As one of God's creations, the Pope was born in sin just like we were, and needs Christ's forgiveness just like we do. None of them ever had the power to pardon anyone else's sins, including their own. Only Christ has that power, the very One whose power they have long since tried to usurp, I might add…

"As sinners, we have the power to forgive the trespasses of others, just like we ask of them, but only God can pardon sin.

"In that light, just like us, every pope who's ever lived and breathed on this fallen planet will either be sent to hell after the Great Judgment, or redeemed from that wretched place, by the blood of Jesus and nothing of their own doing. There is no in-between place."

"Amen to that brother, Tom!" said Tamika, sitting next to Isaac.

Charles said. "As we close the session, let me confess to you all that I don't believe Romanero was really dead. Healed, yes. Brought back to life, no. Think about it, the one who supposedly healed him is called the 'False Prophet'. Much like his title suggests, everything he does will be false, including raising Antichrist from the dead.

"God granted Satan the power to pull off this great miracle, as part of the great delusion that's taking place in these end times, plain and simple, for it is written…"

Dick thought to himself, *this is better than any Sunday mass I've ever attended in the past!*

187

33

HANS GREINHOLD RETURNED TO work, to a very warm reception from his fellow guards, most of whom he didn't know. The only two he recognized were Dietrich and Sofia. The three of them had worked at the same prison before it was destroyed. Had they been working on that fateful day; they surely would have perished along with everyone else.

The new guards stared at Hans with awestruck smiles on their faces, eager to make his acquaintance and even more eager to learn from him. His reputation for being a cold and calculating torturer was legendary.

"Welcome back!" Sofia said empathetically. "I was sorry to hear about Gretchen. She was a good woman. And to lose your three teenage children. They will surely be missed."

Hans nodded his thanks to her.

"Sorry about the loss of your leg, Captain," said Dietrich, to the man who had taught him so many useful techniques in the art of torture, which he thoroughly enjoyed inflicting on the dissidents in their torture chambers, until they were destroyed in the global quake.

Hans wanted to reply by saying, "Compared to what I did to so many of my brothers and sisters in Christ, I got off easily!" But it wasn't the right time.

A new female guard whom Hans didn't know gushed with pride. "So nice to finally meet you! Your reputation precedes you. I hope I will be highly thought of at this place someday, just like you!"

Greinhold looked away from the woman, without thanking her.

Instead of fist-bumping anyone with his free hand, or hugging them, as was his custom in the past, he limped very slowly and gingerly to his chair, his mind torturing him every step of the way.

Sofia and Dietrich shrugged their shoulders and exchanged confused glances. It was so unlike Hans to act this way. He seemed nothing like the man they knew before the global quake.

With his prosthetic leg, no one expected to see him burst through the main door with determined confident strides, eager to torture Christian dissidents, like he did in the past. They were all briefed up front and fully expected to see their comrade in this condition.

But it was as if his entire persona had been severely altered. Perhaps it was because there weren't any torture chambers at Romanero's new death camps. Everyone sent to these places went straight to the guillotine, without first losing fingers or tongues. They could already hear him saying, "This is too easy of an ending for those parasites!"

But what concerned them most was, while they still displayed the same murderous expressions on their faces that Hans was always known for—evil poured out of them like perspiration—there wasn't a trace of it to be found on Greinhold's face.

Where was the brash, foulmouthed, blood thirsty, over-the-top personality he was known for? Instead of displaying those characteristics one needed to possess to work at this place, he seemed terribly anxious.

The newer guards looked at each other, clearly disappointed by his odd behavior. And something about his softer facial features bothered them to no end. What they saw on his face sort of resembled the vermin they were being paid to exterminate.

They silently hoped that once he got back into the flow of things, his blood thirsty personality would resurface.

With his work uniform on, no one could see that he had no welts or abrasions on his tattoo-covered body. No one bothered asking if he had been attacked by those demonic locusts. They all assumed he had.

Not knowing what else to say to their leader, as Hans took his time lowering himself into his chair, the first batch of Christians were brought out to the six guillotines he was in charge of overseeing.

The half-dozen men and women under his employ quickly secured the arms and necks of the first group of dissidents in the stocks, then waited for Hans to give the command—which usually was nothing more than the nod of his head, or the flick of the wrist—but no such command was given.

After a prolonged awkward silence, Dietrich finally asked his boss, "Are you okay?"

Hans started trembling uncontrollably. He lowered his head and massaged his scalp with his left hand. "No, I'm not..." His voice was anguished. "I can no longer participate in the killing of Christians."

Dietrich glared at his mentor in astonishment. "Why is that?"

Hans tipped his tear-filled eyes up at him. "Because I recently became one myself..."

Shock and disbelief filled every face in the room—guard and prisoner alike!

Dietrich cringed, snorted laughter, then grew serious. "If this is a joke, I'm not laughing. None of us are, Hans!"

189

Save for the soft sniffling coming from some of the believers who were about to be put to death, the room became eerily silent, still.

All prisoners at this place were mindful of this man's reputation as a coldblooded killer. All had been warned about his sadistic tendencies toward his detainees, which easily dwarfed that of his co-workers.

Now that Hans was back on the job, they expected their collective conditions to worsen considerably. They silently praised God for rescuing this once wretched man. Truly, it was a miracle!

Hands trembling and knees wobbling, Hans took a few deep breaths, then recited aloud the very first Bible verse he had ever memorized, which thanks to Hana Patel, was Romans 1:16. "For I am not ashamed of the Gospel, because it is the power of God that brings salvation to everyone who believes: first to the Jew, then to the Gentile!"

He followed it up by declaring, "I can't thank Hana Patel enough for posting that verse online a few months ago. I was already saved when she made her bold proclamation, praise Jesus, but I was still living in fear and never shared my faith with anyone.

"For the first time in my life, after I got saved, I was turned into a coward. God used that woman to give me the strength to rise above my fear, to make this declaration now," he said softly, fully mindful of the repercussions of his declaration, and what would soon become of him.

In short, he knew there could be no turning back now.

Using his crutches as leverage, Hans slowly rose from the chair he was seated on and started removing his work uniform, down to his underwear. If his brothers and sisters weren't allowed to wear clothing, neither would he!

This caused global prison camera #1368 to suddenly become a point of interest, for the many on the planet who enjoyed scrolling through the more than 10,000 cameras livestreaming everything that happened at Romanero's death camps.

Stuck in their homes all this time with nothing else to do, watching beheadings on their phone screens had long since become part of their daily activities, as they eagerly anticipated receiving the mark.

They were suddenly curious to know why this prison guard was undressing in front of the prisoners. Viewers started texting friends, neighbors, and family members, urging them to view it for themselves.

In no time, *#camera1368* had more than 300,000 viewers, and counting!

Prior to the global quake, before all former prisons were demolished, this usually happened when dissidents were in the process of having fingers removed or tongues cut out.

But this was becoming equally interesting…

The other reason Hans stripped all the way down was that he wanted everyone to see that he had no lingering welts or abrasions on his body, from the five months the planet had been under assault from those hideous beings.

Hans flashed an anxious grin over at the prisoners, then stretched out his left arm as far as it would go, using his right hand to grip his cane, as he did a slow 360. "Here's proof that I was saved before God sent the five-month plague to our planet. Not a single mark or abrasion on my body! If God can save someone as wretched as me, He can save anyone!"

The prisoners tried looking up at him, but it was difficult with their heads in the stocks.

Hans glanced up at the camera mounted on one of the walls. He wanted everyone watching online, including his fellow Christ followers living in fear, to hear his words. His eyes became moist with tears. "Listen to me very carefully, even if you were stung by them, it's not too late to escape the coming judgment by trusting in Jesus. Just like God's angelic messenger keeps declaring, anyone who takes the mark will be forever doomed! Please take this warning seriously! Repent of your sins and trust in Christ for your salvation, and not Romanero."

Many who knew Hans, including his co-workers watching at home, couldn't believe their eyes and ears. "Hans? It can't be!"

Hans very calmly put his free hand out in surrender, and said to his coworkers, "No need to detain me, I'll come freely to you. My only wish is that you'll let me be the next to be beheaded. If you take me into custody and torture me the way I used to torture my brothers and sisters," he said, his voice cracking, "I won't, under any circumstances, renounce my faith in Christ, no matter what you do to me."

He glanced back up at camera #1368. "Nor will I take the mark of the beast. Never! Jesus is my Lord and Savior, and I am not ashamed!"

Every prisoner who heard his declaration joyously shouted, "Amen", not caring if they were beaten for their insubordination. They wouldn't be alive soon anyway, at least not physically!

The six guards under his employ stared at each other in stunned silence. No one knew what to say or do in response to his outlandish

191

comment, until Sofia received a text message from her superior. *Silence him now! This man needs to be made an example of. Off with his head!*

The female guard showed her colleagues the text message, just as camera #1368 had surpassed more than 500,000 viewers.

Two guards wasted no time subduing their now-former boss, without the slightest struggle from him. "Looks like you got your wish, after all."

With all six guillotines presently occupied, one of the detainees had to first be removed, so Hans could take his place. They quickly secured his hands and neck in the stockades.

Now mere moments away from leaving this planet, Hans felt more despicable than even the thief on the cross, not the one that Christ said would be with Him that day in Paradise, but the other one who had mocked Messiah until his last dying breath.

If anyone felt condemned in his trespasses and unworthy of God's salvation, it was Greinhold. But now that he finally understood the true essence of the Gospel—that Christ died even for filthy sinners like him, and he had been redeemed by His blood, the difference between the two men was eternal.

Whereas that man's soul was transferred to perdition on the very day that Christ was crucified, Hans was about to be forever comforted by his Lord and Savior. He couldn't fathom the depth of God's love that was being shown to him, a vile sinner of the worst kind!

Just like with the Apostle Paul, this "guilt" thorn in his side that kept torturing him even post-salvation, wouldn't follow him into Paradise.

And that was because it wasn't his sinful hold on Christ that had secured his salvation, but Christ's sinless hold on him. Because of Christ, Hans had absolute confidence that his soul had been made right with God, which meant his Maker had forgiven every despicable sin he had ever committed in life, including the diabolical atrocities he had committed on His own children.

Before the order was given for the blood-stained sharpened blades to drop down on their victims' necks, six feet below, his former co-workers paused to see if the man who had taken so much pleasure in torturing and killing the very vermin that he was now willing to die with, could give a logical explanation as to what had caused the big change in him.

With his head and hands secured in the stocks, they could only shake their heads in disbelief, as Hans wept tears of unbridled joy.

His soon-to-be former co-workers thought his tears represented regret for making such a foolish decision, a surefire sign that he had contracted the same mental illness that all prisoners at this place had, but nothing could be farther from the truth.

Greinhold's hands trembled violently in the tightly secured stocks, but his soul rejoiced, knowing beyond a shadow of a doubt he would soon leave this wretched world behind, and be forever comforted in the loving arms of his Savior. It was too much to take in all at once.

Finally, he said, "Now that my life journey's about to come to an end, I want to publicly thank You, Lord, for forgiving the many grotesque sins I have committed against You, and against so many of my brothers and sisters whom I look forward to seeing this day in Paradise."

The five dissidents in the stockades with him still trembled in fear, knowing their heads would soon be severed from their bodies, but it was as if God was using this man to quiet their nerves a bit, and calm their weary souls, comforting all of them greatly.

Hans' weeping intensified. "I can't think of one good thing I ever did in my entire life before my conversion. Jesus knew this, yet He still died for me! For those of you who are seized by guilt and constant nightmares, and feel there is no hope for you, let my words comfort and speak to you, especially my fellow coworkers who may be living in hiding. May the guilt you feel be erased as you focus on God's grace and His love and His forgiveness, and not your own wretchedness."

Head down—he had no choice—tears fell from his eyes to the ground like projectiles. Everyone watching him on camera saw them.

Camera #1368 had trended so quickly that even Romanero was informed of what was going on. He shouted at the monitor, "Enough! More than a million viewers are watching him make a fool of himself! Kill him now!"

In between loud sniffles, Hans said, in a voice that was sorrowful, repentant, and grateful, "Thank You, Lord, for welcoming this beggar into Your King..."

Before Greinhold could even finish making his final declaration on this side of eternity, the blade was dropped and his head was severed from the rest of his body, along with two of his brothers and three of his sisters in Christ, whose names he didn't know.

As the six of them were transported to Heaven, simultaneously, in the blink of an eye, to be forever comforted in the arms of Jesus, Hans already felt a special closeness to them that he had never felt before with any other human beings. It was an eternal closeness.

Totally unaware of this, the prison guards were so befuddled by what had just transpired before their very eyes, disappointed even, that they didn't know what to say to one another.

Dietrich dropped his head sadly, looking like he was on the losing team in the World Cup. *What happened to my captain?*

As they removed the six headless corpses from the stockades and tossed the severed heads into a pile, which would increase by a factor of a thousand this day, only to be repeated every day until the last Christian heretic made his or her way to their guillotines, all were struck with a single thought: Was the mental illness that Hans had recently developed transmittable?

If it was, they hoped they wouldn't be the next ones to catch it...

34

AFTER WHAT HANS GREINHOLD, Benjamin Shapiro and Hana Patel all did to Salvador Romanero, with so many watching, the pressure to locate and silence dissidents was at an all-time high.

Peculiarly, even one week later, Romanero had never ordered the Greinhold video to be taken offline, even with millions watching it every day. Now that the mark was being administered globally, he felt no need to. Soon, he would know for sure who was who.

Like countless millions of others on the planet, Megan McCallister and Rachel Stein were eager to receive the mark. But since they were still too fearful to go outdoors, they made an appointment to have it administered at their apartment, in Concordville, Pennsylvania.

It took a week, but local authorities finally came knocking on their door at the crack of dawn. Since Zachary wouldn't be receiving the mark at this time, they wouldn't bother waking their son, who was still asleep in his crib.

Megan and Rachel grinned excitedly upon seeing the mark proudly displayed on the two officers' bodies. The male officer had it displayed on his forehead, while the female had it displayed on her right hand.

But the two law enforcement officials were also there for another reason, which had nothing to do with administering the mark. Namely, they wanted the two recipients to hear part of a surveillance conversation that had recently been recorded at a location, in nearby Chadds Ford.

What made this location so significant was that it housed hundreds of Christian dissidents, perhaps even thousands, including many children. It was also believed that some very well-known individuals resided there, chief among them, Jefferson Danforth, whom Salvador Romanero never thought was dead to begin with.

But they weren't about to share this tidbit of information with the two women. Everything pertaining to the "Montpelier Project" was being handled with kid gloves on. With all 500 locations on the strike list, they were ordered under no circumstances to share information with anyone, especially since they knew beyond certainty that Jefferson Danforth was residing at the Chadds Ford hideout, with his new wife, Amy.

Their hope for now was that the two recipients would be able to positively identify Dick Mulrooney's voice.

Even before Romanero had access to the microfliers, thanks to their encounter in New York City, three years ago, when Brian Mulrooney and Charles Calloway had smuggled Tamika Moseley out of the city, before ultimately bringing her to Chadds Ford, they already had all three of their voices stored in the universal voice recognition system.

They weren't the slightest bit concerned about the crimes Moseley had committed back then. What mattered most was apprehending her for the even more serious crime of being a Christian dissident.

Tom Dunleavey's voice was also stored in the system, initially from past masses he had preached before leaving the Catholic church.

They also had Clayton Holmes and Travis Hartings identified as the leaders of the rogue defiant group. They had originally captured their voices on the LSAR website.

While the two men were never seen or heard on the Chadds Ford property, their voices were easily identified from the many messages the two had sent to their many so-called safe houses globally.

When the microfliers snatched their voices out of thin air, at the Chadds Ford hideout, it was easy for law enforcement to connect the dots.

The female officer asked Megan and Rachel, "Okay, tell us again about your belief that Brian Mulrooney's father is living in the vicinity?"

Megan explained, "Shortly after the global quake, Dick came to Pennsylvania hoping to find his wife and steal her away from Brian. He even stayed with us a few nights. At that time, he was fully determined to find out where they were living. All he wanted was Sarah back. After that, he didn't care what happened to his son."

Megan frowned. "Brian did so much damage and hurt so many people. He was my sister's boyfriend for more than five years, before he suddenly dumped her for that other woman," she scoffed. "His father betrayed us just like Brian betrayed my sister."

"How so?" the female officer asked, already mindful of her sister Renate's suicide, which was a direct result of Brian and Jacquelyn getting married.

Megan glanced up at the ceiling, then gasped, "We woke one morning, to find a letter he wrote apologizing for leaving so abruptly. He said he had to go back to New York, but if we ever found Brian's hiding place, he would hurry back to Pennsylvania."

The female officer asked, "Do you still have the letter?"

"I threw it away," Megan lied. There wasn't a chance she would let them read it. If they did, they would discover how Dick had refused her seductive advances, after she had begged him to impregnate her, and how he said he was going back to New York, to prevent from falling into temptation with her. In her mind, it was none of their business. Nor was it relevant to the conversation. It would remain stuffed inside her top bedroom drawer. "We haven't heard a word from him since."

"Why do you think that is?" the male officer pressed on.

Megan sighed. "One reason is he never gave us the money he had promised us. We took that man at his word and look where it led us! We feel betrayed by him, used! Turns out he was just like his son after all."

Without bothering to ask the amount, it wasn't important at this juncture, the male officer pressed on, "And the second reason?"

Rachel snorted frustration. "We tried telling you people so many times on the phone! We even told you about his obsession with that convenience store on two-oh-two, not to mention that he disconnected his phone a month or so after he left us high and dry, but nothing was ever done about it. Geez, it's been three years now!"

Megan added, "Even before he came here, we told you our belief that Brian and Jacquelyn Mulrooney were living somewhere in the area. They are the reason we came here in the first place. So, why are you suddenly so willing to help us, after we tried getting your attention all this time?"

The officers exchanged unpleasant glances. "Let me assure you both that your inquiries haven't fallen on deaf ears. We want to find them just as badly as you."

"Oh yeah, why's that?" Rachel asked the male officer.

"Because we also believe they're staying in the area. And so, I ask, why do you think Dick disconnected his phone?"

Rachel stared at her fingernails. They were badly chipped and in desperate need of being manicured. Once the money started rolling in again, it was at the top of her list of things to do. "One possible factor is he discovered his son's and wife's whereabouts, joined their cult, and went into hiding with them even if only to win Sarah back."

Megan added, "Dick was a desperate man. In the few days he was here, he spent each waking moment out searching for her."

The male officer nodded at his female counterpart. It was time. "If we play something for you, do you think you could identify whether or not it's Dick Mulrooney's voice?"

197

Megan and Rachel looked at each other, before Megan answered, "I think so…"

Without saying another word, the female officer pushed play on her police issued SAT phone. Two voices were heard talking among themselves, a male and a female. It was a tearful, intimate embrace.

When it was finished, the man asked, "Does the voice sound familiar to either of you?"

The two women stiffened on the couch, then nodded at him.

"That's him alright!" Megan said, another burst of betrayal rising in her voice.

The male officer couldn't ignore the hatred he saw in her eyes toward that man. He left it alone for now, and jotted notes onto a legal pad. "You're one hundred percent sure of it?"

"When did you record it?" asked Rachel.

"A few weeks ago," came his reply.

Megan asked, "So you know where he is?"

"I'm not at liberty to share that with you at this time," said the male officer with a shrug. "But what I can say is, if it is him, it confirms your suspicion, and ours, that he has defected to the other side."

Megan folded her arms over her chest and glared at the man; her head turned one way then the next. "Why can't you tell us where he is?"

"We're still in the process of linking many dissident locations, before making our move. Besides, it's also for your overall protection."

Rachel threw her hands in the air in mock protest, and snorted frustration. "Oh yeah, how's that?"

The female officer answered this time, "We have reason to believe they will defend themselves to the death, if need be. I'd hate to see either of you go there, only to be killed before receiving your reward money."

Megan kept protesting, "I don't get it, if you know where they are, why don't you arrest them now, before they try escaping?"

The male officer nodded that he understood their dilemma. "I assure you if that happens," he said very calmly, "we'll be all over them."

Rachel still wasn't convinced. "We're following all the rules. We're happy to receive the Mark. But we really need this money," she said, totally exasperated. "We're strapped for cash!"

Aren't we all! he thought, keeping it to himself. "Rest assured, ladies, as soon as the order's been given from the top, now that you're about to receive the Mark, once they've been captured, the money will be credited to your account with the simple push of a button."

Megan desperately blurted out, "We also believe Tamika Moseley and Charles Calloway are living there!"

The female officer glanced over at her male counterpart, before her eyes volleyed back to Megan, ever so suspiciously. "You know them?"

Megan nodded. "They were part of Brian Mulrooney's wedding in Michigan." She lowered her head sadly. "He's the reason my sister killed herself."

The two officers nodded empathetically again, already knowing that. "We'll do all we can to make sure you're compensated for them as well. That's all we need for now, unless you have more questions."

The married couple glanced at each other. Satisfied that all their questions had been answered, they nodded their thanks gratefully.

"We're good for now..." Megan said on behalf of herself and Rachel.

The female officer smiled warmly. "Thanks for your help, ladies. You can receive the mark now..."

Megan and Rachel both chose to receive the mark on their right hands. They didn't want it on their foreheads. It would be too tacky.

They livestreamed the process on their social media accounts, for all to see. Both were giddy with laughter. Part of their excitement came from the potential $6K they stood to earn, when the six dissidents they had identified were apprehended.

They were already spending the money in their minds...

The glow on their faces indicated to their online friends that, for the first time in a very long time, things were finally looking up for them. Their hope, as they shared in Megan's and Rachel's happiness, was that things would quickly improve for them as well.

Some of their followers had already received the mark. The rest of them were scheduled to receive it in the coming days.

Tragically for all of them, by the time they realized that the end result of taking the mark on their bodies meant that their souls would be forever doomed, it would be too late...

35

WHEN HANA AND CRISTIANA Patel arrived at the Singapore safe house, Hana was both shocked and a little dismayed to discover that it was really a boathouse, which was owned by a woman named Fong.

Yasamin Dabiri had arrived 20 minutes earlier, with her son, Navid.

The two fugitives clung to each other for dear life, sobbing tears of joy and relief. So much had happened since they last saw each other two years ago, most of it bad.

When they released their grips, Hana caught Yasamin staring at her. "I know, I look nothing like when we first met, right?"

Yasamin put her hands on her much thinner hips, now that the disguise was off. "I'll admit that it took a second or two to adjust to your spiked hair and your attire. But at least you look younger than you did last time. Wait until you see me in the morning disguised as a grandmother! I just removed my costume before you arrived."

The way Yasamin said it caused Hana to burst out in laughter, for the first time in too long to remember. "Finally, we can talk face to face, without the fear of being spied on!"

Yasamin grinned from ear to ear. Her big black eyes were fully aglow for the first time in what seemed like forever. "I've been waiting for this day for a very long time. I can't tell you how many times I was bored out of my mind on the way here, with no phone, no Wi-Fi, and no one to talk to. The only time I ever felt free to speak my mind with you since you left Dubai, was on the VPN conference call we had with the *ETSM* leaders."

Hana replied, "I know. But this is so much better because now we can talk face-to-face, without any distractions…"

Yasamin said, "Just hope we can survive fifty straight days and nights at sea, with two young kids. It oftentimes felt like the walls were closing in on me on the way here. How much more claustrophobic will I feel when we're trapped in a tiny compartment for seven weeks instead of two?"

Hana couldn't stop yawning. It had been a long first leg of the journey. "I know what you mean. Although I was on a boat with three other Christians, and I had a little more freedom than you, two weeks was still more than enough for me!"

Yasamin sighed. "At least we'll have each other to lean on, right?"

Hana licked her lips which were chapped from overexposure to the salty sea air. Her face was usually covered with a ski mask while out at sea, but her lips were always exposed to the elements. "Right!"

Fong had waited for Hana to arrive before introducing herself to the two fugitive women. "When our safe house was destroyed by the flood waters that ravaged so much of our small country, hundreds of thousands of our citizens were killed, including dozens of our own residents.

"I inherited this hundred-foot yacht from my late father. I was surprised it survived the tsunami waves, even if just barely. It sustained extensive damage from bow to stern, but at least it didn't sink like so many other boats and ships in Singapore had, praise God."

Fong shook her head sadly. "But even before that horrific day, mostly due to a lack of use, the engines barely started. And the hull was covered with barnacles. Still is, in fact. Back in the day, when my father was still alive, he spent more than two hundred thousand dollars a year maintaining the vessel. Those days are long gone. It may not be the best place to hide, but we had no other options at our disposal. If there's one good thing about the marina being obliterated, it's that I no longer pay monthly slip fees..."

Fong motioned with her left hand, as her eyes surveyed the main cabin. "As you can see, every inch of space of this once-luxurious ship is being used for housing exiled believers."

Hana asked her, "Does anyone ever disembark?"

"No, never," came the reply, with a prolonged sigh. "It's just too risky. All it would take is for one of us to be spotted to bring the rest of us down."

Hana and Yasamin both nodded that they understood.

"As you might imagine, life on board the ship is miserable most days. It's difficult living in such crammed living conditions, with meager daily food rations. We don't have much to live for. We're all eager to leave this cruel and heartless planet and be with Jesus...."

After being out at sea all this time, the two women understood Fong perfectly well. As much as they had looked forward to being on dry land for a change, there wasn't a chance that Hana and Yasamin would complain about it. They were just grateful to still be free of the enemy.

At least by being on the boat, they wouldn't encounter anyone on dry land proudly displaying the mark on their right hands or foreheads, scanning everyone within their sight, with their mobile devices, hoping to get paid for their efforts.

201

Donald Johnson joined Hana and Yasamin after a quick shower. "So, you're the global troublemaker! Or should I address you as the First Lady of childbirth, part two!" He made no mention of how different she looked. There was no need to. He understood completely.

Hana grinned shyly at him, then lowered her head. "I suppose so."

Donald gave Hana a comforting hug, and kissed Cristiana on the forehead. "It's an honor to finally meet you both."

Hana said, "Thanks for everything you're doing for us." Cristiana was too tired to reply. She just wanted to sleep. Navid was already asleep.

Donald grinned at her. "It's my pleasure. Brian and Jacquelyn are so excited to meet you."

Hana tipped her eyes up at him. "Brian and Jacquelyn?"

Donald winced at his own carelessness. "That's right, you know them as Brad and Joan Henricksen!" *She'll know soon enough anyway*, he thought, mentally forgiving himself.

Hana yawned into her right fist. "So, that's their real names…"

Donald nodded. "By the way, I only used half of the supplies that were allotted to me on the long voyage. I felt queasy most days and didn't feel like eating. So, you should have plenty of food, water, medicines, Dramamine, and plenty of batteries for the lamps, to survive the long passage to the States."

Yasamin said, "What I would have done for Dramamine on the first leg of the trip!"

"Dramamine or not," Hana snorted, "I'm not looking forward to being confined at sea for nearly two months this time!"

Donald chuckled at her comment. "It wasn't always easy. But truth be told, I didn't mind the solitude most of the time. But when I did get lonely, those were the loneliest moments of my life. Each time my mind was free to wander, it would race back to my wife and son, and my extended family of believers in Pennsylvania."

He sighed. "I always wondered if they were still safe, and whether or not I was doing the right thing by leaving them. The only thing that ever helped me rise above the frequent loneliness, was reading the Bible and praying to God."

"You and me both!" Yasamin said in reply.

Hana asked Donald, "So, what's the plan from here?"

"In the morning, you'll be met by a young man named Vishnu, who will help you board the container ship. He will look after you whenever he can, like he did for me on the long passage here. He's a good man and a true brother in the faith. He truly loves the Lord. But since he will be the only other believer on board, you should always keep your guards up."

Yasamin said, "We will."

Donald added, "After the four of you set sail to the States, I'll board a smaller vessel for the Philippines. I just pray we'll be successful on our journeys, ladies, and that we'll see each other again in the States. It would be nice to see our kids playing together someday soon."

Yasamin asked, "How many children do you have, Donald?"

With an endearing expression on his face, he said, "One, a son named Luke. He just turned one."

Yasamin's eyes lit up at the thought of it. It gave her something else to cling to in these perilous times.

Donald went on, "Now that the mark's available, Vishnu will get off the ship with you in Jacksonville, and stay at a safe house in Florida, before traveling with you to Pennsylvania."

"Okay," Hana said, glancing at Yasamin who nodded agreement.

"Just hope I'm not too far behind you…" The original plan was that Donald would travel back to the states with Vishnu on his next voyage to Singapore. But with the mark now available, Uddin's next trip to the States would be his last.

Donald was grateful that the Lord had led them to Sergei Ivanov, and that the man from Russia was willing to use his 30-foot motorized sailboat to take him to the Philippines, to hopefully rescue Analyn, and bring her back to the States.

Johnson's mood quickly soured when he turned on his SAT phone, which hadn't been used in seven weeks. Now that it was charged, he wanted to inform his wife that he had arrived in Singapore. She knew not to message him under any circumstances.

He had two unread messages from Clayton Holmes, which were sent two months ago. He clicked on the one that said READ FIRST. It was short and to the point. *Do not open the other message without earbuds on!* Johnson reached for his earbuds and listened to the terrifying message. A large dose of fear shot through him.

Hana and Yasamin saw the frightened expression on his face. Whatever he was listening to, it wasn't good.

Donald gulped hard, then put his finger up to his mouth. In a soft whisper, he warned somberly, "There's a strong possibility that our safe houses are being spied on with the use of microfliers…"

The two women glanced at each other and shrugged their shoulders, not knowing what they were. Then again, not even Johnson knew.

After they both listened to the message for themselves, Donald took turns whispering in their ears, "We need to be careful about everything we say from now on, even here on this boat."

He tried shielding the fear he felt by saying, "The good news is, once the two of you are in the bowels of the cargo ship, you should be able to talk freely among yourselves. I seriously doubt there will be microfliers down there. Still, always be careful. Understood?"

Hana and Yasamin both nodded that they did.

But Donald had a sinking feeling that it was already too late, that the three of them had unknowingly said too much. If the enemy was mindful of this hiding place, and they had homed in on the conversation, death would be a certainty for everyone living at this safe house...

Johnson pushed that dreadfully morbid thought as far from his mind as it would go, then let everyone else on the ship listen to Clayton's alarming message, then cautioned that it would be best if they maintained a strict code of silence for the time being.

Before calling it a night, Donald sent another secure text message to Analyn Tibayan. *I'm in Singapore. Something bad has happened. All I can say for now is, five days from now, I want you to go to the place I used to take you for ice cream, the place you said was destroyed in the tsunami when we spoke on the phone. You know the place!*

Be there at sunset. If I'm not there, keep going back there every day until I finally arrive. If I'm not there within two weeks, chances are good I was captured, and I won't be coming. For now, we must avoid all contact. I'll explain everything later. I've come a long way for you. Please be there. I'll see you when I see you. Lord willing, that is...

36

AT ONE A.M., HANA and Yasamin were rustled from their sleep three hours earlier than expected. "It's time to leave," Fong said softly, quietly. Now that they were potentially being spied on, she silently feared their safe boat wouldn't be in existence very much longer.

Hana squinted in the darkness, surprised by this wakeup call of sorts. "I thought we were leaving at 5 a.m.?" She had finally drifted off to sleep roughly an hour ago, after spending most of the night taking care of her sick daughter, who was running a high fever.

In a soft whisper, Fong explained, "After hearing Clayton's message, we've decided to move it up to now. Not only will there be far less people at the dock now, but we've been blessed with foggy skies.

"I know you're exhausted, but it must be this way. Sorry. Once you're on board the container ship, you'll have plenty of time to sleep. But for now, you have thirty minutes to get ready…"

Yasamin got up off the bed, and did a few stretches, before beginning the tedious process of putting on her grandmother's disguise, already dreading the thought of being detained again in the belly of a massive cargo ship. Cristiana and Navid lay sleeping peacefully, totally unaware of what was going on.

Thirty minutes later, Fong went below deck to notify them that Vishnu Uddin was outside waiting to receive them, in a smaller boat that would take them straight to the container ship.

Without formally greeting his passengers—that would hopefully come later—the tall, dark skinned, 43-year-old man from Bangladesh warned, "We must hurry!"

The five stowaways quickly lowered themselves on board Sergei Ivanov's 30-foot sailboat. The new fellow believer in the faith, who had emigrated to Thailand from Russia, would take Vishnu, and the two women and their children to the cargo ship.

Donald Johnson would remain on board with him, as the two would set sail to the Philippines.

Uddin and Ivanov had both been briefed on the "microflier" situation, so they weren't surprised to see their crestfallen faces, as they assisted the women and children down onto the boat.

Vishnu didn't look much better himself, after being told his name had been dropped into the conversation the night before. His paranoia was heightened to all time levels.

Uddin thought to give the two grownup stowaways uniforms to put on, like he did with Donald Johnson, but since they had the two youngsters with them, it would have been pointless.

He studied their disguises very carefully. At first glance, it looked like Yasamin was traveling with her three grandchildren. There was nothing about her features that might suggest to him that she was wearing a disguise.

Whoever had helped transform her into an elderly woman, had done a masterful job. Having seen her image so many times on TV, he knew she looked nothing like the person seated across from him now.

Vishnu couldn't say the same about Hana's disguise. While she certainly looked like the punk rocker teenage boy she was trying to project to the outside world, upon closer inspection, even shrouded in the fog, she started looking more like a female rocker to him than a male one.

In short, her disguise was nowhere near as believable as Yasamin's.

Vishnu silently prayed it wouldn't become a problem at some point along the way. At any rate, after the bold statement Hana had made—with millions watching—before escaping the clutches of the Antichrist of the Bible, he felt honored just being in her presence, Yasamin's too! It was evident in his overall demeanor.

When they reached the container ship, Vishnu checked his smart watch to make sure the GPS was disabled, so no one on board the ship would be able to track him along the way, and force him to explain why he was spending so much time at that particular part of the vessel.

Fully mindful of the gargantuan risk he was taking, his heart rate was jacked so high, he was surprised he was still able to focus on the task at hand. If caught, how could he possibly justify to his bosses that they would be harboring two of the world's most wanted women on their ship, of all people? The answer was obvious: he couldn't.

Perspiration formed on his forehead, as his eyes darted left and right. Seeing that the coast was clear, he said, "Follow me!"

The two women shivered at his command, then obeyed.

"Protect us, Lord!" Hana said. "And please silence our children until we're in the room."

"Amen," said Yasamin in reply.

Vishnu hurried the four stowaways on board the ship at the lowest possible entry point, quickly leading them down to the bottom deck.

Much like he had done with Donald, he breathed a huge sigh of relief upon reaching the converted stockroom that had been changed into a living space of sorts, for his sisters in Christ to occupy for the next 50 days or so.

Satisfied that no one had spotted them, he dragged a sleeve across his sweaty brow, opened the steel door and hurried them inside, quickly closing the door behind him. "Here we are, my dear sisters," he said, "your new home for the next seven weeks."

Hana and Yasamin let their eyes drink in their newly enclosed environment and could only sigh.

Yasamin tried to remain upbeat. She bit her lower lip. "At least it's bigger than the last room I stayed in."

Cristiana wasted no time dropping onto the hard steel floor and fingering through one of the coloring books she had seriously marked up on the first leg of the journey, searching for a clean page to color on next, as Navid lay sleeping on a thin mattress on one of the steel-frame beds.

The kids didn't know it yet, but the two weeks they had just spent at sea for the first leg of the journey, were a mere preparation for the 50-day passage on which they were about to embark to America.

Despite the fear of knowing what getting caught meant, a tinge of excitement ran through Vishnu's tall and lanky body, that he hadn't felt in months. Part of the reason for this was that he was finally living out the name his parents had given him at birth—Vishnu meant "Protector".

His surname was common in many South Asian and Middle Eastern Muslim countries and was derived from the Arabic words "Ud", meaning "of", and "din", meaning "faith". For his family, it meant faith in Islam. It no longer meant that to Vishnu.

While he very much felt like he was protecting Donald Johnson on his long passage across the globe, it couldn't compare to how he felt now that he was protecting the two women on Salvador Romanero's Top 10 Most Wanted list.

The very thought caused his black eyes to blaze nearly as much as the battery-operated lamp he was carrying. Even so, he was determined to keep his enthusiasm in check. "There's a second room you can use if you like. Donald slept in this room and used the other one as a bathroom. But do with them what you want."

Seeing both women hugging themselves to keep warm, he assured them, "Once the engines are turned on, you will no longer be cold. If it gets too hot, turn on those fans," he said, pointing up to them, "to suck in more air and oxygen from the outside. If you need to air it out, you can also open those vents atop the converted stockroom containers.

"The reason for the steel screens covering them is that we have a serious rodent infestation on the ship, especially down here on the bottom deck. I'm a little surprised we didn't see a few rats already."

When Hana and Yasamin both gulped hard at the same time, Vishnu left out the part about the rodent problem worsening since the tsunami. They were already terrified enough by his creepy warning.

He went on, "So long as you don't leave your doors open, you shouldn't find them in your bins. To the best of my knowledge, these rooms are virtually soundproof. So, if your children start crying or if they get too loud, you should close the vents immediately. The last thing we'll need is the loud sound of crying children echoing throughout the ship."

The joy on his face was replaced with a pained expression. "Then again, just hearing female voices would surely arouse suspicion in anyone hearing it. Sorry to have to tell you this, but I must warn that since I'm the only male crew member on this ship who professes faith in Christ, there's no telling what the others might do if they ever discover that we have two female stowaways on board."

Vishnu paused, seeing them both shrinking in fear. "Especially if they become aware of your true identities, which wouldn't be too difficult since you're both famous. Even though I'm responsible for this part of the ship, others may occasionally come down here for various reasons. If anyone finds you…" He paused, then added, "Let's just pray for God's protection in this matter."

Yasamin had wrestled with these very same thoughts on the voyage from Dubai, but just hearing this man say it petrified her even more. She gasped. "I should have dressed like an elderly man instead…"

Vishnu breathed loudly through his nose, then grimaced. "Truth be told, it wouldn't matter. Once your disguises were stripped off, and your true identities were revealed, before even thinking of turning you in for the huge reward they would receive, I shudder to think about what they would do to you before handing you over to the authorities."

Both women thought about the atrocities that were being perpetrated against their sisters in the faith, in Romanero's death camps. They prayed it wouldn't happen to them on this container ship.

Vishnu frowned, then wiped more nervous perspiration from his brow, sensing what they were thinking. "This is the danger I face for harboring two attractive women on a huge container ship full of unconverted men, who won't be with a woman for many weeks to come. This was something I didn't have to worry about with Donald."

Seeing more fear creeping onto their faces, he switched gears again. "The good news is that no one bothered brother Donald on the way to Singapore. Even so, I highly recommend that you always keep these doors locked from the inside, so no one on the outside can gain access if they hear voices or any other unusual activity, like kids screaming."

After they both nodded in agreement with him, he went on, "Those buckets over there should be used as makeshift toilets. There's one for each of you. Are your children potty trained?"

Hana said, "For the most part, yes. But Cristiana wears a diaper to sleep at night."

Yasamin said, "Navid too…"

"I'll make sure to bring two more buckets tomorrow for the kids to share. I'll also dispose of their soiled diapers. If you have to relief yourself, or if you feel nauseous or seasick, use them. Sorry, but given the circumstances, it's the best I can do for you …"

The looks on their faces conveyed to Vishnu that there was no need to apologize to them for anything. If anyone should be apologizing, it was them, for potentially putting his life in danger.

Yasamin didn't need to hear this. She had already been through it, and she knew the routine full well. But not Hana. Everyone on the fishing vessel on which she and Cristiana had sailed to Singapore were believers. So they had full access to the bathroom along with the rest of the boat.

Uddin went on, "It won't always be smooth sailing. It will get rough at times, so you may want to make sure the lids on the buckets are always fastened tightly, to avoid unnecessary messes."

Once again, neither woman had to be told this, but they nevertheless let him finish his spiel.

"I'll collect the buckets from you as often as I can, plus bring fresh buckets of water for bathing and washing your clothes. But whatever you do, do not attempt to drink it. It will surely make you sick. Thankfully, Donald left plenty of bottled water for you to drink."

Vishnu paused when he thought he heard something. When the sound of footsteps drifted away from them, he went on, "Don't be alarmed if I'm unable to check on you for the remainder of the day. The first and last days are always the busiest for the crew. But if it lasts longer than two days, it could spell trouble for us.

"Whenever I'm able to check on you, I'll knock on the door three times, pause a moment, knock two more times, pause again then knock four more times. That's how you'll know it's me. Understood?"

The two women nodded that they did.

Vishnu grinned at them nervously. "If you're wondering why I chose that combination, it reminds me of Romans three, verse twenty-four. But to best understand verse twenty-four, it must be combined with verse twenty-three."

Hana glanced at Yasamin, who shrugged her shoulders.

Vishnu chuckled to himself. Unlike Donald Johnson, his two sisters were newer to the faith and, therefore, newer to the scriptures. He recited it for them, "'For all have sinned and fall short of the glory of God, and all are justified freely by his grace through the redemption that came by Christ Jesus.'"

Vishnu grinned at them again. "Paul didn't say some have sinned, he said all! Only those who understand the first part, that they are sinners in need of God's redemption, can ever be freely justified by His grace."

Hana and Yasamin both said, "Amen" at the same time.

Vishnu surveyed the room to make sure he didn't forget to tell them anything. Satisfied that he hadn't, he said, "The only time I'll padlock your bins on the outside will be if I ever sense danger. Other than that, they will remain unlocked so you can go from one room to the next whenever you need to."

Yasamin asked, "Will we ever get to go outside for fresh air? I ask because I never got to on the way here. I felt claustrophobic being trapped in the room the whole time."

Vishnu nodded at her compassionately. "I'll do my best to make it happen, but it will have to be at night, much like I did with Donald when most of my crew mates were sleeping."

"I understand," came the reply, with a sigh.

Vishnu glanced at his smart watch. "I should go now. But I promise to check on you whenever I can, and bring whatever food and water I can manage to sneak away from the kitchen, starting tomorrow. If, by chance, I can't do that, Donald left you plenty of food to hold you over."

"Thanks for everything you're doing for us, Vishnu," said Hana, gratefully. "We know you're taking a huge risk."

"It's my honor and great pleasure, ladies!" he said, meaning it. "I know you're frightened after hearing the message on Donald's phone. But let me comfort you both with these words that he said to me on the way here, 'Keep fighting the Good fight. Pray for me as I pray for you. God is with us!'"

The way Vishnu said it so tenderly, so endearingly, forced tears from their eyes. The smile on his face reminded both women that their smiles had vanished long ago.

Yasamin said, "Thanks, Vishnu. We will surely pray for you all throughout the day, until we arrive in America..."

Vishnu grinned from ear to ear, fully exposing his crooked teeth. "Likewise, my dear sisters. I know it will be difficult being at sea for so long with two young children, but try to make the best of it..."

Yasamin sighed, then hugged herself a little more tightly to cut off the chill pressing through her coat. "We'll do our best."

Vishnu hugged his two sisters in Christ, then left them, so he could take a three-hour nap before roll call...

Yasamin closed the massive steel door, locked it on the inside, and took her time removing her bothersome disguise.

Dressed as a teenage boy, there wasn't much for Hana to do. She hung the piece of paper on the wall, on which her late husband had written the scripture Mark 8:36—*What shall it profit a man to gain the whole world yet lose his soul...*

She said to Yasamin, "This piece of paper caused so many arguments between me and Yogesh, before we took that disastrous trip to the Middle East. Now it's one of my most cherished possessions."

Yasamin looked up and read it, then said, "I can only imagine..." Her response was intended for both points that Hana had made.

Hana then hung the one that she had handwritten next to it, with Romans 8:28 written on it: *For God works all things for good, for those who love him, who have been called according to his purpose.*

This was to serve as a constant reminder that her God was very much in control of the situation, and was working all things for good, even if it didn't presently seem that way.

Whenever she felt lonely or frightened for her life, and the life of her daughter, she would read it and meditate on it.

Yasamin asked Hana, "Would it be okay if we shared one room? I don't want to be alone, especially at night."

Hana sighed relief. "I was hoping you would say that."

"Say, why don't we keep the buckets in the other container, and use it as a bathroom, like Donald had done?" asked Yasamin.

Hana replied, "We can also use it when one of us needs a nap, or if we ever need to separate the two children if they get too hyper and need timeouts."

"Good thinking. I'm sure they'll be difficult to handle at times. But we'll manage, right? Four hands are better than two. And we can always watch the toddlers in shifts."

Hana smiled wearily. "My thoughts exactly…"

37

CLAYTON HOLMES SENT A secure voice message to all safe house managers. "Greetings beloved! Now that the mark is officially being administered, I confess it's unsettling knowing there are millions of people out there who have already received it, and have downloaded the facial recognition app onto their phones.

"Even as I speak, these eternal enemies of ours are out there looking for us! Equally frightening is knowing multitudes more will receive the mark and download the app each day.

"I must say it was a stroke of genius on Romanero's part to link the two together. Don't misunderstand me, everyone who receives the mark will do so willingly, but imagine how those who may still be on the fence must feel seeing so many already out in the streets, scanning everyone they see looking for people like us?

"We must assume at this point the vast majority are destitute and need to earn income. Now that they can't buy, sell, or trade without the mark, it's only going to get worse for them until they do. Once they see firsthand the potential income that they stand to lose by putting it off, it may entice them to take it sooner than they had originally intended.

"I'm sure in this tattoo-laden culture in which we live, many on the planet who are spiritually blinded won't have a problem marking up their bodies with another tattoo. 'What's one more?' might be the reply of so many, not knowing how consequential their decision would be.

"On the other hand, thanks to Yahweh's one hundred and forty four thousand sealed servants, and God's three angelic messengers, these still on the fencers are also being bombarded with the Word of God every day, without fail. No one can escape it at this point.

"Either they will wait until the very last minute to take the mark, or after seeing so many miraculous things being done by the God of Israel, He will rescue them at the last minute. That must be our constant prayer.

"Truly, these are unprecedented times. Now that Satan's been cast down to the Earth, the spiritual warfare has never been more intense! I can almost envision God and Satan fiercely wrestling over every last soul.

"But I take comfort knowing God will never lose a single soul that belongs to Him! How amazing that the largest soul harvest in human history is happening right before our eyes, even with the Word of God being outlawed.

"It still blows my mind that Revelation seven, verses nine are being fulfilled before our very eyes. "To refresh your minds, it declares, "'After this I looked, and there before me was a great multitude that no one could count, from every nation, tribe, people and language, standing before the throne and before the Lamb.

"'They were wearing white robes and were holding palm branches in their hands. And they cried out in a loud voice: 'Salvation belongs to our God, who sits on the throne, and to the Lamb.'

"One example of God being on the move is something that happened with a prison guard in Europe. I know most of you no longer have internet access, but if you can watch the video of Hans Greinhold, who was recently beheaded after joining our side, it's a must-see!

"I can't tell you how many tears of joy I shed watching it. Not only did it serve to restore the joy of my salvation in Christ Jesus, that man reminded me yet again that no one is beyond God's reach.

"The chain reaction his testimony has created all throughout the prison system can only be attributed to the power of God. Because of Hans, many who were excited to receive it never showed up for their appointments, including a new female guard who had a front row seat to her supervisor's death by guillotine.

"According to the online article I read, this young woman had greatly anticipated having the Mark on her body, but after witnessing it up close and personal, she never showed up for her scheduled appointment.

"What makes this news so astonishing is, given the present financial condition of the planet, prison guards are among the few who have stable jobs to go to each day, with excellent health benefits.

"Suddenly, they're being converted, and quitting their jobs, with no advance warning, and going into hiding. Only God can change hearts so quickly! His mercy and grace are too wonderful to fully conceive...

"God also used Hans' testimony to strengthen many who were already converted, but they were living in fear like he was. Thanks to him, they're finding the same strength he had shown, and are freely laying down their own lives for their faith in Christ...

"Prison guards aren't the only workers being converted to Christianity. Many representing all professions, after encountering the Most High God of the universe are being transformed spiritually, quitting their jobs, and are fleeing their former lives and going into hiding...

"And how about Benjamin Shapiro? If you haven't yet heard about him, he's one of our residents and Salvador Romanero's former doctor. He was so inspired watching Hans Greinhold lay down his life for the faith, that he wanted Yahweh to use him too.

"Instead of joining his former boss in Jerusalem, where he was supposed to give a speech about the chip that will be injected three months from now, he sent an urgent blanket e-mail to everyone on Romanero's staff, informing them that he could no longer be Salvador's personal physician.

"Shapiro brazenly stated in his e-mail to them how everything that was happening in the world, was clearly outlined in the Bible. Not only did the Word of God clearly and definitively prove that Jesus was Who He said He was, the Savior of the World, but it equally proved that Romanero was the Antichrist of the Bible.

"He then said the reason Salvador outlawed the Word of God, was that it clearly indicted him as being the Antichrist of the Bible. He told his former colleagues that even though they had no way of accessing Bibles for themselves, they all had access to Yahweh's three angelic messengers, and His one hundred and forty four thousand sealed servants, who could confirm everything he was sharing with them straight out of the Word of God. Benjamin ended by pleading with his former colleagues to not take the mark. He told them if they did, they would surely perish within the next three and a half years."

Holmes shook his head in awe. "If God can rescue Hans Greinhold and Benjamin Shapiro, no one is out of His reach. There can be no denying that our King is shaking the planet one last time, by using his servants and messengers to warn them against receiving the mark.

"It's with that in mind that I urge you all to contact anyone you may be having dreams about, or those you feel God has placed on your heart. Make VPN phone calls. If they are receptive to the Message, point them in the direction of the closest sealed servants in their area, so they can receive a copy of *The Way* for themselves.

"I know this goes against every protocol our organization has ever had in place, but Travis will be sending an expanded email list to all safe house managers later today, with the locations of the closest safe houses in your area. Since so many of our plans at the outset have already fallen through, it's getting to the point where it doesn't matter anymore. We all know what's coming.

215

"We still don't know how many of our locations have been targeted, but we believe the majority of our safe houses, not to mention the safe houses of millions of others of our brothers and sisters around the world, who aren't part of our organization, won't be around too much longer.

"Another reason we're doing this has to do with one of our members. After his safe house was bombed, he traveled eight hundred miles to make it to the only other safe house location he knew, mostly on foot." Clayton said, regarding Richard Klein.

"I'll spare the details, but it was inspiring to say the least. If his achievement did anything, it exposed a major flaw within our organization. This flaw was necessary at the outset, but given this new climate, it no longer fits our safety protocols.

"By having access to local safe houses in your area, if your place is destroyed, and you survive, you can hopefully find refuge at one of the other safe houses. On the other hand, if your safe house isn't on Romanero's strike list, once the bombs stop falling from the sky, you can go to the other safe houses and help your brothers and sisters in need.

"Since we as a Christian organization can't do much to further the cause, aside from printing more booklets and housing all who are sent to us for as long as we're able to, I very much feel like a spectator watching it all unfolding before my very eyes.

"Even though we're commanded to 'Fear not', it's impossible at times not to fear. It's a natural reaction, but not a spiritual one. Truth be told, I still tremble at times, especially at night when I'm in bed trying to sleep. And that was before I knew we were being spied on!

"But God understands our fear. Even King David feared for his life on several occasions. But as we fear, we must always do our best to keep our eyes on the prize, which is eternity with Christ Jesus. He is the Prize!

"All that said, if you have missions to carry out, namely meeting with unsaved loved ones and sharing the Gospel with them, now would be the time to do it.

"Father, be merciful to sinners as You are to us. May many more of our unconverted friends and loved ones reach out to You while the message of salvation is still being offered to them. Use us to bring the Gospel message to them, for Your glory we pray in Christ's name, Amen.

"Finally, don't forget to use earbuds when sharing this message with your fellow residents. Keep fighting the good fight! Pray for us as we pray for you! God is with us! We love you all very much."

38

TOWERING HIGH ABOVE THE blizzard of microfliers still out identifying dissidents, God's three angelic messengers kept making their bold proclamations known for all to hear.

Up until now, many teenagers had done their best to hang in there until Romanero finally followed through on his shaky promises of a bright future for all. But after waiting for three and a half years, they couldn't point to a single thing that he had changed for the better.

The emptiness they felt since the disappearances never went away, it only intensified as the days and weeks passed. This led many to battle suicidal thoughts once again, until God used the third angelic messenger to open their eyes and capture their hearts, with the only Truth on the planet that was genuine—the Word of God.

The soul-piercing warning coming from the third messenger, against taking the mark of the beast, was causing a seismic shift to take place in the hearts of so many of Salvador's younger on the fence supporters.

Even without having access to Bibles, they weren't only listening, but as Christ Himself had uttered on several occasions, "He who has ears to ear, let him hear," they were hearing, and absorbing their words like a sponge absorbs water.

Many were gaining access to the booklets the 144,000 were passing out every day. As a result of reading them day and night, they were being transformed by the power of the Holy Spirit unto salvation.

Many of these youngsters, after literally having the "hell" scared out of them, tried sharing the Gospel message with their unbelieving parents, but all they got in return was constant scolding, and threats to take them for psychiatric help, or even turn them over to authorities.

Now convinced that Salvador Romanero was the Antichrist of the Bible, they were leaving their unrepentant parents behind, and finding shelter at Christian safe houses planetwide, with the help of God's 144,000 sealed servants.

But it wasn't just youngsters who were being awakened spiritually. Many newly converted spouses were also being saved, and were leaving their unconverted counterparts, and taking their young children with them.

This had led to some of the most heated arguments in so many homes on the planet. Before leaving their unconverted spouses for good, they begged them not to take the mark, but their pleas fell on deaf ears.

But even those who still chose to follow Salvador Romanero weren't blind to what was going on all around them. It wasn't a cause for comfort.

They, too, were fed up with their leader, for letting the 144,000 Jewish heretics take their children away from them, without retribution.

It started long before the three angelic messengers appeared in the sky above, but it had increased a thousandfold since they appeared.

If Romanero valued their children so much, why wasn't he doing anything about it? Wasn't this a clear case of kidnapping? Shouldn't this have been the last straw?

They were convinced that the man who wanted to be addressed as "Savior" or Messiah" couldn't silence the flying angels. But why hadn't he ended the existences of the 144,000 by now, like he had done to their Two mentors? In their eyes, they were even more dangerous, because they were stealing their children away from them.

If Romanero waited too long before he finally silenced the 144,000, like he did with the Two Witnesses, the fear among these still on-the-fencers was that all their children would be taken from them.

On top of that, it was no secret by now that the booklets that the 144,000 were handing out to everyone, titled *The Way*, was a condensed version of the Christian Bible that Romanero had outlawed three years ago. Yet, every word in those booklets came straight from the Word of God. Why weren't there any repercussions for this most grievous act?

Had anyone else been caught handing them out, they would surely be dead by now. So why were the 144,000 still getting away with it?

The only logical answer was that Romanero was powerless to silence them, plain and simple. He was also powerless to prevent the mass exodus from happening with their young and teenage children.

As the days kept passing, and nothing was ever done about it, it was becoming painfully obvious to some of Salvador's followers that by keeping Yahweh's Word hidden from them, he wasn't enlightening anyone, only further blinding them.

Now realizing they weren't moving closer to the truth, only drifting farther away from it, many of Romanero's still on-the-fencers would start looking for "truth" elsewhere, and would find it in the only place it could be found, in Christ Jesus…

39

DAY 3 AT SEA

AS HANA NURSED CRISTIANA to sleep, hopefully for the night, she had no idea about what had recently taken place in Europe, with the prison guard who had credited her for giving him the strength to make his bold declaration for Jesus, before he offered up his life with more than a million viewers watching.

She combed through her daughter's scalp with her fingers, searching for the pesky head lice Cristiana had contracted in their days of living underground, which had unfortunately worsened on the boat ride from Chennai to Singapore. They wouldn't go away.

Hana hoped that they wouldn't attack her scalp next. She glanced over at Yasamin, and sensed her new best friend in life was jealous that she couldn't produce milk for her son, but not in a bad way, it was more of in a longing way.

When the ship encountered a rogue wave earlier in the day, Navid was thrust off the cot, and banged his head on the hard steel floor. He had a golf ball sized lump on his forehead. Nothing could stop him from crying and screaming at the top of his lungs.

As Yasamin gathered her son in her arms hoping to comfort and quiet him, Hana reached for the step ladder to close the vents.

After 20 minutes of constant wailing, Hana expected someone to bang on their door to arrest them all. The stress became so unbearable that she was tempted to pull the bottle out of Navid's mouth and offer to breastfeed him, if it would calm him down and stop his crying, like it always did for Cristiana in similar situations.

It wasn't uncommon in her culture, nor was it uncommon in the so-called utopia that Romanero was creating. Hana remembered seeing many new mothers on her laptop screen, breastfeeding the children of dissident mothers who were arrested for their faith in Christ.

If Navid was a little younger, she surely would have offered to nurse him, if it would calm him down. But since he was a month shy of turning 3 years old, she refrained.

What finally ended up calming him down was when Cristiana came to the rescue. She kneeled beside Yasamin and stroked Navid's hair.

"Don't cry, Navid, it's okay." It took a while, but Cristiana had finally succeeded.

That was only one time the kids had gotten too loud throughout the day. Each time they fought among themselves, Hana and Yasamin would separate them. At one point, Hana took Cristiana to the other room for a 30-minute time out, until she promised to be good again.

Even with the vents closed, their nerves were constantly on edge.

Yasamin had dealt with this on the first leg of the long journey, and hoped it would be a little easier this time with Hana there to help her. Even though they had each other to lean on, it was still stressful.

When Hana was convinced that Cristiana was down for the count, she gently laid her daughter on the cot.

A few minutes later, Navid finally dozed off as well.

With their children now sleeping, the two women were grateful for this much-needed break.

Yasamin prepared two cups of ginger tea in the microwave. She handed Hana her cup. "America, here we come!"

Hana replied, "Lord willing." They tapped cups. She blew into her cup and watched Cristiana and Navid sleeping together, as the cargo ship swayed back and forth, and could only marvel at them. She took a small sip of tea. "Don't you wish you could be a kid again?"

Yasamin took a second to consider the question. "Absolutely! It would be great not knowing the danger we would face if we got caught, or that three years from now this world will no longer exist the way we know it. I just pray our children will still be alive when Christ returns..."

Hana replied, "If we make it to the safe house in America, it's pretty much a given. That's why I'm risking it in the first place. Of course, I'm eager to meet Brian and Jacquelyn. But ultimately, I want Cristiana to still be alive when Christ returns..."

Yasamin gripped her teacup with both hands and held it close to her face. She could feel the steam tickling her nose. "Imagine our children spending a thousand years together in Christ's Millennial Kingdom."

Hana smiled at the thought, then saw her image in the small dirty mirror. She frowned. Whereas Yasamin still resembled her true likeness without her disguise on, she still looked like a punk rocker.

The sheer glamour she had displayed on the day of the award celebration was so far removed from her present reality. So much so that it was impossible for Hana to believe that she felt so beautiful back then, like a celebrity in fact!

Prior to winning the contest for being the first woman on the planet to give birth after the disappearances, those who knew Hana best described her as kind, timid, shy, and rather plain looking, homely even, much like she looked now.

A few makeovers later and she looked like a super model with her slim body, silky-smooth dark skin, long shiny-black hair, sparkling eyes, and a brilliant smile that would cause her eyes to sparkle even more. And thanks to some friends in very high places, her image had even appeared in a handful of fashion magazines before everything in her life fell apart.

Hana sighed at her image in the mirror. "Before winning the contest, Yogesh always told me I was beautiful. I thought he was just being nice to me because he was my husband."

Yasamin looked at Hana over her teacup. "You are beautiful, Hana. Your hair will grow back."

Hana waved off her comment. "I never thought so, not outwardly, anyway. But when heads started turning in my direction in the Middle East, my thinking quickly changed. It seems like many lifetimes ago. If only they could see me now..." *How the mighty have fallen!*

Yasamin interjected, "Who cares how we look, so long as we get to where we're going, right?" She took another small sip from her cup. "When I sat with you in the hotel lobby in Dubai, before you went back to India, all I kept thinking about was how traumatic the transition must have been, going from being interviewed by the press and Hollywood filmmakers one day, to suddenly being interviewed by the police, as part of the investigation process over your husband's death."

Hana frowned in the near darkness. "Everything about that day is still one big blur to me. I didn't know if I was coming or going..."

Yasamin took a small bite of a cracker, then took her time chewing on it before swallowing. "If it happened to me, I would have gone insane."

Hana asked, "Do you remember the last thing I told you before I left for the airport?"

"How could I forget? You told me to be careful with everything I said, because they were watching and listening, right?"

Hana nodded at her. "But what I didn't tell you was what happened the night before, up in my suite."

Yasamin raised a curious eyebrow. "What happened, Hana?"

Hana grimaced. "Shortly before Yogesh was killed, I received a threatening call from a woman, warning me not to tell anyone about my belief that I was already pregnant before the contest was announced. Before hanging up on me, she told me to turn on the television, so I could watch my husband's plane being shot down…" Her voice trailed off.

Yasamin put her hands up to her face. "Really? How cruel!"

Hana's shoulders slumped. A shiver shot through her. "My first thought was how could she possibly know about my belief that I was already pregnant? The only one I told was Yogesh. No one else. That's when I knew we were being spied on.

"I became frightened for my life. This is why I was always so reluctant to message you when I returned from that trip. I've wanted to tell you about it all this time, but you already know why I didn't…"

Yasamin asked, "Do you think Romanero put her up to it?"

"Definitely!" said Hana, with a hard nod of the head. "She knew in advance the plane would be shot down. Who else had that kind of knowledge?"

Yasamin grimaced. "I always sensed they were listening to my conversations too. Since my late husband was a Christian, what they put me through during the interview process, before awarding me custody of Navid, was grueling. They kept glaring at me as if I was lying to them, even though I was telling the truth…"

Hana brushed off a shiver. "I'm sure your premonition was spot on."

Yasamin took another sip from her teacup. "So, you were already pregnant before Romanero announced the contest?"

Hana nodded exhaustedly. "Something else I've wanted to tell you for the longest time, but there wasn't a chance I would do it online."

Yasamin wondered how many other mothers were also pregnant beforehand. "This is just one more proof that Salvador Romanero is the great deceiver," she snickered. "Who does that man think he is, taking credit for something that only God can do, which is to create life?"

Hana agreed with her friend's assessment. "At least we managed to escape from his evil clutches before it was too late."

Yasamin became teary-eyed. "Thank You, Jesus!" She took another sip from her teacup. "Tell me more about Brian and Jacquelyn…"

Hana shrugged her shoulders. "Not much to tell, except that God used them both to rescue me and Yogesh from Salvador Romanero. It's funny how the hatred I have toward that man is the very same hatred I once harbored toward the Henriksens, Mulrooneys rather, before I got saved.

"When they sent my husband a Bible, it didn't take long before I noticed a drastic change in him. When Yogesh accused Romanero of being the Antichrist, I blamed Brad and Joan for it. I also blamed them for my husband's death.

"When I returned home, I was so angry at them that I contributed one hundred thousand dollars to help aid in their captures. Now they're like my human guardian angels."

Yasamin gulped at the thought. "Let's just hope they never locate them. If they do, we'll be captured too."

"Imagine that, funding my own capture," Hana scoffed at herself. "I admit I'm frightened every day for my safety, but being involved with the End Times Salvation Movement gives my life a lasting purpose."

Yasamin nodded at Hana. "I agree. Life is much more fulfilling now than my former life ever was."

Hana scratched her scalp. "I think it's because we matter not only to God, but to our brothers and sisters in Christ as well. When I was in the spotlight and had lots of money, it didn't take long for me to discover just how fake my rich friends were."

Hana wiped a tear from her eye with the sleeve of her sweater. "They proved just how plastic they were when things went bad for me. Without even reaching out to me, they ghosted me like I never even existed. True friends don't do that.

"But at least the friends we're making now are genuine," said Yasamin in reply. "And eternal! I'm eager to meet even more of them in America."

"Me too." Hana frowned in the near darkness. "Eager as I was to leave the safe house in India, the bond that we formed was unbreakable that it was difficult leaving them."

Yasamin grinned at her best friend. "And to think that I was convinced your husband had truly lost his mind!"

Hana chuckled at the way she said it. "Me too. Now that we believe what he did, if it's mental illness, I feel blessed to also have it. Yogesh will be shocked to see me in Heaven."

Yasamin said, "It still blows my mind how we are two of the most-wanted fugitives on the planet! I mean, who are we?"

Hana agreed, then gulped back fear. "We are simple women trying to raise our children in these turbulent times…"

Yasamin noticed and searched her memory for something positive to say. "I can't fully express to you how I felt when I watched your livestream. Something went off inside me that was the most amazing sensation I've ever experienced, which I now know was the Spirit of the living God stirring my soul…"

Hana confessed, "Truth be told, I was even more frightened after I did it, especially once the GPS locators were removed from our bodies. It represented a finality of sorts. There could be no turning back.

"When we were moved underground, I kept second-guessing myself." She grimaced at her words. "Would you like to know what soothed my soul underground more than anything else?"

Yasamin pulled on her sweater to cut off the chill. "Sure…"

"It was what you said on the VPN call we had with the *ETSM* higher-ups. Your words took all those negative thoughts away."

Yasamin raised a confused eyebrow. "What did I say?"

"You said even before I went online to make my declaration for Jesus, that you had already concluded that there was too much evidence pointing to the God of Israel as being the one true God, to ignore as Truth."

Yasamin straightened up on the chair she was seated on. "It's true! Even before I had access to a Bible, how much more confirmation did I need? How much more proof did I need?"

Hana asked her, "Can you tell me again? I really need to hear it again."

You and me both! Yasamin took a moment to formulate her thoughts, then, in her rich Middle Eastern accent, said, "Not only did Israel's Messiah cause my husband to vanish in thin air, but Yahweh also protected His people when Jerusalem fell under attack.

"And what about the Two Men breathing fire out of their mouths before their deaths and resurrections? As much as the world hated them, who could deny the special powers they had?

"And what about the young Jewish preachers out there spreading the Gospel among the constant chaos? Surely, they're being supernaturally protected by the very God we now serve."

"I totally agree with you," said Hana, "and I have no doubt they're being supernaturally protected. One of them was camped outside my house, a young man named Yitzhak. After the global quake, people started flocking back to pay homage to Cristiana, only they knew her as Salvadora.

"Some of them came to protest what had become of my life. Yitzhak showed up every morning among the stragglers, to preach the Word of God to everyone within earshot. He never missed a day. Even after the global quake, while everyone else ran for cover, he was always there. His voice was so loud and commanding that everyone within a quarter mile of the house easily heard him, whether they wanted to or not.

"After a while, as people slowly started trickling back, many became so intrigued by his captivating messages, that they kept coming to hear more of what he had to say. But for their own safety, they would face the house as if they were there for me and Cristiana, when they were really there for Yitzhak. The proof was that when he left for the day, many in the crowd also dispersed.

"I was also listening very carefully! I had no choice—his strong voice had all but demanded my attention! I could only assume he was the same man Yogesh saw in his dreams standing outside our house in the middle of the night, before we went to Dubai.

"All I can say for sure is that God used him mightily to get my attention, and the attention of so many others..."

Yasamin said, "I had a similar experience myself, with a man named Abraham. He used to preach directly across the street from my high-rise condo. Like Yitzhak, he was out preaching on the day of the global quake, even if no one was outside listening to him.

"But with power out, and no TVs or speakers to drown him out, everyone heard his booming voice rising into the air. Every window in my condo was blown out, so I heard every word he spoke, with perfect clarity, in my native tongue, even though others told me they heard him speaking in languages other than mine.

"His messages were so powerful. Like I said, the proof was everywhere that the God of Israel was in control, not Salvador Romanero. I didn't need to read about these things. I got to see them with my own two eyes even before you made your declaration! What blows my mind the most is how everyone else can't see it for themselves."

Hana remarked, "From what we're learning in the Bible, it's because they've been spiritually blinded up to this point..."

Hana's remark made Yasamin think of her parents. "I still remember the day the Dome of the Rock was destroyed, and what the Muslim pilot said during his interview before he was hung on live TV, about the God of Israel deflecting the missile that he himself had fired at a Jewish target, sending it straight into their own holy site!"

She frowned. "My father said it was the beginning of the end for Islam. Turns out he was right..." She shook her head sadly again, at the thought of her family being in Hades now awaiting God's judgment, not

225

to mention her lack of remorse when they were killed by Romanero's blood thirsty forces.

Yasamin took the last sip from her teacup. She was clearly on the verge of tears.

Hana pointed to the wall with the Bible quotations hanging on it, and read Romans 8:28 to her best friend, "For God works all things for good, for those who love him and have been called according to his purpose."

Yasamin said, "Thanks Hana. Exactly what I needed right now."

"Why don't we try to get some sleep while the kids are sleeping?"

"I was just thinking the same thing." Yasamin turned off the battery-operated light, then climbed into bed with her son. "Goodnight best friend. Love you."

"Love you too, Yasamin."

40

WHEN TAMIKA AND MEERA entered the newly reconstructed cafeteria for lunch, they surprised Tamika by singing Happy Birthday to her. Lila Choharjo baked a cake to commemorate her 30th "milestone" birthday.

She also received a greater food portion than everyone else, which was customary for anyone celebrating birthdays or anniversaries. It was a blessing to her on more than one front. "Aww, thanks so much everyone. It's things like this that help keep me going in the midst of the storm."

Isaac looked his wife in the eye. "Sorry I wasn't able to give you a gift this year."

Tamika smiled wearily. "Oh, but you did give me a gift, Isaac. I'm pregnant!"

Isaac's eyes became as big as silver dollars. He gulped hard and had difficulty breathing. The expression on his face indicated that he was no longer sure if he wanted to raise a child in this climate. "Are you sure?"

Tamika looked up at the ceiling and shook her head. "Just like a man to ask that sort of question. Meera just examined me before coming here. We're going to be parents again."

Isaac glanced at a smiling Meera, then kissed Tamika hard on the lips, followed by several soft kisses. "How do you feel, my love?"

Tamika rubbed her chin. "Gee, what can I say? I'm married to the same man for the second time, and pregnant again with his third child, all at the age of thirty! It's exhausting! And you, Isaac?"

"I admit I'm scared, but I'll be by your side every step of the way." Isaac hugged his wife tightly, then rose from the cafeteria seat and declared, "Listen up everyone, Tamika's pregnant!" The way he lisped the "s" his wife's name, was cute to Tamika. And his toothless smile never ceased to cause others to also smile.

As the hundreds in the cafeteria showered the couple with weary congratulatory nods, Tamika lowered her head in embarrassment. Or was it fear? It was probably a combination of both.

"If we have a daughter, I'd like to name her Ruth, after my mother."

Isaac gazed deeply into Tamika's eyes. "Sure, but if we have a son, I'd like to name him Amos John Moseley, to honor Amos Nyarwarta and John Reitz for laying down their lives for me and Dick. We can call him A.J. for short."

Tamika raised an eyebrow. "I see someone's been giving it serious thought…"

"Yes, I have." He asked, "So, what do you think?"

Tamika kissed her husband on the lips. "It sounds perfect, Isaac!"

Tamika noticed Leticia weeping at the table next to theirs. "Are you okay?" She was with her husband, Joaquim, her mother, Marta, and Lila Choharjo, waiting for Julio Sr. to finish patrolling the area before joining them.

Marta asked her daughter, "What's wrong, hija?"

Leticia gasped. "I'm pregnant too, Mama…"

Marta shot a desperate glance at a completely shocked Meera Singh. She nodded her head and put her hands up, as if to say, "I had no idea."

Marta looked over at Lila Choharjo, her best friend at safe house number one, then glared at Joaquim fearfully, before shifting her focus back to her daughter. In between uncontrolled breaths, she said, "Tell me you're joking, hija!"

Leticia tipped her eyes up to meet her mother's shocked gaze. "It wasn't planned, Mama, it just happened."

Marta wasn't disappointed that her daughter was pregnant. They were married, so there was nothing wrong with it. But the timing couldn't have been any worse. *Wait till your father hears about this!*

Leticia knew that look all too well. Her mother was scared for her.

When Julio Sr. arrived, he knew something was up. The fact that his daughter and son-in-law hadn't touched the food on their plates indicated that much. Finally, he raised his hands in the air. "Will someone please tell me what's going on?"

Marta said to her husband, "Tamika's pregnant."

Julio Sr. looked over at Isaac and Tamika. "Congratulations, to you both!" His words lacked confidence on two levels. First, because the timing couldn't have been any worse, and second, he knew there was more not so pleasant news coming. He looked at his daughter seated across from him. "Why are you crying?"

Leticia stared at her food plate, too afraid to make eye contact with her father. She said through soft sniffling, "I'm pregnant again, Papa…"

228

Julio pounded the table out of frustration, causing every plate and cup to vibrate. He glared angrily at his son-in-law. "How could you do this to my daughter? Don't we already have more than enough to worry about? Soon, we'll be forced to leave this place. Who knows what sort of living conditions we'll have there? All we know is it won't be as cozy for us as it is here. Now, you got my little girl pregnant again?!"

Joaquim slumped his shoulders and lowered his head. In a tone that was both soft and respectful, he said, "You know I'm not Julio junior's biological father. This will be my first time being a father for real. I know the timing isn't ideal, but since we'll be going to a supernaturally protected location, I want a child to live in Jesus' Millennial Kingdom, who has my DNA. But I'll always love J.J. like my own…"

Julio gasped loudly, and shook his head, realizing he was out of line. He took a few deep breaths to calm himself down. "Forgive me, Joaquim. You're a great son-in-law, and an awesome husband to my daughter. And J.J. couldn't ask for a better father than you! I guess I just need a little time to accept it. My head's spinning…"

Joaquim sighed. "I understand, sir. The feeling's mutual…"

Leticia threw herself into her father's arms and wept uncontrollably. "We're scared too, Papa, but we need your support."

Julio Sr. felt ashamed of himself, and became teary-eyed. He was one to seldom show emotion. Everything about his demeanor was hard. Everyone on his former construction crew in Rhode Island knew he was a real "crying is for sissies" type of guy. He no longer was that man. He could cry at the drop of a hat now. There wasn't a Christian male on the planet who couldn't relate to him on this level. "Sorry for my outburst, hija. Of course, you have my full support. Both of you…"

Joaquim wanted to comfort his wife, but now wasn't the time. This was clearly father-daughter time…

Julio Sr. stroked his daughter's hair like he did when she was a baby, still unable to fathom how his daughter, who wasn't even 16 yet, would soon be a mother twice over. Then again, he wasn't even 40, yet he was about to be a grandfather twice over.

The conversation plot was about to thicken even more.

Caught up in the emotion of it all, Charles got up off the bench he was seated on. He approached Meera, gulped in air, then did the craziest thing. He took a knee beside the woman. "This is gonna sound crazy to you," he said nervously, "but will you marry me?"

Meera blinked hard a few times. Her head turned one way then the next. Her breathing became erratic, as she scanned the cafeteria to gauge the looks on the faces of her brothers and sisters, all the while trying to wrap her mind around what she had just heard. "Come again?"

Charles shook his head. "I know how crazy it sounds. Truth be told, until just recently, I never thought of you as anything more than my sister in Christ. I started having feelings for you a few months back, but I always did my best to suppress them.

"As my feelings kept growing, I confided in a few brothers here that my biggest objection to proposing to you sooner, was thoughts about my wife and kids. I never thought I would remarry. But just like Clayton confessed in his last message, I'm scared too."

Meera understood his fear completely. She was equally frightened by Clayton's confession.

Charles went on, "Not gonna lie. As the days pass, I feel a little less secure. Since there's not much left to do except hunker down and wait and pray, I don't want to be alone for that.

"Just seeing Isaac and Tamika holding hands caused me to yearn for affection again. You don't have to answer me now. This is something I've wrestled with for a long time. Truth be told, I still feel guilty about my past marital failures to ever consider becoming a husband again.

"Guess you could say this has been one of the thorns in my side. Until this moment, the very notion of being with someone else was never a consideration for me. But since none of us will be married on the other side, we'll all be married to Christ, when I see Monique again, it won't be as husband and wife."

Under normal circumstances, Meera would never consider entertaining something so ridiculous. "But I'm eight years older than you, Charles…"

Calloway put his arms out. "I don't care about that, Meera. I'm not even thinking about the physical side of marriage. I just don't want to be alone."

Charles glanced up at a completely stunned Isaac and Tamika. "Sorry for stealing your thunder, guys, it wasn't my intention, and it certainly wasn't planned."

Tamika waved him off. "Don't sweat it, brother Charles."

All eyes shifted back to Meera, who still couldn't remove the shocked expression from her face.

Like everyone else living on the property, with so much uncertainty in the air, she would love to have someone to hold her in bed each night. Cuddling with her sisters in Christ only went so far. She needed a man to do it, especially on the nights when her body would tremble in fear, as she silently wondered when the next Judgments would strike the planet.

She couldn't count how many nights she had cried herself to sleep, at safe house number one. There were so many. Too many!

Finally, she said, "I won't deny that my feelings for you have deepened ever since you permanently moved onto the safe house, Charles. But like you said, I'll need to pray about it and think things through."

Charles cracked a smile at her. "Of course! Take all the time you need. Well, not all the time..."

The way he said it caused many to laugh.

At that, everyone got back to what they were doing before the surprise birthday greeting for their cherished nurse, followed by the shocking marriage proposal. All things considered; it was just another abnormally normal day at safe house number one...

41

MANILA, PHILIPPINES

FOR THE FIRST TIME since the Rapture, Donald Johnson was back in the Philippines. At first glance, the former Mormon missionary thought his new friend, Sergei Ivanov, had taken him to the wrong location.

Everything he remembered about this once-bustling country, from the 13 years he spent there spreading his former false religion, was gone.

When he arrived in Singapore a little more than a week ago, he thought that country was decimated. And he only got to see it from out on the water. Now that he was in the Philippines, it quickly changed to, *I thought Singapore was unsustainable*!

Then again, perhaps this place looked so much worse because he was more familiar with this country, what was left of it, anyway. Capsized and destroyed boats were everywhere, as far as the eye could see. And the bustling skyline that was Manila before the Rapture, had been reduced to near nothing.

With the sun about to set, Ivanov pulled his sailboat as close to one of the makeshift docks as he could. They were nothing more than a few wooden planks connecting rock and land, not too far from where terminals once stood outside the Mall of Asia.

Donald jumped off the boat even as it kept moving, and steadied himself on one of the wooden planks. "Pray for me, brother."

"I will," Sergei said, with a slight panic in his voice. Ivanov was from Russia. When he turned 25, he grew tired of the cold temperatures, quit his job, and moved to Thailand so he could surf and fish year-round, smoke weed, and eventually meet a nice Thai girl to settle down with.

Before his conversion, Sergei was proud to call himself a hippie. His cobalt blue eyes were friendly and captivating, even if they were usually glazed over from smoking so much weed. His shoulder-length, bleached-blonde hair was straggly. When it was wet, it looked more like a mop turned upside down than actual hair.

When the tsunami destroyed his apartment building in Bangkok, the sailboat had become his new residence. Ivanov had purchased it with some of the winnings he had earned from a handful of prestigious fishing contests he had entered before the Rapture.

While his vessel did sustain minor damage, it was still seaworthy.

Now 32, Ivanov was completely sold out to Jesus. "If she's not there after the sun sets," he said to Donald, "come back as quickly as you can. We can always try again tomorrow. I'll stay as close to shore as I can. If I'm not here when you get back, it means something came up. If that happens, hide wherever you can until I return."

A shiver shot through Donald. "Got it!"

Johnson left at once for where the Mall of Asia had once stood. Analyn was right, Manila looked unrecognizable! There was hardly any infrastructure to be seen anywhere throughout the Capital City.

The widespread damage that was created by the pyroclastic flow from the erupting volcanoes, before ultimately becoming molten lava, caused Donald's heart to sink in his chest.

He also saw the high watermarks on trees that had miraculously survived the mayhem, and on the destroyed buildings that were still visible from the flood waters that had submerged all low-lying sections.

Combined, they completely reshaped the topography in so many places, drowning millions of bodies in the process, including Analyn's parents and her daughter. Johnson was certain it was like this all throughout the Capital City, and beyond. He shuddered to think how many Filipinos had become part of this new foundation of sorts. No doubt it had become the burial site for so many in this country.

It may have taken only a few minutes for the tsunami waves to submerge the Philippines beneath hundreds of feet of seawater, devouring everything and everyone in its pathway, but it would take a hundred lifetimes to rebuild the city, which Johnson knew would never happen.

In a little more than three years, it would all be gone…

He wondered how anyone other than those living in the mountains, and those who had managed to escape to higher ground could have possibly survived what had struck their homeland? Analyn was proof that even many who had reached higher ground were ultimately swept away in the floodwaters caused by the tsunami.

This place felt as apocalyptic as it looked. It was as if Donald had been transported to another planet!

It made him long even more for Christ to make all things new.

Donald grimaced. *How in the world will I ever get to the village where I once preached Mormonism?* But for now, he was on a mission. And that mission was to locate Analyn Tibayan, and hopefully others, and win them all to Christ.

It was easy to see why Analyn was so fearful for her life on the VPN call. *Was she still alive? If so, was she safe? Did she receive the mark?*

Donald pushed those thoughts aside. He could only hope and pray that she didn't take it. If she did, not only would he be heartbroken for her, but there would be nothing else he could do to help her.

If anything, he would have to flee from her presence and hopefully make it safely back to the boat, before someone scanned his image and uploaded it onto the facial recognition app on their phone, then pray that he and Sergei would be able to safely escape the Philippines, without being captured.

Otherwise, unless God led him to someone else to share the Gospel with, it would be a wasted trip indeed.

Now 51, the one thing Johnson had enjoyed most about visiting this country in the past, was the friendly demeanor most Filipinos had always shown toward him. They always made him feel comfortable. So much so that he had serious thoughts about retiring there someday, until God used the Rapture to save his soul and, ultimately, change his direction in life.

With the exception to those who had already received the mark, and were out trying to earn money using their mobile devices, everyone else looked as if they wished they hadn't survived the constant mayhem. They seemed on edge, suspicious, untrusting, and fearful for their lives.

Donald completely understood their plight. Even so, unlike all other past visits to this country, he couldn't wait to leave this time.

He was just glad he decided to leave the backpack full of food, water, and other essentials on the boat with Sergei. Had he brought it with him, it would have made him a bigger target, and the backpack surely would have been stolen by now, even if the would-be thief had to kill him to get it, it would be done. These were desperate times!

Even better, upon discovering that Johnson was a Christ follower, the perpetrator would receive a thousand dollars in his or her new global account, plus be treated as a hero for their efforts.

When Donald saw his first person proudly displaying the mark tattooed on his forehead—a teenage male—his heart pounded so hard, it was like someone was inside his chest banging on bongos.

He looked away and picked up the pace, hoping he wouldn't point his mobile device at him. This was yet another reason why he couldn't wait to leave this place.

As much as he would have preferred waiting until it was dark outside to meet Analyn, it wasn't an option. If he went there at night wearing dark sunglasses, a beige safari hat and a face mask, with exception to the face mask, it would surely arouse suspicion in those out pointing their mobile devices in all directions looking for dissidents.

If there was one advantage, blessing rather, it was that so many people in this country had lost their mobile devices in the flood waters, and hadn't replaced them yet. They couldn't afford to!

Romanero promised to give new mobile devices to anyone needing them upon receiving the mark. The problem for island countries like the Philippines was that, since so many of their islands had been decimated, it was difficult getting to the locations to receive them.

Advantage Donald! At least for the time being.

Like Clayton had said, most people on the planet were destitute, and desperate to earn money. Those who were determined to take the mark would do whatever it took to make it happen.

Since Donald and Analyn couldn't set an exact meeting date, he didn't know how many days he would have to remain camped out at this place, waiting for her. He was grateful that they had agreed upon sunset, so he wouldn't have to spend too much time out in the open fearing for his life. He prayed this would be the day.

When he arrived at the meeting location, his senses were on full alert. He was already upset with himself for letting down his guard in Singapore. He could only wonder if he was still being followed by those microfliers. Not knowing for sure, he had to be extra careful.

Johnson reached the meeting location and walked the massive grounds where the Mall of Asia once stood, hoping to spot Analyn or even bump into her soon.

This place used to be so familiar to him. Now, there wasn't a pile of rubble to be seen anywhere. The entire Mall of Asia had been washed away by the flood waters, and deposited who knows where...

It was impossible to believe that this was where he used to take his students for ice cream, after knocking on doors in the community all morning, spreading their false religion.

Much like the world-renowned mall that had once stood so proudly on this very spot, Mormonism was also built on a faulty foundation.

Donald took in his war-torn surroundings, and could only lament, fearing many of his friends in this country had perished either from the global quake, or from the meteor strike and tsunami that had flattened so much of the country.

But what caused the most nausea to swim through his body, was his understanding that many who had professed faith in God in the Philippines—in one form or another—were left behind.

As it was, more than 90 percent of those living there, before the Rapture, were Roman Catholics. And thanks to individuals like himself, Mormonism had grown exponentially over the years.

In the Southern region of the country—in Mindanao—many Muslims had resided there. Many of them never got to live long enough to potentially be killed by the global quake, the meteor strike or tsunami.

Most were killed by Romanero's forces, when the so-called *Man of Peace* declared all-out war on their religion, killing hundreds of millions of Muslims as a result. Had Johnson not been saved, he may have thought they were fortunate to escape it all.

But he knew their condition had worsened considerably upon dying. So much so that they would give anything to be able to come back to Planet Earth, if only for a second, to profess Christ as their Savior. They learned too late that He already was their Lord, but not their Savior.

The fact that Donald was one of the countless false preachers in this country spreading their false messages which led all who believed it straight to hell, filled his soul with constant dread.

He tried contacting many of them over the past three years, but to no avail, until Analyn miraculously replied to his anonymous message.

And just like when Christ left the 99 sheep to go after him, if she was the only one left on the planet, with God's help, Donald would do everything in his power to bring her to safety. The fact that he had travelled halfway around the globe indicated that much.

But until he and Sergei were convinced beyond a shadow of a doubt that she was saved, they couldn't attempt bringing her back to the States.

Johnson's eyes narrowed when he spotted a young woman roughly 50 yards away from him, eyes fearfully darting left to right, anxious expression on her face. *Could that be her?* Whoever it was, she clearly looked lost, all alone, and frightened for her life.

If it was Analyn, she had been reduced to a mere skeleton of her former self. The poor woman looked so malnourished. Even from this distance, she looked filthy, with unkempt hair that probably hadn't been washed in many weeks. And she probably hadn't eaten in days.

The instant Analyn recognized him, she sighed relief then ran straight into her ninong's arms. She held onto him for dear life, releasing a river of tears, soaking his shirt in the process.

Having recently lost everything that was dear to her—including her entire family—she didn't want to release her tight grip on him.

Donald couldn't ignore the foul odor attacking his nostrils. It made him gag a few times. The clothing she had on looked as if it hadn't been washed in many weeks. Her shirt and shorts were full of holes, and her shoes were threadbare. Her fingernails and toenails were grimy, and her toes were blackened with caked-in dirt from life on the streets.

What sickened him even more than that were the scars and abrasions he saw all over her body. But what he didn't see on her right hand or forehead was the mark of the beast tattoo.

Donald breathed a huge sigh of relief. "You didn't take the mark..."

Analyn nodded her head. "You told me not to, right?"

"Thank you, Lord," he mumbled to himself. Donald couldn't hold her stare without becoming teary eyed.

Never in his life had he seen such hopelessness stenciled onto the face of another human being before. It screamed, "Please don't leave me here to die, Ninong. There's nothing here for me..."

Her comment gutted him. Donald felt even more guilty for having led her astray now, than he did before the call. Even so, although she was one of the sweetest girls he had ever known, he had to keep reminding himself that while she wasn't the enemy yet, she was still among the unconverted.

Finally, through soft sniffling, the woman he hadn't seen in more than four years said to him, "I can't believe you came all this way just for me, Ninong. No one's ever done anything like this for me before. I don't know what I'd do if you weren't here."

"It's the least I can do for misleading you spiritually for so many years," he whispered, seeing the unbridled fear in her eyes.

Johnson scanned the area hoping they didn't look too out of the ordinary. Grateful people stood out like sore thumbs on this crazy planet.

Another thing he hoped was that the bees and mosquitoes he saw flitting this way and that, weren't microfliers in disguise spying on them, which Analyn probably still knew nothing about.

He asked her, "Where did you sleep last night?"

"The same place I was at last time we chatted. It's not too far from here."

"I see. How many others sleep there?"

Anayln took a deep breath and exhaled. "It depends. Sometimes ten or twenty. Other times more than that. It always changes."

237

Donald grimaced. "You'll sleep on the boat tonight with us."

Us? Analyn pushed that thought out of her mind. Whoever it was, she trusted Donald and knew she would be safe with them. "Really?"

In a near whisper, he said, "You need food and water, a change of clothing, and a good night's sleep. I doubt you'll find those things at the boarding house."

Analyn's shoulders slumped. Relief flooded her weary soul. She started weeping again, as a new wave of relief washed over her stressed and fatigued body. For the first time in many weeks, she felt safe, as safe as she could be given the circumstances...

"I also brought two outfits for you to wear. Someone very special gave them to me to give to you."

"Your wife?" she asked.

Donald shook his head. "Perhaps in time you'll know. For now, let's get you back to the boat." He prayed for God's protection, and they left at once, hand in hand, heads down, only looking up occasionally to see where they were going. He was prepared to protect her to the best of his ability. Even if it meant getting badly injured fending off potential troublemakers along the way, male or female, so be it.

Sergei saw them approaching and silently praised God that Donald had made it back with Analyn. He plucked a bottle of water and a pack of peanut butter crackers out of Donald's backpack, then handed them to Analyn. "Welcome on board, Analyn. I'm Sergei."

Analyn nodded her thanks to him, then guzzled every drop of water out of the bottle in just a few seconds. She then practically inhaled the peanut butter crackers.

Donald asked Analyn, "Do you still have a toothache?"

"Not at the moment, Ninong. It comes and goes."

Donald pulled Anbesol out of the backpack and handed it to her. "Next time you have one, this will help."

"Thanks, Ninong, but what I really need is a feminine napkin."

Donald looked skyward and softly whispered, "Thank you, Yasamin," then pulled a box of tampons out of the backpack for her.

Analyn gripped the box with both hands like she was gripping a mug of hot chocolate. "You're a real lifesaver, Ninong."

"Happy to be able to help, Analyn..."

After taking a much needed and refreshing shower on board the sailboat, it felt good to be clean again. It also felt good knowing she would be safe for the night with these two men.

238

As much as Donald wanted to sit Analyn down, and share the Gospel with her—he could hear the panic clock ticking in his head—what she needed more than anything right now was a good night's sleep. She couldn't stop yawning.

He would share the gospel with her come sunrise…

The sailboat had two twin size beds in the main cabin, one for Donald, one for Analyn, and a queen size bed which Sergei had slept on since the tsunami destroyed most of his country.

Once she was settled in bed with a blanket pulled up to her neck to cut off the chill, she said, "I love you, Ninong."

Donald smiled in the darkness. "Love you too, Analyn…"

At that, she rolled onto her side and drifted off to sleep, without ever fearing being groped or raped by someone…

42

FORMER SECRET SERVICE AGENT Anthony Galiano sent a secure text message to Clayton Holmes: *Call me ASAP!*

When Clayton called Galiano, he came straight to the point, "I just gained access to a confidential e-file list, which gave the green light for the bombing of numerous dissident camps to commence in six weeks."

When Jefferson and Amy Danforth left the subterranean safe house in Coeur d'Alene, Idaho, for Pennsylvania, Anthony Galiano, and his former co-agent, Daniel Sullivan, had remained there, along with President Danforth's former National Security Adviser, Nelson Casanieves, his former Chief of Staff, Aaron Gillespie, and his former Joint Chief of Staff, William Messersmith.

The reason they remained behind was so they could maintain control of the advanced technologies their former boss had left behind. They used these technologies to patch into the global system, the facial recognition app, and many other top-secret government files.

Galiano warned his friend, "All five hundred locations that are part of the 'Montpelier Project', are on the list of enemy locations, and have been targeted for destruction." The concern in his voice was evident.

He went on, "Romanero wants them all destroyed simultaneously, so no one knows what's coming until it's too late. It's also being done so if there are survivors, they won't have time to alert other locations."

Clayton felt dizzy, like he was going to faint. His hands trembled so fiercely that he nearly dropped his phone. "Do you have an exact date?"

Agent Galiano sighed into the phone. "Not yet, but I'll keep monitoring the situation very carefully, and will update you if anything changes. If I were you, I'd get busy putting relocation plans in place."

Holmes replied, "It's already in the works. But thanks for the head's up, Anthony."

Galiano asked, "Anything else I can do for you, Clayton?"

"Yes. Can you have Daniel Sullivan contact Jefferson Danforth?"

"Is everything okay with him?"

"As good as can be expected, I suppose. I'll spare the details for now, but it's about a dream he's having. If you can ask Daniel to call him, I'd appreciate it."

"Consider it done, Clayton. I'm sure Sullivan will know how to get in touch with him."

"Thanks, Anthony. Stay safe out there. It's getting crazy."

"You too, Clayton…" The call ended.

Thirty minutes later, Jacquelyn Mulrooney knocked on Jefferson Danforth's cottage door. "Hi Jacquelyn. Is everything okay?"

"Daniel Sullivan's on the phone."

Jefferson sighed relief and took the phone from her. "Hey, Daniel. Thanks for getting back to me so quickly."

"Of course! I hear someone's having dreams…"

Danforth answered, "Yes, about my former brother-in-law, Tyler Stephenson. Do you remember him?"

"Melissa's older brother, right?"

"Correct. Ever since Clayton said in his last address that if we're having dreams about certain individuals, now would be the time to reach out to them. Anyway, in my dream, Tyler was a believer."

Sullivan removed his reading glasses and massaged the bridge of his nose. "That's interesting…"

Jefferson sighed. "I'm not the only one. Many residents are having dreams about people they believe God wants them to share the Gospel with, including our head nurse, Tamika. She told me yesterday that she started having dreams about a woman she went to nursing school with. The first round of dreams never panned out. But in her new dream, Nila was an *ETSM* nurse."

Sullivan breathed warm air onto his glasses and cleaned them, using the bottom of his shirt, silently wondering where his former boss was going with all this.

Jefferson went on, "But since we're one of the groups that will be safely relocated, Clayton advised us to wait until we're at the new location before reaching out to anyone."

Daniel rubbed his chin very slowly. "Makes sense…"

"Yes, it does. But as you might imagine, my situation is different than with most others..."

"How so, sir?"

Jefferson cleared his throat. "You already know Romanero knows I'm alive, which means my kids will find out about it soon enough."

241

Sullivan leaned back on his desk chair. "Let me guess, you want me to track them down for you…"

"I know I'm asking a lot, but I'd rather have them hear about it from you, than to hear about it in the news. I also want William and Janelle to know I'm remarried, and that I'm a Christ follower. I pray every day that they will come to faith in Christ."

"Speaking of your children, sir, I heard through the grapevine that the surveillance on them has been elevated…"

Jefferson wasn't surprised hearing this. "We both know why. Romanero knows I'm alive, and wants to catch us in the act, even though they think I'm dead. Which is why I want to reach out to them before they hear about it from the wrong news sources."

"Understood, Sir…"

Jefferson stood and paced the small cottage living room. "Another problem we have is that I don't know where Tyler lives, or if he's even alive, for that matter. If he is alive, he could be in the D.C. area, or he may have moved back to Wisconsin. I have no way of knowing…" He paused, then started sniffling into the phone. "That goes double for my children, William and Janelle. I haven't seen them in more than two years."

Daniel's heart ached for his former boss. He still vividly remembered the day when Air Force One was shot down with his wife on board. He thought it could never get worse than that day. Yet, it always did…

He said, "If Tyler's alive, Sir, I'll find him. And after him, your kids. But it will probably take a while. It's dangerous for our kind to venture outdoors, let alone drive cross country without any form of currency…"

Jefferson paused, as his eyes drank in his fairly new surroundings, then said, "If I didn't have the dream, I would never ask you to do it."

Sullivan sighed into the phone. "I know, sir. It'll be risky, but I'll do my best to track him down…"

Jefferson sniffled softly into the phone again. "I don't know what I'd ever do without you, Daniel. You have been my tried-and-true friend throughout it all."

Danforth's comment forced a tear from Sullivan's right eye. "It's always been my pleasure serving and protecting you, sir."

Jefferson sat on the couch again. "I'll ask everyone here to pray for your safe passage, and for God's protection every day."

Sullivan took a deep breath through his nose and exhaled. "Thanks. I'll surely need it…"

Jefferson rubbed his forehead with his free hand. "These are unprecedented times…"

"I'll say. Never thought the day would come when there would be a surplus of human organs in the world. With so many Christians having their organs harvested before they were beheaded, it created a surplus. So much so that Romanero recently put an end to it. What would have been a dream scenario before the Rapture, has become a reality post-Rapture."

Jefferson said, "Doesn't surprise me to hear you say that. I can't wait for it all to be over. I'm tired, Daniel. I just want to be with Jesus…"

"Perhaps the reason you're still alive, sir, is that God wants you to rescue your children from Romanero…"

Jefferson sighed. "That's my constant prayer, Daniel."

"Well, now that I'm sort of involved, I'll join you in that prayer."

"God bless you for this, Daniel…"

Sullivan half smiled into the phone. "Let me get back to what I'm doing. I'll be in touch, as soon as I have a plan in place…"

"Sounds good, Daniel…"

At that, the call ended, and Jefferson handed the phone back to Jacquelyn.

43

DAY 31 AT SEA

"HAPPY BIRTHDAY TO YOU, Happy birthday to you, Happy birthday, Cristiana and Navid, Happy birthday to you!"

When Hana and Yasamin finished singing to their children, the two were all smiles as they blew out the candles on the cupcakes, that Vishnu had managed to smuggle out of the kitchen, and their birthday dinner, which consisted of beef lo mein, rice and egg rolls.

It was a simple celebration. But having been tucked away in the belly of the ship for four and a half weeks now, Hana and Yasamin were thankful for the break from the monotony that was unavoidable on clandestine voyages like this.

Hana kissed Cristiana on the cheek and hugged her tightly. "Three years ago today, for ninety-seven seconds, you were the only child on the planet!"

"Really, Mama!" came the reply, even though she still didn't fully understand what her mother had just told her.

Hana kissed her on the cheek again. "Yes sweetie…"

Yasamin followed it up by saying to Navid, "And eight minutes later, *you* came along, sweetheart!" There wasn't a chance she would tell him she wasn't his biological mother. Usually, parents who adopted children didn't tell them until they were teenagers.

And even then, it was often received by them as terrible news, at least initially. Since Navid would never grow to be a teenager, at least not the way they understood it now, chances were good she would never tell him.

At any rate, after all this time at sea, the two mothers had developed a routine that they tried sticking to. By far, even when all the vents were closed, the greatest stress they felt was when their children were awake. The two toddlers were highly energetic and unruly, at times, and needed to be separated a couple of times each day.

The good thing about childly boredom was that it never lasted long, which was a blessing in their present situation. But it was in those moments that Cristiana would tell her mother that she wanted to go home, thus exacerbating the situation even more…

When the kids resumed playing with their toys, Hana prepared two cups of ginger tea. "Could you imagine what Romanero would do if he ever discovered we were on this ship?"

Yasamin shrugged her right shoulder. "Perhaps he already knows. If we were recorded by those microfliers in Singapore, how could he not?"

Hana scratched her itching forehead, hoping she hadn't contracted head lice from her daughter. "If so, do you think he would ever order a drone strike on our ship?"

Yasamin drank in a large gulp of air mixed in with an equal measure of fear. "Not with our children on board. You know how desperate he is to get them back! After everything we did to embarrass him, I'm sure if they weren't with us, he would order the ship destroyed, even with so many crew members on board."

"I agree. No doubt he knows it's their birthday."

Yasamin blew into her teacup a few times before venturing a sip. "The fact that he granted me full custody of Navid, he may be more furious with me than he is with you."

Perhaps I'm not archenemy number one after all... Hana thought fearfully. She watched the kids playing innocently on the hard floor. In a near whisper, she said to Yasamin, "Let's just pray no one is there to arrest us when we arrive in America."

That comment put an end to the discussion. With no place to escape to on this massive ship, both women suddenly felt like sitting ducks.

The ship rocked hard at times against the rolling waves, causing Hana to spill some of her tea on her sweater.

"Just glad brother Donald left plenty of Dramamine for us. I sure could have used it on the first leg of the trip."

Hana sighed. "You and me both! Cristiana battled several bouts of nausea on the fishing boat, and vomited most days. All I could do was hold her in my arms and sing her favorite songs to her. I think our bodies are more accustomed to being out on the water after all this time."

"True, but why does the U.S. have to be so far away?"

"I know. It seems like we've been on this ship forever."

"Well, at least we're past the halfway point. We have less than three weeks left…"

Hana sighed again. "It still seems like forever…"

When the kids were finished coloring with their crayons, the women bathed them before taking their afternoon naps.

Hana nursed Cristiana. "May I ask?"

Yasamin was watching her breastfeeding her daughter, so she knew the question had been directed at her. "Sure, anything…"

"You're very good with Navid. Why didn't you and your husband ever have children?"

Yasamin frowned. "We tried conceiving for many years, but I could never get pregnant. Then suddenly my husband vanishes from the face of the earth, and next thing you know I'm a mother."

She took another small sip of her beverage. "Did you know Navid means, 'glad tidings, good news.'"

Hana shook her head.

Yasamin closed her eyes. A tear escaped from underneath her left eyelid. "I just wish I would have been more receptive to the Good News my husband tried sharing with me, before he vanished…"

Seeing that Yasamin was on the verge of tears, Hana shifted the focus away from her family. "Whatever happened to Navid's biological father?"

"He was later linked to the massive terrorist group that set off all those bombs in America. When he returned to Africa, global police shot him dead in the front yard, in broad daylight. He never got to meet his son."

She shook her head in bewilderment. "I'm sure you still recall why his biological mother was killed…"

Hana nodded. "For refusing to name her son, Salvador, right?"

"Correct, not even as a middle name. Poor woman…" Yasamin frowned. "I also think it was because she was a Muslim. Many of my family members met that same fate for their faith in Islam. When Romanero ordered the killing of Muslims everywhere, you would think that would have been my warning to get away from him. But I didn't…"

Yasamin grimaced. "I believe the reason they told me all this was to keep me in line. I mean, if they did that to Navid's biological parents, why would they think twice about doing it to me?"

Hana gripped her teacup with both hands to warm them. "Knowing Romanero the way we do now, I'm sure you're right."

Yasamin frowned. "Ironically, I was never told their names. And I never bothered asking for them. Guess I was too excited about my new lifestyle, and too selfish and brainwashed to even think to ask. I was just happy to be the mother of their child…"

She sighed. "I won't deny that I thoroughly enjoyed living in the lap of luxury, even if only briefly. Not only had I become the talk of the town, whenever I was out in public, I was practically worshipped by so many. It felt good."

Hana sighed. "I confess that I enjoyed it myself. One of the biggest regrets I had back then was that I was always too busy entertaining my fake celebrity friends to have time to take in more of the metropolitan city. Now that I finally had the means to do whatever I wanted, my hope was to travel the world with my family someday."

Hana's voice quivered. "Yogesh changed all that with the whole world watching. When I returned from the Middle East, I became a recluse. I was always too fearful leave the house." She sighed again. "With exception to my brief visit to Dubai, and the night we spent in Singapore on the boat, Chennai is the only city I ever knew. Now it lay in ruins…"

Yasamin said, "How far we have fallen without a dollar to our names, no identification, nothing. And do you know what?"

Hana raised an eyebrow. "What?"

"I'm okay with it. I'm just glad to be free of Salvador Romanero!"

"Me too. We're so blessed to belong to Jesus now, and no longer *that* monster!"

Yasamin smiled wearily. "Shall we?"

Hana knew what her best friend meant, and reached for her Bible, as Yasamin pulled one of the battery-operated lamps closer so they could better see what they were reading.

Nothing soothed their weary nerves more than reading the Bible and praying together, especially when the kids were asleep, and they could focus all their attention on it.

As late bloomers to the faith, their goal on board this container ship was to learn everything they could about the One who had saved them on a bloody cross, more than 2,000 years ago.

"I believe we left off in the Gospel of Matthew…"

AT ROUGHLY 2 A.M., Hana and Yasamin were still studying the Word, when they heard three soft knocks on the door leading to their container.

Both women were startled and became frighteningly still.

Yasamin held up her hand, as if saying, "Be patient." They listened and waited until they heard two more bangs, followed by four more.

"Vishnu?" asked Yasamin.

"It is I," came the soft reply.

"Thank God," Yasamin said to Hana, sighing relief. She unlocked the padlock and opened the door, to find their brother in Christ holding a battery-operated lantern, which served to stab at the darkness permeating the underbelly of the cavernous ship ever so faintly.

"Would either of you like some fresh air?" he asked softly, careful not to wake the children. "If so, now would be the time. But we only have a few minutes. I believe it's your turn, Hana."

The two women stared at each other. Yasamin shrugged her shoulder. It had already been one week since Vishnu took her outside for a few minutes. She hoped she wouldn't have to wait another week before it happened again. "Go now. I'll be fine…" she said softly.

Vishnu handed Hana the same work uniform he gave to Yasamin last time, and an oversized black hoodie, to help cover her feminine features, in case they bumped into one of the other crewmates.

Hana put them on, covered her face with a facemask, then hugged her best friend, before following Vishnu up to the top deck.

"Whatever you do," he whisper-shouted, desperation dripping from his words, "please don't scream if you encounter a rat or two. I saw many on the way here."

Hana nodded that she understood his command. It wasn't easy climbing the many flights of stairs, as the ship did its best to navigate the choppy seas, but she somehow managed. But for Vishnu, it was a breeze.

When they made it outside, Hana took her time breathing in the salty sea air, which bore the strong smell of a red tide.

It wasn't the most pleasing of aromas, but the fact that she had smelled it so strongly for 15 straight days, on the first leg of the journey to Singapore, her nostrils had sort of grown used to it.

At any rate, this marked only the second time she had seen the night sky in 31 days. Her heart ached for Cristiana and Navid. They never got to leave the stowaway compartment.

Aside from the few lights on the ship, and the faint moonlight and stars, it was otherwise complete blackness. It was as if all ships were destroyed by the tsunami, save for the one she was sailing on.

Her mind was forced back to the night she saw Yogesh staring out into the darkness from their balcony, three years ago, clearly deep in thought. She could only assume that his thoughts back then, were similar to the ones now running through her mind, namely escaping from the Antichrist of the Bible...

Hana held onto the rails for balance, closed her eyes, and slowly breathed in the chilly night air. Even with the strong smell of dead fish thick in the night air, she nevertheless wished she could remain top deck until they reached the U.S. It was so peaceful.

Vishnu, on the other hand, was as nervous as could be. Eyes fearfully darting left and right, he frequently craned his neck back looking for any unusual activity, namely his fellow crew members approaching them, or the two guards on the top deck keeping watch yelling down at them.

After 20 minutes had passed—which felt more like two minutes to Hana, but two hours to Vishnu—he motioned that it was time to go.

The look on his face was a stark reminder that he was only one man among many who were clearly the enemy. Having been stuck on this boat for three weeks now, if someone discovered she was a woman, there would be no place on the ship to escape.

Happy as he was to do this for his sister in Christ, he couldn't wait for it to be over, so he could take her back to her container, then catch a few hours of sleep before his 5 a.m. shift began.

Just like that, they were heading back down to the solid-steel bowels of the ship again. Not counting the worn thin mattresses on the fold up beds they slept on, everything else was made of hard steel metal. It felt like she was being escorted back to her prison cell.

When they reached the shipping container/home, Vishnu softly rapped on the steel door again, using the 3-2-4 signal that Yasamin knew to expect.

She opened the heavy steel door to find Vishnu staring at her again. The constant ogling started soon after they had boarded the ship 31 days ago. But it was done so cutely and so shyly that he never made her feel uncomfortable.

But Vishnu couldn't help himself. The more he saw her without her disguise on, the more her stark beauty took his breath away. She looked even better in person than she had on the dozen or so times he saw her on TV, or on his phone screen. She didn't act stuck up or arrogant like she appeared to him back then.

Uddin was tall and lanky, and extremely thin. He had wavy dark black hair that was mostly unkempt on the ship. Even with severely crooked teeth, when his smile surfaced, it was quite captivating. It would cause his big black eyes to shine all the more, as if exposing part of his soul.

From a physical standpoint, Yasamin didn't consider him a handsome man. But he more than made up for it with a godly character that comforted her immensely. His words and actions were genuine and trustworthy. She felt safe with him. Hana did too.

Many men his age constantly tried wooing her, but she never gave them the time of day. The three men she had dated in her brief time living in Dubai were all in their early 30s. They were anything but godly!

After seeing and interacting with the 43-year-old man on all but three of the 31 days she was on board this ship, Vishnu was making it difficult to not fall in love with him. Especially since on many levels, he reminded her of her late husband, Navid, only Vishnu was 12 years older.

Uddin's knees grew weak seeing the way Yasamin was staring back at him, with a warm smile on her face. "Since I'm here, let me take two of those buckets for you." He stuttered his words. "I'll replace them before I start my early morning shift…"

"What would we ever do without you?" asked Hana, noticing the endearing exchange between them.

Vishnu glanced at them both wearily, yet with a glimmer of hope in his eyes that comforted both women tremendously. "To God be the glory, my dear sisters. I hope you both rest comfortably tonight."

Hana replied, "You too. If anyone needs sleep, it's you!"

"Indeed," he said, his mouth stretched in a wide yawn. He picked up two waste buckets, leaving the third bucket to last them throughout the night, and disappeared into the darkness of the underbelly of the massive ship.

Hana said, "Donald was right. He really is a true brother in the faith in every sense of the word."

Yasamin smiled dreamily. "Yeah. There's just something about him."

It was 2:30 a.m., and both women were tired.

Just as they turned off the battery-operated lanterns to sleep, they both heard in the darkness, "'If anyone worships the beast and his image and receives a mark on his forehead or upon his hand, they, too, will drink the wine of God's fury, which has been poured full strength into the cup of his wrath. They will be tormented with burning sulfur in the presence of the holy angels and of the Lamb.

"'And the smoke of their torment will rise for ever and ever. There will be no rest day or night for those who worship the beast and its image, or for anyone who receives the mark of its name.'"

Even in the belly of this rodent-infested cargo ship, in a soundproof room, the four stowaways heard each word that was uttered with perfect clarity, just like they did with the two angelic messengers.

Even the countless millions presently living in subterranean locations heard it loud and clear.

Cristiana and Navid were awakened by the Voice, but they weren't the least bit afraid. They knew it was one of God's angelic messengers. Whenever the kids heard their voices during their waking hours, they shared looks of excitement and amazement each time. Their faces would glow and the smiles on their faces would always comfort their mothers.

But the same couldn't be said for everyone else on board the massive ship. With exception to Vishnu, who was no doubt praising God for the messenger, everyone else on board the ship was no doubt in panic mode again. The first few times they heard it, every alarm on the ship went off, signaling that danger was fast approaching.

By not having access to the Word of God, the Voice terrified them each time they heard it.

Hana became so excited when she heard it, that she turned the light back on, opened her Bible to Revelation 14, and read verses 9-11 aloud, so Yasamin could hear her.

251

"Simply remarkable…" Yasamin shook her head very slowly from side to side, wishing she had known these soul-stirring truths before the Rapture, like her husband had.

"Indeed, it is…" said Hana, extinguishing the lamp again.

While everyone else on board would remain in panic mode throughout the night, Vishnu and his four stowaways in the belly of the ship, would sleep in Heavenly peace, if only for this night…

44

MANILA, PHILIPPINES

DONALD JOHNSON, ANALYN TIBAYAN and Sergei Ivanov were out on Manila Bay, docked 500 meters away from the coastline. As much as all three of them would have loved to leave the Philippines, never to return, they couldn't until they knew for sure that Analyn was saved.

Sergei stared at the welts and abrasions on her arms. "I can only imagine how much it hurt being stung by them…"

Analyn frowned, then hugged herself, as if mentally fending them off again. "So much! My body ached for many days after each sting. But no matter where I tried hiding, I couldn't escape from them. They always found me."

Seeing the terror in her eyes gave Sergei the impression that she still feared being stung by them, even though they were gone. "They had no power to sting me, but they were still a fright to see."

"So, it's really true that they had no power over Christians?"

Sergei replied, "Look at us, and answer the question for yourself! You won't find a single mark on our bodies from them, or on the bodies of any true Christ follower."

Donald added, "We were mark free then, and will remain mark free now!"

Analyn knew what he meant, but she still couldn't wrap her mind around it all.

Donald asked her, "What are your thoughts on what the third angel proclaimed…"

Analyn sighed. "The first time I heard it, I covered my ears trying to block it out, like I did with the first two angels. I was mad at God and didn't want to hear what he was saying. It never worked. But I must say the third angel frightened me the most."

Donald rubbed his chin. "Why's that?"

"It made me think about what you told me before you came here, about those taking the mark being forever doomed."

Donald nodded at her empathetically. "How much more should you believe it now that God sent an angel to proclaim the very same warning?"

"Hmm…" Analyn pulled her knees up to her chest and squeezed them tightly.

Donald cleared his throat. "The reason I risked my life to come here was so I could look you in the eye and tell you the book of Mormon is riddled with contradictions. It took being left behind after the Rapture for me to finally discover this. I've since learned that the Bible is the only Book that makes sinners right, through Christ Jesus."

"I'm confused, Ninong. I remember you teaching me about Jesus last time you were here…"

Donald held out his hands, palms out. "The Jesus I spoke about back then isn't the Jesus I serve now. The one I, we, serve now," he said, his line of vision swinging back and forth from Sergei to Analyn, "isn't a created being like the one I once taught about before. The Jesus we serve was never married. And Lucifer isn't His brother. Far from it! Nor did Jesus come from a star called, Kolob. The Jesus we serve is God!

"What I'm trying to say is that Mormons and Christians do not worship the same Jesus. The Jesus of the Bible is the Savior of the world. But the Jesus of the book of Mormon comes straight from the pits of hell."

Donald studied Analyn's eyes very carefully. "When it comes to God's salvation, saying you are saved and actually being saved are two very different things. I mean, look at me. I thought I had it all figured out last time I was here when, in truth, I was still lost…"

Analyn asked, "Okay, so how will you know if I'm saved or not?"

Donald said without hesitation, "If you are truly saved, you'll know it, and we will believe you. Only God knows the heart, but Scripture says, by our fruits we will be made known to others…"

He glanced over at Sergei. They couldn't discern her thoughts, but she was clearly confused, deflated, malnourished, and still battling severe exhaustion. Despite that she slept soundly for more than 10 hours the night before, she still couldn't stop yawning.

Sergei nodded at Donald as if reading his thoughts. They would continue in the morning…

As they settled down for the second night on board the ship, Donald silently prayed again that God would rescue this poor woman. If He did, it would make the pain he felt from missing his family worthwhile.

He once again left the battery-power lamp on until Analyn fell asleep, before turning it off to save on the battery usage.

Just as Donald was about to fall asleep, suddenly in the darkness, in a loud booming voice, they all heard it again, loud and clear: "If anyone worships the beast and its image and receives its mark on their forehead or on their hand, they, too, will drink the wine of God's fury, which has been poured full strength into the cup of his wrath.

"'They will be tormented with burning sulfur in the presence of the holy angels and of the Lamb. And the smoke of their torment will rise for ever and ever. There will be no rest day or night for those who worship the beast and its image, or for anyone who receives the mark of its name.'"

When Donald turned the battery-operated lamp back on, he saw Analyn trembling in fear. Having seen so much devastation and smoke from the many collapsed buildings and fires, the thought of experiencing that dreadful sensation of the smoke of her torment rising for ever and ever, frightened her to the core of her being.

Especially after hearing the angel declare there will be no rest day or night for those who worship the beast and its image, or for anyone who receives the mark of its name.

If the message from God's holy angel was meant to scare her into paying closer attention to the true Gospel message, he had succeeded.

She wondered if the kindness Donald and Sergei had shown her, the past two days, had something to do with the tender heart she felt now.

After all, Donald left his wife and child behind and risked his life, just for her? Who else would travel all that way in a world full of constant turmoil?

Analyn looked over at her ninong on the cot, on the opposite side of the room. She wiped tears from her eyes. "Can you tell me about the Jesus of the Bible? I'm ready to listen to you now, really listen..." Her voice trembled with each syllable.

"Hallelujah!" Donald was also exhausted and needed more sleep. But how could he sleep now after hearing this? He sat up on the bed and pulled a copy of *The Way* from his backpack, handed it to Analyn, then knocked on Sergei's small bedroom door.

Sergei was also awakened by the Voice—it was impossible not to hear it. "Come in..."

Donald entered. His face was all aglow. "Analyn wants to know how to have God's eternal assurance."

Sergei practically leapt off the bed and raised his arms toward the ceiling. "Praise Jesus!" He joined Donald and Analyn in the main cabin of the sailboat.

255

Analyn sat on her bed and listened, as the two men took turns reading the Word of God to her, until she had a complete understanding of why Jesus had to die for her.

Analyn excused herself from them and walked outside to the bow of the boat. Now that she understood she was a hell bound sinner, if she didn't make an about face and repent of her sinful lifestyle, and trust in Christ alone for her salvation, she would be eternally doomed.

She raised her hands skyward, and cried out to her Maker in the darkness, and prayed to God in her native Tagalog.

Even if Donald and Sergei could hear her words, they wouldn't understand her. But God heard her every word and understood it with unmistakable clarity. He also knew her repentant cry was sincere and genuine.

The end result was that the One who saw her unformed body from the foundation of the world, and knit her together in her mother's womb, had just pardoned all her sins, thus activating her future citizenship in Heaven. And that meant no matter what happened to her from this point forward, she now had what Donald had described to her several times as God's eternal assurance. It felt good.

Donald and Sergei wept tears of joy, when Analyn came back inside and threw herself into Donald's arms. "I believe, Ninong, and I want you to know I'll never take the mark of the beast, never!"

Sergei raised his hands up to the ceiling, praising God and sobbing tears of joy at the same time. When the first two messengers appeared earlier in the sky above, Analyn was mildly impacted by what they had proclaimed. But now her entire countenance had been changed.

She wiped tears from her eyes. "I love you both so much and I feel a special closeness to the both of you that I've never felt toward anyone before. I'm eager to learn all I can from you about these times…"

Donald was the next to wipe tears from his eyes. "I wanted to tell you earlier, but I had to be absolutely sure that you were saved first…"

"Yes, Ninong?"

"Sergei has agreed to take us to the States on his sailboat. All he wants in return is a place to live, if we ever make it there. He recently drained the fourteen thousand dollars he had left on his global monetary card, by purchasing food, water, fuel, and many other things we'll need for the long voyage, so we should be fine. But we will adhere to strict food rationing, just in case."

Analyn's face lit up. She wanted to pinch herself to make sure she wasn't dreaming.

"The bad news is that God's judgments are far from over. It's about to get even worse, if you can fathom that. The seven bowl judgments, which we'll do our best to explain to you in the coming days and weeks, are next to come.

"For now, you must know that since they will surely be released during our time at sea, there are no guarantees that we'll make it to the States. Sorry to have to tell you this, but I thought you should know in advance..."

Analyn sucked air in through her nose and breathed it out of her mouth. "At least I won't be alone. I'll be with the two of you."

Donald grew more somber. "As much as I wanted to spend a week or so trying to locate some of the others, after seeing the widespread devastation in your country, I don't know if it will be possible."

Analyn gulped hard. "Even if you could go back to my village, you won't find anyone there. The entire village was wiped out..." she said, trying not to recall the faces of those she had known all her life, but knew had perished in the floodwaters.

Donald's heart burned within him. But Analyn was right. It would be too dangerous to go there all for nothing. He asked Sergei, "When can we leave?"

"I say now. With more and more people receiving the mark, every day we're out in public will make it even more difficult to escape. Even being out here on the water is dangerous.

"If the Coast Guard approaches us and wants to come on board to search the boat, it could spell trouble for us. And if thieves ever stormed the boat, it wouldn't be good."

The way Sergei said it forced Analyn's mind back to her nightmarish days of living on the streets. "I'm ready to leave now!"

Sergei added, "You should know we will be out at sea for a very long time, perhaps as long as seven months."

Analyn nodded that she understood and was ready. "That will give me plenty of time to learn about the Word of God."

Donald silently rejoiced hearing this. Her statement made his whole journey worthwhile. Wave upon wave of relief washed over him. He was so overjoyed that he embraced Analyn and didn't let go of her, as they both shed tears of joy.

"May I ask, Ninong?"

"Sure, anything…," came the answer.

"Who gave you the clothing to give to me?"

Donald paused for effect. "Hana Patel!"

Analyn looked confused. Then it dawned on her. "The woman who was the first to give birth after the disappearances?"

Donald grinned from ear to ear. "That would be her! Before we parted ways in Singapore, when I told Hana and her friend Yasamin I was going to the Philippines to rescue you, and hopefully others, they handed me a backpack full of the things they thought you would need."

"I don't know what to say, Ninong…"

"No need to say anything. But do I have a story to tell you…"

Analyn said, "I love good stories, especially those with happy endings."

Sergei stared at Analyn. Now that she was a believer, she appeared so much more attractive to him. Everything she said was attractive. Her smile was attractive. Her mannerisms were attractive.

He grinned to himself, and silently praised God for preserving his sailboat from the destructive flood waters a few months ago, and for bringing the three of them together.

Even with God's seven bowl judgments looming, he looked forward to being out at sea for who knew how long with this young woman, so they could get to know each other even better. *Thy will be done, Lord…*

45

JACKSONVILLE, FLORIDA

AFTER FIFTY LONG AND grueling days at sea, followed by spending three nights at David Wilcox' safe house just north of Jacksonville, the journey to Southeastern Pennsylvania began for Hana Patel, Yasamin Dabiri, their two children, and Vishnu Uddin.

Wilcox gladly volunteered to drive them on what they had all hoped would be the final leg of what had already been a long and tedious journey.

Mindful that many of their locations had been spied on, who knew if his safe house would still be standing when he returned to Florida.

If he returned...

After having a quick breakfast, the safe house residents all laid hands on them and prayed for God's supernatural protection, before they left the property under the cover of darkness, at 5 a.m., in the back of a 15-seat passenger van—which like so much of their fleet—had been converted to transport caskets.

For this trip, three coffins were needed. Just one glance at them forced Hana's mind back to when Cristiana was placed inside the gray plastic container in the back seat of the van, in Chennai, before two men ultimately carried her to the fishing boat that took them to Singapore.

When she opened the lid and saw her daughter lying inside with a lollipop stuffed in her mouth, tears filling her big black eyes, fear etched onto her face, it was a look that Hana never wanted to see on Cristiana's face again.

Her eyes screamed, "Don't ever leave me again, Mama!"

All Hana could do was hold her in her arms that day, telling her how proud she was of her, hoping it would never happen again.

How much worse would she feel if she had to stuff her daughter inside a casket, of all things, if they got pulled over by law enforcement?

Had Hana not been saved, she would have never agreed to such a preposterous notion! But as one of the most wanted fugitives on the planet, what choice did she have?

Then again, despite the many precautions they were taking, if they were pulled over, the instant Wilcox was asked to produce identification,

259

the fact that his name wasn't registered in the global database would be enough to detain them, until they all could be positively identified.

Upon discovering that he was smuggling two of Romanero's Top Ten Most Wanted fugitives in the back of his vehicle, that alone would warrant global coverage.

The arresting officers would become instant heroes, and overnight millionaires. Cristiana and Navid would be reacclimated into Antichrist's global institutions, as the four adults were executed on live television, followed by a celebration over their collective demise, Hana's and Yasamin's especially.

Yasamin was thinking similar thoughts herself. Having travelled all this way, they would fervently pray that it wouldn't come to that.

Though technically not a fugitive yet, if they were pulled over by law enforcement, Vishnu would hide in one of the three coffins.

If it was ever opened, once he was identified, he would have a lot of explaining to do—namely why he chose to get out of Dodge before receiving the Mark with the rest of his crewmates.

But there could be no explaining why he was riding in a vehicle with Hana Patel and Yasamin Dabiri. The instant they made the connection, Uddin's fate would be sealed.

They prayed that if it ever came to that, and they had to hide in the caskets, Cristiana and Navid wouldn't create such a commotion that it would arouse immediate suspicion, which, in turn, would give the officers a reason to inspect the coffins, looking for alive bodies where only dead bodies should be.

To make room for the three caskets, the three rows of bench seats had to be removed from the vehicle. Since Vishnu was the largest passenger, he occupied the front seat, as the other four passengers were squeezed very tightly in between the front seats and the three caskets.

They sat on the floor on stacks of blankets, without the use of seatbelts. To make matters worse, they had to share their tight floor space with a 36-gallon steel fuel tank that was full of gasoline, so they wouldn't have to stop to refuel along the way.

They couldn't even stop at convenience stores to use the restrooms when the need arose. Everyone would have to relive themselves in the brush just off the highway...Though the kids were nearly potty-trained, and only wore diapers at night, they wore them for this trip.

Surprisingly, they made it through the state of Georgia with only a few short construction delays. Halfway through South Carolina, they saw their first ROAD CLOSURE sign, roughly 10 miles south of Santee, just as Donald Johnson had told them to expect.

Wilcox had prepared an alternative route in advance, without the use of GPS. It added three hours to the trip, but it was so much better than being stuck on I-95, with no way of crossing the bridge, except by boat, which they couldn't pay for anyway.

When they reached the state of Virginia, David exited the highway and parked the vehicle in a vacant parking lot, situated near a patch of woods, so he could take a desperately needed nap.

Hana also napped. Although she hadn't been on a ship in more than a week, her body still felt a little queasy, and discombobulated from having spent so much time at sea.

When she first arrived at the Florida safe house, she felt wobbly and had to hold onto the towel rack each time she showered, to keep from slipping and falling. Now that her condition had finally improved, she had to endure the 800-mile trip in a van in which she had no seat to sit on, giving her that same dreadful wobbly sensation again.

Whenever she felt like complaining, she would tell herself, "So long as we don't have to board another ship, it's just perfect!"

As David and Hana slept, Yasamin and Vishnu took the kids for a walk in the nearby woods to stretch their legs.

As the kids ran around and played together, Vishnu, who was never married, explained to Yasamin that the woman he once loved had died a few years before the Rapture, when a fire ravaged their tiny village, killing many who lived there, including his parents.

"I was at sea when it happened," he said sadly. "When I returned home and discovered what had happened to my village, I wept bitterly for many days." Vishnu gasped. "Now that I know their eternal whereabouts, I feel like weeping again…"

Yasamin hugged Vishnu, then held him until she was convinced that he had finally brushed those morbid thoughts away.

Not that either one had any doubts before this loving encounter, but this was the moment they both knew God wanted them to spend their remaining days together as husband and wife.

They held hands all the way back to the van. Even though Yasamin was disguised as a grandmother, Vishnu knew whose hand he was holding. Underneath her disguise was the most beautiful woman he had ever laid eyes on. He smiled at the thought.

261

When they were back in the van, David and Hana were awake.

As David steadied the vehicle back onto the highway, in broken English, Hana, Yasamin and Vishnu took turns praying for God's ongoing protection, as Cristiana and Navid watched a children's DVD.

Wilcox was both deeply touched and comforted by their heartfelt prayers to the God they served. It was moving that he frequently brushed tears from his eyes. It was a remarkable sensation, to say the least.

They finally arrived at safe house number one at 4 a.m., 23 hours after leaving the Sunshine State. This trip would have taken roughly half that time before the Rapture.

Titus and his wife, Ingrid, were waiting for them when they pulled up to the rear property entrance. Titus quickly waved them in.

Jacquelyn was also there to greet them. Brian wasn't feeling well again, so she left him at home with their sleeping daughter.

Jacquelyn leaned her head inside the vehicle, not sure at first glance who was who with their disguises on. It didn't take long to deduce which one was Hana and which one was Yasamin, mostly because Cristiana was lying on what looked like the lap of a teenage boy, which Jacquelyn could only assume was Hana.

Jacquelyn nodded to David Wilcox. She knew he was the point guard on this trip, but this was their first-time meeting in person.

She whispered to the man in the passenger front seat, "Vishnu?"

He nodded at her with a tired grin.

Jacquelyn attempted a smile of her own, but she had difficulty producing one. Donald Johnson had contacted them when he arrived in the Philippines, explaining his encounter with the now-former seaman from Bangladesh. Now that the mark was mandatory, Vishnu had already been cleared from above to join them at safe house number one.

In that light, Jacquelyn had fully expected to see him there. "Welcome home, everyone!" she uttered softly, concern splashed all over her face.

Fatigued as they were, now that they had arrived safely, Jacquelyn's words washed over them.

Hana lowered her head remorsefully, then said to Jacquelyn, "I'm sorry for all the trouble we've caused you. We already know our conversation in Singapore was recorded."

If she was upset by their carelessness in Singapore, it didn't show. It was bound to happen at some point. She was mildly surprised that her anonymity had lasted this long. Now that she had been positively identified as Joan Henriksen, she felt like an international fugitive twice over.

Jacquelyn replied, "Think nothing of it, Hana. Even if your voices hadn't been recorded over there, our days at this place were already numbered."

Another strong dose of guilt swam through Hana's frail body.

Jacquelyn noticed it, and said, "But we can discuss all these things in the morning, after you've rested. Just glad you made it here safely."

"Thank you, Joan, I mean Jacquelyn," said Hana, with another hearty yawn. Although this didn't come as unexpected news, after everything they had all endured to finally make it to America, it was the last thing any of them wanted to hear. It was quite deflating. "Where's Brian?"

"Sleeping. He's practically bedridden these days."

Yasamin asked, "Was he injured in the global quake?"

Jacquelyn shook her head. "My husband's lungs have weakened substantially since the Rapture. It started when we first moved onto the property, but it's gradually gotten worse. The mold and dust in most of the cottages did serious damage to his lungs. The explosions that rocked America on Universal Children's Day only made him worse. It seems like he catches a new cold every two weeks or so. He was told by our resident doctor that his lungs won't regenerate…"

Hana lowered her head. "Sorry to hear that," came the sad reply.

"All we can do is keep praying for him." Jacquelyn twisted her lips one way then the other. She wanted to cry, but after everything their two new residents had already endured—including losing their husbands—she remained strong for them. "Brian will be so happy to see you."

Hana smiled wearily again. "I can't wait to thank him for what he did for me and Yogesh. Both of you, in fact."

For whatever reason, when Hana called her late husband by his name, Jacquelyn was reminded again that the most famous woman and child on the planet were now in her presence. Then again, since the former President of the United States of America and Benjamin Shapiro were also residing at this place, it only figured.

Jacquelyn refocused. "You can see him in the morning when you wake up. You've had a very long trip. Would you like separate cottages, or would you like to share one?"

"Share," Hana and Yasamin both said in unison.

After everything they had endured since being reunited, they had grown so close and were grateful to God for allowing them to spend their final days on Earth living at the same safe house. They never wanted to be separated again.

Jacquelyn asked Titus, "Can you take David and Vishnu to the male shelter?"

"Copy that!" came the reply.

"Thanks, Titus…"

46

AT 8 A.M., AFTER managing a three-hour nap, followed by a soothing lukewarm shower, Hana dropped Cristiana off at the newly constructed daycare center, then strolled the property, careful to steer clear away from the areas that were uprooted in the global quake, two years ago.

She invited Yasamin to join her, but with Navid sleeping soundly in her arms, she didn't want to wake him. Besides, this was her first time sleeping in an aboveground bed since her escape from the Middle East.

In no way was this small cot nearly as comfortable as the massive king-sized bed she got to sleep in each night in Dubai, but after spending a combined 65 days at sea, hidden inside two storage containers on two massive cargo ships, it was just perfect.

Uncertain about when they would be forced to flee this safe house, Yasamin wanted to take full advantage of it by sleeping in a little longer.

Hana was eager to meet her new brothers and sisters in Christ. As she drank in her new surroundings, she was equally comforted knowing guards were on duty 'round the clock, protecting the property as best they could. Even though it had been severely damaged by the global quake, she could see why everyone living there had loved this place so much.

Yet, after being informed of the recent developments, she wouldn't allow herself to become too attached to her surroundings. The strained expression she saw on Jaquelyn's face the night before told her all she needed to know—their time at this place would be short!

Hana saw a young girl holding hands with a child, walking as briskly as the toddler would allow. Their heads were down, playing guessing games with things on the ground, to hopefully conceal their identities from possible microfliers out spying on them.

Not that it mattered all that much. According to Anthony Galiano, they had no doubt already been identified.

When Hana heard the youngster say, "Okay, Mommy", her first thought was that this girl looked too young to be a mother. She brushed that thought aside and asked, "Excuse me, but can you point me in the direction of where the Mulrooneys are staying?"

Leticia stopped walking and stared at her for a few moments, wondering who it was. This wasn't a place where strangers loitered on the grounds. But since Jakob frequently sent new believers to them, Leticia new for certain this woman was a believer, but who was she?

It took a few seconds for the young mother to realize who it was. The spiked hair had thrown her off. After finally realizing who it was, Leticia's mouth was agape. "Hana Patel?"

Hana nodded at the young girl and smiled, thankful to be recognizable again, at least among her brothers and sisters in the faith.

She was also thankful to no longer be wearing clothing that made her look like a rebellious teenager, and grateful that her hair had grown a couple of inches since being chopped off nearly three months ago.

Combined, these things helped her feel even more like her old self.

Leticia was practically awestruck upon seeing her. It was reminiscent of the way her mother had reacted when she met Lila Choharjo for the first time, when the former Hollywood actress arrived in Chadds Ford. "Praise God, you made it! How was your journey?"

Hana's teeth chattered in the brisk chilly wind. "Very long! I can't remember ever feeling this exhausted."

Leticia nodded at her. "I can only imagine after so many days at sea. Since we had no contact with you, none of us knew if you were safe, or when you would finally arrive. I prayed for you every day."

Hana's face lit up. "Thanks so much. Just hope I can adjust to this cold weather," she said, visibly shivering. "I'm freezing!"

Leticia laughed at the way she had said it. "I can't tell you how empowered I felt the day you made your online declaration for Jesus! Holding up those cards was a brilliant idea! I still get chills thinking about it."

"Glory to God, right?" Hana blew into her gloveless hands to warm them. "What's your name?"

"Oh, I'm sorry. It's Leticia Guzman."

"Is that your son?"

Leticia nodded. "Julio junior. JJ for short." She rubbed her belly. "I have another one on the way…"

"Congratulations!" Hana said, not sure if she really meant it. "May I ask how old you are?"

"Fifteen."

In another lifetime, Hana would have winced upon hearing this young teenager tell her she had a husband and a young child, with one more on the way. It was fairly common in some circles in India, but she never thought it would happen in America. "Are you married?"

"I surely am! Just finished having breakfast with my husband, before he went on guard duty. Speaking of kids, how's Cristiana?"

Hana yawned heartily, not at all surprised that this young woman knew her daughter's name. "She's fine. Just dropped her off at daycare."

"Which one? There are seven of them on the property."

Hana twisted her neck back and pointed at the building from which she had just left. "That one over there…"

A smile formed on Leticia's face. "That's the one I work at. I'm on my way there now to begin my shift. I'm excited to meet Cristiana."

Hana remarked, "When she saw the room full of children, it was like I no longer existed."

"I'm sure the toys also had something to do with it. How would you feel if you were three years old in this crazy world? I know I would be anxious to play with new friends, especially after being stuck on a ship for so long. Don't take it personally."

Hana surveyed the property. "You're right. Besides, this is the first real daycare center she's ever been to…"

Leticia said, "The fact that our children have zero exposure to the outside world is a major blessing. Our kids will never have access to cell phones, unless they will be used in the Millennial Kingdom. Funny thing is, had you told me that before the Rapture, I would have thought it to be cruel and unjust punishment. Now I praise God for the blessing!"

"Prior to the Rapture, many teenage churchgoers were constantly exposed to endless temptations on their mobile devices, video games that were full of carnage, pornography, online gambling, and on and on.

"But now that they're being paid to kill us," Leticia said softly, not wanting her son to hear it, "why play online video games when they can do it in the real world, and actually be paid for it?"

A shiver shot through Hana upon hearing this. But she was also comforted knowing that Cristiana would be taught the Word of God at this place, in preparation for the Millennial Kingdom, without having those worldly evils being sprinkled in.

Leticia said, "Caring for so many children can be tedious work at times, but it's well worth it."

Hana smiled in reply, then blew into her gloveless hands again to warm them.

"I know you're cold. You should go…"

"I hope to see you later when I fetch Cristiana."

267

"Hope our kids will become close friends…"

"I'm sure they will, Leticia."

Leticia smiled her reply, then pointed Hana in the direction of the main house, and they parted company.

When she got to the main residence, she knocked on the door. A man opened it. "Sorry to disturb you. I'm here to see Jacquelyn."

"Good morning, Hana. Welcome to safe house number one!" Jefferson Danforth said warmly. Even without being briefed—those days were long gone—he knew who she was. "How was your trip?"

"Very long," came the shivering reply, unaware that she was talking to the former President of the United States. "Just happy to be here."

Jefferson was mildly surprised that she didn't know who he was. *Do I look that different?* "This is supposed to be our summer season. But it still looks and feels like winter, minus the snow…"

It suddenly dawned on Hana who this man was, who she thought he was anyway. She cocked her head one way then the other. If it was the former U.S. President, he looked so much older now, and frailer than when she had seen him on TV and online. "Are you who I think you are?"

"Jefferson Danforth at your service!" he replied jokingly, flashing his once world-famous smile at her, which wasn't so flashy these days.

"But I thought you were…"

"Dead?" Jefferson asked her.

Hana lowered her head. "Yes. Sorry."

Jefferson beamed. "Until just recently, only a handful of people on the planet knew I was still alive. Soon, everyone will know, I'm afraid."

His comment had turned Hana's legs into jelly. It forced her mind back to Jacquelyn's comment when they first arrived at the safe house. She sensed even more now that their time at this place would be shorter than she had anticipated.

Had she not been introduced to so many world-renowned individuals, in the few months in which she was being hailed as one of Planet Earth's heroines, she would have been petrified at the very thought of being in the man's presence. "It's a pleasure meeting you, Sir."

"Believe me when I say, the pleasure's all mine. I feel like I'm the one in the presence of greatness!" Perhaps it was an infamy thing for being the first woman to give birth, post Rapture, but he was more awestruck seeing this mere nobody, before she gave birth, than he was when meeting with global leaders, and scores of other famous human beings.

She's certainly braver than them—her husband too, for that matter! Even in the most perilous of times, Jefferson was amazed at how humans could still elevate certain individuals in their minds and hearts, and place them on pedestals. *Apparently, this is even true with former Presidents...* Hana stared at the man who was so despised in the many elitist circles to which she once belonged. He didn't appear to have a mean bone in his body. If anything, he seemed genuinely kind, caring, and certainly unpretentious—nothing like the monster her former friends had groomed her to hate back then.

Amy Danforth heard the commotion and joined her husband at the front door. "Hello Hana," she said warmly, softly, thankful that she had survived the long voyage.

Jefferson said, "This is my wife, Amy."

Hana raised a curious eyebrow. *Wife?* She brushed aside the thought. After her encounter with Leticia Guzman, this was nothing. "It's a pleasure meeting you, Amy."

"Likewise. Please come in."

Once Hana was inside, her eyes did a quick survey of the house. She wasn't the least bit surprised to see so many deep lines on the walls and on the ceiling, presumably from the global quake. Despite how drafty it was inside the house, she immediately felt the warmth on her face.

Hana saw a couple seated on the living room couch.

Jefferson made the introductions. "Hana, meet Brian's parents, Dick and Sarah Mulrooney."

"Nice meeting you both..."

Dick and Sarah got up off the couch. "Pleasure meeting you, Hana!" Dick's face was aglow. "We've been waiting for this day for a very long time. We've prayed for you every day."

Hana smiled shyly, grateful for the many prayers that had been offered up to God on her behalf, mostly from folks she didn't know. Now that she understood the power of prayer, it comforted her to no end.

Sarah gave Hana a comforting squeeze. She could feel her body trembling from the colder climate. It never got this cold in India."

Benjamin Shapiro introduced himself to Hana. "I'm sure you won't mind me telling you this, Hana, but I recently took the top spot on Romanero's Top Ten Most Wanted List. Better me than you, right?"

Hana gulped hard and remained silent, not knowing how to reply to his soul-stopping comment.

After Hana was introduced to everyone else in the living room, Sarah asked, "Would you like me to get Jacquelyn for you?"

Hana looked down at her feet. "Yes, please," she said shyly, "if you wouldn't mind…"

"Be right back." Sarah took her time trudging her way up the stairs.

A few moments later, Jacquelyn descended the steps leading to the living room, carrying her daughter, with her mother-in-law in tow. "Good morning, Hana!" she said softly. "Did you get enough sleep?"

"I slept soundly for three hours. I'm sure I'll need a nap later, but for now I wanted to get out and meet everyone, and walk the property."

The two women embraced. "Meet our daughter, Sarah."

Hana's face became aglow. "Aww, so precious!"

"Thanks. We couldn't be more blessed! Brian's still sleeping. Let me see if I can wake him."

Hana said, "You don't have to do that, Jacquelyn."

"Are you kidding?! You know how long he's been waiting to finally meet you! He'll be more upset if I don't tell him you're here. But like I said last night, he hasn't been feeling well, so I'm afraid you'll have to see him up in our bedroom."

"That would be fine."

"The stairway was badly damaged in the global quake, and can be a little dangerous for first timers, so watch your step."

Hana nodded that she understood, then carefully followed Jacquelyn upstairs.

47

WHEN THEY REACHED THE landing, sadness covered Jacquelyn's face. "I hope Brian has the strength to make it to the end. He spends more time in bed these days than out of it. Doctor Singh said it's double pneumonia this time."

Hana shot her a sideways look. "Double pneumonia?"

Jacquelyn explained, "It affects both lungs instead of just one. He has shortness of breath, congestion, phlegm, severe body aches and full-blown fatigue. So, even with a facemask on, you may want to keep your distance from him. This means no hugging for now. I'd hate to see you catch it."

Hana nodded at Jacquelyn. "I understand." Like most others on the planet, with the constant temperature changes, and the many unhealthy elements still filling the atmosphere, she was among the growing majority who had increasing difficulty boosting her immune system. The last thing she wanted was to catch another cold.

Jacquelyn stuck her head through the curtain, to find her husband in bed with his eyes closed. "Honey, are you awake?"

Brian yawned into his fist. "I am now. Did they arrive?"

Jacquelyn smiled. "Early this morning, but I didn't want to wake you. Hana's with me now. Are you up to seeing her?"

"Are you kidding? Absolutely! Send her in…"

Jacquelyn craned her neck back at Hana, then pulled back the curtain covering the door frame, so she could enter inside.

Brian took his time sitting up on the bed. He was thrilled to be meeting one of his heroes in the faith. "Welcome to safe house number one, Hana! Finally, we meet in person!" Brian glanced up at the ceiling. "Thank You, Lord, for delivering them here safely."

"Amen…" said Hana and Jacquelyn in reply, softly, gratefully.

Brian coughed into his hand. "Please pardon my appearance."

Hana ran her right fingers through her scalp. "Look at me! I should apologize to you," she said through her face mask. "At least I no longer have to dress like a punk rocker…"

"Compared to the disguise your husband wore during his escape from Dubai, your disguise is mild."

Hana was curious and asked, "What was his disguise?"

"When he left the arena that day, some of our operatives were outside waiting for him. They led him to a nearby tent, and ordered him to take off his suit, before disguising him as a Muslim woman. He wore a full burka, fake breasts, and all."

The way Jacquelyn said it forced laughter from Hana. It didn't last. "Many of our operatives also died that day or were thrown in prison."

Brian said, "Just wish I could have met Yogesh. This was where he was headed until…" He paused. There was no need to finish the sentence. "Though we hardly knew each other, I came to love and respect him so much. How could I not after what he did with the whole world watching? God used him to draw multitudes to Him."

Hana lowered her head in shame. Just hearing this massive amount of praise being heaped upon her late husband caused more guilt to mushroom through her. She sighed. "Do you think he'll forgive me for not standing by his side in Dubai?"

Brian said, "Truth be told, the only forgiveness you need, you already have in Christ Jesus. I assure you when Yogesh discovers you trusted in Christ, he'll be so overjoyed that forgiving you will never come to his mind. That was his constant prayer for you. Ours too, for that matter."

Hana became teary-eyed. She whispered, "Wow!"

Jacquelyn smiled. "What an amazing reunion it will be!"

Brian asked, "Were you aware of the prison guard who recently became a believer?"

Hana shook her head. Ever since she escaped from her home, she had virtually no contact with the outside world.

Brian coughed into his fist. This caused his lungs to hurt again, but he didn't care. "His name was Hans. The way God used him very much reminded me of how he used you and Yogesh."

Hana was curious as ever. "How?"

"The day before the Mark became mandatory for all prison workers, he went to work for the first time in two years, after being badly injured in the global quake."

The look on Hana's face conveyed to the Mulrooneys that she had no idea where Brian was going with this.

Jacquelyn took over. "The reason my husband's telling you this is that he credited you for the first Bible verse he ever memorized. He recited Romans, one sixteen for all to hear, much like you did with more than a million viewers. It went viral from there! He even credited you, for giving him the backbone he was lacking as a Christian…"

Hana stiffened, surprised by what she just heard. Tears flooded her eyes. "Really? He said that?"

Jacquelyn shook her head, then smiled at Hana. "And that's only one person. If our inside source is correct," she said, without mentioning Agent Galiano by name, "hundreds of thousands of prison guards, government officials, local and global law enforcement, and scores of new mothers, who were all slated to receive the mark on the first day, never showed up for their appointments…"

Brian adjusted his weight on the bed. "I can only imagine how many others got saved after hearing your bold declaration. I still get goosebumps thinking about it. Unlike the fortune that was recently stripped away from you, the treasures you're storing up in Heaven are eternal."

Now that Hana better understood what storing up treasures in Heaven was all about, much like her husband was still doing—even in absentia—the feeling it gave her was priceless. It didn't last. She took a few deep nervous breaths. "Can you tell me about the new developments?"

Brian shifted his weight on the bed ever so slowly, then motioned for his wife to answer the question for him.

Jacquelyn sat on the edge of the bed. "Just like the Singapore safe house you were at was being spied on by those microfliers, many others have also been compromised, including this one, I'm afraid."

Hana's eyes widened. "How do you know?" She braced herself.

Jacquelyn bit her lip. "When we first purchased the land, we were grouped together with five hundred other properties in the U.S. and Canada. Long story short, the woman who sold it to us was killed in an explosion not too far from here. They recovered Rhonda's cellphone and eventually discovered the properties after conducting a search of her phone."

Hana became even more panicked hearing this. Exhausted as she was, the notion of being relocated yet again was quite deflating. "Are we still being spied on?"

"Not to our knowledge. The air above us is checked twenty-four-seven for microfliers. We haven't found a single one since we first became aware that we were being spied on."

Hana's shoulders slumped. The thought of being relocated yet again fatigued her to no end. "When will we have to leave?"

Jacquelyn pressed her lips together. "Still not sure. But it could happen any day now. All we know is that it won't happen until Romanero plucks as many children out of our care as he can. But we've been warned to be ready to flee in a moment's notice."

The expression on Hana's face mirrored what she saw on Jacquelyn's face the night before. "Where will we go?"

"Fear not. We have another location not too far from here," Jacquelyn said, careful not to mention Kennett Square just in case, "but we're still unsure as to when we can leave. We're told this will be the final shift, and our kids will be safe there…"

"I understand." What caused even more fear to surface on Hana's face was knowing the relocation wouldn't come from another one of God's judgments, but from the man she had once pledged her undying love and respect to—Salvador Romanero.

There was a knock on the doorframe. "Who is it?"

"It's Meera, Brian…"

Brian said, "Sorry to break up this wonderful meeting, but it's time for my checkup…"

After the two women were introduced, it dawned on Hana who this woman was. Meera had sent her a handful of emails trying to witness to her, in her native tongue. All went unanswered. "Please forgive me for not replying to your messages. I wasn't a believer yet, and I was paranoid."

Meera waved her off. "Think nothing of it, Hana. I'm just glad you arrived safely…" They embraced.

As Meera began her examination on her patient, Jacquelyn and Hana returned to the living room to find Yasamin, Vishnu and David Wilcox seated on the couch together, engaged in conversation with their new brothers and sisters in Christ. The first thing they noticed was that Vishnu and Yasamin were holding hands.

Jefferson Danforth asked Vishnu, "How was the trip?"

This was Vishnu's first time being in the presence of a global leader. It was a little overwhelming. He took a deep breath and exhaled. "It went a little too smoothly, if you ask me."

Jefferson flinched. "Really?"

Vishnu nodded at him. "The one thought I keep wrestling with even now, is how I was able to sneak four stowaways off the ship so easily. It was a blessing to be sure, but it was just too easy. Truth be told, I don't know how we escaped that day."

Yasamin raised a curious eyebrow. "Oh?"

"There were so many moments when I thought for sure we would be caught. The first time was when I informed you all that the Florida coastline was in view, and it was time to be moved into a much-smaller shipping container top deck."

Vishnu took a moment to explain to everyone in the living room, "It is customary for the container ship to be ordered to stop five miles out from the coastline, so locals could board and inspect the ship before bringing it to dock, with the help of three tugboats."

With everyone brought up to speed, he glanced over at Hana, "Remember when you were being moved into the smaller shipping container, and Cristiana kept whining that she wanted to go home, which prompted Navid to do the same?"

Hana nodded. Her eyes were a little brighter, after being washed by her own tears upstairs.

"I knew the kids couldn't wait to get off the ship. They were tired of being stuck in a stowaway compartment." Vishnu shook his head in astonishment. "But the tension I felt was through the roof. It was a miracle that my coworkers didn't hear the commotion going on."

Vishnu looked to his left and said to Yasamin, "That's why I waited seven hours before finally opening the container door."

Yasamin tightened her grip on Vishnu's hand. "For a moment there, we thought you forgot about us…"

"How could I forget you, Yasamin?"

Everyone in the room picked up on a certain sweetness in his voice. It caused Yasamin to blush. She looked down at her feet. The fact that she was already paler than usual, from spending so much time in a storage container, made her pink cheeks easier for everyone to see.

Even Hana, who was more dark-skinned than Yasamin, looked gaunt like, due to a lack of exposure to the sun.

Tom Dunleavey straightened in his chair, silently wondering if he would soon be officiating another wedding that the State of Pennsylvania would never know about. When he was first asked to officiate marriages at safe house number one, he was hesitant at first.

Before the Rapture, he would have never agreed to marry couples so quickly, especially without having them first take marriage courses in advance. He no longer felt that way. How could he, when the divorce rate at all *ETSM* safe houses was at zero percent?

Another thing that had bolstered his decision to officiate marriages so quickly, was that the couples he married at safe house number one never had adulterous thoughts, never cheated on their spouses, and never needed marriage counseling. They were just grateful to have someone to cling to during these desperate times. It was the most amazing thing!

Before the Rapture, the divorce rate among Christians was as high as all other demographics. They could have learned so much about what true Christian living in marriage was all about, just by observing them.

Vishnu felt awkward by the rush of attention and got back on point. "To my great relief, when I opened it, the children were sound asleep. Hana carried Cristiana and Yasamin carried Navid, as I carefully guided them off the ship. I was sweating bullets, as the saying goes…"

Amy Danforth said, "I can only imagine…"

Vishnu took a few deep breaths, having just relived the harrowing experience. "But here's the thing, this wasn't my first time being part of a human smuggling operation. I'm sure you know I also helped Donald Johnson get to Singapore."

Jacquelyn answered for everyone, "Yes, we know…"

Vishnu nodded at her. "Anxious as I was to sneak him off the ship, I expected it to be even worse with two women and children. The most difficult and dangerous part of the smuggling process has always been getting stowaways off the ship. How much worse with two children, and their mothers wearing disguises?"

The now former seaman was still having difficulty processing it all. "No one was bribed this time. And yet, I was able to sneak them off the ship, past the crew and coast guard, and straight to David's vehicle without the slightest struggle. It was too easy…"

David interjected, "When we arrived at the Jacksonville safe house, I informed Hana and Yasamin that their conversation at the Singapore safe house had been recorded, just as we all had feared. The enemy heard Donald address Hana as the 'First Lady of childbirth, part two', not to mention that he belonged to a group of believers in Pennsylvania.

"But his biggest mistake was when he addressed Brad and Joan Henricksen, as Brian and Jacquelyn Mulrooney. I fully expected global authorities to break down the doors to arrest us all. But it never happened."

Vishnu added, "I asked David how he knew for sure the conversation had been recorded. He told me the Henriksens were already on Romanero's Top 10 Most Wanted list, but the updated list had the names Brian and Jacquelyn Mulrooney on it." He rubbed his throbbing forehead. "And yet, we made it all this way. It was far too easy. Deceptively easy…"

After listening to the conversation very carefully, Benjamin Shapiro weighed in, "I'm sure your assumptions are spot on. It really was too easy.

It confirms that we really are on his radar. Romanero undoubtedly knows by now that Donald lives here, not to mention Brian and Jacquelyn, President Danforth, and perhaps even me too."

Benjamin shook his head very slowly from side to side. "If so, I know how the man operates. He undoubtedly gave the order to let you travel safely here, so he could catch all of us together…"

The room was silent as everyone tried absorbing what Dr. Shapiro had just told them.

Finally, Jacquelyn asked him, "So, what should we do?"

Benjamin pressed his hands together. "The only thing we can do, keep praying for God's protection."

After a while, Wilcox shook his head. "It's mind boggling to think how an innocent conversation on a boat in Singapore, has potentially done massive damage to our global organization."

Yasamin said to David, "Sorry for causing you so much trouble. Because of us, you may never get to return to Florida."

Wilcox waved her off. "I've already accepted that I may never return to the Sunshine State. But it's okay. Florida isn't so sunshiny anymore. This is my home now, until Christ returns for us…"

48

FORMER U.S. SECRET SERVICE Agent Anthony Galiano read the report; his heart nearly failed him. He sent a secure text message to Clayton Holmes: *Change of plans! Call me!*

Clayton was with Travis and Lee Kim at their safe house location, in Northwest Georgia. He showed both men his SAT phone screen. Travis reached for his water bottle as Lee Kim lowered his head in fear.

Holmes wasted no time calling the former secret service agent. "What's up, Anthony?" As much as he wanted to turn the speaker on for the benefit of his two brothers, he couldn't take that chance. He would brief them after the call.

Galiano didn't mince words. "Romanero moved the bombing campaign up one week. Thanks to Dr. Shapiro's email, many of Salvador's staff stopped showing up for work, including some of his top military officials. Because of this, he decided to move it up before one of them eventually leaked it to the millions of dissidents, whose lives he hoped to end in the coming days.

"He also ordered all strike locations to be surrounded by law enforcement in case it was leaked, and those living at those places tried escaping before the bombing occurred. I'm sure he would have moved it up even sooner, but a global campaign of this magnitude requires careful planning. Even moving it up one week was a monumental task."

"What a madman!" said Clayton angrily, clenching his fists as tightly as he could. Hartings and Kim became even more fearful seeing his reaction. They weren't sure they wanted to know what had caused it.

"You're right about that!" said Galiano. "The only thing we have going for us, is that we know the exact time when the bombs will start falling from the skies planetwide."

Clayton asked fearfully, "And what time will that be, Anthony?"

"At precisely six a.m., eastern standard time, a week from now. We must use this intel to our advantage, and pick up the pace on our end, and relocate all children to their final residences."

Clayton Holmes rubbed his suddenly throbbing head. "Agreed. Is there anything else we should know?"

Galiano sighed into the receiver. "I'm afraid there is. The reason no one's heard from Manuel Jimenez was that he was detained at the

Mexican border. Microfliers recorded him and Donald Johnson in Florida, praying with another man, before Johnson and Jimenez parted company just north of Jacksonville. The other man was identified as David Wilcox. Do you know him?"

"Yeah," said Clayton. "He manages one of our safe houses in Jacksonville. He was coordinating things down there for us with Donald and Manuel."

"I see. At any rate, Jimenez surrendered peacefully without putting up a struggle. He was beheaded three days later." Galiano sighed again. "After checking the prison camera archives, I can confirm it. Fearful as he may have been at the notion of having his head severed from the rest of his body, he also felt a great sense of relief.

"The reason I say this is that he kept repeating the words, 'This isn't my home! This isn't my home'. Then, just before the blade was dropped, he shouted, 'I'm coming home, Jesus!' It was quite inspiring. At any rate, we must assume they also linked him to safe house number one."

Clayton whispered the words to Travis and Lee, "Manuel Jiminez was captured in Mexico and beheaded..."

The two men lowered their heads sadly, but also joyfully, knowing their friend and brother in Christ's struggle was finally over.

Galiano said, "There's something else you need to know..."

"What is it, Anthony?"

"When Donald Johnson resurfaced in Singapore, law enforcement was ordered to detain him and everyone living on the yacht. But after it was confirmed that Hana Patel and Yasamin Dabiri were with him, they were told to stand down. They were less than a mile away from the yacht when the new order was given, by Romanero himself.

"According to the e-mail, he didn't want Hana and Yasamin to be detained in Singapore. He wants to let it all play out, to see where it might lead. Once they boarded the container ship to America, and Donald was on board the sailboat for the Philippines, Romanero ordered the hundred-foot yacht in Singapore to be destroyed, along with everyone on it. I can confirm that this has since happened.

"It gets even crazier. When Johnson was in the Philippines, his face was scanned more than 50 times, and checked against the facial recognition app. But it always came back as 'restricted'. They also know the boat he sailed on belongs to Sergei Ivanov, and that Donald had met a young woman named Analyn Tibayan in Manila."

279

Galiano rubbed his throbbing forehead, and went on, "When Hana Patel, Yasamin Dabiri, and Vishnu Uddin arrived in the U.S., they were monitored all the way from Florida to Pennsylvania.

"Once they were five miles away from Chadds Ford, all surveillance stopped, so those living there wouldn't catch on to him. You already know how interested Romanero is in that location, mostly because of you know who," Galliano said, referring to Jefferson Danforth.

"We must assume he wanted them to make it there, knowing it was already on the destroy list. Besides, if they didn't arrive, it might create a preemptive evacuation which, in turn, might cause a domino effect with the other Christian hideouts."

Clayton shook his head in despair. "What can I say, Anthony, my mind is completely blown!"

"Same here! I mean, talk about the irony of all ironies! They were being temporarily protected by the Antichrist of the Bible, without even knowing it."

Not knowing how to reply to his outrageously bizarre statement, Clayton said, "Thanks for bringing us up to speed again, Anthony. You're a good man. Stay safe out there in Idaho."

"You too, Clayton."

At that, the call ended. It would be the last time they would speak to one another on this side of Heaven…

49

SIX DAYS LATER

ON THIS THEIR LAST day at safe house number one, since strength came in numbers, most residents were gathered at the sanctuary one last time to pray together, and hopefully calm each other's nerves a bit. Once the sun was down, they would be caravanned off to Kennett Square, in shifts, under the cover of darkness.

Even though they all had God's eternal assurance, no one could hide the fear that was clearly stenciled on their faces. How could they hide it, knowing the safe house they had all come to love would soon be blown to smithereens?

They all knew this day was fast approaching, but when Romanero moved the strike date up a week, it left them with little time to transport some of the things they would need in Kennett Square.

The reason for the delay in transferring their children to the next safe house was that children from several other safe houses were also being relocated there. They couldn't have everyone arrive in Kennett Square all at once.

Everyone started arriving at the sanctuary after lunch, which they all knew would be their last cooked meal at this place. They would eat MREs for dinner later.

Lila Choharjo occupied a pew with Julio and Marta Gonzalez, and Joaquim and Leticia Guzman. "Look at the bright side, Marta," Lila joked to her former cafeteria co-worker before she was promoted to nurse a few months later. "At least you didn't have to worry about washing the dishes first, or mopping the floors before coming here!"

Marta wanted to laugh at her friend's joke, funny as it was, but she was too frightened.

Then again, even Lila didn't laugh. She, too, was scared spitless.

Thankfully, with exception to the lone fallout shelter that Dr. Shapiro sent to safe house number one—which Julio Gonzalez, Tony Pearsall, Joaquim Guzman, and Shamus Harmon had buried off property at the back of the land—all other resources that Romanero's former physician had blessed them with, were shipped directly to Kennett Square.

Aside from the many pints of blood, medicines, canned and jarred foods, fish tanks, hydroponics equipment, all things children—toys, books, and clothing—and generators that had already been relocated to the next safe house, everything else would be left behind.

As much as they would have loved to ship the larger generators to Kennett Square, there wasn't enough time. Even if there was, they no longer had access to the large equipment that was used to help reconstruct the Chadds Ford property at the outset.

Even if they still had access to those things, they were so massive that it would be too risky to even attempt such a monumental task.

On top of that, they barely had enough fuel to make the many required trips from Chadds Ford to Kennett Square, then back again, before the 6 a.m. global bombing campaign began.

Just as Charles was about to say, "Let us pray…" many heads turned when Brian Mulrooney walked through the sanctuary doors, slowly and with great effort, bundled in the warmest clothing he had. He looked terrible!

Everyone knew he was practically bedridden at this point. He was the last person anyone thought they would see walking through those doors, especially with double pneumonia!

Jacquelyn accompanied her husband, shaking her head in confusion. Once eye contact was made with Meera and Tamika, she shrugged her shoulders and mouthed the words, "He's so stubborn at times…"

But Mulrooney was insistent that he wanted to pray and worship with his brothers and sisters in the sanctuary one last time, before it was leveled. Even though the Place they would soon inhabit by being children of the Most High God would make this place look like a bad case of eyestrain—especially post global quake—it was the only place Brian and Jacquelyn had ever known together, as husband and wife.

Both had come to love safe house number one and had hoped they would get to remain there until Christ returned. Since their wish wouldn't be granted, there was no other place Brian would rather be than inside the sanctuary one final time, with his brothers and sisters in Christ.

He already made it clear to Titus that he and Jacquelyn wanted to be the last ones to be moved off the property. One reason for this was that they wanted to spend their last night together in their bedroom, knowing they wouldn't have this sort of privacy at the next safe house.

Since Titus would be busy all through the night, relocating passengers to Kennett Square, he felt no need to challenge the couple.

The problem was that their decision had created a chain reaction of sorts, in that Dick and Sarah, and Isaac and Tamika, had decided to do the same, for the very same reason.

Even had that not been Brian's wish, Dr. Singh still would have ordered it, especially since he had defied her order to remain in bed, so he would have the strength to leave the property with everyone else before sunrise.

Brian took a seat in a vacant pew in the second row, careful not to get too close to anyone else. Had he not had double pneumonia, he surely would have been the one chosen to address the group at this crucial moment.

"Are you sure you should be here, Brian?"

"I'll be fine," he said to Charles, in strained grunts.

Calloway began, "Let us pray. Lord, we all knew this day was coming. We didn't know every detail, but we knew it was coming. None of us know how many of our safe houses will be destroyed by the enemy. Only You know, Lord. All we know is, aside from our locations that will house children, there are no guarantees that our other locations will still be standing in the next few hours.

"For the multitudes of our brothers and sisters who will no longer be alive in the coming hours, we rejoice in advance for all of them, knowing their suffering will soon be over. Not gonna lie, that outcome sounds downright comforting now.

"Since we will be going to one of the safe houses that will house so many of our little ones, we ask for Your protection in getting us all from here to there. Thank you, Father, for trusting us with taking care of Your children, until our Lord returns in a little more than three years. We love you…"

Charles opened his eyes and looked at the many seated before him. He sighed. "No doubt, it seems like we're losing the fight. But would you rather win now only to lose in the end, brothers and sisters, or lose now to win in the end?

"We must never stop believing God's promise that we will win in the end! Down here, we keep suffering tragedy after tragedy. We are strangers in an alien land which belongs to the enemy. But soon we'll be going to a Place where graves don't exist, where we'll have an eternity to celebrate our victories in Glory. Amen?"

"Amen!" came the reply in unison.

"So let this eternal Truth comfort your souls as much as it does mine, despite the constant horror we face."

Everyone was comforted by Calloway's words, yet it was evident that they were equally petrified. With the clock inside their heads ticking more loudly with each passing second, reminding them of the impending danger that was headed their way, it was impossible to disguise the paranoia they all felt...

MEANWHILE, CLAYTON HOLMES AND Travis Hartings wanted to go to Kennett Square, and hunker down with their brothers and sisters there, but since the raid was moved up one week, they ended up going back to the very last place they ever wanted to go, the tiny subterranean safe house in Ellijay, Georgia.

Dr. Lee Kim accompanied them this time. The very thought of going back to that place was wrought with terrifying memories.

On the other hand, because it was so nondescript, they seriously doubted that it would be among the many locations that would be destroyed. They would soon find out...

50

JACQUELYN STARED AT BRIAN quizzically, upon seeing her husband straining hard to look outside the curtain covered window behind the pulpit, where the stained-glass windows used to be before they were blown out in the global quake.

A strong gust of wind had momentarily forced the curtain open, exposing a faint wisp of sunlight which dimly illuminated the few remaining trees scattered about the property.

Brian shifted his weight on the bench and waited for it to happen again. When another gust of wind blew, partially opening the curtain again, his face became aglow. "Talk about God's assurance! Hallelujah!"

"What are you talking about, honey?" asked Jacquelyn quizzically, nervously, wondering if the many meds he was taking were causing him to hallucinate. She whispered in her husband's ear, "Are you okay?"

Brian waved off her concern and slowly stood on his feet. He gripped the pew in front of him with his left hand, for balance, and used his right hand to take a puff from his asthma inhaler, before pointing at the window. "Charles, can you pull back the curtain for me?"

Calloway shot Brian a sideways look, then nodded at him, without first asking for an explanation.

Brian nodded his thanks to his big brother, and spiritual mentor, then glanced around the sanctuary. "See that dim sunlight on those trees out there?"

"Yeah," Charles answered for everyone, "what about it?"

No one could overlook the astonished expression on Brian's face. "Doesn't it blow your mind how that beam of light came from more than ninety million miles away?"

Tamika was sitting in the front row with Isaac. She craned her neck back at Brian. "Have you suddenly turned into a philosopher?"

Mulrooney chuckled softly to himself, until it made him cough again. He took a moment to deposit the phlegm that had gathered in his mouth into a tissue, and stuffed it back inside his coat pocket. "Think about it, with all the judgments we've already faced, and with a constant haze hovering above the planet, from the countless clouds of smoke and who knows what else is up there drowning out the sun, we can't see a mile away in any direction…"

Tamika wondered where he was going with all this. "And?"

Mulrooney coughed into his fists several times. Each cough made his jowls flap a bit. "Yet, dim and faded as it is, that beam of light still found a way to penetrate through it all, by traveling ninety-three million miles, even as the sun is setting, no less. It's mind-boggling!"

Brian paused for a moment to let his comment sink in. "With exception to God's three angelic angels and the one hundred and forty four thousand still out there preaching, it's difficult seeing God's hand at work anywhere else on the planet.

"I believe the Most High is reminding us at this most pivotal time in human history that He is still in control, and He's still here with us! Who else could possibly orchestrate this monumental miracle? Perhaps He sent it as a preemptive way of strengthening those of us who will live another day, so we can take care of the children.

"Either that or He sent it to comfort us, knowing what will soon become of many of our brothers and sisters at their safe houses. Who knows? All I know is that He sent it to remind us that He is still in control."

Brian paused to take another deep breath. "Even though my flesh trembles in fear, knowing what's about to become of our beloved safe house, this was never our home to begin with. We must always remind ourselves that we're going to a far better place soon.

"I believe God is using this sunset to revive my weary spirit. It should remind us all again that God is still in charge, and our hope must remain anchored in Him, in good times and in bad.

"Yes, this miracle of sorts should constantly remind us that the very One who sent the sunset is the same One who has our souls safely and securely in His hands. Talk about assurance! How could we not be deeply comforted seeing this?"

Many "Amens" were uttered all throughout the sanctuary.

At that, Brian sat down.

Clayton Holmes, Travis Hartings, and Dr. Lee Kim were listening from the Ellijay, Georgia safe house, but the speaker on Hartings' SAT phone was muted. All three were strengthened by Brian's words of encouragement. "Way to go, Brian!" Hartings shouted softly to his two brothers in the faith.

Wow! Jefferson Danforth thought, raising an eyebrow, totally astonished by Brian's words. He and Amy were seated 15 rows behind him. "Now that you put it that way, Brian, you're right. it really is mind boggling!"

Brian craned his neck back at the former U.S. President and nodded at him.

Jacquelyn reached for her husband's hand and gave it a comforting squeeze, shaking her head in amazement. "What can I say? My mind is blown!"

Dick said to Sarah, "Simply fascinating!" *Good one, Mr. Hotel Man!*

The looks on their faces said it all—they were blown away that something they had all seen thousands of times, but had taken for granted, was suddenly significant enough to bolster their confidence in their Lord, to the extent that they couldn't believe they never saw it that way before the Rapture.

Meera whispered in Tamika's ear. "Now I know why Brian's here, even against our strongest protests."

Tamika straightened up on the bench. "Yeah, so God could use him to comfort us all now."

"Precisely!"

Calloway offered, "Brian's right! Now more than ever we need to be ever mindful that our Maker is still in complete control, even when it doesn't seem that way. Our remaining time together at this place should be focused entirely on that eternal truth!"

Mary Johnson bounced her son, Luke, on her lap. "Thanks for your timely words of wisdom, Brian. It couldn't have come at a better time." she said, amid soft sniffling. "It's just what I needed to hear."

Isaac listened and was blown away by the love and transparency he felt in this sanctuary. While he didn't have many cherished memories at this place, like everyone else, the one thing his mind kept recalling was how Amos Nyarwarta and Officer John Reitz had offered up their lives for him and Dick, and how it had led them to this beautiful family of believers.

In the near decade he had pledged his complete loyalty to Allah, he never experienced anything quite like this. What he had always felt in that circle was a brotherhood who were willing to commit violent acts toward all who disagreed with their beliefs. When he renounced faith in Islam, they even tried killing him!

Eyes glancing around the sanctuary, Isaac, not Abdul, knew beyond a certainty that if he ever renounced his faith in Christ—which he never would—there wasn't a person in this building who would express murderous thoughts toward him for his apostasy.

If anything, they would pray that he would ultimately come back to his Savior. But having violent thoughts toward him would never be part of the equation! *This is my true family, my eternal family!*

Frightened as he was, now that he would soon be a father again, he wanted to be around for him. Overcome with emotion, Isaac stood and shouted, "Hallelujah!" at the top of his lungs.

Hands raised high above his head, he started singing,

> "I love you, Lord,
> and I lift my voice,
> to worship You,
> Oh my soul, rejoice.
> Take joy my King,
> in what You hear,
> let it be a sweet, sweet, sound in Your ear..."

Tamika glanced up at her husband. Chills shot all throughout her body. Isaac motioned for her to join him.

Tamika rose to her feet, and clutched Isaac's left hand, as they shouted out their declaration together in this song of praise to Jesus.

The fact that they were just moments away from being relocated, not to mention that Tamika was pregnant with the couple's third child, at the worst possible time in human history, yet they still praised God with everything that was in them, was awe inspiring.

Amy Danforth was the next to stand. Her mind was brought back to that glorious day at Camp David, when her former boss, now husband, declared to everyone that day, that he had recently become a Christ follower.

While she wasn't nearly as frightened back then as she was now, she nevertheless felt that same comforting peace she had felt that day.

She joined Isaac and Tamika in song and praise.

> "I love you, Lord,
> and I lift my voice,
> to worship You,
> Oh my soul, rejoice.
> Take joy my King,

in what You hear,
let it be a sweet, sweet, sound in Your ear…"

Amy reached for her husband's hand. Instead of shrinking in his seat, Jefferson stood alongside his wife and lent his voice to praise the One who had saved his soul from eternal destruction, a little more than three years ago.

He glanced around the sanctuary and smiled wearily. *Now this is what I call faith in action!*

Charles Calloway watched his brothers and sisters all praising God together, and giving Him glory, from up on stage. It was one of the most wonderful sights his eyes had ever seen.

He, too, was at Camp David on that wondrously beautiful day, when then President Danforth first professed his faith to them.

He was also at the cabin situated on the Tennessee-Georgia border, on the night he got to praise the Lord with his late Aunt Evelyn, Ernest Stone, and Amos Nyarwarta.

That praise and worship session lasted all throughout the night. What he saw unfolding before him now, very much reminded him of that time.

Even though that *ETSM* safe house was later leveled in the global quake, claiming the lives of many of his cherished loved ones, whom he still missed every day, it nevertheless was one of the greatest nights of his life, post Rapture.

Charles never would have participated in something like this before his spiritual conversion. Now it was as natural to him as breathing air into his lungs. He dropped to his knees, raised his hands Heavenward, and joined his brothers and sisters in praising the Lord.

"I love you, Lord,
and I lift my voice,
to worship You,
Oh my soul, rejoice.
Take joy my King,
in what You hear,
let it be a sweet, sweet, sound in Your ear…"

After a while, everyone was on their feet, hands lifted high in worship, shouting their declarations to Jesus. One song led to another, and before

289

you know it, they had spent nearly two hours in song and praise of their Maker.

As much as they would have loved to keep singing all throughout the night, with the sun now setting in the sky above, and darkness slowly flexing its muscles, they hadn't a moment to waste.

Before leaving the sanctuary, Titus ordered the first group of residents to be transported to Kennett Square, to proceed to the back of the property, where five vans were already there waiting, as everyone else went back to their cottages for the very last time.

Jakob had already assured them that they would be supernaturally protected when transporting all children to the Kennett Square safe house. This meant even the microfliers, spy drones, law enforcement surrounding the safe house, and the satellites up in space presently spying on them, would be powerless from capturing their images the entire time they were in transit.

In short, they wouldn't see or feel Yahweh's supernatural force protecting them from harm, but they would all benefit from it...

51

4 A.M. THE FOLOWING MORNING

JACQUELYN WAS AT BRIAN'S bedside with her in-laws, Dick and Sarah, Tamika Moseley, Meera Singh, Tom Dunleavey, and Charles Calloway. Hana Patel also decided to remain behind at the last minute, in case this would be her last time seeing Brian on this side.

Everyone else had either already been relocated to Kennett Square, or they were still in the process of being relocated. Tony Pearsall told them he would be back within the hour to take them there next.

Jacquelyn felt Brian's forehead. "He's burning up!" she bemoaned. Although his body was chilled to the bone, his clothing was soaked all the way through with sweat.

"He's in no condition to travel anywhere," said Tamika in reply, "let alone get out of bed."

Jacquelyn became increasingly panicked with each breath she took. "True, but he doesn't have the luxury of remaining in bed until his condition improves." She sighed. "If it improves…"

All Tamika could do was grimace at the notion.

Jacquelyn kept looking up at the bedroom ceiling, as if anticipating bombs falling on them any second now. Heartrate jacked through the roof, the clock inside her head kept screaming at her. "We have to leave now, sweetie, the van's waiting for us…"

Brian clung to his wife's hand, and squeezed the blanket covering his body even tighter with his free hand, to cut off the chill he felt. "Sorry, my love," he said as loudly as he could, which wasn't too loud, "as much as I don't want to be separated from you and Sarah, I don't have the strength to make it off the property, let alone travel to the other location.

"Chances are good that the global police have already surrounded the property. Even if I made it past them, which I seriously doubt, the drive alone might kill me. I should have listened to Meera and Tamika yesterday, by remaining in bed. Had I done that, perhaps I would have felt well enough to make it to the next location."

Jacquelyn became even more panicked. "You must try, sweetie…"

Brian gasped. "I wish I could, but I don't have the strength to."

291

Jacquelyn blinked tears from her eyes and glanced up at the ceiling again. She wanted to keep pleading with her husband to try and find the strength to hang in there, but she knew it would be fruitless. He looked even more deathly ill now than when he walked to the sanctuary the day before. "Can you at least go to the fallout shelter?"

"I can try, but only if someone carries me."

Charles gazed deep into Brian's eyes, his mind suddenly full of the many memories they had created together, beginning in his hotel suite at the Waldorf-Astoria, when Brian received Christ as Lord and Savior. "I'll carry you, brother. I'll even stay there with you if you want. It'll be my honor."

Tears flooded Brian's eyes as he nodded his thanks to his big brother, whom God had used to rescue his soul from perdition a few days after the Rapture took place.

Charles asked Meera, "Is there enough medicine to leave behind for him?" He knew the fallout shelter was stocked with enough food and water to last 12 people more than a week, so with it just being the two of them, they should be fine.

Meera answered, "Everything Brian will need is in this bag. There's enough medicine to last a little more than a week. There's also an intravenous hookup for him down there…"

"Good thinking…" Calloway said, cutely.

Meera lowered her head shyly, embarrassed at the attention his comment had garnered.

Brian covered his wife's hands in his. "If this is goodbye, for now, anyway," he said, coughing loudly, deeply, too weak to cover his mouth, "I know we won't be married on the other side, but I want you to know the greatest honor of my life was having the blessing of being your husband."

Brian gazed deeply into Jacquelyn's moist eyes. "And to think I met the most amazing person in my life on the worst day in human history! We helped each other get through that day, and we've been there for each other ever since. You've been my constant! Thanks for making me the most blessed man on the planet the past few years."

Jacquelyn brushed more tears from her eyes. "I don't want to be without you, Brian. I'll stay behind with you."

Brian slowly shook his head from one side to the other. Even that hurt. "As comforting as your words are in my ears, Sarah needs you."

The bedroom grew silent until Dick said, "He's my son! I'll stay with him. He's going to need someone to take care of him underground. He'll never survive it alone with double pneumonia. Lord willing, we'll join you in Kennett Square after the dust settles."

Sarah shot an astonished look at her husband. A few short months ago, he hated Brian. Now he was willing to die with him. She couldn't have been prouder of Dick. Had he not made the offer, she would have...

All eyes shifted to Tom Dunleavey when he said, "I'll stay behind with him. It's the least I can do after everything he's done for me." He glanced at Charles. "Your leadership skills far outweigh mine. You will surely be needed in Kennett Square. Besides, I'm a single man. I'll never get married or have a child. Perhaps someday you will again..."

Out of nowhere, Meera blurted out, "Yes, he will."

Charles' mouth was agape for the longest time before he could finally speak again. "Does that mean you'll marry me?"

"Yes, I will. But I don't want to have a child."

"I understand completely." Charles kissed Meera on the cheek, then refocused his attention back to Tom, who hadn't yet finished speaking.

"It took me three and half years to finally find the courage to look death square in the eye, by way of laying down my life for another, like Christ had done for me. This is my big opportunity.

"Besides, I'm tired of living in hiding, and weary of rebuilding after each new judgment. And with the seven bowl judgments soon to come, not to mention the great quake that Clayton said will be even worse than the global quake, I don't know if I'll have the physical, emotional or the mental strength to endure it all. In case you haven't noticed, I'm not twenty-one any more..."

Even at this most crucial moment in time, his comment caused laughter to fill the bedroom, even if only for a second or two.

Tom grew serious again. "Truth be told, ever since my heart attack, followed by the global quake, my mind's been steadfastly focused on the afterlife. Being in the presence of the Lord Jesus Christ is where I want to be. Why cling to this pigsty of an existence, when my Savior is preparing a place just for me, that will be perfectly suited for me in all ways? Why would I want to delay it any longer?

"If going down to the bomb shelter with Brian means death for me, I'm fully resigned to it. If, on the other hand, we survive, I'll take it as a sign that God still isn't finished with me..."

293

Tears filled Brian's eyes, but he was too weak to dry them, as memories flooded his mind about how he and Tom had first spoken on the phone the day after the Rapture, followed by a meeting that both men were convinced was orchestrated by God, which led to a friendship that was so deep and strong, it felt to both men like they had been friends forever. Brian nodded his sincere heartfelt thanks to Tom.

Dick glanced at Tom but couldn't hold his stare. The man who had sickened him for so long, for shamefully leaving the Catholic priesthood, was now willing to die with his son. It was too intense to put into words.

Jacquelyn dried Brian's eyes with her shirt sleeve.

He gazed deep into his wife's tear-drenched eyes. "I know it's the last thing on your mind right now, but if this is the last time we see each other, if you feel the need to remarry, if only to not be alone at night, I want you to know you have my blessing."

A lone tear slowly made its way down Jacquelyn's left cheek. "Can we please not talk about this now?"

Brian grunted as he adjusted his achy body on the bed. "You know my prayer all along was that we would remain husband and wife until Christ returned. Nothing's changed, honey. I just don't want you to feel conflicted later, if it ever comes to that…"

Jacquelyn wept more intensely.

Brian added, "If this is it, please tell baby Sarah that I couldn't have been blessed with a better daughter than her. I hope our Lord changes nothing about her when she becomes part of the Millennial Kingdom. She's simply perfect in all ways…"

A new batch of tears streamed down Jacquelyn's cheeks one after the next, this time accompanied by loud wailing.

Titus radioed them to inform them that he was waiting outside, having just returned from making his twelfth trip to Kennett Square.

"We'll be right down," Charles said in a soft whisper. Then to everyone gathered in the room with him, "I hate to break this touching moment, but it's time to get a move on…"

"Can we pray first?" asked Brian.

Charles replied, "Of course, we can, brother!"

52

WHEN CHARLES FINISHED PRAYING, there wasn't a dry eye in the room.

Jacquelyn hugged her husband as tightly as she could, not wanting to let go of him. Her hands squeezed his upper back and shoulder, as she clung to him for dear life.

As much as the pressure from her hands hurt his fatigued body, there wasn't a chance he would ask her to let go. She hadn't even left yet, and he already missed her.

When she finally released her grip on him, Brian said, "Goodbye for now, my sweet Jacquelyn. I'll see you when I see you. If not here, surely on the other side." He then said to the others, "If this is it, I look forward to spending eternity with you all someday."

Hana Patel was also weeping. She dried her moist eyes with her coat sleeve, and said through soft sniffles, "I wish to thank you again, Brian, from the bottom of my heart for what you did for me and my husband. I can't help but think that your kindness to my family was partly the reason why God has restored yours."

More tears surfaced in Brian's eyes. If this turned out to be his last day on Earth, it would be a touching send-off to say the least.

Once again, Charles was the one to break the emotional silence. "All of you go now. Tell Titus I'll be there shortly." He hoisted Brian up off the bed and placed him over his left shoulder. "Make sure he's bundled up good."

Through heavy grunts and wheezing, Brian said, "Wait, my Bible..."

He was referring to the Bible that his childhood friend, Justin Schroeder, had sent to him before he was taken in the Rapture, along with a handwritten letter that God had used to open Brian's spiritual eyes and ears. These were two of Brian's most prized possessions in life.

Jacquelyn grabbed it off the end table on his side of the bed, and tucked it into her husband's right arm, silently wondering if Brian and Justin would be reunited this day...

She bent down and kissed Brian on the lips, told him she loved him again, hopefully not for the last time, and left her husband.

As she walked to the rear of the property also for the very last time, she cried a new river of tears.

Tamika scrambled to throw on a jacket, then grabbed Cocoa, as Isaac grabbed Revelation. The couple dashed down the stairs of their humble dwelling place, and headed straight to the waiting van.

Before descending the steps for the very last time, with her husband by her side, Sarah peeked her head into the bedroom she had occupied the past three years, knowing she would never sleep in that bed again.

As much as she didn't want to leave the place that she had grown to love with all her heart, she had no choice—in a little more than an hour, the house would no longer be standing.

WHEN THEY ARRIVED AT the fallout shelter, Charles gently laid Brian onto the bed inside his pod, then covered him with the blankets he took from the bedroom, as Tom eased himself into his own pod.

Calloway glanced over at Tom. "What you're doing is right up there with Yogesh Patel, Amos Nyarwarta and Officer John Reitz. Talk about being on the front line! Regardless of what may come, I'll always consider you as one of my heroes in the faith. Both of you, in fact."

Tom's eyes became moist with tears. He was deeply moved by his words. "I can't tell you how much I appreciate hearing that…"

Charles smiled just enough for Tom to see it. "Hope to see the two of you again soon. If not, you'll be in a much better place than me. But we can know for sure we'll see each other again."

He became even more choked up. "I'm not sure how it all works up there, but if you bump into Monique and my five kids, tell them I love them, and I'll see them soon…"

Tom could tell that Charles was still struggling with the guilt he felt. "I don't know how it works either. All I know for sure is you won't be married to Monique on the other side. Meera, neither, for that matter. So, don't feel guilty about marrying her. After all, it's why I volunteered to do this."

Charles said through soft sniffling, "I love you both so much, and I'll always be grateful for the blessing of friendship and brotherhood we got to share over the past three and a half years."

"Love you too, Charles," both men said at the same time, their voices shaking and their hearts thundering inside their chests.

Prior to his conversion, Calloway would have been too macho to show this sort of raw, genuine emotion toward others. But now that he was truly saved, it flowed easily through him. "As much as I'd love to stay, I can't keep them waiting any longer."

Tom said, "We understand. Go now. Escape while you can."

Before closing Brian's pod, Charles asked, "Would you like me to turn off the light? Or should I leave it on?"

Brian turned his head to the left, to look at Tom lying on a mattress inside his pod. "My eyes will be closed anyway, no matter what, so it's up to you, brother."

"Since it'll soon be off for good, I say leave it on."

Charles glanced at Brian. "I agree. I'll leave it on to remind you both of what you told us in the sanctuary yesterday. You'll never know how much your words strengthened me. More than you can ever imagine."

Tom said, "That goes double for me, Brian."

"Even when this light's extinguished," Charles added, "never stop thinking about that beam of light that traveled ninety-three million miles to penetrate all obstructions, for all of us to see. Even though you can't see it down here, it's still there. God is too. He's got our backs, right?"

Brian nodded at him, then started coughing again.

"When you feel it's safe to come out, all you'll have to do is push that button. If it doesn't work, you can still open the pod manually, by pulling that lever," Charles said, pointing to it."

"Thanks Charles," Brian said weakly.

Tom asked, "When will someone come to check on us?"

Charles frowned. "As soon as we're able to, brother. Perhaps it'll even be me…"

Tom said, "If I don't get to meet Charles and Meera Calloway on this side, I look forward to seeing you both again on the other side…"

The way Tom said it was like further confirmation to him. He smiled at the thought. "Likewise, brother…"

At that, Charles left the fallout capsule…

SALVADOR ROMANERO WENT LIVE again, using the global push alert system he first used after the Two witnesses were resurrected. "Greetings global citizens! Since time is of the essence, I'll come straight to the point. Something huge is about to happen. During the five months we all suffered at the hands of Israel's God, we positively identified hundreds of thousands of enemy camps and safe houses planetwide.

"Due to the intensive planning that has been ongoing since that time, I couldn't publicly divulge anything to you. But the time has come to take back the children that have been stolen from us, and lead them to safe passage, before their impressionable minds become even more corrupted by the enemy! It's been long enough! It's time for payback."

Romanero paused for a moment, then said, "Do not be alarmed by what will soon unfold globally. What many of you will soon experience will not be another global quake, though it may feel like it. It will be a coordinated attack on the enemy.

"The instant we confiscate the children from their hideouts, most enemy camps will be utterly wiped off the face of the earth, simultaneously, just as I kept promising they would.

"I want the adults to be alive so they can experience one last bout of sheer terror, when bombs strike their hideouts, before they all meet their demise. It's time for them to suffer as we watch and rejoice."

Romanero glanced at his watch. "Three, two, one. Go get 'em!"

With swiftness of foot, more than a million global soldiers and law enforcement officials stormed each property on the strike list.

Their orders were specific—confiscate all children as quickly as possible, then flee the grounds before the bombing commenced. They all took pride knowing they would soon be hailed as global heroes.

One hundred of these soldiers were sent to the enemy camp in Chadds Ford, Pennsylvania. They spread all throughout the property in rapid succession, breaking down cottage doors looking for children.

As all this was happening, a text alert was sent to everyone living within 10 miles of the targeted enemy camps. This was particularly beneficial for individuals who were deaf or whose eardrums were damaged due to the recent meteor strike.

It read: *If you haven't already left the area, do it now! You have 30 minutes! If your properties are damaged or destroyed, by way of collateral damage, they will be repaired or rebuilt at no cost to you. May you all be blessed in my name…*

Twenty-five minutes later, one of the soldiers sent to the Chadds Ford safe house, approached his commanding officer. "They're all gone, sir…"

The man's eyes popped. "What do you mean they're all gone?"

"We searched everywhere," he answered, trying his best to stabilize his breathing. "Someone must've tipped them off."

The commanding officer became so furious that he slammed his mobile device to the ground, shattering it into many pieces.

He used the soldier's phone to forward the disappointing news to his superiors. "They got away, sir. All of them! Someone tipped them off."

The commanding officer got an earful back, as if it was all his fault. When the call ended, he gave the order to his soldiers, "Everyone off the property now!"

They quickly left for the military command center, which was set up in a former shopping center parking lot, five miles southeast of Chadds Ford. Once it was safe to return, they would encircle the enemy camp, in case anyone survived the blast. Survivors would be immediately shot.

53

MEANWHILE, THE DRIVE FROM Chadds Ford to Kennett Square was a somber one, filled with many fearful tears and despair.

Jacquelyn didn't have the strength to look at Charles in the passenger front seat, as he brushed tears from his eyes. The soft sniffling alone felt like constant hammer blows to her heart.

As much as she wanted to ask Charles to share his final moments with Brian and Tom with everyone, if she did that, it would only add to the heartache she felt, for leaving her husband in the first place.

Part of her wanted to beg Titus to turn the car around, so she could join her husband in the pod and take care of him. But if she did ask him, there wasn't a chance he would acquiesce to her emotional wishes.

Aside from potential law enforcement officers pulling them over, nothing would stop Titus from guiding the vehicle to Kennett Square.

Even surrounded by those whom Jacquelyn loved dearly, by not having Brian by her side, she felt even lonelier now than she did when her first husband was killed at Michigan Stadium, after the Rapture.

What made it even worse was that she didn't have her daughter to cling to, for comfort. Sarah was already at the Kennett Square safe house.

The dreadful sensation they all felt intensified by leaps and bounds when, 30 minutes after they left Chadds Ford—roughly eight miles away—they heard a faint sound in the sky. Everyone inside the vehicle knew what it was.

The closer the bomb got to its target the louder it screamed, before ultimately striking the surface below, with a deafening explosion.

Even this far away, everyone in the van heard and felt it loud and clear. It shook the ground beneath them, nearly causing some of the windows on their vehicle to be blown out.

No one had to ask what had just happened.

Safe house number one was no more...

Dick craned his neck back and saw the mushroom cloud of smoke the bomb had created.

Sarah couldn't bear to look. She gasped loudly, then lowered her head and wept uncontrollably. Dick pulled his wife closer hoping to comfort her, knowing how impossible it would be, at least for now.

Jacquelyn wept so fiercely that her shoulders kept twitching. It was as if part of her had just died. She started suffocating as her lungs fought for each new breath. Her hands shook so much that she tried to calm them by squeezing her kneecaps. It didn't work.

Since Brian and Jacquelyn were one in God's eyes, it was as if she could almost feel the flesh being ripped from her body. If he didn't survive, her heart wouldn't stop beating, but it would stop feeling for any other man until the very end.

After a while, Sarah said through soft sniffling, "Never thought we'd outlive our two children."

Dick replied, "We don't know that yet. It all depends on where the bomb struck. If they were outside the scope of the crater, perhaps they survived. Let's keep praying for God's protection over Brian and Tom."

"Look how far away we are, Dick!" she snapped, purely out of frustration, "If we felt it so strongly from this distance, how could Brian and Tom possibly survive what just hit them?"

"I understand," Dick said, as calmly as he could, "but we were assured the capsules were built to sustain a blast like that."

Sarah took comfort knowing she would see Brian again, no matter what, but the pain in her heart from knowing she would never see Chelsea again made her wish she had been in the pathway of the bomb.

Her weeping intensified...

SINCE BRIAN AND TOM were encapsulated in the fallout shelter pods, 30 feet beneath the Earth's surface, they didn't hear the property being stormed by the 100 global military and law enforcement officials.

It took a while for them to hear the screeching sound coming from the sky above, but they eventually heard it loud and clear. It screamed in their ears as if they both were mounted on it.

Since they were in the bomb's direct pathway, their hope was that they wouldn't hear it coming, or feel the ground shaking all around them.

But since they did, all Brian and Tom could do was pray, then wait and see if they would still be alive in the coming minutes.

Brian thought about the late Justin Schroeder again. He couldn't wait to see his childhood friend and tell him how much God had used him to rescue his soul from hell.

Had he not included the letter with the Bible, that Brian found in his apartment the day after the Rapture, he may not have read it.

He also wanted Justin to know the Bible that was intended for his parents had ended up in his own mother's hands. So, in that light, God had used his efforts to win them both to Christ. Brian's father, too, by extension. Would this be the day he would get to tell him?

He was about to find out…

With trembling voice and limbs, Tom said to Brian, "One thing is certain, we're about to see firsthand if this capsule can withstand a twenty-kiloton nuclear blast."

Brian closed his eyes as tightly as he could. "Whatever may come, I hope we see each other again immediately after impact. Either we'll both survive, or we'll be with the Lord a few moments from now."

"Amen! Thy will be done, Lord!" came Tom's reply, in a voice that was quite anticipatory either way. "I love you, Brian, and I want to thank you again for being my closest friend the past three and a half years."

After a moment of tearful, fearful silence, Brian said, "Love you too, brother Tom…"

Mulrooney coughed a few times, then joined Tom in uttering the words, "Thy will be done, Lord!" over and over again, until the bomb made impact with precise, punishing force, quickly destroying his beloved safe house, and everything within close proximity to it…

"So when you see standing in the holy place 'the abomination that causes desolation,' spoken of through the prophet Daniel—let the reader understand—then let those who are in Judea flee to the mountains. Let no one on the housetop go down to take anything out of the house.

"'Let no one in the field go back to get their cloak. How dreadful it will be in those days for pregnant women and nursing mothers! Pray that your flight will not take place in winter or on the Sabbath. For then there will be great distress, unequaled from the beginning of the world until now—and never to be equaled again.'" (Matthew 24:15-21.)

Epilogue

Will Donald Johnson, Sergei Ivanov, and Analyn Tibayan survive the long voyage at sea, with God's seven bowl judgments pounding the planet?

If they do make it to America, now that safe house number one has been destroyed, will Donald ever see his wife and son again?

Will Brian Mulrooney and Tom Dunleavey survive the bombing?

Will Tamika Moseley's dream about her college friend lead to disappointment again, or is Mila Mirano an *ETSM* nurse like she saw in her dream?

With the majority of their safe houses no longer in existence, what will become of the End Times Salvation Movement?

Now that Yahweh is gathering His remnant, what will become of Israel?

Will Daniel Sullivan find Jefferson Danforth's brother-in-law and children?

Find answers to these questions and so much more as you continue in this prophetic series...

Thanks for taking the time to read the eighth installment of the CHAOS series. I would be most grateful if you shared your thoughts on Amazon. Even a short review would be appreciated. May God continue to bless and keep you.

Once completed, there will be 10 installments. Look for the ninth installment of the series to be available for pre-release in September 2023.

To contact author for book signings, speaking engagements,
or for bulk discounts, email @ patrick12272003@gmail.com.

TO ORDER PATRICK HIGGINS' BOOKS IN PAPERBACK FORMAT
(AND SOON IN HARD COPY) AT DEEP DISCOUNT PRICES:

www.patrickhigginsbooks.com

All books purchased on the site will be personally signed by the author and dedicated to the readers. They make the perfect gifts for holidays, birthdays, anniversaries, Mother's Day, Father's Day, and on and on.

Order signed copies now for family members, friends and loved ones.

About the author

Patrick Higgins is an Amazon bestseller and award-winning author of the end times prophetic series, *Chaos in The Blink of an Eye*. The "CHAOS" in our world is well documented in this series, which won the Radiqx Press Spirit-Filled Fiction Award of Excellence, after the first installment was published.

The latest recognition for the CHAOS series was winning the 2024 International Impact Book Award (Best Fiction - Christian Fiction).

To date, more than 15,000 positive ratings/reviews have been posted on Amazon and Goodreads, on the first 9 installments...and counting!

Look for the final installment to be released in 2025.

He also wrote *I Never Knew You,* winner of the 2021 Readers' Favorite Gold Medal in Christian fiction, 2021 Independent Author Network (IAN) book of the year winner in Christian fiction, and Finalist in both the 2022 American Best Book Awards, and the 2021 International Book Awards, *The Unannounced Christmas Visitor*, which won both the International Publishers Awards (IPA) and the 2018 Readers' Favorite Gold Medal Awards in Christian fiction, *The Pelican Trees*, and *Coffee In Manila*.

While the stories he writes all have different themes and take place in different settings, the one thread that links them all together is his heart for Jesus and his yearning for the lost. With that in mind, it is his wish that the message his stories convey will greatly impact each reader, by challenging you not only to contemplate life on this side of the grave, but on the other side as well.

After all, each of us will spend eternity at one of two places, based solely upon a single decision which must be made on this side of the grave. That decision will be made crystal clear to each reader of his books.

Higgins is currently writing many other books, both fiction and non-fiction, including a sequel to *Coffee in Manila,* which will shine a bright, sobering light on the diabolical human trafficking industry.

Thanks for taking the time to read the eighth installment of the CHAOS series. I would be most grateful if you shared your thoughts about this story on Amazon. Even a short review would be appreciated. God bless and keep you always.

To contact author: patrick12272003@gmail.com
Like on Facebook: https://www.facebook.com/patrick12272003
Twitter: https://twitter.com/patrick12272003
Instagram: https://www.instagram.com/patrick12272003
Amazon: https://www.amazon.com/Patrick-Higgins/e/B005ANHSU2
Goodreads: https://www.goodreads.com/author/show/10796904.Patrick_Higgins
Bookbub: https://www.bookbub.com/authors/patrick-higgins
Looking for an editor? Contact Susan Axel Bedsaul, the Complete Editor
Excellent Results. Reasonable Rates – complete-editor@outlook.com